beauty
OF A
MONSTER
redemption
part two

A novel by
ELEANOR LLOYD-JONES
KATIE FOX

Epigraph © JmStorm

Editing, Cover Design, and Formatting: Schmidt's Author Services

ISBN: 9781726737708

For more information on the authors' work, and to keep up to date with new releases, please visit the following links:

Eleanor Lloyd-Jones
www.eleanorlloydjones.weebly.com
www.facebook.com/eleanorlloydj
www.facebook.com/groups/eljelephant
www.instagram.com/eleanorlloydjones
Follow Eleanor on Twitter: @EleanorLloydJ

Katie Fox
www.authorkatiefox.com
www.facebook.com/authorkatiefox
www.facebook.com/groups/katiesfoxyreaders
www.instagram.com/authorkatiefox
Follow Katie on Twitter: @authorkatiefox

Playlist

Music was instrumental in inspiring this story, and each chapter has specific songs that relate to certain scenes. These can be found underneath the chapter headings.

If you would like to listen to it as you read or after you have finished, please follow the link below to find a chronological list of songs.

https://spoti.fi/2xYil8w

Dedicated to...

To our superfans, this one is for you.

And if she is in your life, you must
know she believes you're a battle
worth fighting.

JM Storm

Chapter 1

Stitches by Jaclyn Davies
Lean On Me by Sizzt Rocket
Bleeding Out by Molly Hunt
Truth by Raelee Nikole

THE SOUND OF *footsteps on the tiled pathway grow closer as I crouch down behind a rose bush, my hand pressed over my mouth to suppress the giggle that's bubbling in my chest and about to break free.*

"Joey? Where are you?" The boyish sing-song voice floats through the air like a gentle breeze, and at the sight of a pair of white trainers, I push myself up and spin around, taking off in the opposite direction. Childish laughter fills my ears—not just my own, but his too—as the figure closes the distance between us.

It's joyous and carefree.

It's familiar.

My curls bounce against my shoulders with every swift step, and the dirt on my dress begins to fade.

I run towards the large maze, and as my fingers brush against the soft leaves that make up the walls, I'm lifted off my feet.

My hands instinctively wrap around the strong arm of my captor—the same arm that's circled around my waist and banding me to him.

Goosebumps form on my skin as he whispers in my ear.

"Gotcha." His voice is deeper now, more mature: a man's voice.

Not another second passes before he turns me around so I'm facing him, and I have to stop myself from reaching up to cup his face.

"Will?" His name rolls from the tip of my tongue on a whisper of disbelief. It sounds foreign, as if I have no right giving it a voice. Intense blue eyes full of pain and regret stare down at me, and a feeling of helplessness slowly trickles the length of my spine.

I want to erase it all, every emotion that holds me in place and keeps me from moving.

I want to take away his sorrow.

Rough and calloused fingers sweep up my arms before tenderly skimming across my collarbone. Prickles of heat dance down my chest, and I'm once again knocked off balance, this time thrown into a whirlwind of lust and desire.

"Joey..." He begins to lean in closer as his hands curl around my shoulders, his touch gentle. He's everything I need. His nose brushes along mine, and his lips hover just above my mouth, his breath warm.

Unable to resist, I push onto my toes, wanting to kiss him, and a roll of thunder cracks loudly in the sky. Dark grey clouds form overhead, swallowing the light and shrouding us in complete darkness. Pain shoots down my arms as his hold on me tightens—as his nails cut into my sensitive flesh.

"I hate you, Josephine Bell." His voice has changed again. It's seething and anger-filled. "I hate you."

Another roar of thunder has my heart beating violently against my ribs, and a scattering of rain falls to the ground.

Only it's not rain.

It's tears.

My tears.

Blinking slowly, Joey squinted against the harsh, bright lights that beamed down from the ceiling. Muffled voices hummed only just in earshot, gradually becoming clearer as the steady beat of the machine beside her forced her back to reality. Every inch of her body felt heavy—like a weight she had no strength to move—and she struggled to push herself upright.

"Hold on, sweetheart. Let me help you." Little John leaned forwards, grabbing the remote that controlled the position of Joey's bed and pressed the button until she was sitting comfortably. He looked at her with worried eyes. "How are you feeling?"

How *was* she feeling?

She hurt.

She hurt everywhere.

The wound across her temple throbbed, the stitches serving as a reminder that her accident had been more than a simple fall, yet the excruciating pain paled in comparison to the pulsing ache in her heart.

Three days had passed since she'd walked out of Will's office.

Her feet had moved with a sense of urgency as she'd searched for the first escape she could find. Her head had been empty aside from his words—the soul shattering truth that had torn her entire world apart—and as she'd stepped out of the manor and her eyes had landed on the stables, she'd made the split second decision to take Roya, the need to leave being the only thing that had mattered.

However, here she was—seventy-two hours later—with Will's confessions still swirling in her mind, as alive and real as they'd been the moment they were released from their lockbox.

"I'm okay, Dad." As the lie floated from her mouth, Joey resisted looking at her father. Not only were her eyes an open window straight to her broken heart, but she couldn't stand seeing that look of 'I told you so' staring back at her.

He *had* told her.

He'd warned her to stay away from William, but she'd deliberately ignored him, falling instead for the man whose life she'd unwittingly helped to destroy.

Relieved to see his daughter awake, John reached out and took her hand in his, squeezing it gently, his thumb caressing her skin. She'd drifted in and out of consciousness over the last forty-eight hours, and seeing her awake and communicating was comforting.

When he'd received the distraught call from Bea, fear like never before had gripped him by the chest, and his inability to get up and easily go to her had become a frustration all in itself. Joey was all he had—all he'd ever had for the last twenty-nine years—and if anything was to happen to her... well, he didn't even want to entertain that thought.

"Are you hungry? Dinner isn't for another two hours, but I can take a walk down to the cafeteria for you if you'd like. Maybe grab those crisps you like so much from the—"

Joey began to shake her head. "No, thank you. I'm good." A shot of pain soared across her temple, and she winced. She squeezed her eyes shut, blowing out a breath as if it would help relieve the ache, and then reopened them, allowing her gaze to drift lazily towards the door of her private room.

Her heart stuttered in her chest.

Danny stood leaning against the frame with a gentle smile on his face and a small bouqet of flowers in his hands. His blonde hair was perfectly mussed and a thin layer of golden stubble covered the hard cut of his jaw.

Several silent moments passed—an unspoken conversation bouncing between them—before he straightened himself and walked towards her, grabbing the arm of the nearest chair and pulling it up beside her bed and setting the flowers down on the table.

Little John pushed out of his seat. He could read the situation clearly, realising the pair needed some time to themselves. "I think I'll take that walk anyway. Need to stretch these old legs of mine. Better make use of them while I still can." He dropped a quick kiss to the top of his daughter's head, and, with his cane in hand, left the two of them alone.

Danny licked his lips and stared down at the floor, his fingers weaving together between his thighs. There was so much to say, but he didn't know where to start or which words to use.

Gingerly lifting his head, he looked right at her.

Even wrapped in an ugly hospital gown, her uncombed hair piled messily on top of her head, she was beautiful. "Hey, you."

Joey smiled sadly, her lips pulling tight as she curled her hands nervously around the blanket on her legs. "Hey."

"I'd, uh… I'd ask you how you're feeling, but I kind of get the idea you've been asked that enough. And, well…" His eyes rolled over her face and then briefly over the white bandage wrapped several times around her forehead. "Truth be told, you look pretty damn great."

A repressed laugh forced itself out of Joey's mouth, and Danny's attempt at flattery instantly lightened her mood. She knew he was only trying to eliminate the air of awkward tension surrounding them, and she was thankful: awkwardness and silence were two things that had no business existing in the first place where they were concerned.

"Yes. You would be correct. And thank you, but you don't have to lie to make me feel better, y'know." Allowing her gaze to trace the lines of his face and that dimple that was once again on full display, Joey felt an overwhelming rush of emotion crash into her. After everything that had happened, he was there. Danny was there. She wasn't sure she even deserved his friendship, but there was no hiding the tears that quickly filled her big brown eyes. "Danny. I'm so sorr—"

"Hey." He shook his head. "None of that, okay?" She didn't need to be sorry. Sure, he'd been hurt, but he knew better than anyone that you couldn't control the way you felt or who your heart chose to love. Moving from his chair, he sat down on her bed, wanting to be closer to her. "You don't need to be sorry."

"You tried to warn me. You tried—" Joey's words stopped on a choked sob, and Danny wrapped his arms tightly around her small frame, dragging her into his chest and stroking a gentle hand up and down the length of her back.

"Forget what I said. I was just upset." Danny retreated a little, smoothing his thumbs beneath her eyes to wipe away the tears that had fallen, careful to avoid the stitches. "It doesn't matter anymore. The only thing that matters is that you're okay." He gifted her another smile, and as they stared at each other for a few long beats, Joey felt a spark of hope flicker inside of her.

She wasn't okay—far from it—but having Danny there with her made it all a little easier.

Reaching over, he swept away a loose curl that had escaped from her bun and tucked it behind her ear. "What were you thinking, huh? Taking off with Roya like that?"

Joey gave her head a shake, the movement once again causing her head to throb and her eyes to squint against the pain. "That's just it. I wasn't thinking at all. I needed to leave and that was—"

"But you know she hasn't been trained to handle that kind of terrain, Joey. You know she's not ready for the woods."

She did know. She knew fine well, yet she'd taken her anyway, ignoring Olivia and the other staff and figuring it would be the quickest route home. "I know. I know. I'm sorry. I'm so sorry."

"What happened anyway? Did she get spooked? Did she trip?" Staring at her and trying to make sense of the situation, Danny lifted his hand to the back of his neck, massaging away the stress and tension that had been there for days.

God.

He'd been so worried about her and just couldn't understand how she could have been so reckless. "Please tell me you didn't have her jump anything."

"It all happened so fast. I don't remember much, but there was a fallen tree in the path. I hadn't seen it, Danny, at least not right away, and by the time I realised it was there, it was too late. Roya stopped and I was thrown through the air. All I remember is the pain before everything faded to black."

Danny's chest fell on a long and heavy huff of air. Lecturing her on things she already knew wasn't going to do either of them any good. "I'm just relieved you're okay. We all are." Shifting around and scooting back, he curled his arm around her and gently pulled her into his side. "Promise me you won't do anything like that ever again."

Joey rested her head on his shoulder, her eyes flicking up to meet the hazel pools full of worry staring at her. "I promise."

As the two of them sat there, Joey let out a contented sigh at the comfort of being so close to him, and she squeezed him tighter, some of the last words he had spoken to her before her world had fallen apart replaying in her head. "I was afraid I'd never be able to do this again."

Danny smoothed his thumb up and down the soft skin of her arm. "Do what?"

"Lean on your shoulder."

STANDING OUTSIDE THE door, her coat buttoned and her handbag in the crook of her arm, Bea waited a moment with her head bowed.

It had been almost two weeks since she'd seen Joey. Helplessness had overwhelmed her in the corridor outside Will's office that day when all she'd wanted to do was wrap the girl up in her arms and tell her that everything would work out just fine.

She'd contemplated bringing flowers, or at least something to say 'get well soon', but flowers seemed too cheerful and God only knew that no one was feeling particularly cheerful at the moment. Joey wasn't going to be getting well any time soon, because it was more than her head that was broken, so had Bea settled for a small tub of home-baked biscuits: a little bit of sugar to keep her energy levels up.

Lifting her arm, she rapped her knuckles gently on the door and waited for an invitation to enter.

She was about to turn to leave, assuming Joey was asleep, when the young woman's soft voice, laced with an almost tentative undertone, stopped her.

The knock echoing around the room had pulled Joey from her mindless daze, and as she granted entry to whoever was standing just beyond the large door, her heart started to beat a little faster. She sat up straighter, adjusting the covers around her waist, and held her breath as Bea appeared around the barrier separating her from what seemed like the entire outside world.

Tears burned the backs of Joey's eyes, and she struggled to keep them from falling. She was so tired of crying, but seeing Bea—this woman who was so much more than a friend or a work colleague—had a swell of emotion clogging her throat. "Hey, Bea."

8

Bea forced a bright smile on her face, the pained expression that graced Joey's cutting her to the core. Seeing her looking so pale and tired instead of the vibrant and sparkling young woman she was used to seeing took her by surprise. "Well. Aren't you just a sight for sore eyes, sweetheart." She walked over to the bed and around towards the window where she sat in the high-backed chair, regretting the question that then tumbled freely without much forethought. "How are you feeling, dear?" How was she feeling? She expected that she felt like her heart had been trampled on, amongst other things.

Joey held her gaze.

The old woman was only attempting to make small talk, but that was just another 'thing' to add to the ever-growing list of 'things' Joey was tired of. For Bea's sake, she forced a counterfeit smile on her face. "I'm getting there. How are you? Is everything okay at the manor? I mean, with Graham and stuff…"

Bea stilled.

The manor.

Well, the manor was just not the manor anymore, not with Joey gone. Even with all of the curtains still drawn open each morning, the light had gone. The light had gone from their hearts and the light had gone from Will's eyes, but that wasn't something she needed to burden her with. "We're all getting along, dear. Graham is fine. But I'm not here to talk about all that. I'm here to check that you are looking after yourself—to check you're eating. I'm here to check you have everything you need and that your father is being cared for properly with you in here. How is your father, Joey? Is he doing okay?"

Inhaling a deep breath and holding the air in her lungs for a few seconds, she released it slowly. "I haven't had much of an appetite really, and well, Dad's okay. Emma is with him most days and Danny has been kind enough to bring him to see me as much as he can. Hopefully, I'll be going home soon." Joey paused, her next thoughts practically ready to jump from her tongue as Bea reached out and patted her hand with her gentle one. She still had questions, so many questions, and if there was anyone who could answer them—anyone who could maybe help her understand a little bit more—it was Bea. "Why didn't you tell me, Bea? How could you all stand around watching as I fell hopelessly in love with him and not tell me?"

Bea dragged in a deep breath, holding Joey's eyes, and squeezed her fingers around the young woman's hand. There was no wavering. There was no hesitation in her response, because as painful as all of this was, as troubled and broken as everyone was feeling, this was the only way it could have happened. Any other way and this big mess would just have gotten messier. "You know that it wasn't our story to tell, my love. It was…" She gave a tight smile before continuing, his name like a sworn secret on her lips. "It was William's story, Joey. You know this."

Joey shook her head, sighing. "But you all knew. Every single one of you knew and you refused to say anything." Hadn't any of them stopped to think perhaps that their silence was part of the problem? That it had only contributed to Will's inability to heal? "I've been a part of this from the beginning. I'm part of the reason he is the way he is. How am I supposed to live with that? How am I—" Joey stopped, her breath failing her as the truth and all the secrets once again punched her straight in the chest. Swallowing down, she mustered enough courage to ask the questions that haunted her every waking and sleeping minute. "How many times? How many times did he try hurting me? Was it really that bad? Was it really as bad as he made it out to be?"

Bea dropped her eyes to the bed, picking Joey's hand up and encasing it in her own. This was harder than she'd imagined. She knew the truth was going to rip the girl apart, but having to speak out loud the most hurtful bullets of all was something she hadn't prepared herself for. She hadn't envisaged that it would be her that would have to fire the final arrow. Lifting her head to meet Joey's expectant but almost imploring expression, the pleas from the girl's heart so visible on her face, she gave her a tight smile and nodded gently. "It was bad. He was angry, Joey. He was fourteen years old and really, really angry. He was angry with himself—and still is, as you know—but that anger became misplaced and he found himself targeting someone else so that he could try to... I don't know, move on, I guess. And unfortunately, you became his target. He needed someone to blame and so he blamed you." Bea took another deep breath. She hadn't really answered Joey's question fully.

How many times?

She didn't know. She hadn't kept count.

It took a few moments for Joey to gather her words, but when she did, they all poured out. "I don't know what to do. I don't know how to make this right or how to take away his pain. I don't know how to get him to look at me as the woman I am and not as that stupid little girl who, in his eyes, destroyed his entire life."

She stared at Bea, hoping the old woman, who always seemed to have the right answers, would have them for her now.

But for once, she had absolutely none.

Bea had absolutely nothing.

Her blue eyes held an immeasurable amount of sadness, and the tears Joey had been trying so hard to keep back, broke free. "Do you know what hurts the most, what makes this so hard? In spite of everything that I've learned and all that I know, I still love him. I love every broken part of him, and every time there is a knock on that door or a creak of its hinges, my heart can't help but beat a little faster in the hope that it will be him walking through it." The tears streamed down Joey's cheeks, hotter and faster than they ever had before, and there was no stopping the quiver of her chin or the painful lump in her throat that made it difficult to breathe. "I want him to walk through that door, Bea." Her voice left her on a sob. " I want him to walk through that door, but he's not going to, is he?"

Chapter 2

BEA UNBUTTONED HER coat and unfastened her headscarf before setting off towards the kitchen. She got a mere five or six steps before Graham appeared in front of her, seemingly out of nowhere.

"Good gracious." Bea's hand flew to her chest and her eyes fluttered closed as she tried to still the racing of her heart. "Scare an old woman, would you?"

"Sorry. I just wanted to catch you before I head out." Graham slipped his hands into his pockets and tried to disguise a frown.

"Well, follow me down to the kitchen. I'm a little late back and I need to get dinner started. Come on." She scuttled along the corridor, Graham by her side, and the pair of them in a companionable, yet emotion-filled silence.

After hanging her belongings on the back of the door, and tying her apron around her waist, she began pulling pans and utensils out, lining them up before busying herself in the fridge. "So. What was it you wanted, Graham?"

Still near the door, his hands clasped uncomfortably in front of him, Graham rocked back onto his heels and released a long breath through pursed lips. He looked over at Bea and waited until he had her attention. "How is she?"

Bea stopped what she was doing and rested her hands on the countertop. "She's Joey. She will be absolutely fine."

He eyed her for a moment and then slid his hands back into his pockets.

There was a strong and sturdy wall erected around Beatrice Sykes, but he could see right through it. He walked slowly to stand next to her, picking up a potato and beginning to peel it. "And how are you?" He turned his head to the side to catch her eyes and didn't miss the glassy look in them. He put the peeler and the potato back down and turned to face his long-standing colleague. She was holding it together as if her strength would hold everyone else together, too, and she didn't need to. She had kept this secret, carried the weight of this troubling tale, for so many years and every second had been done with a smile and a twinkle in her eye. She needed to know she didn't have to keep it up, not every moment of every day.

Graham ducked his head a little and smiled at her sadly. "Bea. You seem to forget that I know you better than most people. You don't have to hide from me. You don't have to stay strong for me."

Bea blinked, allowing the tears that had collected uncharacteristically to trickle over her lashes. Graham reached out and brushed them away with his thumb and wrapped a strong arm around her shoulders, pulling her gently to him. "You don't have to be the answer to everyone's problems all the time, Beatrice. You are allowed to lean on others when you need to." His grey eyes softened and he allowed his hand to rub supportively up and down her arm.

He had to be the strong one now.

He had to be the one to keep everyone upright until this mess was sorted out.

He would do whatever it took to make sure that the people he cared about were okay. Everyone had to be okay. There wasn't another option.

"It's all such a mess, Graham. I know you probably want to shout a million 'told you sos' at me, but what other choice did I have?" Bea turned to face him, her head tipping back slightly as a pained frown that he had never seen before changed the whole look of her face. "Did I bring this? Was this my fault for being a meddling old woman?"

He shook his head. "Don't do that, Bea. You have nothing but a heart of gold and despite this old cynic, you did what you thought would be best for everyone. You should not apologise for any of it. Yes, it's messy. Yes, there are broken hearts all over Christendom right now, but you know as well as I do that hearts mend—they do—and I think it is our job to keep on pushing for that. William and Josephine are hurting, but it won't last forever. Okay?"

Bea allowed a final tear to trace the path of its friends before pulling in a deep breath and wiping her fingers over her cheeks. She took a step back out of Graham's embrace and smiled, patting his chest. "When did you get all wise and sentimental about affairs of the heart, Mr Kent? I never put you down as a romantic."

He straightened himself up and shrugged. "I have been known to have my moments, Mrs Sykes."

She laughed and picked up a knife to chop the potato that he had peeled. "I shall remember that."

The pair worked together side by side for a few more minutes before Graham made his excuses and left to continue with business, leaving Bea with her own thoughts. She wasn't a meddling old woman, she knew that. She was just as wise as Graham and had just as much insight into how people's hearts beat for others'. She'd seen the love in the eyes of the youngsters for long enough to know that it was all meant to be, but once again, they needed a little help—they needed a little push in the right direction—and she wasn't going to stop trying until all avenues had been exhausted.

Pouring the ingredients into the huge crock-pot and placing the lid gently on top, she flicked the switch on before heading out of the kitchen and down towards the north wing, a mug of coffee in her hand.

There had been few sightings of William over the last week or so. He'd buried himself in his work and closed the door on the outside world once more. Bea's heart ached to see him smiling again. Her visit to the hospital had almost broken her, but hearing Joey's confession—hearing that despite everything, she was still very much in love with him—had been a gentle breeze below the wings of hope, and her plan was to cling onto it for as long as was necessary.

On reaching his office door, Bea stilled a moment, fixing an expression on her face that would not scream of anything other than 'good afternoon', and then lifted her hand to knock. She knew he was in there, so his silence caused her to knock a little harder and to clear her throat. "William. I have a coffee for you. Can I come in?"

The shuffling of papers and the scrape of a chair on the hardwood floor had her standing a little straighter as she waited for him to come to the door. It opened faster than she anticipated and made her flinch as Will suddenly appeared in front of her, dishevelled, unshaven and void of emotion.

"Willi—"

"Thanks, Bea." Will reached out, taking the mug from her hand, and stepped back in order to close the door, but before he had the chance, she reached out and clasped her hand around his forearm.

"I was wondering if I could have a minute." She smiled gently at him, holding his tired eyes with her own, and waited for him to react.

It took him a moment as he stood there, unsure whether or not to let her in. The only thing she could possibly want to talk about would be Josephine, and as topics of conversation went, that one wasn't at the top of his list. "I'm snowed under. It'll have to wait." He went to shut the door again, but again, Bea stopped him, this time by halting the door on its journey to shut her in the corridor.

"I just want a minute. Please."

Bowing his head, Will pulled in a deep breath and stepped to the side. He knew better than to shut her out. She would always find a way of worming her way in, in that extra special 'Sykes' way. "Just for a moment. I really am busy."

The old cook nodded and stepped into his office, glancing around the space with her hands clasped in front of her. Will gestured for her to sit down and rounded his desk to his chair. The pair of them had known each other for so long that there was no need for pleasantries or polite pre-chat. Bea was there for a reason and she wouldn't beat about the bush.

He sat back in his chair and linked his fingers over his chest, waiting until she found the words she was looking for.

"I went to see Josephine today. In the hospital."

He'd been expecting exactly that, and so his expression didn't falter. His heart, however, took off in his chest at the mere mention of her name, and a swirling of nervous energy in his stomach had him dragging air in through his nose discreetly. He didn't have anything to say, and Bea took that as her cue to continue.

"Her wound seems to be healing well." She dropped her eyes to her lap. "But... well, her heart isn't doing too good." She lifted her lids and looked at him, waiting for something—some indication that he was interested in what she had to say to him. "She's hurting. Her heart is broken, and you and I both know that you're the only one who can fix it —"

"Bea, please —"

"Let me finish. You're the only one who can fix it, and she knows that too. I'm not suggesting for one minute that you should go storming in to whisk her off her feet in an instant. I know how these things work. I had my heart broken once, too, you know. I know it takes time, but can you find it in you to go and see her? Can you show your face so she knows you at least care? That poor girl is lying in the hospital broken and bruised in so many ways because she thinks you hate her. She thinks you threw her away because you hate her."

Will shifted uncomfortably and leaned forwards, placing his elbows on the desk and dropping his head into his hands.

"You don't hate her, do you, Will?" Bea pushed to her feet and walked tentatively around the side of the desk, placing a gentle hand on his shoulder. "You don't still blame her do you?"

At her words, Will kicked his head up and turned his head sharply to look at Bea. His voice was loud and angry. "Of course I don't blame her. She was a kid. She was a six year old kid. I'm not completely stupid." He shook his head and covered Bea's hand with his own. "I'm sorry, Bea. I didn't mean to shout at you. I'm just…"

Just what? What was he?

He didn't even know.

The only word that popped into his head was 'empty'. He was completely drained of everything: emotion, drive, happiness, hunger… it had all gone that day in the woods. Everything she had made him feel just trickled away as he saw her lying there, and there was nothing he could do to start filling himself back up again. It was tragically impossible, but how could he explain himself to anyone? How could he make everyone see that simply having her

18

around was not going to make anything better for anyone? He'd made a decision because he was scared to death of himself, and he couldn't have her around because she would end up being scared of him too. It was better for everyone if she just hated him—if she believed he didn't care about her—and that was just the way it had to be, regardless of what anyone else thought of the situation.

"Just let her see you care. Let her see that you don't hate her."

Will stood up and walked over to the window, his eyes immediately finding the rose garden, and as he slid his hands into his pockets, his mind betrayed him for a moment as it floated like a feather on the wind back to the day he had watched Josephine Bell wander lazily in and out of the bushes—the day his heart had beat a little louder and his eyes had seen a little clearer.

She was his everything.

Everything that she was made everything better, but he would ruin her. He would break her strength and shatter her kindness, and he couldn't be the one to change Joey. He couldn't be the one to turn her bitter, hateful and scared. This way, at least she had a chance to survive, and he was damned if he was going to selfishly keep hold of her just because he needed her in order to keep himself afloat.

No.

It was his job to let her go, to give her a chance to be loved by someone who would nurture her and allow her to shine like the bright star she was—someone who was worthy of her love.

He snapped out of his daydream and turned to face Beatrice. "No."

Bea frowned. "Why?"

He walked back to his chair and picked up the letter he had been reading before she came in. "Because it's better for her if she thinks I hate her."

"And how did you come to that conclusion?" Bea began to move back towards the chair but stopped beside it, placing her hand on the back of it, watching as Will practically dismissed her with his avoidance.

"Because then she can hate me back."

Pulling her lips in tightly, Bea dipped her chin to her chest and squeezed the leather upholstery. "Well, she doesn't."

"Doesn't what?" Will continued to shuffle bits of paper and slurped on his coffee, not once meeting Bea's eyes. He was becoming increasingly uncomfortable and needed to distract his mind with work more than ever.

"She doesn't hate you."

"She will. In time."

Bea smiled to herself and walked towards the door. Gripping the handle, she pulled it open and began to step into the corridor. She halted and looked back over her shoulder at the broken man whom her heart beat so hard for—the man whom she loved like a son. "I wouldn't be so sure of that, sweetheart. I'll bring you some dinner shortly." She closed the door quietly behind her and pressed her fingertips against it before shuffling off down towards the servants quarters.

Will stared at the door, at the emptiness of his office, as he was left with Bea's words. They swam around the room like a whisper and troubled his already troubled mind.

She had to hate him. There was no other option.

He was too dangerous, and he would *not* see her hurt.

Chapter 3

Cold by Jorge Mendez
Look Away by Eli Lieb, Steve Grand

WITH HIS HEAD bowed low and his hands gripping the steering wheel of the Bentley, Will pulled in a series of deep breaths to shut out all internal chatter that was telling him this was a good idea, and equally those telling him it was a bad idea.

He had to do this no matter the outcome; he had to see she was okay.

He glanced up, peering out through the front windscreen at the bright squares of light from the hospital windows that glowed in the dark night. They were strange places, hospitals: bustling and busy, alive and awake at all times of the day. He watched as patients and their loved ones entered sporadically through the Accident and Emergency entrance with their midnight ailments and problems, hobling and clinging to one another for physical and emotional support. Here and there, paramedics wandered in and out, assisting people from the backs of ambulances, giving precise and timely feedback to doctors and nurses about their first response attention. He watched, interested, as a young pregnant woman was wheeled in, clutching her bulging stomach and wailing in pain whilst her husband talked animatedly to one of the ambulance drivers, who was doing her best to calm him down without being rude. It was a strange scene to watch, one that almost filled him with momentary joy for the guy who was about to become a father.

What a feeling that must be.

But then real life kicked him in the gut again and brought him back to the horror of his situation.

He wasn't sure how long he continued to sit there, watching, but after a while, Will switched his engine back on and rolled the car slowly into the multi-story car park, pulling into one of a number of empty spots. Mechanically, robotically, he climbed out and approached the pay metre.

1 hour - £2
2 hours - £4
3 hours - £6

He fumbled around for change in his pocket and slipped two pound coins into the slot, his foot tapping as he waited for his ticket, and after displaying it in the window of the car, Will began the two minute walk from to the hospital wards, moving from the harsh fluorescent lights of the car park to the dim street lights that lined the minor roads and paths around the hospital.

Navigating the wide and bright corridors, Will located the signs that led to Ward 23—the signs that led her: to Josephine Bell.

Up until Bea had left him in his office a few days before, no one had troubled him with talk of Josephine. They had left him to his work, not questioned him about his whereabouts nor if he would be home for dinner, but now that silence had been broken. Now, the erected walls around him were shaking again, and he could not get rid of his thoughts of her, not that he'd had much luck with that anyway.

Since the accident, since he had left her there on the ground in the woods, it wasn't just the nightmares of his past that kept him awake at night. Josephine was in every damn dream he had.

Up until Bea had left him in his office a few days before, he had been able, as always, to bury himself waist deep in his work in daylight hours, all thoughts of anything pushed aside until the end of the day.

However, now her name had been spoken aloud, and all of his attempts to shut out reality during the day were futile.

He pushed open the large double doors that led down the final corridor, which was bathed in a softer light as patients slept, and stepped through them, halting on the other side. He hadn't even thought to prepare himself for all of this. He had just made his decision and moved with it — he had made the decision to come for his own peace of mind. Standing there, though, with only one hundred metres to go, his heart plummeted to his stomach at the prospect of seeing her. Everything screamed at him to turn back around, to return to his nightmare-filled house, and deal with the fucking mess he had made. He didn't deserve peace of mind. He didn't deserve to feel relieved about any of this because it was his mess. He had caused every single bit of pain and hurt that every one of these people were feeling, so why the hell did he think he had the right to come and feel better about any of it?

A soft female voice dragged him from his thoughts. "Are you okay there?"

He snapped his head to the side, his eyes roaming over the stranger for a second or two before remembering where he was when her nurse's uniform became apparent. He ran his fingers through his hair and looked back down the corridor of the high dependency ward.

"Visiting hours technically finished here a few hours ago."

Will turned back to face the young woman. "I…"

"Who was it you were hoping to see?"

Will dropped to a crouch on the floor and let his head fall into his hands as he tried to steady his heartbeat. "I don't want to visit really. I just..." He stopped and got a grip of himself. "I just want to know she's okay."

"Josephine?"

Will's eyes locked with the nurses in confusion, his brow twitching slightly with questions.

"She's the only female we have on the ward, so when you said 'she' I just put two and two together." She smiled kindly. "Come on. I'll let you have a couple of minutes with her." She began walking down the corridor and Will watched her for a few moments before his feet took on a life of their own and followed her. After a few steps, she stopped and turned to face him. "You'll have to be quiet: she's asleep."

Will nodded obediently and the pair continued side by side until the nurse stopped again and turned to grab the handle of a door.

Without thinking, Will reached out and placed his hand on her arm to stop her. "No."

Confusion floated across the woman's face.

"I'm sorry. Just... I think it's better if I stay out here. If I can have a moment alone at her window perhaps?"

The nurse shrugged. "Whatever you prefer. I'm happy to let you in if you're quiet."

"No. It's okay. I'll... the window will be fine."

With a curt nod, the young woman moved away. "I'll be back in a few minutes then."

Will smiled tightly and watched as she moved back to the nurses station at the other end of the corridor and then inhaled deeply.

An icy fear ran up and down his back —fear of what he would see, fear of how he would feel and fear that she would wake up and see him.

If she woke up and saw him, he didn't have a clue what he would do.

When he'd talked himself into coming, the idea that he would actually be in the same room as her hadn't even entered his mind. He'd never planned to sit by her bed and hold her hand the way a man who loves her should. He never planned to brush the hair from her cheek and talk to her softly about how sorry he was and how much he wished he could turn back time, go right back to the beginning and make it all better. There was never a moment that he'd imagined he would be sitting there with his forehead pressed gently against her arm whilst he begged for her forgiveness, but as he neared the window, his heart in his mouth and his lungs high in his chest as he held his breath, all of those things were the only things he wanted to do.

Except he knew better.

He stood in front of the clear pane of glass with his chin dipped and his hands in his pockets and finally, slowly and with pain in his heart, lifted his eyes to see her.

Josephine lay on her back, fast asleep, her arm across her stomach and with a cannula in the back of her hand. The thin blue hospital blanket had slipped to the floor, leaving her tangled up in a starched white sheet, and Will found himself having to suppress the urge to walk in, pick it up and to tuck it around her again.

Her face was turned ever so slightly towards him, but he held off looking at it for as long as possible. Instead, he let his eyes roam down the length of the bed, noticing her leg that was bent up and out of the sheet, the silky skin of her calf exposed. The room was full of flowers and cards, not one thing from himself, and he closed his eyes at the thought. That room should be full of gifts and get well love from him, but how could he begin to give her those kinds of superficial wishes? How could any of that stuff express how he really felt?

Will's furrowed and pained brow twitched as he finally allowed his eyes to travel up the length of her body and rest on her face. Her long brown locks curled around her ears and under her chin and her lashes dusted the apples of her cheeks.

She looked so peaceful and rested.

There was no sign of the tears she had shed that day, or the heartache that had creased her features as he'd let her walk out of his office door, out of his life, with no hesitation.

Without prior thought, Will lifted his arm up and touched the glass with the tips of his fingers and let them linger there as he took in the curve of her shoulders and her jawline, remembering how in love with her he still was, but the sound of the nurses shoes padding across the tiles disturbed him and had him huffing his demons out of his nostrils.

He let his fingers slip from the glass.

"All good?"

Will turned to face her and nodded. "Thank you."

"No problem. I'm sure she will be thrilled to know you came. Who shall I say visited?"

Will looked back at the window and through the glass, committing to memory how peaceful and trouble free she looked without him.

She's better off thinking you hate her, Will.

He pulled in another deep breath and stepped past the nurse, heading slowly back down towards the exit with his hands in his pockets and his head low. "No one. Thank you."

Chapter 4

Run Away Heart by The Strange Familiar
Roots Before Branches by Room For Two
All I Do by Yuna
Paperboats by Nessi

Two months later…

A CLIPBOARD IN hand, Joey stood in one of the
exam rooms at Paws and Tails, listening carefully and
taking notes as Dr Watson finished rattling off the
information for the patient's file. She smiled politely at the
owners—a young couple who had just added the newest
furry addition to their small but growing family—and then
crouched down to pet the border collie pup that was
tugging and making cute growling noises at the hem of her
trousers.

"You're a playful one, aren't you?" She tickled him
behind the ear and then ran her fingers through his soft
coat.

It was the middle of March and the day marked the
start of her sixth week working at the surgery as an
assistant to the vets and the other technicians, a position
that had been graciously offered by Danny's uncle under
Danny's recommendation, and she couldn't have been
happier or more thankful, the new job keeping her busy

and her mind off of everything that no longer mattered — off the one person she was trying so hard to forget.

Fifty eight days and five hours had gone by since she'd walked out of the entrance hall of Wildridge manor, and while the hole in her heart was just as painful and hollow as Will's words had left it that day, it was time for her to move on. She needed to finally take charge of her life, and, for once, she needed to put herself first. Accepting Will's offer to pay for her education was not something she could bring herself to do. She just couldn't. As kind as the gesture may have seemed, it felt wrong.

But it was more than that.

It had felt like a kick to her chest, as if everything they had been and everything they'd shared could simply be erased with the endless supply of funds in his bank account.

She'd told him she didn't want his money, and she'd meant it.

Not all of his offers were to be avoided, however. After her first full month of working, Joey had sent Will a rent check for the house. She had been determined to make ends meet on her own, but when it arrived back in her mailbox a few days later, she knew any attempt at paying him would be futile.

Living rent free in the house had its benefits, though. It meant that she was able to keep up with the monthly bills on her own and still be able to put some money aside to afford her course fees once university officially started in September. The only thing left to do now was apply.

Straightening herself, Joey gave the pup's owners another smile and headed for the main reception area. For a Monday afternoon, the office was unusually quiet. A handful of people sat patiently on benches with their pets resting beside their feet — surprisingly obediently — waiting for their name to be called.

Not having a lot of experience meant Joey was left to some of the smaller tasks such as filing paperwork, taking notes during examinations and cleaning the exam rooms after each appointment, but regardless of how menial her duties were, she loved it. She loved being around the animals and the staff—who had welcomed her with open arms from the very first day—and she loved that she was finally able to focus and work towards achieving her dream. She passed the paperwork to Alice, one of the receptionists, who quickly imput the information into her computer before handing it back to Joey to put away.

As she sorted through the paperwork and placed it into the appropriate folders, the chiming of the bell hanging over the front door floated to her ears, stealing her attention. She turned her head to see Danny walking straight towards her, the dimple on his cheek on full display.

He stopped a few feet away, setting his keys down on the counter, and Joey's lips lifted into a smile. "Hey."

"Hey."

Dr Watson appeared beside Joey not a moment later and Danny raised his hand, waving to the balding, elderly gentleman dressed in his white coat. "Uncle Frank."

"Daniel." He lifted his chin in a nod and glanced down at the watch strapped to his wrist, before flicking his gaze back to his nephew. "What are you doing here? Shouldn't you be in the middle of teaching a lesson, or shall I assume you're giving the word 'slacker' an entirely new meaning?"

Danny smirked, running his finger under his nose. The old man loved giving him a hard time, but it was all in good fun. "My afternoon lesson was cancelled, so I figured I'd stop in and check on our girl—see how she's getting on."

"Miss Bell is getting on just fine. I can assure you, she's a fully capable adult who doesn't need checking up on." Pinching the metal frame of his glasses between his fingers, he slid them back up to the bridge of his nose as he read over the prescription in his hands. "I was getting ready to ask if she would mind accompanying me tomorrow to

Lakewood Stables. Richard called, he thinks one of his older mares may have come down with something and would feel better if I stopped by to check her over."

Surprise soared across Joey's features and she glanced at her boss, quickly nodding her head. "I'd love to."

While Paws and Tails was a vet's surgery that welcomed a variety of animals, Dr Watson himself specialised in equine care, meaning that a lot of his time was spent making visits to the surrounding farms and stables instead of remaining within the walls of an exam room. Being able to accompany him on one of those visits was an opportunity she didn't want to miss.

Joey loved horses, and not being able to interact with them on a daily basis like she once did while working at the manor had been a hard adjustment for her to make. She hadn't seen Roya since that day, and every time she thought of her, she was reminded of all that she'd lost. Of course, Danny had encouraged her on numerous occasions to visit her horse, but how could she? Going to the manor wasn't an option, no matter how much she missed Roya. She couldn't risk being caught on the grounds, but more than that, she couldn't bear the possibility of seeing Will. Reliving memories that were bound to surface if she stepped so much as a foot on the property would be way more than she could handle.

No. It was best for everyone if she kept her distance. The plan was to close the wound in her heart, not remove the sutures that were starting to form and watch helplessly as it bled all over again.

"Do you mind if I take Joey to lunch?"

Danny's unexpected question knocked Joey from her thoughts, and she turned towards Dr Watson to await his response.

"Why the hell are you asking me? She's the one that has to sit with ya."

A soft chuckle erupted from Joey's chest, the banter between the two men confirming how close they were. It was no wonder Danny loved horses and people as much as he did. In the short time she'd gotten to know Dr Watson, it had become clear they were not only related, but their relationship resembled more of a father and son than an uncle and nephew. Swinging her head back to Danny, who stood with an incredulous expression on his face, she rolled her lips between her teeth, stopping her grin in its tracks.

The corners of Danny's mouth twitched. "I was just making sure it was okay if I stole her away for an hour or two. Next time I won't bother asking." This time he didn't wait for his uncle's reply. He stared right at Joey. "Fancy going to lunch with me?"

She crossed her arms over her chest and shook her head in amusement, before glancing at Frank for his reassurance and approval. It wasn't quite her lunch hour just yet, and he had been so generous already with offering her the job, the last thing she wanted to do was have it seem like she was taking advantage of his relationship with Danny.

Frank cocked his head to the side, gesturing her to go. "Go on. We're not busy anyway."

"Thank you. We shouldn't be long." She tossed her thumb over her shoulder, this time speaking to Danny. "I just need to grab my cardigan and bag from the back. I'll meet you in the car?"

"Sure thing." Grinning, Danny picked his keys up from the counter and spun around, striding happily out the door.

"What are you hungry for? Anything in particular?"

Joey shook her head as she closed the passenger side door and set her handbag down on the floor between her feet. "No. Wherever you want to go is fine with me." She grabbed hold of the seat belt and began to buckle herself in, lifting her chin to look up at Danny at the same time it clicked into place. "I appreciate you doing this, but you didn't have to, y'know. I'd packed a lunch."

Of course she had.

Danny knew the wage she received was only just a little bit more than what she needed to get by, and every extra penny she earned was stashed away for university, and hopefully, a vehicle in the not too far future.

"I figured as much, but my afternoon schedule is empty, and I wanted to see you. It's been a while and I thought it would give us a chance to catch up." He knocked his shoulder playfully against hers. "I've missed you, Just Joey."

Warmth from the sound of Danny using her nickname—one she hadn't heard in quite sometime—swept down her chest, and a genuine smile stretched across her lips. "I've missed you, too."

After making sure she was safely in her seat, Danny started the car and pulled out of the car park, heading in the direction of the first food place that called to their stomachs. The decision to take her to lunch had been spur of the moment and rather whimsical, but he was glad to be able to steal her away and spend time with her, even if it was brief. She'd been so busy lately with work, and the desire to do nothing but return home after her hours had finished meant she confined herself to the house like a recluse.

"Have you had a chance to get your application submitted for uni yet?"

Joey licked the sudden dryness from the corners of her mouth, the idea of her returning to school after all this time making her feel nauseous. "Not yet. I'm working on it."

"Well, if I can help you in any way, just let me know."

"Thanks." She paused, contemplating his offer before speaking again. "Actually, do you think maybe you can give me a lift to the admissions office? I'd rather get it dropped off in person than have to mail it, and they are usually closed by the time I get home." She hated asking him, knowing it was a huge inconvenience on his part, but there was no way she'd make it there in time with having to rely on public transport.

"Yeah, of course. Just say when." Scanning the row of shops, he tapped his thumb along the steering wheel. "So. Going on a house call tomorrow, huh?"

Joey bit down on her lip and nodded her head, a beaming smile on her face attempting to break through. "Yeah. I'm kind of excited about it. Not that I don't love working at the office, but it will be nice to be able to get out for a change and interact with the horses."

"I bet."

Joey's ecstaticism about the opportunity, the way her face had lit up as his uncle asked her to accompany him, reminded Danny of all the reasons why he'd initially fallen for her. Even now, he still cared about her—immensely— but he also knew that underneath her supposed happiness was a barely beating heart whose broken pieces belonged to the only man capable of fully putting it back together, the same man who had been responsible for breaking it.

"I'm nervous too."

"Nervous?" Danny's head snapped around, confusion narrowing his brows as he tooks his eyes from the road and stared at her. "Why are you nervous?"

She shrugged. "I don't know. I just... it's been a while and—"

"Joey, there is absolutely nothing for you to be nervous about, understand me? My uncle thinks very highly of you, and if he thought for one second you weren't prepared to handle it, he would never have asked you to go with him. I mean that."

Joey pinched her lips together to stop herself from arguing back. Danny was a great friend, and she'd always live with regret for hurting him the way she had. "Thanks, Danny. It means a lot. This all means so much. I'm not sure what I'd have done if you hadn't recommended me to Frank."

"It's what friends are for, right?"

She smiled in agreement. "Right."

A silence filled the car, although not an uncomfortable one: they had moved past that over the last couple of months. The bridges that Joey had once thought were burned between them were now re-erected and standing stronger than ever. They were back to the laughs and the jokes, all things she had missed greatly during the span of weeks when there had been no communication between them whatsoever.

"So, my schedule on Thursday is pretty much empty aside from a ten am lesson."

"Oh?" Rolling her head lazily to the side, she stared at him with a raised brow. "And is there a reason why you're telling me this?"

"Well..." He scratched at the coarse stubble dusting his jawline. "I was thinking I could speak with Uncle Frank and maybe he'd be willing to give you a paid day off so you could come by and see Roya for a few hours."

"Danny—" Joey sighed, feeling the creeping of tension that invaded her muscles every time they had this conversation. "We've been through this."

"Just hear me out, okay? I know. Trust me. I know all your reasons for not wanting to come, but you can't sit there and tell me you don't miss her."

"You know I do."

And she did. God, did she ever. Words couldn't express how much she missed her, the bond between them stronger than she ever would have thought possible, but she couldn't. She couldn't go there. She knew Roya was in great hands with Danny, and hearing his updates about her would just have to suffice for now.

Pulling into the car park of a small pizza shop, Danny killed the engine and turned his entire body to face her. He could read her mind and her thoughts and decided it was about time to put her biggest concern to rest. "He won't be around."

Silence stretched between them for a few seconds as Joey swallowed down slowly, a look of unease rolling across her face at the mention of Will.

"For what it's worth, he's drowning himself in work. You can come and see her and leave before he even returns home. You don't have to see him. He doesn't even need to know you were there."

A pulse of sadness throbbed in her chest at Danny's words.

She shouldn't care.

She didn't want to care.

Will drowning himself in work and alcohol was what he excelled at. He had been right. He had chosen this. He had chosen to suffer in his sadness and remain in the dark, to find his comfort in the temporary vices that only ever kept his hurtful past a few sips away. She was done caring, but that was beside the point. "Danny, I don't—"

"You don't have to be there for long. Just stop by for an hour or two and spend time with her. I think it will do you both some good. She needs it, Joey. We don't include her in the lesson rotation, which means the only time she ever gets ridden is when either I or Olivia have free time. Come see her. Please."

He wasn't going to let this go.

Joey huffed out a weary breath. "I'll think about it, okay?" She cocked her head to the side and reached for the door handle. "Come on, let's go eat."

Stepping off the bus, Joey hooked the strap of her handbag over her shoulder and started in the direction of her house. After working all day, she was ready to get home, eat dinner and slip into the comfort of her bed. She couldn't wait for the day she didn't have to rely on public transport or someone else for a ride.

Hitting the play button on her playlist, she allowed the sounds of her music to carry her the rest of the way, ignoring the signs of life surrounding her. As exhausted as she was, the brief fifteen minutes walk at the start and end of each day were the ones she looked forward to the most. They were the only times when she didn't feel like she needed to pretend to be okay. She didn't need to wear a smile for the sake of everyone else around her.

As she climbed the steps onto the front porch, she tugged her headphones from her ears and stopped to look at the rose bush beside her. The buds were starting to emerge, a sign that they would soon be in full bloom, and she ran her fingertips gently over them before turning and unlocking the door.

"Hey, Dad. I'm home." She shrugged off her cardigan, draping it over the arm of the sofa and placing her handbag on top of it as she moved into the kitchen, expecting to see her father sitting at the table. Instead, he was positioned in front of the sink, washing the dirty dishes she had been too tired to get to the previous evening. A pot of homemade chilli sat on the stove simmering, and a frown tugged at her mouth. "What are you doing? You should be resting." Walking up beside him, she reached out to take the plate he was in the middle of scrubbing clean. "I'm home now. I'll take care of it. Go relax."

Little John refused to hand it over. Yes, there were days when his body didn't quite do what he wanted it to, days where it hurt simply to get off the couch, but today wasn't one of them, and Joey had been working so hard, he wanted to do this for her. For once, he didn't want to feel completely helpless. "I'm just fine, d'ya hear me? I know my limits and when enough is enough."

Sighing in defeat, Joey pushed onto her toes and pressed a kiss to her father's cheek. Choosing her battles was something she was slowly starting to learn, and given her exhausted state, this was one war she didn't have the energy to engage in. Turning around, she sat down at the table, watching as he finished.

"How was work today?" His voice carried over his shoulder, and she smiled to herself, recalling her lunch date with Danny.

"It was great. Danny stopped by to see me. He took me to lunch."

"He did?"

"Yeah, he did."

A sense of relief fell over John at his daughter's words. Lately, she had been so distant, occupying her time with work and closing herself off from what seemed like the rest of the world. He understood why, but the happiness he'd seen in her on Christmas Day and the days that followed had completely vanished, and he was eager for it to return, to see it dance in her eyes again. He hoped that if anyone had the ability to help reignite her spark, it was Danny. "That was nice of him. That boy cares about you, y'know. A lot. He's a good kid, Joey."

Joey folded her arms across her chest, picking at a piece of lint on her shirt sleeve. "I know. He is the best."

And he truly was.

There was not a doubt in her mind he'd make a great husband and an even better father, but the only person he would ever be in her heart was a friend. She knew that. Danny knew that. And while her father may have secretly wished it had been Danny she'd fallen for, even he knew that.

"He wants me to go see Roya."

John paused, and as a permeating silence thickened the air, both of their thoughts travelled to the manor and to the one person neither of them had spoken about since that day—since Joey had discovered the heartbreaking truth. Will was a topic they both had avoided, but Little John wasn't sure if it was intentional avoidance on her part or his own. Drying the last dish, he moved over to the pot of chilli and spooned two large scoops into a bowl, bracing himself for whatever conversation lay ahead. Surely she still had questions, and it was only a matter of time before she started asking them.

"Do you really think that's a wise decision?"

Sitting herself up a little straighter, Josephine shrugged. Of course going to the manor wasn't a wise decision, but there was a large part of her that was desperate to see the horse Will had gifted her, and that alone made her mind waver.

Setting her food down in front of her, John grabbed his own and two mugs from the cupboard, filling them full of hot tea before joining her at the table.

"Thanks, Dad." Joey cradled the drink in her hands, the weight of her father's gaze causing a shiver of trepidation to run down the length of her spine.

They were back to him.

Somehow, they were back to the conversation they both knew they needed to have but one that neither had any idea how to begin. She sat, staring at her him, searching for words. If she was going to have any successful chance of moving on, she needed to bring it up. "It makes sense now—all of it: why he hates me, why he didn't want me there, why you tried to warn me away from him." A lump formed in her throat and she quickly chased it down with a sip of tea. Her fingers ran absentmindedly around the rim of the mug as she placed it down on the table, and she looked up at her father through her lashes, sadness pouring from her big brown eyes. "You won't ever forgive him, will you?"

Little John's brows knitted as he contemplated Joey's question. Will had only been a boy at the time—of course he had—but John had continued to work for Nicholas and eventually William over the years, and he'd seen the way hate and anger had consumed the younger Marshall-Croft—how it had changed him. He was no longer the same boy who'd played hide and seek with Joey in the rose garden. He'd become heartless and cold: an empty shell of a person, void of the bright young soul that had once burned with optimism and ambition.

But how could he possibly explain that?

How could he make her understand?

John's love for his daughter and his need to protect her was far more important than forgiving a man he wasn't sure could be redeemed.

"Joey. Sweetheart..."

Joey swirled her spoon around the chilli. She wasn't hungry, and it quickly dawned on her she really didn't want to be having this conversation at all. "No. It's okay, because it doesn't even matter." Pushing her bowl away, she stood to her feet. "I'm tired. I'm going to go up to bed to get an early night."

"Josephine, please." He couldn't allow her to walk away. Twenty-three years of lies and avoidance had been enough. "We need to talk about this."

"Talk about this?" A laugh full of contempt forced itself from her chest. "After all this time, and *now* you want to talk about it? What do you want to know, Dad?" She clenched down on her back teeth, attempting to rein in her emotions. "Do you want to hear how I fell in love with him and how over the course of a few short months he somehow became my everything? Or how there is now this emptiness inside of me that I don't know how to begin to fill?"

John looked at her sadly, guilt stinging his heart. She was so strong and beautiful, but he knew his daughter better than he knew himself, and, right then, she was barely holding herself together.

"Do you have any idea what it's like to walk around feeling like you're only half of a whole? Because that's how I feel—that's exactly how I feel." The corners of her eyes burned and her vision blurred. "But you know what? I'm going to be okay. I didn't need him in my life before and I sure as hell don't need him now."

She continued to speak the words out loud as if saying them was for her own reassurance, and John rose from his chair. He walked towards her and pulled her to him. Pain was something he dealt with nearly everyday of his life, but as he wrapped his arms around his daughter and listened to her speak into his chest, he realised it didn't come close to the ache he felt at seeing her like this: only half alive and so completely broken.

"I don't want to need him." Her voice came on a whisper, the lump in her throat now painful and making it difficult to breathe, much less speak. Her words were honest and true. She *didn't* want to need him. She wanted to live her life and forget William Marshall-Croft, forever.

Chapter 5

"JUST SORT IT and send me the paperwork, Simon."

"Man, chill the hell out. The paperwork is done. I can drop it off this afternoon on my way home from the office."

"Fine. Good. Do that then."

Will hung up and dropped his phone to the desk before pulling his laptop towards him and continuing to type out the letters and e-mails that'd had him tied to his desk all morning. A handful of new properties were in the process of being bought and he was keeping all of his fingers crossed regarding finalisation of the contracts that week. Simon, as usual, had deftly managed the transitions with little input from Will, which meant he was able to set up more meetings for more properties, all of which were keeping his head above water and his mind thoroughly occupied.

Weighing in the back of his mind was the sale of the manor, which was still not certain. The pressure from the interested companies was starting, and Will was in a state of limbo. Simon had made a valid point that night at the ball about it being dead money. The house and surrounding land was enormous and here he was, rattling around inside

41

of it for the sake of sentiment. He knew it wasn't smart business, and so that part of him was leaning towards setting up a series of meetings with Green Frog: the one company that Simon seemed more keen on than any of the others who had put offers in.

He stood from his desk and walked over to the window, placing his arm on the glass and resting his forehead against it. It was a view he once was ambivalent towards. Ambivalence had then turned to something he'd cherished, and now, looking out on that rose garden and all the memories that came with it—memories of the woman he loved and how he had turned her away—there was an overwhelming sense of regret. Was this the sentiment he was clinging to now? Or was it still the past and all the thoughts of his mother that had him hanging on to his childhood home? He wasn't sure he could separate the two now. Every inch of the place reeked of his mother now that the secrets were out, but every hallway echoed with the sound of Josephine Bell, and he wasn't sure which haunted him the most anymore.

Of course, the stables were still something he needed to think about. If the estate were to be turned into a theme park, there would be no room for the horses, and uprooting the whole riding school could be damaging in more ways than one.

Will's fingers curled into a fist and he tapped the side of his hand on the window a few times whilst he tried to get his thoughts in order, his eyes closed and his jaw ticking rhythmically as he clenched his back teeth.

It was the most difficult business decision he'd ever been faced with.

"Am I going to have to continually badger you, Will? Can you not see that all of this makes sense in every way? Every avenue you explore will wind up at the same destination. Sell, Will. Just fucking sell. What other option is there?"

Will sipped on a luke-warm cup of coffee as he sat across the room from Simon. What other option *was* there? Well there weren't any more were there? It was stay, or sell.

Stay or sell.

"I just can't see what's keeping you here, old boy. Not to be disrespectful or anything but, the family is gone, the filly is gone..." He chuckled a little as Will's head snapped up to look at him and he held his hands up in defense, shaking his head. "Sorry, man, but you have to admit that you're eventually going to be better off without her. You'd lost your game head with her around. Business would not have done well had she stayed. Am I right, or am I right?"

Will didn't answer. There was nothing to say. None of Simon's opinions about Josephine were worth a second thought, because no, he *wasn't* better off without her, but that wasn't why she was gone was it: *she* was better off without him, and that was the end of it.

"And once you sort this out—" Simon kept talking, gesturing towards Will with his arm outstretched. "This... mess you're in—you'll be laughing. You realise you're still in yesterday's clothes, I assume? And when was the last time you shaved, man? I hope you don't think you can turn up to meetings with these people looking like a tramp." He paused and smirked. "And smelling like one." He chuckled to himself but continued with his stream of babble. "You know, if you don't start making plans soon, these companies are going to get restless and will end up pulling out. They don't like to be messed around. They'll take their money else—"

"Just drop it for now, Simon. Please. I am well aware of all of this. It's my job to know. I am also well aware of the fact that if they really want my property, they'll wait. So for now, they will have to wait. I am not ready to make decisions." Will flicked his eyes towards Simon, whose brows were raised and mouth was down-turned in a way that let Will know he was backing down for now. Another thing he was aware of was the physical state he was in, and having it pointed out to him by Simon just made the whole mess even more messy.

"You're the boss."

Will eye-balled him for a moment before releasing his next question. "You'd advise I go with Green Frog, right?"

A satisfied smirk tugged at the corner of Simon's mouth before he sat himself straighter in his chair and then leaned forward, clasping his hands between his knees. "Croft, I think that would be a *very* wise move."

"Toast?"

Graham shook his head. "No, thank you. I'll finish this tea and then I suppose I should get a move on."

Beatrice pulled out a chair and joined her colleague for a short time before the breakfast rush. "How has he been this week?"

He pushed himself into the back of the upright chair and let out a sigh before reaching out to fiddle with the handle of his mug, his eyes downcast. "No better. Possibly worse. I don't know, Beatrice. I mean, he's working, that I can say. He's throwing himself into that every single day and certainly not letting me have a moment's peace, but I've found him passed out at his desk a couple of times this week, still fully clothed, an empty bottle at his side. I feel like he's not even giving himself the chance to try to sleep. He's working through his pain, inebriated, until his body just gives up. Or so it seems." Graham lifted his eyes to meet the concerned ones of Bea. "I'm worried about him, honestly. We all are, I know. But he just seems to be sinking deeper and further away and I have run out of ideas to pull him back."

Beatrice reached over and patted Graham's hand. She knew exactly what he was saying. She was constantly scraping full plates of food in the bin and the washing pile wasn't nearly as big as it used to be. "We just have to keep trying, I suppose. I mean... well... you know my thoughts on the matter."

Graham gave Bea a sad smile. "Josephine might be the answer, Mrs Sykes, but we can't force that, now can we. Those two need to work out their differences by themselves, that is if they even want —"

"They still love each other. Very much."

"Does that mean they want to make it work, though?"

"The heart wants what it wants, Mr Kent. I don't think there is any denying that. I think they know, but they just need to admit it to themselves and each other. And if I am in a position at all to be able to help that along, then you know damn well I will be jumping feet first into that pool. Meddling old woman or not. He is my life, Graham, and I just can't watch him wash *his* life away with whiskey. Diana would never forgive me."

Graham pulled in a sigh and lifted his mug to his mouth as the kitchen door opened and Danny strode in cheerfully.

"Morning, Danny, dear." Bea pushed from her chair and moved towards the kitchen counter. "Tea? Toast?" She pulled the bread from the bread bin and slid two slices into the toaster without waiting for his response. "We were just chatting about Will." She stopped and looked up at him. "How does he seem to you?"

Danny pulled out a chair and sat down, resting his elbows on the table and sighing. This conversation was sure to be a mood killer. "He's Will, Bea. Same old miserable Will." As he dragged his fingers through his still wet hair, he lifted his chin just in time to catch the look on her face, and quickly held his hands up in the air. "Look, I'm sorry, but he created this mess and I hate that you two feel like you need to constantly pick up all the pieces. Lord knows I'm still trying to pick up Joey's. That man is nothing but a walking storm of destruction."

Graham cleared his throat, lifting his eyebrows and taking another sip of his drink as he glanced over at the pair of them.

With pursed lips, Bea shook her head a little before pouring tea into a large mug. "But he's worse. Right? He's worse than he has ever been. I mean that much is quite clear. Isn't it? And why do you think that is, Danny?" She turned to retrieve the popped toast and threw them onto the breadboard before hastily smearing butter on them. "I'll tell you. Because Josephine is gone. That is why." She kicked her head up sharply and gave him a curt smile. "You agree?"

Danny glanced over at Graham, waiting for an indication from the old man as to whether or not he was going to offer his thoughts on the matter, and when he didn't, Danny spoke up, this time hesitantly. "Yes. But again, he created this mess. He pushed her away. He's the one that didn't realise how good he had —"

"What the *hell* are you all standing around chatting for?"

Three heads swung, wide-eyed, towards the open door where a still-drunk, disheveled Will stood, fists curled at his side, swaying. His shirt was crumpled, his chin was covered in shadow and his eyes were blood-shot.

"Get the fuck to work." He glanced specifically at Danny before he slurred his next words out of his mouth. "I don't pay you to drink fucking tea." He stumbled to the side, his hand lifting to hold the side of his painful head before he turned and left.

Bea dropped her eyes to the jar of jam, dipping the knife inside before giving her shoulders a little shrug. "I rest my case." She spread an unnecessary extra layer on top of Danny's toast before sliding the plate towards him.

Danny reached out to take it, and the old woman held onto it for a moment before lifting her eyes to his.

"He still loves her. He's always loved her. He let her go to protect her heart, Danny. Please don't think less of him for that."

Chapter 6

The Way We Look At Horses by Trent Dabbs
Winter Night by Slow Skies
Say Anything by Ashley Nite
On Fire by Roxanne Emery
Love's To Blame by For King & Country
Boy Who Let Me Down by Sara Phillips

"Thank you so much for doing this. I really appreciate it."

"You're welcome. Are you sure you'll be able to get a lift home?"

"I'll sort it, and if for some reason I can't manage one, I'll walk. I'm hoping the rain will decide to give us a break today." Joey gave a reassuring smile, and Emma nodded almost reluctantly.

She didn't mind helping Joey out whenever possible, and the idea of her having to walk all that way wasn't one she was comfortable with. "Call me if you can't find one. I'll come pick you up."

"I'll be fine. I promise. I don't want to inconvenience you more than I already have." Joey reached for the door handle and stepped foot out of the car.

Emma ducked her head and leaned across the handbreak. "It's not an inconvenience, Joey. You have my number, don't be afraid to use it."

"Thanks, Emma." She pushed the door closed, and as she watched the car and its driver disappear down the gravel driveway, her pulse quickened.

Hesitation and a stomach full of nerves kept her standing still for a few seconds, her eyes closed and her heart beating fast as she tried to calm herself.

She inhaled deeply.

And again.

The smell of recent rain coated the air like a thick layer of smog, and the grey clouds hovering in the sky reminded her of the day she had walked herself all the way to Wildridge Manor. Had she known then the pain her heart would be forced to endure, she may have searched harder for another alternative. But there hadn't been another, had there?

Turning and heading for the door that led to the stable offices, her boots sinking into the soft ground beneath her feet, she hooked her thumbs into the back pockets of her jean shorts. A mix of suppressed excitement and anticipation controlled her movements as her legs carried her through the heavy door and in the direction of Danny's personal space.

Her decision to come see Roya had been last minute after a whole lot of internal persuasion, and even now, her reluctance to remain there was battling with her need to see the horse she had spent the last two months away from.

The door to Danny's office sat ajar, and she pushed on it gently. Peeking her head in, she saw him sitting at his desk, a mountain of paperwork in front of him that she assumed was evaluations and reports. He hated paperwork, and the scowl painting his expression reconfirmed that fact. Sidestepping around the wooden barrier, she allowed herself to fully enter the room, and his head kicked up.

The sound of her footsteps padding across the stone floor took him by surprise and a smile pulled at his lips. "Hey." He tossed his pen down on his desk and leaned back in his chair, folding his hands behind his head. "You came."

"Yeah." Tugging on the corner of her bottom lip with her teeth, she threw her thumb over her shoulder and turned her body with the movement. "I probably won't stay for long, though, I just needed to—"

"See her."

Joey nodded, and Danny continued on without allowing her a moment to elaborate. She was there. Joey was there and that's all that mattered. "She's in her stall. She hasn't been groomed yet today, so if you want to... well, y'know." He flicked his fingers in the direction of the barn. "I don't have to tell you."

"No. No, you don't." A pause of silence settled between them for just a few seconds before Joey spoke up again. "Once I'm done, if you're not busy, do you think maybe you can give me a lift home? If not, that's okay, I'll just—"

"You're not walking. I'll take you home. Just let me know when you're ready."

"Thanks, Danny." Giving him an appreciative smile and pivoting around, Joey slipped quietly out of his office, leaving him alone to return to his work.

As she made her way back out of the building—the unusual emptiness of the place not going unnoticed with the lack of lessons and staff on that day—her thoughts began to wander. They took her back to Christmas Eve, a night that seemed forever ago, as she and Will had walked the same tiled path she was walking now, hand in hand—the night he had given her Roya, the night she had finally admitted to herself that she was in love with him.

Blocking the painful images away, she dragged in a breath to steady her racing heart and pulled on the large door that led into the stable. The rustle of hay and the soft neighs of horses propelled her feet onwards to the last stall on the right and with shaking fingers, Joey grabbed a hold of the cool metal bolt on the door. She slid it from its lock, a sudden nervousness gathering in her chest as she pulled it wide open.

Her heart skipped—or maybe it was more of a jump—as her sight landed on the chestnut mare that had turned her head to look at her as she entered the small stall. She couldn't help it. Tears welled in her eyes as she moved across the distance and stopped directly in front of her, smoothing her hands up either sides of Roya's face. "Hey, girl."

The horse bowed her head, looking away from Joey as she pawed at the ground with her hoof, and her dismissal had Joey unconsciously holding her breath.

"I'm sorry I haven't come by to see you. Life's just been…" She struggled for an explanation. "Well, it's been a little tough lately. I hope you're not mad at me."

There was a second of hesitation before Roya nickered, once again lifting her head and nuzzling herself into Joey's neck as if she understood and was accepting her apology. The warm tears that had collected in Joey's eyes trickled silently down her cheeks as she squeezed them shut and pressed her forehead against Roya's. "I've missed you so much."

Licking a kiss up Joey's salty cheek, Roya stopped as she reached the faint scar that now trailed along her temple, and Joey swore she saw a look of sadness fill those big, brown eyes.

"It wasn't your fault. I should have never taken off with you like I did. We should have never gone through the woods, but after everything I learned, I just needed to get away. It was the fastest route and I wasn't thinking."

Joey stroked her hand down Roya's neck and across her back, continuing to engage in conversation with the horse. Of all the people in her life, this animal was the only one she felt comfortable pouring out her confessions to — pouring out the thoughts that kept her awake at night and the ache in her heart that kept her from letting go and moving on. Perhaps it was because there was a connection between the two of them, or maybe it was the fact Roya didn't have the ability to reply. There was no judgement —

no offers of unsolicited advice that everyone else so readily made available.

For the next hour, Roya soaked up the attention, occasionally neighing or wrapping herself around Joey in the way horses do when they are offering a hug, and Joey relished every single moment. She wasn't sure when, or indeed if, she'd be able to return, and as much as she wanted to relocate Roya to a stable she'd have no qualms about visiting, she knew she was better off here at Wildridge, in the hands and under the direct supervision of Danny.

This was the best place for her.

After walking a few laps around the paddock, Joey allowed Roya to roam free while she perched herself on the fence. Her gaze slid over the property — the neglected pathways that were in desperate need of a sweep and the beds of flowers that needed their weeds pulled — and she momentarily wondered if anyone else had been hired to fill her position.

By the looks of it, the answer was no.

Much to her annoyance, she continued to survey the grounds, the eerie magnificence of the place holding her attention for far longer than she would have liked. She took note of the overgrown bushes and the new trails of ivy climbing the sides of the old house before settling her eyes on the large windows. Every single curtain was still open, allowing the light to flood through the panes, and a sudden urgency to be on the other side of them had her sliding off the fence. It had been a few weeks since she'd last seen Bea, and the smell of freshly baked buns or cakes that was surely filling the kitchen had her walking straight in the old cook's direction. She had no business stepping foot inside the place, but her head and her heart were hardly on the same page these days and she quietly reassured herself she would only be a few minutes.

Curling her fingers around the large metal handle, she slowly pushed the front door open and entered the main hall. A barrage of memories assaulted her from nearly every direction as she stood in the centre, and she took a second to distance herself from the flickers of her past.

Once her head was clear and her thoughts free, she made her way down the south wing, stopping as she reached the door to the kitchen.

A cheerful hum that could only belong to one person drifted through the cracks in the frame, and Joey smiled to herself as she gently pushed it open and stepped inside.

Opening the back door to let in a little fresh air, Bea turned around to the sound of the someone entering the room and her eyes widened as she saw Joey standing there. "Well what a surprise!" She hurried across the large tiles and wrapped her arms around Joey for a hug, holding onto her for just a little longer than she would normally. "And to what do I owe this pleasure?" Bea pulled back and held the younger woman at arm's length, her eyes sweeping over her features and her face beaming.

"I, um…" Joey stood nervously, her heart thumping beneath her ribs as she glanced around the massive kitchen. It had been so long since she'd been there, but everything about it was just as she remembered. An array of baked goods lined the countertops and the sweet smell of butter and sugar lingered in the air. "I came to see Roya, and well, I know I shouldn't be here, but I couldn't help coming in for a few minutes to see you. I hope that's okay."

"Well what a ridiculous question. Of course it's okay. Come. Sit down and I'll pop the kettle on. Tea?" Bea didn't wait for an answer before she trundled behind the kitchen island and began filling the kettle and grabbing mugs from the cupboard.

"Yes, please. Thank you." Dragging out one of the chairs, Joey sat herself on it. "I really can't stay long."

"Not to worry, dear. It's just wonderful to see you. You must tell me all about your new job and how your father is getting along before you go, though."

Within a few minutes, the pair were sitting opposite each other, cradling mugs of steaming tea and enjoying listening to the ins and out of each other's daily lives.

"So Danny's uncle is a good boss it sounds. I think it's wonderful that he's giving you so many opportunities, especially where the horses are concerned."

"Yeah. He's really nice. I can't thank Danny enough for helping me after... well, after everything." Joey set her drink down, forcing a smile on to her face as her eyes fell to the table. She ran her fingers around the rim of the mug before turning her gaze back to Bea. "How is everything around here, Bea?"

"Oh, everything here is fine, dear. We manage. We plod along. Graham is run ragged doing his bits and bobs as ever, Danny has taken on more staff at the stables, so that leaves me cooking for even more people. We keep busy, Joey. We keep ourselves busy." She smiled at her, desperate to tell her that things just were not the same without her, and that things never would be the same again unless...

Bea's thoughts trailed off as Joey began to speak again.

"And what about him? Is he okay?" The questions jumped right off of Joey's tongue, and her eyes widened slightly at the realisation of what she had just asked. Not even twenty minutes of being in this house and she was already breaking every vow she had made to herself. "Nevermind. Some questions are better left unanswered." She pushed from her seat and grabbed her handbag. "I should really be going."

Reaching out, Bea covered Joey's hand with her own, forcing her to halt in her tracks. "He's empty, Joey. He's drained of everything and I'm not sure how to fill him up again." She held onto her a few moments before she shook her head. "I'm sorry, dear. That wasn't fair of me. I just...." Bea stood, too, and picked up the empty mugs, turning towards the sink. "I'm just worried about him. That's all."

"I tried, Bea." Tears clawed at the back of Joey's eyes, and a sudden lump of emotion swelled in her throat. Who was she kidding? She still loved him, as much as she had done the day she walked out of his office door all those weeks ago. "I'm so sorry. I really did try…" She licked her lips and hooked the strap of her handbag over her shoulder. "But you can't save somebody who doesn't want saving."

She stood for another tick of the clock, and then without saying anything, Joey disappeared out of the kitchen door, leaving the old woman alone with the heaviness of their conversation.

Bea ran the hot tap as she pushed the plug into the sink and squirted washing-up liquid into the flow of hot water. Joey's footsteps got further away, and as she placed the cups into the bubbles, she lifted her chin and glanced at the clock on the wall.

Almost six pm.

Her lips pulled involuntarily into a tight smile that held little, but a dash of, hope and she closed her eyes. "He doesn't realise yet that you're the one who will save him whether he likes it or not, Josephine."

Slipping into the corridor, Joey pulled the door closed behind her and walked over to one of the large windows. Her heart was filled with a strange mix of sadness and contentment. She'd loved seeing Bea: the old woman's ability to raise her spirits was something she hadn't realised she'd been sorely missing. She'd grown used to her bubbly and uplifting personality when working at the manor, and the last few weeks without it had served as another reminder of the events that had unfolded.

Inhaling deeply and releasing all that she was feeling in one heavy exhale, Josephine backed away from the window and started her journey down the hallway, knowing it would be the last time she ever walked it. She had no right being there. It wasn't her home and it was no longer her place of employment. She made a decision right there: as soon as she had enough money, she would relocate Roya, even though it may not be the wisest decision. She had no choice. It was finally time to leave this manor and all of its inhabitants exactly where they belonged: in the past.

Joey's feet moved at a steady pace as she neared the main entrance hall, halting only when the front door slammed shut and the cool spring breeze whirled through the corridor, lifting her curls from her shoulders.

Her heart stopped.

Deep, and the darkest shade of blue she could ever recall seeing them, Will's eyes connected with hers.

The pair stared at each other in a moment filled with absolutely nothing—not a shred of emotion, not a single breath taken—before a look of utter confusion drifted across his handsome features. With a furrowed brow, he blinked, as if the image of her standing there was a mere figment of his imagination, and a nervous shiver raced down Joey's spine. She opened her mouth, ready to speak—ready to provide an explanation as to why she was there, in his house, after all this time—but his naturally intimidating and brooding demeanour silenced her in the same way it silenced an entire room.

He still affected her.

Her heart beat faster as she took in every inch of the man standing in front of her. This man whom she had given her entire self to—this man who still owned every single part of her, no matter how much she wanted to deny it.

His brown hair, the soft strands she had run her fingers through countless times, was longer than she remembered, curling around his ears and over the collar of his shirt, and the dark stubble dusting his jaw was thicker, past the point of the prickle that she secretly longed to feel against her palms again. Two months had obviously changed him; it had changed her, but it hadn't changed the magnetic pull she felt towards him. It hadn't erased the memories of them — of his warm breath in her ear or his soft lips on her skin.

Standing there, both of them still locked in a cloud of uncertainty, Joey wondered if there had been another woman in the time they had spent apart. Had there been someone else to keep his bed warm and his nights less lonely?

As soon as the thought surfaced, she rid it from her mind, the mere possibility of the answer being yes stinging her chest in the most painful of ways. It didn't matter. They were done. Everything they had been and shared was locked in a box that had been tossed straight into history.

Tucking her hair behind her ears and curling her arms tightly around her stomach, Joey took a hesitant step in his direction. She needed to offer a reason for her presence, so she opened her mouth to try again, and this time the words tumbled out all at once. "I came to see Roya. It's been too long and I've been — "

Will moved.

He began to walk towards her, and Joey's pulse quickened again beneath her skin, the heat of it spreading through her veins in an unexpected rush. The intoxicating scent of him — a mix of cologne and a subtle hint of hand-rolled cigars — filled her nose the closer he came, and she held her breath in anticipation, waiting to see where his next steps would lead him.

He brushed straight past her.

Without a further glance, he continued down the hall, leaving her to stand there alone, her heart in her stomach and a sadness in her throat she couldn't swallow down.

The ringing in Will's ears wouldn't stop as he marched towards the kitchen.

Nothing would *ever* have prepared him for that moment, and stopping to catch his breath—to steady the quickening of his heart—he realised something: that fire in his chest that had been missing for what felt like a lifetime was back. He felt suddenly alive and he had no idea how to deal with it. He'd spent all of this time pushing and pushing, convincing himself that he could be without her for her sake, but even occupying the same space as her for mere seconds had once again tipped him upside down and knocked him off course. He halted quickly, swinging his fist into the wall with a grunt, his knuckles burning from the force, and grabbed at his hair as he continued down the south wing corridor. This was not how it was supposed to be. She was meant to hate him, to stay away, to never want to see him again.

On reaching the kitchen door, he clenched on his back teeth before bursting through the it to confront Beatrice.

"Before you start huffing and puffing, I didn't invite her here, so please don't throw your blame around, William." Bea didn't even look at him. She bustled around near the fridge, rehousing packs of butter, fruit and salad as she finished off preparing the last of dinner. "She was here to see Roya and just happened to pop her head in."

Will's chest heaved and he sank into a chair at the table and allowed his head to drop into his hands. There was no point even saying anything. It was like the old woman could read his mind, and so he sat there and allowed her to fuss around him in silence.

Of course he still loved her. There was no question of that. The way his body reacted to her being so near would betray any protestations to the contrary anyway, so there was no point in trying to deny it to himself.

But the bottom line was that he needed to forget her.

She needed to forget him.

She needed to move on and live her life, and he had to let her.

Chapter 7

Dynasty by MIIA
Awake At Night by LOWES

Two steps behind her, Daniel followed Josephine out of the restaurant, holding the door open for another couple before swiftly returning to her side. The night was beautiful, the air mild and warm with a cool breeze that occasionally blew across their faces and through their hair.

She turned to look at him as he walked beside her, his hands stuffed in his coat pockets and a smile on his face.

"Thank you for this."

Danny shook his head. She didn't need to thank him. He was her friend, and this was exactly the type of stuff friends did. He was just glad she'd agreed and he'd been finally able to get her out of the house. "You don't have to thank—"

"No, I do." She smiled tightly. "These past two months haven't exactly been easy, and I know I haven't been the most lively person to be around, but I want you to know that I appreciate everything you've done for me. The job with your uncle, pushing me to get my application submitted for uni and then for taking me to drop it—"

Danny stopped, causing Joey's feet to halt their movement. Turning to face her, he inhaled deeply and brushed away a curl that swept across her forehead, tucking it behind her ear. "First off, I don't need lively in my life, okay? I mean, come on, you're talking to the guy who spends most of his time engaging with animals and people under the age of ten, for fuck's sake."

Joey chuckled, and Danny's smile grew wider.

"And secondly, I know this hasn't been easy for you. I know you're trying to move on after everything, but I also want you to know that it's okay to have your moments. It's okay to be sad, and as hard as this is for me to say and for you to hear, it's okay to miss him, Joey."

A heavy breath left her lungs and she bit down on the corner of her lip. "But is it?" Her shoulders dropped with the weight of it all. She understood the point Danny was trying to make and knew fine well everything would get better in time, or so she imagined, but after running into Will at the manor, she felt as though any progress she'd made in her quest to forget about him had been wiped clean. She was back at square one with little hope that she'd ever be able to live her life without him.

As if he could read her mind, Danny interrupted her thoughts. "Look, I'm sorry about the other day at the manor. When you didn't come back to my office, I should have come to find you and got you out of there before he came home, but I was so wrapped up with work, and I've been under so much stress lately, I just didn't realise the time." They both turned and started their journey back down the pavement. "He's still thinking about selling, y'know? And if he does, I don't know what that's going to mean for the riding school."

"Do you think he will? I mean, really? I know he may not always show it, but that riding school means so much to him. It's the last connection he has with his mum and I can't imagine he'd do anything to jeopardise the reputation it has or any of the work she poured into it. As much as he avoids it, his heart and soul lies within every square inch of that place, Danny. You, Bea, Graham… you guys can't allow him to sell it. You can't."

"You know as well as I do, we don't have a say in the matter. Will has a mind of his own, and when it's made up, it's made up." Danny lifted a shoulder and shrugged. "Besides, it's not the school he's contemplating selling, it's Wildridge."

But that school *was* Wildridge. They may have been two different structures but at the end of the day, they were one and the same.

There was a pregnant pause before the next question swirling in Joey's mind sprang from her tongue. "Is he still working with Simon?"

"Yeah." Danny looked at her with a hint of confusion in his eyes, the answer to the question seemingly obvious. "Why wouldn't he be?"

Of course he was. Danny's response was valid. Why wouldn't he be? Will didn't know the truth about the man he was working alongside. Perhaps if she'd had the courage to tell Will what had happened the night of the ball — everything that Simon had said and done to her — the evening would have played out differently. Every day since January would've played out differently. Regardless, mistakes had been made, not just on Will's part, but on hers as well, and now they were both suffering the consequences.

"What made you ask that?"

Joey gave her head a small shake, not wanting to elaborate. The boat of confession had already sailed. "No reason."

Joey had spent the last nine weeks trying to forget about Will and focus on herself and her career, but now her mind swirled with nothing but the memories of them and she found herself wanting to know how he was managing on a daily basis.

Bea's words the other day about the state of Will had sliced straight through her, cutting her open and once again leaving her completely vulnerable, and they still lingered. At the time, she had needed to leave because she wasn't able to bear hearing anymore, but then she saw him in the entrance hall, and when his appearance had only solidified all of Bea's worries and fears, she felt a sadness crash over her for the man she loved. All she had ever wanted to do was try to save him—to heal his heart and help him see the good in himself.

Deciding it best to set aside all thoughts of her former lover, Joey returned her mind to the present, and the pair of them continued their stroll, falling into a comfortable silence as they absorbed the city life around them. Couples walked with their fingers or arms entwined, laughing and smiling, and single men and women hurried down the streets, filtering in and out of the restaurants and pubs that were still open.

She pivoted around, shoving her hands in her coat pockets as she strode backwards. "So what movie did you say we were going to see?"

Danny began to open his mouth to respond at the same time Joey collided with an oncoming body. She turned around quickly, apologies pouring from her lips for her lack of attention, as she knelt down to help the stranger pick up her handbag that had been knocked out of her grasp.

"I'm so sorry." Joey's hands moved frantically, a wash of embarrassment creeping down her neck as she moved to collect up the bits and bobs that tumbled out and were littering the pavement. "I should have been paying attention." Gathering the last of it, she pushed herself up straight and held the strap of the woman's handbag out for her to take. She turned her rosy cheeks and her panicked gaze to Danny who cupped his hand around her shoulder and smiled reassuringly at her.

"Joey, you remember Hannah's mum, no? Ms Evans?"

Joey's attention turned back to the woman beside her, who was standing with two other women who were close in age. If the name alone hadn't jogged her memory, the bright red curls and the green eyes should have been a dead giveaway. "Yes, of course." The embarrassment began to subside and she held her hand out. "Ms Evans, how are you? How is Hannah?"

"It's Amy, please. And we're both well, thank you. We were sad to hear that you'd left Wildridge. We've missed seeing you at Hannah's lessons.

"Yes, well..." Joey stumbled over her words, searching for an explanation and wondering if Amy knew even a fraction of the details surrounding her dismissal. She figured not, but it didn't stop an air of awkwardness from sweeping into the conversation. What was she supposed to say?

Reading the situation and Joey's unease, Danny intervened. "We all miss her, but Joey has decided to pursue her own passion instead and is focusing on her vet's degree."

"That's wonderful, Joey." Amy appeared genuinely happy. "I wish you all the luck and success."

"Thank you." Joey smiled appreciatively and stood back for a moment, watching as Amy's gaze shifted from her own to Danny's, and she couldn't help but notice the flicker of something dancing brightly within them.

She knew the woman was single, and for whatever reason, Hannah's father wasn't in the picture anymore. Did Hannah's mum have a crush on Danny?

Hooking the strap of her handbag over her arm, Amy turned to her two friends and gestured in Danny's direction. "Ladies, this is Danny Watson, Hannah's riding instructor at Wildridge, and this is Joey. She used to work at the manor." Both women smiled, and after a brief exchange of introductions and pleasantries, the conversation turned back to the little girl who Joey now knew was with a babysitter for the evening.

"Hannah absolutely loves you, Danny. She's looking forward to summer holidays and increasing her weekly lessons."

A beaming grin tugged high onto Danny's cheeks, and Joey stifled a chuckle at the way he lit up at Ms Evans's remarks. Joey knew desire when she saw it, and there was no denying the flashes of it arcing between the two people communicating beside her.

"I'm looking forward to it. Hannah has so much potential and her love for the horses is truly something special. You should be very proud of your little girl, Amy. I know I am."

Rocking back and forth on her heels, Joey allowed the pair to carry on for a few more minutes, listening to the banter and occasional giggles that would float into the air. The happiness that poured from Hannah's mum, and the way she would rest her hand on Danny's bicep reminded her of the same happiness she had once felt in the presence of Will.

"I'm so sorry. You'll have to excuse me. I have this horrible problem where I just start rambling. It's so very rude of me. We'll allow you two to get back to your date."

Both Joey and Danny spoke at the same time.

"We're not on a date."

"It's not a date."

If there ever was a picture of relief, it was the expression that spilled out across Ms Evans's face. "Oh, my apologies. I just assumed—"

"No. It's okay." Joey waved her off, not wanting her to form any further conclusions. "We're just friends out for a night on the town."

"Right. Well, we should really be going anyhow. Joey, it was nice seeing you, and good luck again with all your studies." She smiled and sidestepped around Joey, lifting her fingers, which were still clenched around the strap of her handbag, in a small wave. "And, Danny, I'll see you next Wednesday."

A shining grin and his dimple on display, Danny nodded. "Absolutely. Have a good night, Amy." He lifted his chin to her friends. "Ladies."

"Goodnight."

Both Danny and Joey watched as the three women carried on down the sidewalk, neither of them turning away or saying a word until they had completely vanished into the sea of bodies milling about the row of open pubs.

Joey rolled her lips between her teeth and leaned over, punching Danny square in the arm and knocking his solid frame off balance.

"Ow." He immediately reached up, rubbing the ache away from her physical abuse. "What the heck was that for?"

"You are totally crushing on Hannah's mum!"

Danny rolled his eyes at her. "Am not."

"You are too! We all just stood here and watched you two flirt back and forth as if we weren't even present. You like her! You should ask her out on a date."

"Shhh. Keep your voice down." Ragging a hand through his hair, Danny shook his head and laughed. "Come on, Miss Matchmaker." He snaked his arm around Joey's shoulders and tucked her into his side, pressing a chaste kiss to her temple as they started off in the direction of the cinema. "We have a movie to see."

With his thoughts lost to Amy, they made it but a few steps before Joey stopped abruptly, both of their bodies nearly flying forwards with her sudden halt. He glanced down at her, his brow twitching in worried confusion. "Everything okay?"

Joey stood stock still, the blood in her veins pumping vigorously and rushing up to the tips of her ears as her heart beat out of rhythm. All the color drained from her face and those knots in her stomach were back, this time twisting and churning the bile that was on the verge of rising.

Danny followed her gaze, noticing what had captured her attention, and his immediate reaction was to pull her closer, to wrap her up and protect her from the sight before her. He pressed his lips to her ear and whispered, hoping he'd be able to cut through whatever it was she was feeling. "I know what I said earlier, but forget about it, Joey. You are doing so much better without him. You *are* better without him, you hear me?" He had said the words, but even he wasn't entirely convinced. As much as Danny despised the man, a part of him had hoped Croft would pull his head out of his arse and come to his senses. What the hell was he doing?

Forget about it?

Joey clenched her back teeth together to fight against... what? To fight against her emotions? The feelings everyone and their mother knew she had for the man?

Will's past, she could forget. The night of the ball and the events in his mother's drawing room, she could forget. The things he had said to her and the way he turned her away, she could forget. But this... seeing him with another woman wrapped around his arm, one who was clearly a stand in as Josephine's replacement, this she couldn't forget.

Chapter 8

My Favourite Faded Fantasy by Damien Rice
Break Away by Artist vs. Poet
Paralyzed by NF
Grow by Frances

The manor was eerily quiet first thing in the morning these days, and Beatrice didn't like it one bit. There had been a time when Josephine had been up and about at the same time as she had, and they'd enjoyed early morning chatter.

She walked down the corridor towards the north wing, a mug of coffee in one hand and a plate of toast—that she knew she would be tossing into the bin later on—in the other. She would find Will slumped over his desk as usual, she was sure, but when there was no answer after knocking, she began to climb the stairs to the second floor, hoping she would find him asleep in his bed for once.

The top floor of the north wing wasn't somewhere she often went. It was Will's private quarters and she treated it as such. The majority of the rest of the manor was a bit of a free for all for staff, and there were some comings and goings, particularly around meal times, but this was the wing that everyone steered clear of.

Bea halted outside his bedroom door, surprised to find it open and, after peering inside, that the bed had not been slept in.

"Hmm... where is that boy?" She shrugged and turned back around to the stairway, passing the closed door of Will's small sitting room. She stopped and moved back towards it, resting her ear on the wood and listened for clues that Will was inside, and, on hearing a gentle snoring, she did what any mother figure would do if their little ones were hungover and heartbroken: she opened the door and walked into the room with a cheery smile on her face.

"Morning, Willia—" A touch of deja vu trickled through her memory as a half-asleep, half-dressed Will sat up from the armchair and her eyes followed a trail of clothes and shoes across the floor. Her heart picked up a little as it led to the larger chair in the corner and the barely covered form of a long-haired brunette who was curled, still asleep.

William sat up, his naked chest flexing as he stretched his arms and rubbed at his eyes before the events of the previous night flashed before his eyes. He halted his movements, his hands still over his face before he scrubbed them slowly down to his mouth and stood to his feet.

"Is that—" Bea stopped as the sleeping woman began to stir, turning her face towards the pair of them and the realisation that no, it wasn't, hit Bea in the chest like a bullet. She didn't even look at him. She turned and stormed out of the room towards the staircase.

"Beatrice." Will grabbed at the door that was on its way to slamming shut and darted out into the corridor, striding to catch the slower and older Bea. "Bea, wait."

"I don't think I want to hear it, William. It's none of my business. I'll put your breakfast on your desk and leave you to it." She didn't turn around. She continued as fast as she could towards the stairs, her eyes stinging a little and her chest heaving with disappointment. All of her hopes and all of her positive thinking were trashed, and she just couldn't even contemplate how this was all going to play out now.

How *could* he?

A strong hand curled gently around her upper arm, stopping her in her tracks and turning her slowly.

"Beatrice. Please. Can you listen?"

"To what? To how you are just going to let your life dissolve away in front of you? To how you are not even going to try to mend that heart of yours that I have fought for *every* minute of my working life? Goddamnit, William. Get a grip of yourself. Look at you. Just look at you."

Will bowed his head and slipped his hands into his trouser pockets. She was the one person in this world that he knew better than anyone and who knew him in the same way, and seeing her like this, seeing her so fucking displeased with him, almost broke the remaining pieces of his heart in two. He couldn't stand that look in her eyes. "I didn't."

"I'm not interested. I don't care. It's none of my business, and I'll be damned if I am going to waste any more of my day thinking about it." Bea tried to walk away, the coffee and toast still in tact, but Will stopped her again.

"I couldn't. I couldn't go through with anything. I didn't." Will's face crumpled as he remembered the night before and the way this girl had seduced him without even trying. After seeing Josephine at the manor just days before, his head, his heart and everything about him had been full to the brim of her, and this stranger's brown waves and brown eyes had tempted him in a way that now felt dirty. He had been sucked in by her without even realising it, and it wasn't until he had taken her home—a breaking of his own rules in his moment of insanity and where she'd kissed him with that alien mouth—that he had woken up. She had been persistent, and the aching of his dick had, for a time, led him a merry dance around his sitting room. She had begun to undress him, and herself, licking and biting him in all the right places, but she wasn't Josephine. She was the wrong smell, the wrong touch. He didn't light up at the feel of her skin and her eyes—those big brown eyes that she had flashed at him from the dance floor—were empty.

"So why is she still here?" Bea's tone softened as she watched turmoil swirl in Will's eyes.

"Because I'm not the kind of guy to kick a girl out in the middle of the night, contrary to popular belief. I got her drunk so she would leave me alone and then we passed out."

Beatrice nodded. "You're a mess. You know that?" She huffed out of her nose. "Toast?" She lifted the plate and the corner of her mouth turned up a little.

Will plucked a piece of the now cold toast and took a bite. "Yum."

Bea linked her arm through his. They walked silently and side by side until they reached the kitchen where Bea prepared two fresh mugs of coffee and buttered fresh toast. She sat down opposite Will like she had done so many times before and held his eyes for a few moments before speaking. "You can not go on like this. You just can't. I won't allow it."

Will didn't speak. He chewed slowly on his food and allowed Bea to do the talking.

"You miss her—you are no good without her, and I don't mind saying that because it's patently obvious to everyone. The only person who seems to be ignoring that fact is you. It's time you woke up. It's time you admitted to yourself that you've made a bloody great big mistake and that you should have put your trust in her to handle whatever your lives together would bring. She's stronger than you think. She can handle life. She loves you, William. Still."

Will swallowed a large mouthful awkwardly as Bea's words flew across the table.

Did she?

"I think it's time for a re-evaluation. It's time for you to take charge of this life of yours instead of letting your past rule every move you make. We all hurt, but not one of us blames you, William. You have to let go of this fucking — excuse my French — guilt. You need to live your life and you will never be able to do that until you swallow your damn pride and admit that you need help to heal." Bea reached over and covered his hand with hers. "What do you say?"

With his business head firmly screwed on in an attempt to push away Bea's lecture from earlier that morning and all thoughts of Joey, Will slipped into his suit jacket as he jogged down the steps of the manor onto the gravel driveway. He took a left, heading towards the riding school, wanting to run a few things by Danny. The stables were already flourishing better than ever before thanks to his business sense and Danny's expertise, and he wanted to push it to the next level, offering more specialised training for Olympic riders and the like.

He wanted to go bigger — to extend — and in doing so make the transition to move the stables a little easier if the sale of the manor was to ever go through.

Danny was grooming one of the more expensive thoroughbreds as Will approached the main stable, and shoving his hands into his pockets, Will jutted his chin in greeting and cocked his head to the side to let him know he wanted a word.

Danny placed the brush back in the bucket and wiped his hands down his jodhpurs before following Will down the path to the side of the building.

Will leaned his shoulder against the brick wall and waited for Danny to stop beside him. "You remember how to teach dressage, right?"

A condescending laugh almost slipped from Danny's mouth as he stared at Will. What kind of question was that? "Yeah. Of course I do. Why? What are you thinking?"

Will stroked at the stubble on his chin and held Danny's eyes as he thought through his plans—plans that he had sat all morning devising. He pushed himself off the wall and turned to walk off. "Come with me." He led Danny around the side of the offices and past the training paddock to the edge of the manor's immediate grounds. "I want to expand." He cast his eye across the perimeter of the land and pointed far beyond to where there lay a patchwork of empty fields. "I want to go big. We are the most successful riding school in the country. I want to be the most successful Olympic training ground. I want us to train the Olympic Equestrian Team, and I want you to lead that training, just like you used to before you came to us, but here, at Wildridge. I want you to train in dressage and show jumping, and for that, we need more space." He glanced at Danny before continuing. "Logistics, contacts and the business side of it you can leave to me, but once we are set up, I can guarantee they will want us. They will want you back. So. What do you think?"

Danny blew out a heavy breath, trying to process everything Will had just dumped on his plate. It was a lot to think about, and ultimately it would be taking the riding school in a completely different direction—a direction Danny wasn't the least bit thrilled to explore. "Wow. You sound like you've really given this some thought." He licked his lips, staring out at the land and hesitating only for a couple of beats before he shook his head. "I'm not interested, Will."

The muscle along Will's jaw ticked as he squinted out across his empire. "Well, as my employee, you don't technically have the choice, now do you. You are paid to do as I see fit for my business." He turned on his heel to face

Danny and gave him a sarcastic smile, his eyes bright and wide.

Now more than ever, Danny wanted to wipe that smug expression off the bastard's face. It hadn't been why he'd accepted the position at Wildridge four years ago. He'd wanted to work with kids and adults in a stress-free environment. All that Olympic glory bullshit was overrated. It was why he had left and why he'd sworn to himself he'd never go back, no matter how much it paid. "You really are in the business of making people's lives miserable, aren't you?" Giving Will another harsh shake of his head, he began to turn around, annoyance streaming thick through his veins. "God. Joey never even stood a chance."

With a dry throat, Will's features creased with incredulousness as he processed Danny's words. "I beg your fucking pardon?"

"Nevermind. I'm going back to work." Kicking a foot of dirt into the wind, Danny placed his hands on his hips and started walking in the direction of the stables with his head low.

With no forethought, Will lurched forwards and grabbed the back of Danny's collar, spinning him around to face him. "I said, I beg your fucking pardon. You don't get to make comments about my relationship with Josephine and then walk away."

"Your relationship?" Danny laughed at his ignorance and stepped forwards, bringing his face dangerously close to Will's. He was going to say this once and it was going to be the end of it. "Let's set something straight right now. You and Josephine don't have any *Goddamned* relationship, do you understand me?"

"And I suppose you're benefitting just nicely because of that, aren't you. So quick to jump in my shoes, Watson. I saw you. I saw you with her. You couldn't even wait for her to…" Will shook his head and let his words trail. How presumptuous to assume she wasn't already over him. He didn't deserve her to be pining after him and she deserved more than anything to be happy. That was what he wanted, right?

It took all but a moment for Danny to realise Will was referring to the previous evening when he'd wrapped an arm around Joey and dropped a kiss to her forehead, right before they'd both witnessed Will leaving the club with another woman. He shrugged, a cocky smirk lifting one corner of his mouth. How could he possibly feel sorry for this man after all that he'd done? "Yeah, well, someone has to pick up the shattered pieces of her heart that you left carelessly lying around. If it means getting some sweet arse on the side, so be it."

A rage like no other shot through every nerve in Will's body as his arm took on a life of its own, lifting and swinging through the air in slow motion, his clenched fist slamming into the side of Danny's face causing his head to whip to the side. "Fuck you." The roar of his voice muffled the smack of knuckle against jaw, and Will watched as Danny stumbled to the side from the force of his punch.

Regaining his balance and straightening himself, Danny swiped at the blood slicking his lower lip and the sight of it on his fingers tightened every muscle.

Danny moved.

All he saw was red.

He dived forwards, tackling Will by the waist and as both men dropped and performed a series of rolls on the ground, Danny grabbed him by the collar, his other arm in the air ready to swing.

Joey flashed before his eyes and he hesitated.

He couldn't hit him. He wouldn't hit him. Instead, he reached down and fisted the material of Will's shirt with both hands, lifting him closer. "When the hell are you going to pull your head out of your arse, huh?" He spat his words out at him. "I'm not fucking her, Will. I'm doing exactly what you asked of me. I'm watching out for her, as her *friend.* That's all. How can I possibly want someone who is still head over heels in love with someone else?" Danny's tight grip loosened, and as he pushed himself up to his feet, his pulse pumping from the sudden rush of anger and adrenaline, he shoved at Will's chest. "Instead of looking for a fight with me, perhaps you should pour that energy into fighting for her. She is the best Goddamn thing to ever happen to you and you're just letting her slip right through your fingers."

Will let his head fall back onto the dusty rubble of the path and closed his eyes tight. Everything Danny had said to him swam around his brain in a muddle of words. His chest heaved and he winced at the pain in his stomach from being winded.

Twice in one day he had heard the same message and it was like music to his ears: she still loved him. The only problem was him. He was the barrier between his heart and hers, and he was the only one to be able to knock it down. He pushed onto his elbows, his chin against his chest and took a deep breath.

Swallowing his pride and his better judgement, Danny reached down and offered Will his hand in a bid to help him to his feet. "I may not want her like that, but it doesn't mean someone else won't. Go after her. Fight for her, or you're going to lose her for good."

Will looked up at Danny's face and after a flicker of hesitation, he reached out and took his hand, the pair of them closing their fingers around each other's hands in a firm grip of acceptance and middle ground. Will brushed the dust from his trousers and watched as Danny turned on his heel and walked lazily back towards the stables, leaving Will with his thoughts and an inkling of hope that spluttered his heart back to life.

On arriving back to the manor, Will halted by the front door as Graham stood just inside, watching him. He looked down at himself, his clothes dusty and dishevelled, and he shook his head, stuffing his hands into his pockets. "No. I don't want to talk about it." He glanced at Graham as he walked past him into the house.

Graham followed him. "I'm sure you don't, but I'm going to have to insist. It's time I intervened, William."

Will spun around. "I'm sick of everyone intervening. Everyone is so damn quick to tell me how much I have fucked up, how much I have messed up my life. Do you not think I know this? Do you not think that I go out of my fucking mind every Goddamned day, back and forth, telling myself I am stupid?" He turned back around and marched into his office with Graham on his heels. "I don't need people to remind me that I am a fuck up."

"Son. You are not a fuck up. You have lost your way, that's all. And these people, us, we are your family. We care about you and we want to help you back on the right path, that's all. Beatrice is just about losing her own mind with worry about you because she cares so deeply for you. I have tried to sit back and let you work it out, but it's getting to the point now where I am just too concerned. We hate seeing you like this."

The two men sat down in chairs at the same time, Will slumping back into his and pushing his hands through his hair. "Tell me what the fuck I am supposed to do, Graham. Tell me."

The older man leaned forward, his elbows on his knees and his fingertips together. He studied Will for a moment, taking in his appearance and the desperate expression on his face. "Forgive yourself, boy." He held Will's eyes with his. "Forgive yourself so that you're open to being forgiven by others. Just stop being so hard on yourself. Leave the past in the past and start building a future, because believe me, this is no way to live. Go to her, William. Forgive yourself and go to her. Open your heart and let out the love that you keep locking away. Let her in. Let her take up residence there and the rest will work itself out. Do not leave it too late, because regret will eat you alive."

Chapter 9

Alone by Billy Lockett
Fear by Blue October
Numb by David Archuleta

The breeze rustled the bushes as Will strolled aimlessly between them, the memory of the last time he was in the rose garden at the forefront of his mind. It had looked different then: there had been no flowers, only the remains of dried up petals strewn along the paths, and he'd told Josephine that she would need to come back in the spring to see the place in its full glory.

Spring had arrived now, yet she wasn't there — now that each bush boasted a jewellery box of blooms in its own special shape and colour, she wasn't there to see it: her mother's garden.

Absentmindedly, he crouched down and gently cupped a pink flower in the palm of his hand, his fingers either side of the stalk.

She should be here to see this.

She should be here to see this every day.

He stood to his feet and squinted into the distance.

It was time.

Chapter 10

Best I Ever Had by State Of Shock
Bitter Pill by Gavin James
Gravity by Sara Bareilles

"Are you sure you don't want me to stay?"

Following the sound of Alice's voice, Joey glanced over her shoulder and smiled appreciatively. The main receptionist at Paws and Tails stood with her coat draped over her forearm and her handbag hooked over her shoulder.

"Positive. I'm going to be leaving soon myself. I just want to finish putting all of these papers away first."

"Okay. If you insist."

"I do insist. Get an early start on your weekend. I'll make sure everything is locked up."

Alice nodded, confident that she would keep to her word. Joey had been a wonderful addition to the staff at the vets surgery and was quickly becoming a favorite amongst her coworkers, as well as the animals and clients who visited on a daily basis.

She gathered the rest of her things, including her keys that sat on the desk, and headed for the door. "Have a great weekend, Joey. I'll see you Monday."

"You too, Alice. See you Monday!"

The high-pitched sound of the bell that followed Alice's footsteps out of the building signified Joey was the last one on the premises, and as the late afternoon sun poured through the windows and door, warming the entire space, she stood for a moment, relishing the peaceful quiet surrounding her. It lasted all but a few seconds before she realised it was silence that allowed her mind to wander and decided on some background noise to pass the time and keep her busy. Pulling out her phone and hitting play on her playlist, she returned to her work, singing to the music and swaying her hips. She was in the middle of organising the day's patient exams and stuffing them in their appropriate folders when the sound stopped and her mobile rattled across the countertop.

Danny's name flashed across the screen.

Joey smiled to herself, wondering what he could possibly want this time and answered the call. "Yes, Mr Watson?"

"Mr Watson?"

She didn't need to see him to know his nose was scrunched and his forehead crinkled in feigned disgust.

"Why so formal?"

A lighthearted chuckle erupted from her chest. "Well, because you insist on checking in on me as if I'm a disobedient teenager who needs reminding of their curfew all the time."

"Oh, so I'm your daddy now, huh?"

Heavy silence thickened the line, and as Joey processed the words she wasn't entirely sure she'd heard, she burst out laughing, the deep rumble of Danny's own laughter following only seconds later.

"God, please don't tell me that's your latest pickup line."

"Depends. Did it work?"

"Not. At. All." She shook her head, bringing her shoulder to her cheek to hold her phone while she went back to sorting her paperwork. A few more to do and she was free to go home.

"Shit. Guess I'm scratching that one off the list then."

Another giggle slipped from the back of Joey's throat. "Oh, Danny. What am I going to do with you?"

"I don't know, but I do know what you can do *for* me."

She paused, hesitant to ask. She lifted her chin and took hold of her phone once again, crossing her free arm over her stomach. "And what's that?"

"Accompany me to the Association of British Riding Schools annual award ceremony next Saturday night. Wildridge is in the running to receive several awards, and I'd love it if I didn't have to go alone."

Joey sighed, a sudden tightness in her chest. As happy as she was for Danny and for the school, she was supposed to be distancing herself from all of it. How could he expect her answer to be anything other than a resounding 'no'? "I don't know. Why don't you ask Hannah's mum? You like her; her daughter attends Wildridge. It makes sense. It would be the perfect first date."

Danny didn't say anything, at least not right away, and in the time it took for him to find his voice, guilt dug a hole in Joey's chest. Could she do this for him? Just this once? He had been her backbone since that day, and if anything, she owed it to him.

"I've been nominated for their Golden Spur Award for Instructor of the Year."

"You're kidding?" Her eyes widened, and there was no containing the excitement she felt for her best friend. That particular award was highly regarded amongst the association, and if anybody deserved to be recognised for it, it was Danny. "That is amazing. Congratulations!"

"Yeah. It's sort of a big deal. So, you see, you'd be doing me a major honour by accompanying me. Also, I'm pretty terrible at public speaking. It would be nice to have a pretty face to look at *if* and when it's time to get up and give my speech."

Persistent should have been his middle name. She had to give it to him. He was good. Really good. A true charmer who always had a way of knocking down her resistance and making her bend to his whims. "Okay, listen. I'll go under one condition."

"One condition, eh? Come on then, spit it out."

"I want you to ask Amy out on a date. An actual, real date."

Danny blew out a heavy breath, the sound of it floating through the line and straight to Joey's ears. "Jesus, woman. You wager a hard bargain, y'know that?"

She smiled to herself, knowing she had backed him into a corner he had no means of escaping. She looked at her fingers, chipping away at the rest of the nail polish that had already started flaking off her nails. "That's my offer. Take it or leave it."

"Take it." His response was immediate. "The ceremony is formal, so if you need to buy a dress, I'm happy to take you and cover the cost since you are doing this for me."

Joey's heart felt full at his generous offer. "No. No, it's okay. I'll sort it. Thank you, though." Reaching down and filing away the last folder, she closed the drawer on the cabinet and leaned against the desk. "I guess that means I'll see you next Saturday then?"

"Next Saturday it is. I'll pick you up at six pm."

"Sounds great."

"Awesome." His voice was filled with smug pride, as if he'd won a battle he knew he'd had no chance of losing. "Have a good night, Just Joey."

"Yeah, yeah."

Disconnecting the call and retrieving her coat and handbag from the closet, Joey did a final walkthrough of the building, making sure all the lights were turned off and everything was in order for the weekend ahead. Satisfied with her inspection, she grabbed the keys from the desk where Alice had left them and started for the door, pushing it open and flipping through the keys in search of the one she needed. Finding it, she pulled the handle tightly before giving it a little push to ensure it was locked and stuffed the keys into her handbag for safe keeping.

As she zipped it closed and lifted her head, her breath failed her.

She stood unmoving, her heart and her entire world stopping.

A few feet away, Will rested against the bonnet of his Jaguar E, his hands in his trouser pockets and his ankles crossed. His eyes were that ever-perfect shade of blue — deep, dark and intense — staring at her as if he were seeing her for the very first time. His dark brown hair was mussed just the way she liked it and the stubble covering his jaw was once again neatly trimmed.

There he was.

Not the man she had felt so detached from, but the man she'd given all of herself to.

Her body lit up the way it always did in his presence, but the pain in her heart was enough to remind her that whatever she was feeling was fallacious.

How was that possible?

How could a love that once felt so right be the exemplary definition of wrong?

Realising she was still standing there, unmoving, Joey took one more glance at him and then turned away, the memory of him exiting the club with another woman three weeks previous, painting itself fresh in her mind. She couldn't take it. Her heart couldn't take it. She didn't know why he was there, outside of her work, but she knew without a doubt, she couldn't be near him.

Not now. Not ever.

Her hand tightening on the strap of her bag and her stomach a bubbling mess of nerves, Joey hurried across the carpark and down towards the pavement, heading in the direction of the bus stop.

"Josephine. Wait."

The sound of his voice was like an axe to her barely beating heart. It had been three long months since she'd last heard the deep gravelly tone, and she'd spent nearly every one of those days wishing he'd come around and tell her everything she wanted to hear. Now it was too late.

Blocking out his presence, she dug around in her handbag, searching for her headphones. As she pulled out the tangled wire, she increased her pace, shutting down the part of herself that wanted to stop and allow him a chance to speak.

"Josephine."

Will's voice grew louder, more desperate, but she was determined to ignore it. Her fingers trembled as they fumbled to remove the knots in the cord, and as her patience to work them free waned, the thin wire slipped from her hold, falling to the ground and landing beside her feet. "Shit." She reached down to swipe them up, angrily crumpling them into a ball and then thrusting them back into her bag as she once again moved to put distance between herself and Will.

She was in the middle of rounding the next street corner when his next plea halted her strides.

"Joey. Please."

She stopped in her tracks. The only other time he had called her 'Joey' was right before he'd kicked her out of his life, and hearing it now was like a kick to her gut. She hadn't given it any thought when they were together, but now she wondered if it was his way of separating the past from the present—the little girl who had helped destroy his life from the grown woman who had been trying to piece it back together.

Her shoulders dropped in defeat.

Drawing in a deep breath, Joey whipped around, an unbearable tightness in her lungs. "What do you want, Will?"

Halting as she faced him, Will's chest heaved with apprehension and nerves as he willed the words he wanted to say to tumble out of his mouth. Instead, he just looked at her. He drank her in like a man parched. He took in every line of her face, every curve of her like it was the only thing keeping him alive. She was there, within his reach, and all he could do was stare, committing every inch of her to memory in case she disappeared.

He wasn't sure how many seconds passed before his brain kicked into gear, and taking a tentative step forwards, he slipped his hands into his trouser pockets and dipped his head a little. He was on edge, prepared for her to rush off again at any moment, but she didn't. She remained still, her chest rising and falling to the same rhythm as his own.

"Joey."

There was no reply.

He watched her throat as she swallowed, the slight trembling of her bottom lip as she attempted to hold together the strength she was desperate for him to see — all the signs of her falling apart inside that he had learned by heart, and every one of them caused another crack in it.

He took another step towards her, lifting his eyes to meet hers in a bid to speak what his heart was screaming, hoping she would hear it without him having to say a single word after all. If only he could get close enough to her, to wrap his arms around her and pull her to him so that their bodies were finally one again. The love he had for her was all but bursting from his chest, and all he wanted was for her to see it — to see that she was his only answer.

"Can... can we talk?"

Joey pulled her bottom lip between her teeth in an attempt to steady it. She looked away from him, her heart beating fast at his words while her muddled brain tried to

86

process what was happening. It hurt to see him. It hurt to hear his voice, but underneath all that hurt was an intense curiosity that needed to be satisfied. Crossing her arm over her stomach and giving her head a little shake, she turned her gaze back to his. Her hand tightened on the strap of her handbag and a huff of dry air floated from her mouth. "Three months. Three months and you want to talk *now*?"

Will closed his eyes at her animosity. He deserved it, but it didn't stop it from stinging. He moved closer still until he was mere feet away from her and searched her eyes for a hint of something to tell him he wasn't wasting his time, and as he watched the waning sunlight glint off the pools of chocolate brown, he saw it: a glimmer of the past and the life that had danced there when she was his.

And his heart picked up.

He curled his fingers inside his palm to stop himself from reaching out to touch her—to run his fingers down the side of her cheek. He bit on the tip of his tongue to stop from telling her he loved her, so damn hard, because he knew today was not the day she needed to hear it. "Can we go somewhere to talk? Please?"

With her pulse beating in her throat, Joey turned her eyes away from him.

She couldn't do this.

As curious as she was, she couldn't erase three months of heartache and every ounce of strength she'd fought hard to retain. Whatever he had to say didn't matter. Everything they once shared was now just a distant memory—one that didn't need revisiting.

"I don't want to go anywhere but home." Twisting on her heels, she breathed in as much air as her lungs could possibly hold and then started in the original direction she had been heading, not bothering to wait for a reply.

A rush of impatience loosened Will's tongue, and his tone was more harsh than he intended. He shouted after her before following her with long strides, almost grabbing her by the arm until he stopped himself. "Fine. Well then, we will just do it here, in the middle of the street because, damnit, you're going to listen to me. I've wasted enough time as it is, and I don't want to waste any more."

"Yeah, you know what?" Joey stilled. She glanced over her shoulder, knowing that if she turned around to face him again, it would only lessen her resistance, her strength, and she needed to do this—for her. No question. "I can't do this." Without any further hesitation or explanation, she looked ahead, her mind focused only on her immediate task: reaching the bus stop without completely falling apart.

Will once again stood and watched. He watched the way her shoulders straightened and how her steps were measured and precise. He could see, even from his position behind her, that she was struggling to remain in charge of the situation, but because she was strong, the strongest person he knew, she was pushing through the hurt and standing up to what she believed to be the right thing to do.

He let her leave.

He let her walk away from him, because she needed to. She needed to make a stand.

But he would not give up.

Chapter 11

The Black And White by The Band Camino
Things We Lost In The Fire by Janet Devlin
Die Trying by Michl

Rising from her chair and smiling, Joey stood with the rest of the nearly two-hundred guests filling the reception suite at Oulton Hall, applauding Danny's heartfelt acceptance speech. She had never been more proud of him, and seeing the look on his face, the glimmer in his hazel eyes as he spoke in front of a room full of strangers — expressing his gratitude and thanks for an award that was truly well deserved — was worth every nerve she'd battled throughout the evening.

She watched as he lifted the engraved plaque into the air one more time, before stepping away from the podium and weaving his way through the maze of round tables that were draped in white linen and decorated with extravagant floral centerpieces. People continued to clap, and his journey back to her was halted several times by a shake of a hand or a pat on the shoulder. She waited patiently though, and as soon he was within arm's reach, she pulled him into her embrace, squeezing him tightly.

"I'm so proud of you." Tears pricked the corners of her eyes as she stepped back, running her hands up his suited arms.

Danny circled an arm around her waist, yanking her into him once again as he dropped a chaste kiss to her forehead. "Thank you for doing this for me. For being here."

"You don't have to thank me. Besides, we had a deal, remember? I'm not just here for you." Smirking, she tossed him a playful wink, and as he pushed her chair in like a true gentleman, a lighthearted chuckle rumbled from his chest.

"Yeah. I haven't forgotten. And something tells me you'll make sure I won't." With a lopsided grin on his face, he set his award down on the table and licked his lips, His shoulders fell into a relaxed state as he slung his arm over the back of Joey's chair and the pair of them sat for a few minutes, both lost in the energy of the atmosphere before the sound of music filled the air. Guests made their way to the dance floor, and Danny held his hand out for Joey to take. "What do you say? Want to do me the honour of dancing with me?"

Joey's nose wrinkled as she twisted her lips to one side. "I don't recall that being a part of the bargain."

He rolled his eyes. "Screw the bloody bargain." Grabbing her hand, he pulled her from her seat. "Come on."

She shook her head in defeated laughter, watching her steps and being careful not to trip over her own feet as Danny guided them across the floor. He found a spot right in the center, and as her heels clacked against the hardwood, he lifted her hand and spun her around, twirling her a few times before bringing her close.

As he swayed with her in his arms, shared pride and happiness reflecting from each other's faces, Danny's attention was caught by another set of eyes.

Sharp, blue eyes.

After a quick glance at Joey as confusion twitched in her brow when he slowly released his hold on her, and he stepped backwards, gifting a nod of mutual understanding towards his boss.

Tick… The feel of her skin under his hands.

Tock… The graceful movement of her body as he turned her towards him.

Tick… The gasp of uncertainty that left her as their eyes connected.

For a breathless second, she stood, unmoving.

Had he been there the entire time?

Joey allowed her eyes to move down his body, taking in the way his black tux clung to the lean muscles of his chest; the way his shoulders were so broad. He was so handsome, and a momentary flashback of the last time she had seen him dressed to perfection took her back to that night—the night their love had been tested; the night that had become the catalyst to their downfall.

Their downfall…

Three months had passed and it still hurt as much as it had done that day and the days that followed.

Will's rough palms ghosted down Joey's arms, and the warmth of his touch spread across her skin in a rush of tingly heat, stealing her ability to focus on anything except him. Her heart pounded in her ears as his strong hands slid effortlessly around her waist, and as he gently brought her body flush with his own, she was overwhelmed by his unexpected contact. She knew she should step away, break the trance he'd magically pulled her into, but she couldn't, at least not right then. He was holding her, and it felt so good. It felt *right*. The moment itself seemed to freeze as they both stared at each other, their chests rising and falling against the other's.

The feel of her body beneath his hands again was sending Will's mind into a spin. The slinky fabric of her silver dress hugged every curve, clinging to her like a second skin and reminding him exactly what was underneath, and he pulled in a shaky breath through his

91

nose, clenching down on his back teeth to control the urge to show her just exactly how much he missed her, right there and then. Drinking in each of her delicate features, Will pulled his hand from the small of her back and gingerly reached up to move a lock of hair from her forehead, his brows twitching in pain as his eyes rested momentarily on the scar that now adorned her skin—the scar that marked the day he had failed her. He pulled in another nervous breath, finally settling on the chocolate brown pools that had held his future not so long ago.

Was it still there?

He had to be sure before he laid himself bare for her to scrutinise—before he shared every inch of his broken heart with her and spilled his apologies at her feet. He had to know that she wasn't going to reject him forever, and so he looked deep. He held her there in his gentle touch and he searched the depths of her for that glimmer of the Josephine Bell who had loved him with every inch of herself.

No words were exchanged as they stood, completely still, breathing in unison.

The rest of the guests whirled around them to the sounds of violins—smiles painted on their faces; merriment in their eyes—but all of it was lost on them. It were as if they were the only people in the room, and if he could have made time stand still, he would have stopped the whole damn world from spinning because she looked so fucking beautiful.

And she was there.

She hadn't walked away from him.

She was there in his arms, and if this was going to be the last time he got to look into those eyes and feel the warmth of her, then he wanted it to be his only memory, forever.

Joey was lost.

She was lost in Will's gentle touch and his intoxicating scent that even on her loneliest days reminded her of what they once were, what they'd once had and the love they'd once shared, and even now, a simple glance in those dark, intense blue eyes, and she wanted to pick up right where they had left off, as if their past had never come back to haunt them, but it was impossible. The arms that had become her home, that had showed her a love she feared she'd never experience again, had held another. And that thought alone was too much to bear.

A cold sickness swirled in her stomach at the memory, and she took one more look at him before taking a step back and breaking their connection. She removed herself from his warmth, from the safety of his arms. Her eyes drifted around the dance floor, at the couples that were swaying from side to side in loving embraces, before searching frantically for an exit, an escape. Her heart pounded in her chest and in her ears, drowning out the sound of the music, and she took off.

She ran before her mind had even commanded the action.

Darting from the dance floor, she pushed through the crowd of people and weaved around the tables, heading towards the set of double doors that led to a long, narrow corridor. As she slipped into the silence, her dress and her heels impeding her movement, she hurried through the empty hallway eventually pushing through another set of doors. A rush of cool air whipped across her face as she stepped out of the eighteenth century mansion and into the darkness. She moved quickly along a path decorated with neatly trimmed bushes and an array of colorful flowers as she desperately tried to put distance between herself and the night that had started off with positive smiles and cheerful laughter.

What was it about magical evenings ending in disaster?

Out of breath, her lungs burning and chest heaving from exertion and emotion, she slowed her strides. She didn't want to be there anymore, but it was Danny's night. It was his celebration and she was damned if she was going to allow the presence of her former lover ruin it. What had he been thinking anyway, allowing Will to cut in on their dance? Shaking her head and bringing her hand to her mouth to try and stifle the sound of a sob, she breathed deeply. She needed a few minutes to regain her composure and hoped that when she'd gathered enough courage to return to the party, Will would be gone.

He stood, alone, lost and completely deflated, his head bowing slowly in defeat as he dragged air into his lungs before he suffocated with the pain that sliced through him at the loss of her. He felt himself dissolving into nothingness as his whole world fled from him for a second time, and he lifted his eyes, catching those of Danny who sat at a nearby table, his shoulders relaxed and his right leg propped up on his left knee, his fingers wrapped loosely around his ankle.

Even from where he was sitting, Danny had seen the love in his best friend's eyes and the sadness that had enveloped her as Will had held her close. She was hurting, he understood that, but he also knew the remedy for her pain had been standing right in front of her. She just needed to open her heart and put her trust in Will, *in them*, one more time.

"Go." The words fell silently and slowly as Danny mouthed his support from across the room, and Will held the guy's gaze for a few seconds before his determination reignited, soaring through his chest.

He was not giving up.

He was not losing her that easily.

He squeezed his hands into fists, giving Danny a small nod, and then turned on his heel and strode through the crowds of people, his heart thumping wildly at the idea that she might have left and that he might be too late.

94

"Excuse me." He placed his hands on men's shoulders, turning his head with a tight smile when they shuffled out of his way, not even remotely fast enough for his liking. "Cheers. Thanks." He kept moving, the sea of people seeming to get deeper and thicker with each step he took.

Where the hell did she go?

A throng of women, all in glittering ball gowns and sipping from champagne flutes, were directly in his path, and recognising a couple of them, he attempted to duck his head and move in a different direction, but to no avail.

"William! Darling!" A middle-aged redhead reached out and cupped his elbow, guiding him to her side before placing a lingering kiss on his cheek. "Ladies. This is William Marshall-Croft, our most eligible bachelor and all round, well..." She chuckled and batted her eyelashes. "You can see for yourself." A tinkle of giggles swam around the group and Will nodded politely, shaking the waiting hands of three women, who were practically panting at him, and smiled tightly whilst manoeuvring around them with no attempt at eye contact. His attention was focused solely over their shoulders and the direction in which Josephine had fled. "Excuse me."

Pushing through the double doors at the far end of the room, Will burst into the corridor and began to run. "Josephine." His head darted from one side to the other, peering in doors as he sprinted down the length of the hallway. "Joey. Wait." His voice was loud and gruff as his optimism began to wane with each step he ran. "Joey!"

Reaching the end, he pushed through another set of doors and found himself outside at the top of a set of stone steps. He stood, scanning the darkness, his eyes squinting and his chest heaving with fear and exertion. "Joey!" He shouted louder this time, desperate to find her and tell her he needed her. "Joey, please!"

He jogged down the steps and frantically turned around in every direction, his hands folding on top of his head causing his shirt to untuck from his trousers. *"Joey!"* He squatted to the floor, bowing his head low, and dropped his arms letting them hang between his legs as he tried to catch his breath, all hope draining from him with every second she didn't reply.

Tears clouding her vision, Joey rounded the corner of bushes she'd been hidden behind, her arms tight across her chest in a bid to keep herself from falling completely apart. She had been standing there the entire time, listening to his pleas and fighting against the urge to reveal herself. Her gaze landed on a broken and defeated Will and her heart squeezed at the sight of him.

Despite all that had happened between them, she loved him, incredibly so, and therein lay the problem. She was torn between walking away and taking him into her arms, wrapping him up in the solace she knew only she could provide.

Yet she did neither.

She stood with her pulse throbbing in her neck and a painful lump in her throat. "What the hell do you want from me?"

Kicking his head up at the sound of her voice, Will slowly pushed to his feet, careful not to do or say anything that would have her running away from him again. He remained still, his arms hanging loosely by his sides and he opened his mouth to speak. "Ev..." The words got stuck, causing him to clear his throat before continuing, his voice now barely a whisper. "Everything." Will swallowed down and continued. "I want everything from you, Joey. I... I miss you." Running his hand through his hair, and gripping the back of his neck, he dipped his chin a little, but held her eyes with his, a reiteration of his heart falling from his lips without invitation. "I love you."

Joey's lips trembled and her chin quivered as she pulled in a shuddering breath, the words she had wanted to hear him say three months ago—when they would have mattered, when they would have made a difference—rendering her speechless. How could he do this to her? How could he force her out of his life and then return and expect her to carry on as though she'd never left it?

Inhaling deeply through her nose, she gathered as much air as she could, struggling to release it on a controlled exhale. She didn't know what to say, so she allowed her heart to speak for her. "I have nothing left to give you, Will. I gave you all of me and I have absolutely nothing left to give."

Chapter 12

Nothing To Lose by Karl Kimmel
Broken Arrows by Daughtry
Of The Chains by Red

They were the words he'd been dreading above all others: a rejection of the heart. They hit him square in the chest causing him to physically wince, and he almost stumbled back from the force of them.

She could not be done with him.

She could not.

He was finally in a place to accept every part of her and let her into every crevice of his fucked up world, and she had to want him back.

"Joey. Please."

Joey shook her head, a sadness clawing at her throat making it impossible to breathe. "How can you stand there and tell me that you love me after…" She paused, her chest aching as she pulled in another lungful of air, this time releasing it on a heavy sigh. She was at a loss for words, not knowing where to even begin when it came to this, to them. "Everything."

Will shoved his hands into his pockets and sighed. "I know how this looks. I do. And I don't blame you for being angry. But I see it all now. I see everything clearly. My mind was chaos back then. You saw it. You saw me.

Goddamnit, you're the only one who sees me. I was a mess, Joey. But now… well, now I'm less of a mess." He glanced up at her through his lashes, watching her expression and hoping for a change.

"You tried to hurt me, Will. All those years ago you tried to hurt me and you may have failed then, but twenty-three years later and you finally succeeded…" Joey's words trailed as her mind conjured up another possibility for his actions, a realisation she had never once given thought to but now seemed entirely plausible. "Was this your plan all along? Was this why you allowed me to work at the manor? Some twisted revenge scheme to make me fall in love with you just so you could turn around and completely destroy me?"

Lifting his head up, he threw his hands in the air. "Don't be absurd." The words fell from his mouth without forethought and he quickly shook his head and turned around, kicking at the gravel as he did. He took a few steps towards the path that led into the abyss that was the grounds of Oulton Hall, now cloaked in darkness, before spinning back on his heel and walking quickly back towards her, his arms hanging by his sides. "I was a kid, Joey. I was a hurt, damaged kid who had just watched his mother die. I was fucking angry with the world, but mostly, I was angry with myself." He stopped, his chest heaving with emotion as he tried to rid the images of his past that flashed through his mind. Breathing through his nose, he turned his head to the side and squinted, his voice coming out quietly. "You just happened to be in the way."

Turning back to face her, he took another step closer, hoping to God she wouldn't run. "Of course I didn't plan to hurt you. I'm not a monster…"

The tears burning the back of Joey's eyes finally sprung free, and she choked back a sob. Not once had she ever seen Will as anything other than a beautifully broken man in desperate need of saving, but so much had happened between them, so much. She didn't know how to erase the hurt and the pain. She didn't know how to put her trust in the very person who had shattered her heart. "What do you want from me? What do you expect me to do? Am I just supposed to forget everything?"

"Well that would be rather selfish of me considering my own life, my own past. I'm not expecting anything from you, Joey. I just..." He shoved his hand through his hair and fought for the right words to line up in the right order before he did more damage than good. "I guess I'm looking for forgiveness. I'm standing here hoping you can see through all my shit and see that I'm screaming from the inside for you to forgive me. And then maybe, we can go from there." He quirked his eyebrow a little in question and watched her process the words. He was like a ticking time bomb and was sure he was about to explode with everything his heart wanted to tell her.

"You want forgiveness. I can forgive you, Will, but that's about the only thing I have left in my heart to give." Joey watched the expression on Will's face change from hopeful to one of hurt and sadness, and she couldn't stand it. She needed to walk away. "I'm sorry." Hiking up the skirt of her dress, she sidestepped around his broad and sturdy frame, closing her eyes to hide her internal war. Everything about this situation was hard, but then again, love was hard. If it was easy, then it wasn't really love, was it?

Tears slid down her cheeks. She was desperate to get away from him, away from the agonizing ache that burned a hollow hole in her chest whenever she looked at him. Her legs moved in careful strides as she hurried up the pathway that led back to the back entrance of the building.

Anger born of nothing but his own frustrations rose in Will's chest and he opened his mouth, leting loose again with no thought for how his words might be received. "Goddamnit, Josephine. You're not going to make this easy for me are you? Cut me some fucking slack, for fuck's sake."

Joey froze.

Anger grating her nerves, she took several calming breaths before whirling around to face him. "Cut you some slack? Cut you some *fucking* slack?! Are you *shitting* me?" She bit down on her bottom lip, a weak attempt to control her emotions as she stormed back to where he was standing, her hands balled into tight fists ready to pummel him. "Three months. Three *Goddamned* months I sat wondering why I wasn't good enough, what I had possibly done or what I could have done differently to make you see me as Josephine and not Joey—not that *stupid* little girl who destroyed your life. I loved you for every damn second of those lonely and heartbreaking months and you... you were too busy giving that love to someone else."

"What?" Will's face screwed up in confusion. "Someone else? What the *hell* are you talking about?"

"I saw you with her. I saw you." Joey stepped closer, her face an inch away from his as fire burned in her big brown eyes. "Was she worth it, huh? Did she help you forget about your past and help soothe you through your nightmares?"

Will stood in stunned silence, as if he didn't have a clue what she was saying, and it only angered Joey more.

She pressed her hands to his chest, pushing him back, wanting him to just tell her the truth. For once, she wanted the damn truth. "Was she —"

"She was nothing, Joey. She was —"

"No! Stop." Joey squeezed her eyes shut, shaking her head to erase the words that had already started to fall from his mouth. She wanted the truth, but she couldn't bear to hear this. She couldn't bear the thought of him with anyone else and hearing the details would surely obliterate what remained of her heart. "I don't want to hear about her. I don't want to know what she —"

Will reached out and grabbed her wrists, pulling them down so he could look her in the eyes and so she would stop talking. "She was *nothing*." He made sure she was looking at him, watching her as her chest rose and fell, her bottom lip trembling and tears chasing each other down her face. "She was a one night thing that turned out to be nothing at all." He wasn't explaining himself properly and could feel Josephine tensing, ready to pull herself away. "Nothing happened, Joey. Nothing. I was crazy. I was drunk and I was messed up. I thought I could close myself off to everything, and she was in the right place at the right time, but *nothing* happened."

Joey's heart slowed, her breathing changed and her eyes narrowed in confusion. She knew she had sounded bitter and hurt, but only because she was. God, she was. She had carried around the idea of him and this other woman for the last three weeks, and now here he was, holding her, claiming that she was nothing, that she meant nothing, and Joey didn't know how to process any of it, much less her emotions. "But... I saw you. I saw you with her."

Lowering her hands and releasing his tightening grip on her delicate wrists, Will reached up and cupped Josephine's cheeks, his eyes flicking from one of hers to the other. "What you saw was a moment of weakness. What you didn't see was my moment of strength. Did I intend for something to happen? Yes. I did. I wanted to forget you, Joey, because I had fucked up my life sending you away. I wanted to forget you because I believed, and still do, that you are so much better off without me. I *needed* to forget you because I had let you go and it was a choice I was willing to live with so that you could be happy without me. But I changed my mind, Joey." The corner of his mouth lifted into a sad smile. "I changed my mind because *you* are my strength. I was strong because of you, and I realised that without you, I will always be weak." He stroked the apple of her cheeks with the pads of his thumbs, chasing away the fresh tears that were running in rivulets after one another before inhaling deeply. "You once said to me that I shouldn't ever try to change who I am. You said that all I needed to do was to be the best version of myself. Do you remember saying that?"

Josephine pulled in a shaky breath and nodded. Of course she remembered. It had been during the second time they were together, the moment she'd lost a piece of her heart to him.

"Well, I realised that I am only ever the best version of me when I am with you."

The sound of Will's words were like church bells to Joey's ears, and she stood there, soaking them up in case she was hearing things, or in case she woke up from this strange but wonderful dream. Everything he was saying was exactly what she'd been longing to hear, and she was frozen on the spot, glued to the look in his beautiful eyes, her skin humming at the feel of his hands on her face.

Will watched with hope — hope that he had said enough, and hope that he had said the right words. She was so close to him now, closer than she had been for so long, and he was desperate for her to stay that way.

Would she stay?

The pair remained sealed in a prism of the here and now, where nothing else seemed to matter, all the while their eyes locked together, both of them searching for the answers to the mess that lay at their feet.

As if their thoughts were connected by some external power, they moved closer to each other at the same time, their bodies almost flush, Joey's face tilting in a hesitant offering as Will dipped his chin to be near to her. Their lips met in the middle with no second guessing, like a pair of magnets that could not be kept apart, come hell or high water. They pressed gently, a feather-light touch to start, almost like there was a need to re-learn each other's shapes and contours—to familiarise themselves with each other after so long—but they knew each other by heart, and instinct took over and it was like they had never been apart. Closed lips pushed together fiercely—hot and mixed with the trickle of salty tears—and eyes squeezed tightly shut as if doing so would anchor them and keep them from falling apart again. They inhaled deeply through their noses, filling their lungs so they need not come up for air.

The kiss was loaded with a hundred 'I miss yous' and a thousand more 'I'm sorrys'.

Nothing more, nothing less.

Will's hands kept a tight hold of Joey's face, and she reached up to grip just as tightly to his forearms, both of them not daring to breathe—both of them not daring to move.

Joey was desperate to remain in the moment, but as cruel and unfair as reality could be, it came crashing down, pulling her away from the soft, sensual feel of Will's lips and the gentle strength of his embrace. She looked at him sadly, wishing she had all the answers to somehow make everything right, to convince her heart to give him another chance.

Will blinked his eyes open at the loss of her and slowly dragged his hands away from her cheeks as she stepped away from him. He once again searched her eyes to try to work out what was in her heart, but she gave nothing away. She had closed those shutters and flicked those chocolate brown pools of wonder away from him.

"I love you, Joey," he whispered, hoping he could get through to her with those three words he longed so much to hear from her again. "I love you."

A fresh round of tears trickled slowly down Joey's face, and the pain that accompanied Will's heartfelt sentiment pierced straight through her chest like a sharp steel blade. "Will... I can't—" She shook her head and looked up at him, her vision blurred behind a shield of wetness and confused thinking. "I can't do this. I'm sorry."

Taking a step backwards, Will nodded and slipped his hands into his trouser pockets. "Okay." He lifted his chin and squinted up at the clear night sky, roaming his gaze across the brightly lit stars before inhaling deeply and bowing his head. He took one more lingering look at the woman he adored—the woman he would do anything for, give anything to, including all the time in the world that she needed—and smiled sadly. And with crunch of gravel, he climbed back up the stone steps, two by two, and into the grand hall, leaving Josephine in a cloud of heartbreak and troubled thoughts.

Chapter 13

A Love Story by Brian Crain

A light wind blew at the hair that curled around the collar of his open-necked shirt, and Will paused a minute before lifting his hand to knock on the front door of number seven Hazler Lane, standing back once he had done so to glance up and down the road and across the acres of fields behind him. The sun lit up his land as far as the copse of trees that was the barrier between here and the manor. His fingers smoothed along the edge of the envelope that he held in his hands and after there was no answer, he knocked again.

The past month had seen Will an anxious mess, waiting, still hoping, that Josephine would come to him. He had kept his silent promise from the night of the awards ceremony and had given her space and time, leaving her with the words from his heart, but the time had come where he had to admit defeat: she wasn't coming back to him, and he needed to accept that. He needed to put it all to bed, to move on and to let her do the same without having to worry that she might have to deal with him again.

A shuffle and a click of the latch had Will turning his head slowly back to the door and he pulled in a deep breath, preparing himself for the well-rehearsed speech he was about to deliver.

Wishing he had worn a tie and a jacket, he stood tall and connected his brain to the businessman inside of him, locking away his heart and his emotions just as the door began to open slowly.

The loose hold Little John had on the doorknob tightened as his eyes narrowed, equal parts shock and confusion settling into the lines of his face. He'd wondered who had been knocking on the door with Josephine at work and Emma not due to arrive for at least another hour, but he never expected to see William Marshall-Croft on his doorstep. He regarded him warily, his tone clipped and full of disdain. "What the hell are you doing here?"

Pulling in a deep breath, Will smiled tightly. "Hi, John."

"Don't 'Hi, John' me. Why the hell are you here? You have a real nerve showing your face after everything you've done to my daughter. I'd tell you to get off my Goddamn property but seeing as you own it..."

Will looked down at the envelope in his hands and then back up at John. "I just came to give you this. I don't want any trouble." He held his arm out so that John could take it from him. "Here. For you. And for Josephine. No catch. No hidden agenda. Just..." He smiled again. "Just please accept it."

Staring at the white envelope clutched between Will's fingers, John eyed it curiously before reaching out and freeing it from his grasp. He didn't know what Will was bringing to his door, but he tore through the flap and pulled out the thick stack of papers, his eyes scanning over every word as he flipped through the pages. He read quickly, not believing for one second this was a no-strings attached offer, and then lifted his chin, returning his gaze to Will's. "What the hell are you playing at?"

Will put his hands on his hips and squinted to the blue sky, trying to recall the words he had planned, but none of them seemed to be relevant in the reality of the situation. "I'm not playing at anything, John. It is as you see it. I want you to have it. I don't want you to have to struggle anymore. I don't want..." Once again he battled to get his words out. "I don't want Joey to have to owe me anything anymore. She's free to move on with her life and not have to worry about dealing with Wildridge, me or anything else. I guess I'm trying to set her free." He looked back at John. "Does that make any sense to you?"

John arched a brow, still not sure he fully understood what Will was trying to say. "You're setting her free."

Will flinched a little. "No. I don't suppose it does make sense to anyone else." He sighed and dropped his chin to gather his thoughts. "I don't want her to owe me anything. I don't want her to think I still have some sort of hold on her. I want her to be free of that, and I think this is the way to make it happen. I *know* it's the way to make it happen. Am I making sense yet?"

Taking a step back into the house, John hesitated for a moment before pushing the front door wide open.

Something in his gut told him this was the right thing to do, for the sake of his daughter, and he held his arm out, gesturing Will inside. "I think it's about time you and I had a talk."

Will nodded in understanding, slipped his hands into his pockets, took one more look down the street with squinted eyes and stepped into the house behind the old man.

John headed straight for the kitchen, slipping the papers back inside the envelope, placing it down on the counter and then turning around to lean against it for support. He crossed his arms over his chest and stared Will straight in the eyes. "You love her don't you."

Will raised his eyebrows and blew out a breath, shoving his hands through his hair. He glanced at John and pulled his lips in tight, nodding. "Like you wouldn't believe." He let out a nervous laugh. Despite effectively being John's boss, he felt like the lesser person right then. He was just a boy, standing in front of a man, telling him he loved his daughter.

In all the years John had worked for Will, he had never seen the younger Marshall-Croft so vulnerable, so exposed and so *sincere*. He'd been told on many occasions, by Bea, of Will's affections for his daughter—how true they were. But the history between the two men had always been too hard to erase. Perhaps instead of erasing it, it was now simply time to try to leave it where it belonged: in the past. The muscle running along John's jaw twitched and he reached up, running a hand over it and sighing. "You messed up, Will. You messed up real good."

"I messed up because I *was* a mess. My whole life since..." He stopped and looked at John, almost imploring that he understand what he was saying about that day without him having to spell it out. He, more than anyone almost, knew what Will's life had been like, and even if he hated him for everything he had done, he hoped John would now be able to find it in him to understand. "You know what I was like." He paced the kitchen floor slowly before continuing. "I was so angry with the world. I was so angry with everything and everyone. But I was mostly angry with myself, and she ended up being my scapegoat back then." He pinched the bridge of his nose, the pain of the past eating away at him. Forcing himself to remember how he had felt that first day he realised he wanted Joey, he lifted his head. "But then Joey came back." He turned back to face the old man, and the way his eyes lit up at her mere name was not lost on John. "She came back like this... like this... I don't even know how to explain it. Like this ball of energy. This fire and this spirit that, try as I might, I could not ignore." He was on a roll now, and he realised he had never before spoken out loud how much Josephine meant to him and how lost he was without her. "She flipped my whole world upside down and I was swept along with her beauty and her love—her deep and almost unconditional love—for me, for a man I thought would never be loved by anyone because I didn't deserve to be loved. And I fell with her. I fell so hard, John. She was... *is...* my everything. My whole life. But I lost my way for a while back there, and yes, I messed up good. I fucked it all up." He flicked his eyes to John's in silent apology for his bad language. "But I need you to understand why that happened."

"Will—"

"Please, John. Please. Just hear me out."

John pursed his lips and let him continue.

"I sent her away from me because I believed that she was better off without me. I believed that she would grow to resent me because of the way I am. I couldn't let go of what had happened, and even though I know that none of it could be pinned on a tiny child, my messed up mind would always take me back to that day and how I felt, causing me to drink, to have nightmares, to drink more and worse, to become angry and... violent. I was scared for her. I didn't want to put her in a situation where she would be scared of me again—and I saw it in her eyes in the end. She was scared of what I was going to do next, and I couldn't let her stay and be frightened of me. I didn't deserve her love, anyone's love. She was better off without me, and I guess I thought I'd be better off without her as a constant reminder of my past. But I was wrong. Completely wrong. I am lost, John. I am utterly lost without her. I love her with everything that I am and now it's too late because she doesn't want me back anymore. And so I want to set her free. I want you to have this because I love her. So damn much." He paused, his breathing a little laboured from the released emotion. "I'm so deeply in love with her."

"You're setting her free." John finally understood. "You're giving up." He cocked his head and eyed Will, waiting for a reaction, a sign that he may have misread what was now so clear as day. "Giving up is easy, Will. Love is not. Love is hard. Love is *really* fucking hard. It's probably one of the hardest things we will ever have the pleasure of experiencing in our lifetime." He reached over, picking up the papers Will had handed him a short time ago. "This." He held up them up in the air. "This is easy. This is the easy way out. If you love her like you say you do, like I *believe* you do, then don't settle for easy. Never settle for easy."

Will hung on every word John was saying, but shook his head sadly. "And what if the love is unrequited? Surely that's not an easy way out. Surely that's impossible."

John smiled. "It's not unrequited, Will. You just need to keep fighting damn hard."

Tugging her headphones from her ears, Joey walked the small gravel path that led to the front door of her house, her eyes roaming over the landscape that was in dire need of attention. The increasingly warmer temperature and the forever prevalent rain showers meant the grass was growing taller, faster, and the flower beds her father had made a conscious effort to keep beautiful over the years were overflowing with pesky weeds.

Her heart clenched at the sight—at the reminder that her father's health was deteriorating and his ability to perform simple tasks was growing further and further out of reach.

Frowning, she made a mental note to get to it at the weekend over the weekend and continued towards the house, her feet tired and heavy as they climbed the steps of the small front porch. Her fingers curled around the handle on the door and a quick glance to her left halted her movement.

Red and in full bloom, her mother's rose bush was alive and as beautiful as ever, and an immediate smile danced across her face. She reached out smoothing her fingers over the silk-like petals and closed her eyes, losing herself in the sense of calm and peace their presence seemed to bring.

Her chest felt suddenly lighter, and she inhaled a deep breath before pushing open the door, sidestepping around it and hanging her handbag from one of the pegs on the nearby coat rack.

"Hey, Dad."

Little John stood in the doorway that separated the living room and kitchen, his shoulder pressed against the wooden frame. "Hi, sweetheart. How was work?"

"Good." Joey smiled tightly as she moved around the living room, collecting an empty mug and crumb-filled plate that sat on her father's side table. "Tiring."

Work *had been* tiring as of late, and her often restless nights that were occupied with thoughts of Will never helped. No matter how many times she tried to push him from her mind, he always returned. The memory of him on her skin and the feel of his lips on hers assaulted her to the point of distraction, and the whispering of his words on the night of the awards ceremony—those three little words: *I love you*—kept her up long after she would slip beneath the sheets.

Perhaps that's what happens when someone leaves themselves imprinted on your heart: you can't forget them; you don't *want* to forget them because doing so means forgetting a portion of yourself.

Will was a part of her.

He always had been.

Their lives had been entwined even when she hadn't realised it—hadn't remembered he existed—and now that she was without him after knowing what it felt like to be wrapped up and consumed by William Marshall-Croft, she wasn't sure how to return to the once oblivious life she lived.

She finally understood his need for the golden temptress, the whiskey he infused his veins with every night in order to switch-off, to capture even just an hour or two's worth of uninterrupted sleep — his need to feel numb, even if only temporarily.

"Leave them be. I'll get them." Her father's voice cut through her thoughts, forcing her back to the here and now.

"It's okay. I've got them." She headed for the kitchen and placed them in the sink, feeling the weight of his gaze lingering heavily on her back. "You should be resting. How are you feeling?"

"I'm good, but, Joey... sweetheart, how are you? You've taken on so much recently between work, taking care of me and the house. Not to mention re-enrolling in your studies. And you're doing this all with a broken heart. I'm worried about you."

Not wanting to burden him with the complications of her love life, she pulled in a shaky breath through her nose and forced another smile on her face as she turned to look at him. "I'm stronger than I look, Dad."

"I know you are." He resisted a frown, wishing he had the words or even the arms to make it right. It was times like this when he especially wished Claire were still alive. She'd know exactly what to do or say when it came to the affairs of the heart. She'd be able to provide that bond only a mother and daughter could have. "Your mother used to say that all the time, y'know."

Joey turned around, curiosity tugging at her brow. "Really?"

"Yep. She was stubborn, but determined. She'd always try to do things herself that she knew fine well were beyond her capabilities. I'd tell her so and she'd be the first to put me in my place. '*I'm stronger than I look, John,*' she'd say, and I swear, every time those words left her lips, I fell a little bit more in love with her." John smiled fondly at the memory.

Eyes glistening, Joey reached up and swiped away the tears before they had a chance to fall. "I wish she were here."

John moved from his position against the doorframe and across the small kitchen he had spent many nights cooking proper meals in—meals that had been shared only by the two of them. He reached out to his daughter, his pride and joy, and wrapped her as tightly as he could in his increasingly feeble arms. "Me too, sweetheart. Me too." A small tear of his own slipped from the corner of his eye and he rested his chin on the top of Joey's head, running a gentle hand up and down her back.

He'd never felt particularly great at saying the right thing or giving advice—never saw himself as the ideal father-figure. He just woke up everyday and tried his hardest to give his daughter the best life he could, the life she deserved. And now that he was nearing his mid-sixties, he questioned whether or not he had done a good enough job. He couldn't help but feel as though he'd somehow failed her.

Joey pulled back first, her hands coming up once again to wipe away what was left of her sadness and then turned to the counter, reaching for two mugs and the kettle. "Tea?"

"Please." John sat down at the table, his legs and bones thankful for the reprieve. He blew out a sigh as he watched his daughter fix them both a drink, and he struggled to find his next set of words. He knew he needed to mention Will's visit today—he wouldn't keep it from her—but he just didn't know how to approach the conversation.

"Was there any mail today?"

"It's on the counter."

Joey set the two mugs down on the table, sliding one in her father's direction before turning to grab the stack of envelopes.

"Sweetheart, there is something I need to talk to you about. Something I need you to know."

Joey returned to the table and sat opposite her father, taking a sip of her tea. "Okay. What do you want to..." Her voice trailed, a twitch of confusion narrowing her brows as her gaze lowered and her eyes flicked over the familiar stark white envelope with Wildridge's unique seal. She ran her fingers beneath the flap, retrieving the papers folded and tucked safely inside. "What's this?"

John swallowed around the lump in his throat, his fingers tightening around his mug and his lips pressed in a firm line. "It's what I was just about to tell you —"

Joey's head shot up, the words on the paper causing her heart to beat faster and her mind to swirl with a thousand questions.

Only one made it off her tongue.

"Is this... is this real?"

A small nod from her father was the only response she received, and her lungs burned with the inability to catch her breath. "I... I don't understand. Why would he..."

Chapter 14

Leave Me Alone by The Corrs

Out of breath and her arms swinging fiercely at her sides, Joey hurried up the gravel driveway that led to Wildridge manor, her curls springing off her shoulders and heat slicking every inch of her skin in spite of the the cool breeze ruffling the leaves of the surrounding trees. Nothing fuelled her movements and thoughts other than the immediate need to speak to Will, to figure out the reasons for his actions. Deciding she needed to hear it right from his mouth, she had pushed herself out of her chair and darted out the front door, not giving her father a chance to explain or caring about a means of transport.

She'd started the nearly hour long trek on foot, and now here she was, yanking on the large front door of the manor and storming through the north wing corridor, heading straight for Will's office.

Her breath came in short bursts, her chest heaving with exhaustion and a slew of emotions.

Confusion. Anger. Disbelief.

Who knew what else.

Her fingers curled inward, digging into her palms as her feet halted in front of the familiar door to his office—just one of many things that kept him locked away from the rest of the world—and she pulled in a deep and much-needed breath through her nose. She held it high in her chest as she pushed her way inside, uninvited and unannounced.

She looked around, her heart drumming beneath her ribs.

Empty.

Of course. It was Friday. His work for the week was done, which meant there was a good chance he was already halfway through emptying a newly opened bottle of whiskey.

Twisting around, her head whipping in both directions as if deciding where to search next, she took off towards the kitchen. Her legs moved in long, determined strides, her pulse pounding against her skin, and this time, she didn't stop. She stepped right around the kitchen door, spotting a busy Bea at the counter, collecting the day's worth of pastries and cakes to be packaged and delivered to the homeless shelter.

"Where the hell is he?"

Startled by Josephine's sudden and unexpected appearance, Bea lifted her head, her mouth falling open at the same time Joey turned around, rushing back out of the kitchen and into the hallway.

The need to find him powered her steps. She raced up the stairs, taking them two at a time, and moved quickly towards his bedroom, throwing open the unlocked doors to every room on the way in case he was hidden inside any of them. Discovering that they too were empty, she reached his door and wasted no time barging into his personal space.

She stilled.

A whirlwind of memories assaulted her as her gaze roamed over every square inch of the place, the large windows, whose curtains still sat drawn wide open, and his bed—his bed where they had made love far too many times to count. The scent of his aftershave lingered in the air, and an ache burned in Joey's chest. She reached up to caress away the pain, but the attempt was interrupted as Will walked out of his en suite bathroom, his ice blue eyes meeting hers in a moment of stunned wonderment.

Joey stood breathless. Her blood, which had been raging with frustration as she moved through the halls of the manor, now simmered with something much more potent—something she was afraid of feeling again because she had given him her heart once and he'd destroyed it; there was no way she was in a position to trust him enough to put back together the broken pieces.

Shirtless and the button of his jeans undone, Will stood barefoot, and Joey's eyes widened, her throat drying as her gaze took on a mind of its own, drifting from his handsome face, down to his sculpted chest of muscle and finally to the dark trail of hair that disappeared beneath the exposed waistband of his boxers.

Jesus.

Snapping herself out of her Will-induced trance, Joey shook her head and licked her lips, quickly gathering her wits as she reached for the stapled papers tucked into the rear pocket of her shorts. She held them up in the air between them, feeling her frustrations once again take their rightful place, front and center. "What the hell is this?"

Will moved to the edge of his bed and picked up the grey t-shirt that lay folded there, pushing his arms into it and pulling it over his head, his eyes never leaving her. "You know what it is, Joey. That's why you're here." Buttoning his jeans and sitting on the bed, he shoved some socks on before bending down and slipping his feet into a pair of trainers, tying up the laces.

"The house? Are you serious?"

"Deadly."

She tossed the papers at his feet, watching as they fell to the floor in a fanned-out mess. "We don't want your Goddamn handouts."

Will said nothing. He stood up, walked to the other side of the room and scooped up a set of car keys from the top of his drawers, turning to look at Joey as she continued to scream at him. He cocked his head, the corner of his mouth lifting into a sexy smile, his eyes sparkling with humour. "You know, you're pretty fucking irresistible when you're mad. Seriously turns me on."

Joey's eyes snapped to his, her hands balling into tight fists at his audacity. "I'm glad you think this is a joke."

"No joke. You're hot as hell right now." He took a step forwards, a step closer to her, and dangled his keys in front of her face. "I'm going to drive you back to your home now."

"Like *hell* you are." Joey turned around, angrier than she had ever felt in her life, and started for the door. She didn't want his stupid house. And she sure as hell didn't want a ride back to it.

Without a sound, Will moved until he was right behind her, grabbed her around the waist and spun her to face him, their bodies flush, their eyes locked. He watched her face for a few seconds, waited for something to happen and then smiled. "Yep. I am." And with one swift movement, he picked her up, slung her over his shoulder and headed out of his bedroom.

Jogging easily down the stairs, he headed for the front door, with Josephine Bell squealing in protest and pummeling his back with her fists.

"Put me down, Will! Put me down!"

"Ha! Not on your life." Marching with long strides, he rounded the corner of the manor and arrived outside the garages, clicking the button to open the door and then bobbing down before it had fully lifted to scoot underneath.

Upon reaching the Land Rover, he plonked Joey on the roof whilst he unlocked the doors and opened them both.

"You're an arsehole, you know that!"

"Yep."

Once both doors were open, Will reached up and lifted her down, deliberately cupping her arse with his hands before allowing her to slide down his body to the floor. "In you get."

Knowing she didn't have a choice, his broad and sturdy frame blocking any chance of an escape, Joey huffed out of her nose and twisted on her heels, heat crawling over her skin as she sat down on the passenger seat whilst Will rounded the car and slipped into the driver's seat beside her. She tugged on the strap of the seatbelt, cursing under her breath while attempting to get it fastened and when it finally clicked into place, she turned her chin defiantly away from Will, keeping her eyes glued to the window.

A twenty minute drive later, and Will indicated left into the driveway of number seven. He rolled to a halt and pulled the handbrake on, leaving the engine running. "You're welcome." He smiled cheekily at a still-seething Joey, who remained firmly in her seat, her stubbornness and frustration at the way he'd turned this entire situation into one in his favor making her madder than ever.

"Joey."

She turned to look at him reluctantly.

"Get out of the car. Go to your dad, to your home. It's *yours* now."

Chapter 15

You Must Go To Him by Alan Menken

At the sound of someone knocking on the front door, Joey rolled over in her bed, groaning as the early morning sun filtered in through her open window, bathing her entire room in its bright rays. "I'm coming!"

She lifted her head and glanced at the clock perched on the small table beside her bed, squinting in order to read the black hands around its center. What time even was it?

Another knock echoed loudly throughout the old house and she sat up—not ready in the slightest to get out of bed—swinging her legs off the side of the mattress. The tile floor was cool against the soles of her feet, sending a shiver to race the length of her spine as she ran her fingers through her hair, attempting to tame the unruly strands.

Half asleep and blurry-eyed, she padded down the stairs, the old wood creaking beneath her weight, as if it too, was groaning out in frustration.

"Morning, Dad." She turned to look at her father, who was in the middle of exiting the loo, and then carried on across the living room, unlocking the bolts and locks on the door whilst wondering who the hell was knocking so early on a Saturday morning.

Swinging the door open, she rested her head against the frame, speaking around an uncontrolled yawn. "Yes. Can I help—"

"Well aren't you just a sight for sore eyes. I'd be more than happy to spend the day with you looking like that. Sadly, skimpy pyjamas are not really the right attire for what I have in mind."

Joey glanced down at the thin silk top and matching shorts hugging her body—that now under further inspection, seemed to show more than they covered—and resisted the urge to cover herself. She flicked her tired eyes back to their unexpected visitor. "What are you doing here?"

"Good morning to you too, sweetness." Will grinned a heart-stopping grin and reached up to grab onto the top of the door frame, his muscles stretching, his blue shirt untucking from his jeans. "I'm here to take you out for the day."

He was here to do what*?*

Both of Josephine's brows climbed her forehead at the way he was so damn sure of himself, and she shook her head at the same time she began to close the door. "Go home, Will."

He moved quicker than Joey's brain was capable of processing so early in the morning, and his large hand flew to the door, stopping it before she could completely shut him out. She gripped the handle tighter, her blood beginning to boil with frustration and impatience as she pushed with all her weight, determined to make him leave so she could go back to bed and catch a few more hours of sleep. "This is not your home, Will. You gave it to us, *remember?*"

At that moment, Little John walked past the front door, a mug of tea in his hand. Will popped his head around the doorframe and lifted his arm in greeting, plastering a huge smile on his face. "Morning, John!"

John lifted his mug of tea in Will's direction. "Morning, William!"

"Glorious day! I was just telling Joey I have come to take her out for the day."

John nodded. "Jolly good." He looked Josephine up and down. "Best get some clothes on then." Winking at Will, he headed off to the kitchen.

Stunned still, Joey snapped her mouth shut, her nose crinkling at Will and her father's friendly exchange, and she turned to look at John, curious if he was suddenly losing his mind. "*Dad!*"

"Have fun, sweetheart!"

Joey shook her head, completely speechless. What the hell was going on around here? She turned back to Will, who was still standing in front of her, and she narrowed her eyes. "What did you do to him?"

Will dropped his head a little and gazed at the feisty bundle of fire that his heart continued to beat for and stepped a little closer to her, lifting his arm slowly and cupping her face. "Hey, Joey." He smiled a smile that sang of his love for her as he stroked his thumb down her cheek. "How about you go get dressed and we spend the day together, huh?"

Melting a little internally at the feel of him on her skin, Joey closed her eyes, huffing out an exasperated sigh. "Will..."

"Just today, Joey. Just give me today before you write me off completely. Yeah?"

Today. He wanted just today.

Could she do that?

Sighing heavily for a second time, Joey gave in to defeat and pivoted around, leaving the door hanging open and Will standing there as she quietly climbed the stairs back to the second floor. She returned roughly twenty minutes later, her hair still wet from her shower and her body clad in a floaty white blouse and a pair of jean shorts. She

123

slipped her feet into her boots and grabbed her handbag from its place on the coat rack before heading for the door, muttering under her breath as she shoved past Will.

"Try not to piss me off."

Will shook his head and laughed, watching Joey climb into the Land Rover, and turned his head over his shoulder to look at Little John. "Damn hard, right?"

John simply nodded, offering him an encouraging smile. "I assume you have your sword and shield ready?"

The men shared a chuckle and Will raised his hand in a goodbye gesture before jogging down the driveway to his vehicle.

Sliding into the driver's seat, he turned on the engine and settled himself back in his seat. He had no idea how this was going to play out, but he needed to stay positive, and fight—fight for his fucking life for the woman he loved.

Joey sat in her seat, uncomfortable to say the least.

Since when had it become awkward to be in Will's presence?

She attempted to push away the feeling and shifted, turning her gaze from the window and over to him. "Where are we going?"

"Wait and see." Will gave her a glance from the corner of his eye, an unusual feeling of nervousness taking over him. He was never nervous about anything, but this was a massive deal for him, and he needed to get it right. He needed to win her back. "We'll be there soon."

The rest of the journey was silent and became more and more uncomfortable as time passed. Will shifted in his seat, trying to think of something to say to her, but coming up short. This was already a disaster. Joey's silence spoke volumes and Will pulled in a deep breath. It would be fine. They would get there and it would all be fine.

After twenty minutes, Will turned the Land Rover into the driveway of Wildridge, and the look on Joey's face could have killed him.

"The *manor?*" Joey's gaze rolled over the landscape, a heat of irritation sweeping up her neck and over her cheeks. She looked at Will in disbelief. "Are you serious? You said you were taking me out. I've got out of bed to come to the *manor?*" She shook her head, knowing she should have just listened to her gut and stood her ground, making him leave. "Unbelievable."

As Will came to a halt in front of the house, Joey unfastened her seatbelt, her lips pressed in a firm line to prevent herself from lashing out on him, or worse, demanding he take her back home. She'd agreed to give him the day, so now she needed to give him the benefit of the doubt. Still, she couldn't help the mutter of annoyance that slipped out from under breath as she pushed the car door open and stepped out. "I've seen enough of this place to last me a lifetime."

Will closed his door and ignored her comment, walking around the back of the car and in front of her. He set off walking towards the stables, glancing over his shoulder at a stroppy Joey with a shit-eating grin on his face. "Come on then."

Standing still for a moment with her arms crossed over her chest, Joey stared at him curiously. What could he possibly have up his sleeve? This was so unlike him. She twisted her lips to the side and reluctantly followed behind him, the gravel crunching beneath her feet.

Will led them down the path that wound around the corner of the grounds to the stables, and he jogged down the three stone steps before moving to the stalls. Halting in front of one of them, he leaned his forearms on the lower door, a smile taking over his features, and Joey watched him as she got closer.

Her heart soared in her chest.

As irritated as she was, she couldn't help the smile that danced across her face at the sight of Roya, fully saddled. She looked at Will, briefly, before moving over to her horse and running her hands up the sides of her face in greeting. "Hey, girl."

Roya dipped her head, making a sound of excitement and Joey chuckled, happy to see her. It had been a while, and although Danny made sure to keep her updated and bombard her phone with tons of pictures, it was nothing compared to seeing her in the flesh. She nuzzled her face into Roya's nose and whispered. "I've missed you."

Will stood back a moment, watching the light in Joey's expression, and he knew at once he had made the right decision to bring her. "So..." He looked down the path to the other stalls. "I thought you might like to go out for a ride." He turned back to her again, waiting until she was looking at his face. "With me."

Confused, Joey tried to make sense of what he was saying, offering. She didn't understand. After everything that had happened, the uneasiness that had crippled him the last time they'd stood together in the stables, she just didn't understand. "But... you haven't been on a horse since..."

Will stood up tall and pushed his shoulders back, a little uncomfortableness snaking down his spine. He squinted off to the side. " That's not strictly true but — " He stopped and shook his head, laughing gently. "Never mind. So. Ride?"

"You were on a horse. When were you on a horse? That's a huge deal, Will."

"Yeah, well. Things happen." He smiled tightly, ignoring her question completely. "So, I saddled Equinox and Roya is ready to go. So how about it? I thought we could just go where the wind takes us. I happen to own a bit of land over thataway." He thumbed over his shoulder and gave her a cheeky smirk. "So we can pretty much go where we want."

Joey licked her lips in contemplation and only a couple of beats passed before she caved, one side of her mouthing quirking up in the corner. "I promised you today, didn't I?"

126

Will grinned and nodded his head, turning away with his heart pattering a little faster before unbolting Equinox's stall.

Joey's gaze followed his movement, her eyes lingering on the way he looked at his prize black stallion—a look she'd never seen him give another human being never mind a horse—and then at the way his jeans sat low on his hips and his shirt pulled tight against the muscles in his back, reminding her what it was like to have her hands all over them—all over him. She swallowed hard, glancing at his arse before quickly removing all inappropriate thoughts and averting her attention. Happiness ricocheted through her like an out of control ping pong ball, and she squealed at the idea of finally being able to ride again, her body doing a little jump out of pure excitement and her hands clapping together in front of her. It had been so long, and she'd missed the times when riding had been nearly an everyday occurrence.

Pulling open Roya's stall door, Joey walked in and took hold of her reins, guiding her to where Will was already mounted. Grabbing the horn of the saddle, she slipped her foot into the stirrup and pulled herself up, squinting up at Will as she did so, not missing how incredibly sexy he looked on such a powerful animal.

Lord help her.

"Ready?"

Joey smiled, giving him a small nod of her head, and Will pulled at Equinox's reins, leading the pair of them up the path towards the gate that led to the fields and beyond.

Once they got up there, Will slowed Equinox down so that Joey could catch up and ride by his side. "You okay up there? She's not been out for a few weeks, I don't think, only in the paddock, so she will be glad of a run. You fancy picking up the pace once we get over this next field?"

Despite her accident with Roya in the woods, Joey was more than ready. She was ready for the wind to blow across her face and whip through her hair. She was ready to leave behind her stresses and her worries. Riding was the only time she ever could, and she needed that right now more than ever. As she turned her head to look at Will, her chest fell on a heavy breath of anticipation. "Yeah. Sounds great."

The two of them rode quietly side by side, and Joey marvelled at the expert way in which Will handled the stallion. For a man who didn't ride anymore, he was skilled and confident. Joey continued to sneak glances at him, and a smile played at the corner of her mouth. "You're not so bad at this, are you?"

Will turned to face her and shrugged. "It's a bit like riding a bike, I guess. Once you learn how, you never forget. I haven't always hated riding, you know: I used to spend all my days doing it before…" He sighed. He needed to stop avoiding the past because each time he did, it dug its way deeper into his blood. He needed to stop being afraid of it—challenge it instead—and battle his way out of it. "Before my mum was killed."

Joey hesitated, but only for a moment before responding. "It makes sense now I know the full story. Why it's not easy for you to be around the horses, the stable. I can't imagine how hard it was for you."

The conditioned response to a comment like Joey's was for him to lash out verbally, to push away and hide behind his anger and grief, but he was putting his best foot forward for her, and although it was new ground and he was having to take baby steps, he considered each word before he said it to make sure she could see that he was trying, so fucking hard.

"It was really hard. Harder than anything I'd ever had to endure. Harder than most people have to endure I would imagine." He turned his head to look at her again. "But I'm here. I'm good. I can see a light at the end of the tunnel and I'm working on reaching it."

Over the last few months, Joey's heart had ached for this man, but right now, it ached for an entirely different reason. She stared at him, that forever prevalent urge to help ease his pain and sadness still strong as ever. She bit down on her lip, wondering if she should give voice to her next thought and figured, why not. He was obviously trying, that much was clear, and she was willing to take her chances. "The accident... everything that happened. Is that why you don't really speak with your father?"

Will let out a nervous laugh and blew the air from his cheeks. "Wow. We are really doing this, aren't we, dragging out my demons so we can slay them in the fields." He pushed his hand through his hair. "I cut my dad off. This whole mess is because of my reactions. Right from the moment I came back from the woods that day, twenty odd years ago, with you hurt, it spiraled downwards because of the way I reacted to each situation. None of this is Dad's fault. I got angry and I stayed angry. Dad couldn't cope with Mum gone. I know now he didn't blame me as such, but back then I felt like he did, and I just broke all bridges and connections with him, stayed out of his way and our relationship fell apart."

"Did you used to get on well?"

He smiled sadly and nodded. "We were a perfect little family. Really happy. And then I messed it all up."

"Please stop doing that. Stop blaming yourself." Joey shook her head, her heart hurting for the man beside her. "It was an accident, a tragic accident, and while I understand everyone's pain, I don't understand why he didn't try harder. He's your father and as a parent he had a duty of care and responsibility for his son. He may have lost his wife and unborn child that day, but you lost them too, Will. He wasn't the only one hurting."

Regarding her with interest he nodded. "You're probably right, but I was just a kid. I didn't know what I was meant to do or what he was meant to do. I spent most of my time with Bea or hanging out in the woods by myself." He pulled in a deep breath. "When I turned twenty-one, Dad sat me down 'man to man' and gave me the option to take on Wildridge Estate. He spent seven years wishing he could get out of the place because it was so hard for him to be around all memories of my mother. I don't think he realised that I felt the same, but despite the other option being to sell up, I wouldn't have it. I took Wildridge on as a kind of punishment. I decided that I deserved to be in pain and to suffer because of what I had done, and so he showed me the ropes and left."

"All this time you've kept yourself locked in your own personal hell." Joey said the words more to herself than to Will. "And now? Are you still thinking about selling?"

"Oh God. The million dollar question." He shook his head and laughed. I don't know, Joey. It's on the cards still. So many companies are interested. I would make a shit ton of money, and the place would be put to better use. Yeah, there are members of staff who come and go for meals and to use the loo, but it's literally just me, Bea and Graham rattling around the place, and as Simon has said, it's dead money. So I don't know. I'm considering it."

Joey shuddered at the mention of Simon's name, the sound of it alone enough to remind her of the night of the ball and her own secrets she was keeping from Will when it came to his business associate. She schooled her expression and carried on with her next question. "Would your mum want you to sell?"

"God, I don't know." Will steered Equinox around a huge puddle and then back beside Joey. "Probably not. It's our family home; it's been passed down for generations. She's probably turning in her grave just hearing me contemplating it, but I guess I have to do what I feel is right. It's the stables I worry about, although I have considered the idea of expanding, moving them to some other land that I have to help make the decision for me. I approached Danny—I don't know if he mentioned it to you—asking him if he would consider going back to olympic training. He didn't greet the idea with a smile. There's lots to think about I guess, but I am keeping my options open. Simon thinks Green Frog Entertainment are offering the best." He rolled his eyes as he told Joey that they created theme parks.

Joey's nose scrunched, the corners of her eyes wrinkling. "A theme park? Really? Like, rollercoasters and shit?"

A laugh erupted from Will's chest. "Yes, Joey. Like rollercoasters and shit." He reached over and cuffed her chin gently. "Anyway. Simon is in the process of setting up more meetings, so I guess we will see."

"Do you always listen to Simon's advice?"

Will frowned a little before answering. "In matters of business, he is pretty much the only person I listen to, Graham excepted. He's very good at what he does."

"I see." Joey pressed her lips together.

A slightly uncomfortable silence drifted over them for a minute or two before Will broke it with a grin. "Race you!" And with a kick to Equinox's side, and a cowboy 'yar!' he was off, galloping across the field.

Joey's mouth fell open and her hands tightened on Roya's reins. "*Bastard.*"

A command later and she was chasing after him across the open land, her heart feeling lighter than it had done two hours ago.

Chapter 16

Make It Right by The George Twins
Hurt Lovers by Blue
Fighting For You by Quinn Erwin
Love Is War by Runaground
Sale by Britt Nichole

Roya and Equinox munched lazily at the grass: sometimes stopping, their ears pricked at some noise or other; sometimes walking a few steps to the stream that ran through the Marshall-Croft land, lapping at the cool, rushing water.

Joey sat with her feet pressed together as she leaned over, picking at the long blades of grass between her legs, and Will lay relaxed on his side, his weight supported by his elbow and forearm, looking out across the fields. "So tell me about life with Josephine Bell. How's work? Are you enjoying it? Study?"

Scooting herself forwards a bit, Joey lay back on the ground beside Will, placing her hands under her head and looking up at him with a soft smile on her face. "It's great. I love it. Danny's uncle has been absolutely wonderful and the rest of the staff are just as nice, and whilst I don't do much other than clean the exam rooms and file paperwork, I get to be around the animals."

Will gave her a questioning look but remained quiet and she shrugged her shoulder.

"With Danny's encouragement, I've re-applied and have been accepted on the course. I enroll at the end of September. So I can only hope it's a matter of time before I can move up, maybe be offered some more responsibilities."

"You've been busy. I'm thrilled you re-applied. Congratulations on being accepted. You'll be Doctor Bell in no time." He smiled across at her, even though she was staring at the blue sky and didn't reciprocate.

God, she was so beautiful. So much had happened and changed in the last few months, but that was still something that he couldn't get over.

She took his breath away.

He kept watching her as she ran her fingers through the grass at her sides and his heart ached. "It's weird without you around the place, Joey."

Joey smiled halfheartedly, dragging her eyes away from the sky to glance over at him. "I'm sorry, Will. Can't say I miss washing your underwear three times a week."

A laugh huffed out of his chest and he moved onto his back, propping himself up with his forearms. "Well, yes. My boxer shorts are no longer at risk. They remain in tact at all times these days." He narrowed his eyes at her and smirked.

Joey couldn't help it. She laughed, one that twisted her insides, and she shook her head as she recalled that day. "I was so frustrated with you that day. I just..." She sighed. "You were always so miserable and I wanted you to lighten up. Even then, I would have given anything to just see you smile."

A tightness in Will's chest stopped him from replying. It seemed a lifetime ago since they were in that place, fighting with one another, avoiding one another and pretending they hated one another.

His absent response allowed an air of uneasy silence to fill the space between them, and Joey inhaled deeply, wishing this wasn't so difficult. Why did it feel like they were still skirting around the real reason they were here?

Why *were* they here?

She shifted uncomfortably and began to lift up on her elbows when Roya walked over as if sensing the need for a change of subject. Her face came down to meet Joey's and as she licked a kiss up her cheek, Joey fell back to the ground, laughing at her perfect timing.

Saved by the horse.

She reached up, stroking a gentle hand along the mare's nose and then over her neck. "What are you doing, huh?"

Watching the two of them interacting like old friends mesmerised Will for a moment. He watched Joey's slender fingers stroke the horse's neck and the velvety softness of her nose and he smiled again. He seemed to be doing a lot of that today. "So where did the name Roya come from? I never asked you. It took you a while to name her but you seemed so set on it once you'd thought of it. Does it mean anything?"

Keeping her focus on her beloved horse, Joey continued to run a gentle hand over her coat. "It means sweet dream." She paused, trying to collect her thoughts. She had chosen Roya's name for a reason and she wanted to be able to communicate it to Will in a way that he understood, in a way that made sense. "Do you remember the night you gave her to me and what happened that night?"

A frown tugged at Will's brow as he tried to recall the evening. It had been Christmas. He'd thought so damn hard about what to give to Josephine, and the look on her face when it had dawned on her that the horse was her present had been worth every single penny he'd spent on her. The rest of that night had gone downhill after his mood had soured, but as usual, Joey had turned it around with her gentleness, her overpowering love for him and her inexplicable intuition when it came to him. He nodded. "I do. I remember lots about that night. So much happened."

"You had a nightmare. It was probably the worst one I'd seen, and well, that's what inspired her name. I thought it, *she*, could be a constant reminder that dreams don't always have to be dark and haunting. Sometimes they can be absolutely beautiful."

As Joey turned her head back to Roya, the horse whinnied and rejoined Equinox by the river.

Will was taken aback by her words. Everything she had done had been for him, to help him, and he had shoved her way. Yet here she was, agreeing to spend the day with him. She was a marvel. She was the strongest person he knew, and he was desperate to have her in his life again. His eyes ran across the delicate features on her face, her huge brown eyes and the way her hair curled at the ends.

Yes. She was so stunningly beautiful.

Joey could sense Will's eyes on her, and although the butterflies in her stomach were enough of a warning to keep her own set on the sky, she gingerly turned her head in his direction, her gaze meeting his in a moment of intense yearning—yearning for the moment that he'd tell her everything she needed to hear.

She felt as if they had finally made progress today, as if for once he was actually letting her inside, but was it too late? Opening up to her was all she'd ever wanted from him. She'd wanted him to trust her—trust that she could handle all the punches their lives and pasts threw at them and to believe that she'd always remain in his corner of the ring, fighting for them both.

Yet he hadn't.

He'd shoved her away without so much as an explanation. And then there had been the house, the icing on the cake, the smack in the face she hadn't been expecting. Pain had stabbed through her as she'd read the papers, and her immediate thought had been that he was cutting her out of his life, again.

She was angry, but above all else, she was hurt.

After all these months, she was still so incredibly hurt.
And she was scared.

She was utterly terrified to give him her heart again
because there would be absolutely no surviving if he broke
it a second time.

Unable to look at him any longer, the tightness in her
lungs making it near impossible to breathe, she tilted her
head back and returned her gaze to the sky, her chin
slightly quivering and her heart thundering against her ribs.

She lay still for a few minutes, the rise and fall of her
chest indicating her internal struggle, and then she moved.
It was too much. She needed to take control of the situation
and control of her emotions and they needed to leave.

Rolling to her side, Joey pushed herself up off the
ground, her hands coming down to swipe the grass and dirt
from her legs. "I guess we should probably get back."
Brushing her hair from her shoulders, she turned around
and began the few steps towards where Roya was drinking
from the stream.

At her words, Will started to sit up, confused by her
sudden need to get away. "Joey. Stay. Please." There was
desperation in his voice. He knew it; he could hear it.
"Come and sit down with me."

Joey stopped. Her heart pounded in her ears and her
hands balled into fists. She shook her head, trying to push
away everything she was feeling.

She couldn't.

Every emotion she'd experienced over the previous
months finally forced themselves to the surface and Joey to
her breaking point. She whipped around, her blood
pumping so fast it heated her skin. "Why?"

Will frowned again and pushed to his feet, confusion
and fear rushing in equal parts through his body. He
needed to fight. He needed to fight damn hard. "Because
you promised me today, Joey. You promised I could try for
one last day."

136

"No, Will. Not why should I stay. *Why?*" She licked her lips, her vision beginning to blur behind a shield of tears. "Why? Why did you push me away? Why didn't you fight for us?"

Will's jaw clenched, the muscle running along it ticking.

John's words echoed around his head on a continuous loop again, and after inhaling a deep breath, he took two strides forwards and grasped Joey by the shoulders to make her look at him, giving her a gentle shake. "I did fight, Joey. I fought like fuck because it tore me apart to let you go. I fought through all of the times my heart told me to keep you, to let you stay. And I fought them because I didn't deserve you. You didn't deserve to have to put up with me and all my demons. You needed to move on and be the bright fucking shining star that I know you are and will always be but that would have burned out had you stayed. You wouldn't and couldn't see it, but you would have resented me, Joey. You would have resented *us* because you couldn't fix me. I needed to be the one who fixed me, and besides that, I wasn't ready to be fixed. I wasn't ever going to pull my head out of my past until I was ready, and keeping you next to me while I figured that out would have been downright selfish. I've spent my whole Goddamned life being selfish and I couldn't do it with you, not anymore. I might never have figured it out, and so I needed to let you go. I needed to set you free.

"That day when you took off and Danny told me where you'd gone, I was so scared. But that fear was *nothing* compared to the fear that gripped me when I saw your broken body lying on the ground. Fuck, Joey. I thought I'd killed you. Can you comprehend what that did to me? So when I came to the hospital to see you, to see you all fixed and peaceful, I knew I had a second chance to save you — to save you from me. I knew I'd done the right thing. I had to let you go, Josephine Bell, because I love you. Don't you see that? Can't you see that it was all for you? I never wanted this for you. You deserve so much fucking better." Will put his hands on his hips and squinted off to the side, breathless and emotional. He needed a second to calm down. Scraping his hair back off his face, he turned his eyes to her again. "And now? Well now is different because now I have seen the light haven't I. Now I have realised what I have lost and it's kick-started a catalyst in me. I am nothing without you. My life is worthless, empty, and I may as well shut myself away with my whiskey and never come out again. I can't have you when I'm grief-stricken and angry because it's not fair on you, Joey, but if I can just pull myself out of this black fucking hole that has engulfed me for Goddamned years, then maybe I have a fucking chance at loving you the way you *do* deserve." He reached out and stroked her cheek. "I never stopped caring, Joey. I never stopped loving you. Not ever."

Everything stilled around them. The air. Their breaths. Joey's heart. Her eyes were open and wide, hidden beneath a layer of fresh tears as the ones that had collected before raced down her cheeks. Her lips trembled and there was a weakness in her knees from his words. All along she had thought he didn't care, and she'd been wrong.

He cared. He'd always cared.

It was a realisation that had her choking on a hiccuped sob. "You were there? In the woods and in the hospital? Y-you were there and I didn't know —" Joey's chest heaved, and she crumpled. Her legs gave out and she dropped to the ground, her face falling into her hands as sadness warred through her tiny frame.

Will followed her to the floor quickly, wrapping her up from behind in his strong arms and pulling her between his legs so that he could cradle her against his chest. His heart was breaking and he didn't know what else to do.

Joey's tears continued to flow, hot and fast, soaking her hands and the collar of her shirt as they rolled off her face, and the painful ache in her heart finally exploded.

She couldn't breathe.

She couldn't think.

All she could do was cry—cry for the love they'd once shared and had lost, cry for the man who had thought he was too damaged to deserve her love and cry for the woman who had been so incredibly broken without him.

Will lifted a hand, stroking it down the side of her face, and began to rock gently, pressing his lips to the top of her head. He said nothing. He just held her—let her be. He tried to empty his mind because all he could think about was that even after spilling his soul she still might walk away from him, and he could not entertain that.

And so they sat in the late afternoon sun until Joey's breathing began to even out.

When the ache in her lungs subsided and her chest found a steady, constant rhythm, Joey turned. She twisted in Will's arms, the warmth of his embrace and the beating of his heart against hers causing her to finally break down the last barrier between them. She tilted her head back, meeting his blue gaze, her eyes red and puffy from her tears. "I never wanted to be free of you, Will."

Swallowing down a lump of emotion, he searched Joey's eyes for what he hoped her words were saying. They shone back at him with a love he hadn't seen for so long, but there was no mistaking it. He breathed in deeply and without the hesitancy that he'd had in the courtyard of Oulton hall, he lowered his mouth and pressed his lips to hers in a kiss that was a promise for the future. His heart thundered and his arms tightened around her as he felt her whole body melt into his chest. He reached up and smoothed her hair away from her face, pulling back gently and cupping the back of her head. He held her eyes for a moment and then pressed his lips to her forehead, whispering the words she had wanted to hear for an eternity. "I'm sorry, Joey. I love you. Always have, always will."

Joey's heart burst, overflowing with the intense love she had for this man. Her hands slid up his chest, her fingers tightening on his collar as she pulled him closer and she captured his lips again, a sudden urgency consuming her to once again feel his mouth on hers. "I love you." Her breath was warm, her voice a whisper, as she continued to kiss him with passion and fervor. "I love you so much."

Chapter 17

Pieces (Hushed) by Andrew Belle
Surrender by Natalie Taylor
In Love Again by Colbie Caillat

Having her in his arms again had Will's body lighting up and his heart thundering with energy and optimism. He moved his thumb around to stroke the curve of her jaw as he deepened the kiss that he had longed for for so long. But somehow, she still wasn't close enough. He had spent so much lost time away from her, and now that she was back where she belonged, the overwhelming urge to make their bodies as one again was something he struggled to fight. Sweeping her hair from her shoulders and dragging his palms down her back, he pushed underneath her thighs, lifting her and twisting her body so that she was sitting in his lap, straddling him with her legs behind him. They instinctively wrapped around his back and he let out a moan of intense pleasure as Joey's fingers pushed through his hair as their kiss intensified.

"God, I've missed you." His words buzzed gently as a whisper against her mouth, and he inhaled through his nose as he swept his tongue against hers. They were pressed against each other tightly as if letting go would break this spell they were now under. It seemed too good to be true, and in a moment of panic, Will lifted the hem of her blouse, smoothing his palms up the soft skin of her back in case it was the only chance he got—in case someone was playing an evil trick on him and that in fact all of this was some sort of sick joke. But Joey's response was to arch her back, pushing down into his lap and causing his head to spin with desire. The way she responded to him, the way her hands seemed to be aching to touch him in the same way he was aching to touch her, gave him renewed hope.

Pulling back gently, he searched Joey's face as her huge eyes fluttered open sexily and full of love. He reached up to the open neck of her blouse and nervously began to unfasten the first button, silently asking her permission as he did so. She dragged her bottom lip between her teeth before glancing down to watch him, and he inhaled sharply, letting out a huff of sexual frustration at how Goddamned hot she was. He shook his head gently and smiled from the corner of his mouth. "You'll be the death of me, Miss Bell."

Moving at an excruciatingly slow pace, he moved down the front of her blouse, his eyes trained on hers at all times, undoing each button at a time until the material lay open down her breasts. He leaned forwards and kissed each of her eyes as he trailed the tips of his fingers down her collarbone and the front of her exposed stomach.

Joey shivered, her breath catching in her chest each time his fingers found new skin to dance along, and Will could barely contain himself. He wanted to rip her clothes off and ravage her, but now was not the time. Right now he was going to savor every single second he had with her, taking his sweet time to worship each millimetre of her skin.

She was weak with desire and her hands slid lazily into her lap as she tipped her head back to expose her neck. Will moved forwards, placing his mouth below her jaw, and trailed butterfly kisses mixed with tiny licks with the tip of his tongue down the length of her throat.

"Will." Joey's voice was barely a whisper, and he smiled against her skin. She was putty in his hands, just the way he loved it, and he was going to devour her with his love.

Pushing his hands inside her open blouse, he reached behind and unclasped her bra before pushing it and the blouse from her shoulders, leaving her exposed to the cool breeze. Her nipples hardened immediately, and as she let out a shiver, he leaned forwards to swirl his tongue softly around them causing her to shiver again, but this time with need.

He was throbbing now, and it was taking every ounce of his concentration to keep from throwing her on her back.

Joey opened her eyes and tipped her head forwards, pulling Will's face up to look at her. "Make love to me, Will."

Will flicked his eyes from one of hers to the other and then crushed his lips to hers, wrapping his arms tightly around her back and pushing forwards until Joey was lying down in the soft grass beneath him. They kissed like their lives depended on it—like it was all the sustenance that they needed to live on, and Joey's fingers worked at the buttons on Will's shirt. He sat up to help her, shrugging out of it, his muscles flexing in the waning sunlight as he did so, and Joey reached up to drag her fingers along the dips and curves of his torso, remembering the paths they made like she'd never been away.

Bending down, Will swirled his tongue around Joey's belly button and reached up to sweep the rough pads of his thumbs across her nipples, causing her to buck her hips with pleasure, a soft moan releasing from the back of her throat that drove him to distraction. He pulled his fingers down her breasts, all the way to the waistband of her jean shorts, popping open the button and pulling them over her hips whilst Joey lifted herself up to help him.

She lay there, bathed in sunlight in the long grass of his land in just her white cotton briefs and she had never looked so beautiful to him. Her eyes glistened, the gold flecks highlighted from the natural light, and her face radiated warmth and happiness. He was overcome with emotion and took a moment to steady his breathing, just watching her, allowing his greedy eyes to roam all over her.

"What are you looking at?" Joey smiled gently at him.

"You."

"Why?"

"Because you're amazing."

Joey bit her lip again and blinked heavily.

"And sexy as fuck."

She chuckled and reached up to wrap her fingers around the back of his neck. "Then show me how sexy you think I am instead of staring at me."

He needed no more encouragement. Hooking his fingers in the sides of her underwear, he whipped them off quickly lowering himself over her body and worshiping her breasts once more with his tongue. He dragged his hand down her stomach until he found the heat of her arousal between her legs.

Joey instinctively dropped her legs apart for him, and he swept his finger into the wetness.

They simultaneously let out breathy groans, and Joey's eyes fluttered closed. Will kissed her, slowly, deeply and with everything he owned as he slid his finger in and out of her softness, his thumb circling her most sensitive spot until she was twitching and panting beneath him in release.

"Will. Please." She reached for the waistband on his jeans and fumbled with the fastening until they were open, pushing at them until they were over his hips, and then used her feet to push them down his legs. Will reluctantly sat up and removed his boxers, quickly resuming his place between her legs, both of them now naked and both of them ready to combust with desire and love for one another.

He needed them to be skin on skin, and so he slid his hand underneath the small of her back and pulled her flush to his huge chest. "Hold on." His voice was gruff and commanding, and Joey wrapped her arms around his back and her legs around his hips. They were flush and hot and slick with perspiration.

They were close.

They were finally close, and Will took another moment to drink her in, to gaze upon her face and to kiss every inch of it softly before reaching her full lips and inviting her tongue to dance with his in a sensual waltz of love. Joey's cries of ecstasy and the way she pulled herself close to him was his cue. He lay her back down and rested his forearms in the grass beside her head, pressing his forehead to hers and looking deep into her eyes before sliding slowly inside of her. "I love you, Josephine Bell."

Lying curled in Will's arms, her ear pressed to his chest and listening to the steady beats of his heart, Joey snuggled herself deeper into his side, her eyes closed. She was afraid to open them—afraid if she did she would wake up to discover it had all been a dream. She wasn't naive enough to believe that everything was magically right between them. The rebuilding of their relationship was going to take more than an exchange of a few words and an intense and passionate love making session, but it was a start.

And it felt good. It felt so good.

Shifting herself so she was hovering above him, Joey lowered her mouth to his naked torso, pressing feather-light kisses to his collarbone and moving south over the ridges and dips that made up his well-defined chest, her nose trailing along the same path. She inhaled deeply, her tongue darting out to taste his skin, and Joey smiled against it. She lingered there for a moment before sighing and returning to her slow descent. "God, I've missed that smell."

Will watched her, completely turned on by the feel of her nakedness pressed against his, and he cocked his head to the side, his brows pulling together slightly in confusion. "What smell?"

Joey lifted her chin, a blush of red staining the apples of her cheeks as if she were embarrassed to admit her next words. She licked her lips and said them anyway. "The smell of me on you."

Will's mouth turned up at the corners and he grabbed her face with his hands, pulling her to his mouth again. "It's my favourite smell."

Their lips crashed together, their tongues colliding in a heated dance of swirls and nips, a delicate tangle of love. Hands roamed, and the need to have each other again was the only thing on both of their minds, but Joey pulled back, halting both of their movements. She wanted him, and the truth was, she could have spent all day in his arms, allowing him to show her how truly sorry he was and how much he loved her, but she also knew they had a lot to discuss. If they were going to do this, if they were going to be together again, then they needed to start working on the foundation on which they were both standing.

Rolling onto her side next to him, she propped herself up on her elbow, staring down at his handsome face. "I think we've given Roya and Equinox enough of a show, don't you?"

Will stretched his arms above his head and chuckled. "I guess so. We should probably start heading back. But..." He stopped and regarded her carefully in a moment of disbelief. He wasn't ready for her to go home, not by a long shot, and having to drop her there and say goodbye until the next time, after spending so long away from her, was something that he was going to try to avoid for as long as possible. He brushed her hair away from her face, cupping the back of her head and running his thumb across her cheek. "Will you stay? For a while?"

Smiling, Joey leaned forwards and dropped another chaste kiss to his lips. "I thought you'd never ask."

Will's eyes widened a little in surprise. "Yeah?" He ran his thumb along her bottom lip before replacing it gently with his mouth. The look on his face turned more serious for a split second as he contemplated what this could be the start of and how much he had almost lost.

The battle was not over yet, not by any stretch of the imagination, and he needed to keep fighting. "How did I get so lucky?"

Chapter 18

Whatever It Takes by Lifehouse
Safe & Sound by Bailey
Best Part of Me by St. Leonards
Monsters by Katie Sky

Joey waited for Will to step into the entrance hall of the manor before turning around and closing the front door. Her stomach growled as she did so, reminding her that they'd been out the entire day without a single thing to eat. Then again, eating hadn't really been on their minds, had it?

"God, I'm starving."

Will turned around to face her, a predatory look in his eye, and gently took hold of her fingertips, lifting her hands and turning his own so that their palms were flat together before linking their fingers together. He walked closer, forcing her arms into the air with his own and pressing his body flush against her as he walked her to the wall, and in one swift movement, he'd gripped her wrists with one hand and had trapped them above her head. He towered above her, his eyes boring into hers before he nuzzled into her neck, inhaling her and everything she meant to him. "Me too. For you."

Joey closed her eyes, her mouth falling open and her hips bucking right out to meet his, desire coursing through her suddenly warm veins. How the hell was she supposed to resist him and focus on the things they needed to discuss when he said things like that? She pressed her body against his, needing to feel every hard inch of him, but also in an attempt to wiggle her wrists free from his firm grasp. "Will. We really need—" A gasp left her chest as Will's hand crept under the hem of her un-tucked blouse and smoothed across the flat plains of her stomach, catching her unawares as his fingers grazed the place down her side that made her whole body jerk.

"God, I've missed having you in my hands."

"I've missed being in your hands, but—*holy fuck*!" Will's thumb had found its way under her bra and was sweeping gently across her already hardening nipple, trashing any full sentences she was trying to release as her breath was stolen once again.

He continued to kiss his way up her neck and below her ear, the tip of his tongue swirling gently around her earlobe, his hand now exploring every inch of her underneath her shirt.

"Will, we really shou—" A small, needy moan bubbled out of her throat as he continued his seductive assault, and as her body shivered—not from being cold, but from being totally and completely aroused—she surrendered. "Oh screw the Goddamned talk."

His eyes closed as he lost himself in her. "Hmmm?"

"Never mind. Just take me the fuck to bed, Will."

Releasing an exaggerated and playful growl from the very depths of him, he chuckled against her skin and dragged his hands down and around her body until they cupped underneath her thighs so that he could lift her effortlessly. Joey's arms snaked around his neck and the pair lost themselves in a deep kiss of need and urgency as Will stalked down the north wing corridor and up the stairs to his room. He kicked open the door and all but threw Josephine Bell onto his bed to the sound of her squeals, and after kicking the door shut, he reached over his shoulders, grabbing the back of his t-shirt and pulling it over his head before dropping it to the floor.

"I'm going to eat you now."

And as Joey wriggled her way up the bed, laughing, she bit down on her full bottom lip, entirely aware of what she had coming to her.

Will kneeled onto the mattress after her, dragging her by her feet until she was under him, and he was over her in all of his Marshall-Croft magnificence.

Slumping down on the edge of the bed, dropping two plates and forks beside him, Will dug into the white carrier bag and pulled out the plastic tubs, reading the scrawl on the top of the first one. "One chicken chow mein, m'lady." He passed it over to a naked Joey who sat with his sheets wrapped around her, her hair tousled in that 'just fucked' way that he loved so much. He pulled out two foil cartons of rice and a bag of prawn crackers, setting them between the two of them as he pushed himself up to sit back against the pillows before emptying his food into a huge steaming pile on his plate.

She groaned as she shovelled the first forkful of food into her mouth. "Oh my God. This is so good."

Will smiled over at her, his own mouth full of sticky beef pieces. "Best Chinese takeaway in the whole of Christendom." He turned back for another forkful and then looked at her again. "Only ever the best for my girl."

Warmth rolled across Joey's chest at his words. He was trying, she knew he was, and she was fully ready to give him that second chance. "My girl?" Her lips twisted to the side in a half smile/half smirk. "I like the sound of that." She scooped another heaping forkful of chow mein into her mouth before setting her plate on her lap and reaching for a napkin to wipe her face clean.

A sudden hesitation clogged her throat as she turned to face the beautiful man beside her, and she swallowed down slowly.

This was Will.

This was the love of her life, and if they were going to have any fighting chance at making it work between them, they needed to be open with one another.

No more secrets.

No more lies.

"You know we need to talk, right?"

Will glanced at her.

Of course he knew. He was just wary of the fact—nervous. He didn't want to get it wrong, say the wrong thing that would have her bolting out of the door like one of his horses. He wanted to keep her here, wrapped up in him for as long as she would stay, but yes. He knew.

Taking a long drink of his water, he placed the glass carefully on his bedside table, his plate next to it and then reached for Joey's too. Once the bed was clear, he wrapped his arm around her shoulders and pulled her snugly into his side, kissing the top of her head. He would talk until the cows came home if it meant he could keep her forever, so he needed to take a deep breath and do what needed to be done. "Yep."

Joey's chest felt lighter already, and she tilted her head back, looking at those blue eyes that belonged to her entire world. "If we're going to do this, then you need to let me in. No more secrets. I need you to trust that I will always be here for you. I'll always fight for you, no matter what." She paused, pulling in a lungful of air before continuing. "I once asked you not to hide from me, remember? I wanted to see every single side of you, and I still do."

His lips moved and pressed even harder to the top of her head as her words of openness wrapped themselves around his heart.

This woman was everything.

He had been a fool to shut her away from him, and sitting there with her body against his, he almost cursed out loud at his stupidity. She'd only ever wanted to love him, to see him, and he'd pushed all of that goodness away for the sake of his pride, his insecurity and his fear that he was not worthy of her. Looking at her now, he knew what an insult that was to Josephine. She wasn't stupid. She was a strong woman with a heart and mind of her own; she wasn't the kind of person to give her love away to someone who did not deserve it. He could see that now.

He inhaled deeply.

There would be no compromise. This would be an all or nothing deal, and he was in.

He was all in.

He held her face in his hands and looked deeply into her expectant expression. "I love you, Josephine. If you need all of me for this to work, then baby, I'm here. All of me. I promise you that now. I just—" He paused for a second, lining up the words in the right order. Talking so openly was not something he was used to doing in regards to affairs of the heart, but he needed to push through and keep up that fucking fight. "Will you let me take it slow? Can you have patience with me? There might be days where I find this excruciatingly difficult. There might be days when my past is right fucking here." He prodded his forehead hard with his forefinger, his face contorting a little at the pain that he was so used to feeling. "I promise you now I will not hide from you, but some days, I might just need to not talk, until it…" His voice trailed off as emotion that he was not used to feeling seemed to take his words away. A flutter of a frown across his brow had him clearing his throat and shaking his head to rid the onslaught of sadness and fear that was clawing at his back and making the fight more difficult. "Joey." He held her a little tighter. "I can't do this on my own."

Holding back the tears that were quickly building, Joey reached for his hand, bringing it to her mouth and placing soft kisses against his knuckles. She looked at him, wanting to make sure he heard her next words loud and clear. "I can do that for you, Will, because I love you. I love you so much. But I need you to do something for me." She cupped his face, slowly dragging her thumb across the sculpted bone of his cheek. "I need you to stop hating yourself. If you're going to have any chance at loving me the way I deserve, the way you think I deserve, then you need to learn to love yourself, every single broken piece. And it's going to be hard, and at times it's going to hurt, but know that I'm going to be right there, loving them too."

The way I deserve.

Those words alone scared the shit out of him, and he pulled in a shaky breath. What if he couldn't live up to that? What if he came up short? What if after pouring in every single effort that he could muster, he still wasn't good enough for her?

Quit it, Will.

It was a vicious circle, but he needed to climb out of the pool. He contemplated smiling and nodding, but she wanted all of him: she wanted all of his fears and hesitations and it started right there in that bed. He was a successful businessman and had people eating out of his hands in all corners of the country, yet lying next to this beautiful woman, he had never felt so vulnerable. "What... what if I can't love you like you deserve? What if I fail?"

A single tear trekked down Joey's cheek and she shook her head. "That's not possible." Taking hold of his hand, Joey guided it to his chest, resting it right over his heart. "You feel that?" She didn't bother to wait for a response.

"I've felt the love this heart is capable of giving, and it's more than enough, Will. More than I'll ever need."

Leaning forwards, he pressed his forehead against hers, his heart beating fast at the intense feeling of what was happening to them both. "I will love you with all of my heart, Joey. Everything I have to give, I will give it to you until you feel that you have what you deserve."

Dusk was closing in, and the light in the room was dimming as the two of them lay in each other's arms in what felt like a much lighter air of quiet understanding. Such a lot had been said that day, and they were both feeling the relief and the release. Will lazily twirled strands of Joey's hair around his fingers as she moved her fingertips up and down the skin of his bicep, and for several minutes, they just lay entwined, their breathing steady, their minds at peace.

Joey thought back to the time they'd spent apart—the way it had affected her and the way it had affected him — and the question that was forming in her immediate thoughts sat at the back of her tongue, burning her throat the same way that vicious drink he relied on did the last time she'd tasted it. She glanced over at him and sighed, not wanting to upset him in anyway but knowing she needed to just come out with it. She needed to know if this was going to continue to be a problem—another obstacle for them to conquer. She pressed her lips together before swallowing down all her fear and blowing out a shallow breath. "Are you still drinking every night?"

Will reached up and pinched the bridge of his nose tightly, as tightly as his eyes were squeezed shut. He didn't want to disappoint her with his answer. He couldn't bear to hear it in her voice or in the way her breathing would hitch slightly, but this was a new start, right? This was where everything changed for the better, and with everything laid out on the table, palms open and cards face up, he could get through this with her by his side. He huffed out of his nose and nodded silently before sitting up a little and pulling her closer so that her cheek rested on his chest. "I have had a drink every night since the day I understood the effects it had on one's ability to remember things. I think I was sixteen the first time I had a sip. At first, it was just funny to get wasted on my dad's expensive liquor when he wasn't in the house, but one day it hit me that whilst I was lolling around trying to walk up the stairs without tripping or slamming into a wall, my brain had also switched off my past and made me really fucking sleepy. It became a crutch, Joey. And it's remained a crutch." He pulled her lip from between her teeth where she worried on it. "When you left... well, when I sent you away, I had more to forget and if we're being honest here, which we are, I think I have slowly become more dependent on it for a good night's sleep than ever. I had so much shit whirling around once you had gone and—" He sighed loudly. "I don't like it. At all. I hate that I can't sleep without it, and believe me when I say I am desperate for the day when I can do just that. So yes. I still drink every night. But I don't want to drink every night."

Joey's chin quivered, all the sadness she felt for him bubbling right up to the surface. As much as she hated it, oddly, she understood. "I can't imagine for one second what it's like, but we can work through it, okay? We can get you help. You can see a doctor, maybe someone to talk to. I know those aren't your ideal options, and I know you've said you've been down that road before, but there are other ways to numb the pain and dull the nightmares. There are healthier ways, and we won't stop searching until we've tried them all. I promise. And even then, we'll keep searching."

"We." He smiled and pulled her so she was lying flush on top of him, her legs between his and the warmth of her nakedness seeping into him. "I like that word." He kissed each of her eyelids. "In fact—" He kissed the tip of her nose. "I think—" And then pressed his lips to hers. "It's my favorite word."

A heavy sigh filled with relief floated from Joey's chest and the remaining stress that had been tightening the muscles in her neck and shoulders slowly melted away. "It's not going to be easy, I know this. I am prepared for this."

Will hooked his hands under her arms and pulled her further up so that she was straddling his waist and so that their foreheads were pressed together. "Well, it just so happens that I don't want easy with you, Josephine Bell. I want love."

Chapter 19

Be OK by Too Far Moon
Fall In Love by Jurrivh

"Shit."

Will jumped back as the knife fell from his fingers, bounced onto the kitchen counter and fell point up to the floor, narrowly missing his foot—his bare foot. Sighing, he bent at the knees and picked it up, wiping it on the arse of his pyjama bottoms, before continuing to cut the loaf, muttering to himself. "Fucking stupid anyway when you can buy it pre-sliced."

He moved over to the fridge and pulled out eggs, bacon, milk and butter, and with them balanced in one arm, his chin securing the top item, he returned to the countertop and set about cooking.

Cooking.

He snorted at the word.

He'd never cooked in his life aside from that one time, and even then she'd had to come to his rescue.

Ripping open the pack of bacon, he carried it and a frying pan over to the hob, lighting the front burner and placing the pan on top. The first rasher landed flat and smoke began to billow quickly. "Oh for fuck's sake. What now?" He stood with his hands on his hips, looking around the kitchen for a clue. "What the hell have I done wrong now?" Quickly grabbing the spatula, he slid it under the bacon only to find it stuck. "Oil. I forgot the Goddamned oil." He slid across the floor and grabbed it from the shelf, flipping the lid open and pouring a small amount in. He watched as the bacon began to make that wonderful sizzling sound, and a grin tugged at the corner of his mouth as the rasher flipped over easily this time.

He nodded to himself. "Just c-a-a-ll me Heston."

Adding a few more rashers, he reached over and opened the window to let out the smoke and set about preparing the eggs.

Now this he *could* do.

His mind went back to that night so many months before when Josephine had shown him — her hand covering his gently, sending sparks of sexual energy flying around them — and that same feeling of utter lust that had consumed him back then crept into his stomach and pooled in his groin as he stood there whisking, just the way he'd been taught. God, he'd wanted her so badly that night, but standing there, making breakfast for her while she slept in his bed, under his sheets, smelling of him, he realised he wanted her even more than that now.

That night he hadn't known what he was missing.

Now, he knew every inch of her.

Now, he knew what she tasted like when she kissed him.

Now, he knew what it was like to move inside of her with her sexy little body arching beneath him.

Now, she was written across his heart indelibly.

And so he ached for every part of her so much more, and he was ready to do anything and everything it might take to build a strong and infallible tower of love for them to live in, together.

He lifted the glass bowl, full of perfectly whisked eggs, and moved over to the pan where the bacon was looking a little frazzled.

"Crap." He turned off the gas, reaching up to grab a small copper pan to pour the eggs into.

After a few minutes of stirring and inspecting, he decided they looked pretty much like scrambled eggs should look, if a little watery, and he high-fived himself internally when at the last minute, he remembered the pepper. She liked pepper in her eggs.

Holding the grinder over the pan, he twisted and peered in. It didn't look like much, so he twisted again, and again, until the little black specs started to become noticeable. He gave another a stir and then another twist of the pepper grinder. How much pepper was enough anyway?

After buttering a few slices of toast, he grabbed a tray, poured fresh orange juice into a glass and arranged the eggs and bacon on a plate, just like she had that night: bacon rashers on top.

Did it look okay?

Would it taste okay?

He moved his eyes across the tray nudging the plate one way, then the other, repositioning the glass more than twice and changing his mind about how to present the cutlery until it drove him insane before glancing around the kitchen to see if there was anything he had missed, a swirl of butterflies dancing in his stomach.

Fairly satisfied that it was satisfactory at least, he picked up the tray, grabbing a napkin at the last minute, and headed towards the door. But then an idea struck him. He moved quickly back to the north wing, opening his office door and placing the tray on his desk. Without a sound, he walked to the front door and slipped out into the early morning, closing the door gently behind him.

Eyes still closed, Joey wriggled herself deeper under the covers, attempting to block out the mid morning sunshine filtering through the large windows in Will's room. For the first time since stepping foot in the manor, she cursed the light shining through the glass panes that was rudely forcing her from her peaceful slumber. She wasn't ready to get up—wasn't ready to pull herself out of the sweet dream she'd been having or away from the delicious scent she had spent so long missing.

This was heaven.

She was absolutely sure of it.

After a few seconds, her mind blissfully lost to the previous evening and the countless times Will had made love to her, she rolled over onto her side, fully expecting to be met by the warm, firm body and gentle hands that had held her in their comforting grip all night.

Only there was nothing.

She rolled again, knowing the bed was rather large, but when she collided with dead air and cool sheets, she lifted her head, allowing the duvet to tumble to her shoulders. A frown twitched at her brow at the empty spot where Will had slept, and she slowly pushed herself up, twisting at the waist. Her heart beat a little faster in her chest at the thought he'd had another nightmare and had slipped out of the room to keep from waking her as he'd done often before, but she had hoped after their intense and passionate love making sessions he would've managed at least a couple hours of uninterrupted sleep.

Biting down on her lip to prevent the frown from forming there too, she pushed the blankets from her legs so she could swing them off the side of the bed but was stopped by the sound of the door's hinges creaking open.

Peeking around the side of it was the handsome face she had been in search of, and Joey smiled, her chest feeling one hundred times lighter than it had a few seconds ago. "There you are. I was wondering where you got to. I was just getting ready to come find you."

Will pushed the door further open with the ball of his foot, sidestepping around it and into the room, his fingers gripping the tray he carried in his hands, and Joey's eyes widened in surprise.

"Will…" Her next breath came on a sharp gasp and the smile on her face grew twice its size as she realised what he was carrying and where he'd been.

He hadn't… had he? Was Bea in the house?

He wore a look of uncertainty on his face as he padded across the room and sat down, carefully placing the tray full of food on the bed directly in front of her. Joey's stomach growled, hunger suddenly waking at the smell of food. She looked at the plate, bacon rashers not perfectly cooked, but cooked nonetheless, and a single rose—a beautiful orange rose that she'd never seen in her life before. Her heart nearly burst right out of her chest and she stared at Will in complete awe.

He *had*.

"What did you do?"

"Um…" Will dipped his head and pushed his hand through his hair, smiling out of the corner of his mouth at the delight on her face. "I cooked you breakfast."

"You certainly did." Joey stared at the tray, her smile still large and in place, not sure where to begin. Reaching out, she picked up the beautiful flower that lay beside her plate and twirled the stem between her fingers as she brought it to her nose and closed her eyes, inhaling its soft, subtle scent. She held it there for a moment before replacing it and grabbing a piece of bacon, her stomach growling again in hungry anticipation. She could tell already it was overdone, but she didn't care. He'd gone out of his way to do this; she knew fine well he had no idea how to cook, and well, she was going to eat it. Taking a bite, she stared at Will who was waiting for her reaction, and she schooled her expression, her eyes widening as she swallowed down the burnt pieces. Quickly grabbing a hold of the glass of orange juice, she took a sip, washing down the remains of the crispy shards.

Will raised his eyebrows hopefully. "It's okay?"

She nodded her head enthusiastically, her lips pulled tight. "Mmmm. Yummy." Moving the other two rashers aside, Joey picked up her fork, fluffing the eggs a bit before scooping some up and bringing them to her mouth. He couldn't screw up eggs, right? She parted her lips, almost hesitant this time, and tentatively pushed the food into her mouth, rolling the eggs around in her mouth for a couple of seconds before the overwhelming flavour had her choking and reaching for the napkin. Her eyes began to water and she downed another large mouthful of orange juice, desperate to rid the burning sensation from her tongue.

What was he trying to do? Kill her?

"Holy shit, Will." She covered her mouth as she coughed. "How much pepper have you put in here?"

Death by pepper.

"I… I thought you liked pepper in your eggs." Will's eyes closed and he shook his head, disappointment churning around his body. "I've fucked it up haven't I." It wasn't a question. He reached out to grab the tray. "I'll bin it. I'm sorry." He stood up as he caught hold of the edge of the tray, but Joey stopped him, taking hold of his hand and pulling him back down.

"No. Don't." She could clearly see his frustration with himself and she wanted him to know how much his effort meant to her. "I love it. So the bacon was burned and the eggs inedible. So what? It's perfect." She smiled reassuringly at him and leaned forwards, cupping his cheek as she pressed a gentle kiss to his lips. Pulling back, her

162

eyes fell on the orange rose that still lay across the tray, and she picked it up, holding it up between them. "I've never seen a more beautiful rose in all of my life."

Will glanced down at the flower, reaching out to stroke one of its petals gently. "Simply The Best."

"Your mum's favourite."

Will nodded. He turned his body and took hold of Joey's hands, maintaining eye contact and smiling softly. "Simply The Best, because that's what you are to me, Joey. You're simply the best thing in my life. You're simply the best thing that has happened to me, and I know that my life will be the best it can be because you're back in it." He reached up and dragged his thumb across her bottom lip before moving forwards and capturing it with his own. "I love you."

He began to break away from their kiss and Joey halted his movement, pushing the tray of food out of the way and crawling into his lap, her arms wrapping tightly around his neck and her fingers threading through the soft strands of his hair. "I love you." She pressed her lips harder to his, an intense need to have him right there and then gripping her as she felt his growing erection through the thin material of his pyjama bottoms, hard and thick against her inner thigh. Joey moaned at the feel of it, and, forcing Will onto his back, she quickly worked to free him from the cloth barrier between them.

And then she dedicated the next hour just to him, showing him exactly how much she loved him.

Switching off the engine, Will sat back in his seat and turned to look at her, a sad smile on his face. "Here we are then."

"Here we are." Joey glanced out of the window at the house that now belonged to her and her father and she sighed, a tightness in her chest that hadn't been there a few short hours before. She didn't want to leave him, but she had work the next day and she couldn't just drop the life she had been living simply because they were back together. "Thank you for the lovely weekend."

Will reached out and pushed his hands through her hair, his mood deflating at the thought of her getting out of the car and leaving him alone. "I'll see you again, right? You won't forget..." He shook his head, laughing to himself. "This is it, right? No more dancing around? We're doing this. Yeah?"

Sensing the insecurity in Will's tone, Joey moved herself closer. She didn't know how else to reassure him other than pressing her lips to his and kissing him with everything she had. She retreated a little, resting her forehead against his, her hands still cupping his face. She looked him straight in the eyes. "This is it, Will. We're doing this."

He nodded, his smile widening a touch. "So I'll see you soon?"

Joey placed another soft kiss to his lips before moving back into her seat and collecting her handbag. "Definitely."

"Good." He smiled again, much brighter this time, but there was still a sadness behind his eyes.

Leaning over and giving Will one more final 'see you later' kiss, Joey yanked on the handle of the car door and stepped out, glancing over her shoulder and flashing him a smile as she turned and walked up the path that lead to the front door of the house. Her mobile pinged seconds later, and she stopped, fishing through her handbag to find it. She pulled it out, staring down at the message on its screen, her lips spreading into a shit-eating grin.

Fuck me, I love your arse. But not as much as I love you xx

She quickly turned on her heels, darting back down the path and to Will's window which was still down, and threw her arms around his neck, kissing him hard. "I love you." Their tongues danced for a few moments—greedily, passionately—before she released him from her hold. "I really should be going."

"Yes, go, before I rag you around on the back seat."

Joey chuckled as she forced herself to take a step away from him and return to her original journey towards the front of the house. She stopped only as she reached the door, tossing Will a loving smile and a small wave before disappearing inside.

Her father sat on the couch, his mouth falling open the second she appeared and Joey held her hand up in the air, halting whatever words were about to jump uninvited from his tongue. "Don't, Dad. Just don't even bother."

"He loves you, Joey. The house was a gift of love, nothing more, nothing less."

Smiling, Joey nodded her head. "I know."

Chapter 20

Smoke by Didrick, Amanda Fondell
Lower The Tone by Rae Morris

Will reached around Joey's slightly swaying body to turn the key in the front door, pushing it open for her to step inside the manor. "In you go, piss head." He smiled at her and put his hand in the small of her back to guide her in the right direction. She giggled and stepped inside, spinning on uneasy feet to face him as he closed the door behind him.

"Piss head? I had two drinks, Will. Count them." She held her fingers up, splaying them apart in front of his face, using her other hand to wiggle them as she counted. "One. Two." And then she stopped, her nose scrunching up in confusion as if she'd forgotten what number came next. She bit down on her lip, trying to recall how many glasses of wine the waiter had filled for her throughout their meal, but to no avail. "How many did I have again?"

A laugh huffed out of Will's chest as he closed his hand over the top of Joey's fingers, pulling her gently to him. "The majority of the first bottle and then some." He kissed the tip of her nose and pushed his fingers into her hair to grip it gently at the back of her neck so he could tilt her face up. "You're still just as sexy when you're drunk though." His eyes bore holes in hers as he filled himself up with her soul and pushed his lips to hers greedily, speaking against them. "So damn sexy."

Joey entertained his kiss for a moment before pressing her hands to his chest and pushing him away, a sparkle in her eye made even brighter from the alcohol swishing around her bloodstream. "You're so bad. And so damn horny all the time." Her voice was obnoxiously loud, but in her intoxicated state she didn't really care. She was having fun. She was enjoying herself. What was the harm in that?

Dipping his chin slightly, Will glared at her through hooded eyes, a hunger igniting in his belly that had nothing to do with food. "You need to lower that voice of yours, Miss Bell, or I'm going to have to chastise you. The olds are asleep upstairs. Hush it, woman." The corner of his mouth lifted into a sexy grin and he tugged a little harder on her hair before kissing the corner of her mouth.

She gave him an exaggerated eye roll, and before he had a chance to take his attempts at seduction any further, Joey manoeuvred herself around his frame, a giggle of laughter floating from her chest as she staggered down the hallway in the direction of the kitchen.

Pushing open the door, she tottered around the centre worktable and over to the cupboards, pulling out a pint glass. She quickly filled it from the sink and after taking a small sip, she spun on her heels, looking at Will who had followed behind her, and grinned. "We should bake!"

With his shoulders pressed back against the wall, his ankles crossed and his arms folded over his chest, Will raised his eyebrows. "You think? After last time? I think not. Not in your state. You were bad enough sober." He stood up straight and began to walk to where Joey was leaning her lower back against the sink unit. "You made way too much mess." He stopped a couple of feet from her and stretched his arm out to run his thumb along her bottom lip in that way that drove her crazy and allowed himself a moment to drink her in. "I'm not in the mood for cleaning up mess tonight. I have other things in mind."

A devilish smile curling her lips, Joey moved closer, her glass still in hand as she pressed her body against his in an effort to pull a reaction out of him. "What's wrong, Will? Afraid I'm going to beat you again?"

"Hmm…" Will raised his eyes to the ceiling as he stroked his chin. "I seem to remember that I was the one who won that little game, Josephine Bell. I think you'll find that if you dig deep into that memory of yours there will be a—" His words were stolen from him when, as fast as lightning, Joey pushed onto her toes and poured the liquid from her glass over his head causing ice cold water to trickle down his neck, his back and into his ears. He closed his eyes momentarily, pulling in a breath born of shock but one used to compose himself ready for retaliation, and then snapped them back open, a wild emotion flashing in them as he pinned her with them, sure he could hear the patter of her heart speed up.

"Run."

Swiftly setting the glass on the counter, and biting down on the inside of her lips to stop herself from laughing, Joey darted around Will and headed for the kitchen door, slipping her petite frame through it and hurrying down the south wing corridor, frantically searching for a place to escape to and hide in.

Her heart pounded beneath her ribs as playful fear ignited her pulse, and as her legs moved in quick strides, she glanced over her shoulder to see if Will was gaining on her heels. Not seeing him, she quickly ducked into the sitting room and eased the door shut, tiptoeing across the hardwood floor and crouching down behind the sofa. She cupped a hand over her mouth in an attempt to stifle the sound of her breaths and to prevent herself from laughing.

His hair wet through and with the water soaking into his shirt, Will clenched his jaw and smirked to himself. She was going to get what she had coming to her, and he was going to enjoy every second that he spent giving it to her. His heart pounded away at the very idea of catching up with her and devouring her, his memories of the last time they had played this little game flickering in his mind, and he yanked the kitchen door open, looking both ways down the dark corridor to try to work out which way she had gone. His head snapped to the left as he heard the click of a door shutting and he almost laughed to himself at the game of hide and seek that had begun. His long strides reached the dining room, and he nodded, sucking on his bottom lip as he remembered catching up with Joey in the exact same room. Reaching up to grip the door frame above his head he leaned forwards until his mouth was near the edge of the door. "I know you're in there, Miss Bell."

Joey's eyes widened at the sound of his voice.

Oh fuck.

She clamped her hand harder, attempting to stop the squeal of surprise at how quickly he'd found her from escaping her mouth. Making sure no part of her body was showing, she remained completely still behind the couch, her heart thudding loudly against her ribs in nervous anticipation of what may happen next.

Will leaned his forehead on the wood, listening carefully for the sounds of her moving, but there was nothing. She was good at this game. He smiled to himself again. "Have you not learned your lesson from last time? There's no escaping this room."

"Is it too late to call a truce?"

A hearty rumble of laughter erupted from Will's chest causing her already warm blood to grow hotter, and he thumped the side of his curled up fist against the wood. This woman—this woman whom he loved with all of his heart—was finally back in his life bringing all of her light and love. He couldn't imagine being happier than he was feeling. He dropped his hand to the door knob and gripped it tightly, making sure he rattled it a little first. "You know very well that I don't believe in truces, Miss Bell." He turned the knob enough to crack the door a little. "I'm coming to get you now. Okay?"

As the sound of the door swinging open echoed through the quiet room, Joey peeked around the arm of the sofa, trying to put together a plan of action. He'd caught her last time, just, but if she was smart about her moves, she had a good chance of outrunning him this time. It was a game she wasn't ready to lose.

Watching as he stepped into the room, his movements calculated, she crawled onto her knees, getting ready to push to her feet the second he got close. He strode towards her quickly and with purpose, and as he neared her position behind the sofa, Joey pushed to her feet to make a run for it. Will's reactions were lightning fast, though, and as she lurched forwards in a drunken stumble, his arm snaked around her middle and he scooped her up, as a squeal of joy errupted from her, giving her absolutely no chance of escape.

Dropping her to the floor, he spun her around to face him but immediately lifted her by the waist again before slamming her down on the keys of the grand piano, the minor notes mingling in the air in a less than melodic symphony. Joey gasped, her eyes wide as Will trapped her between his thighs, his hands either side of her on the keys. His eyes were hooded and full of lust and as he pressed his forehead against hers, his palms sliding the skirt of her dress up her thighs, he closed his them and rubbed his nose down the length of hers. "I love you so fucking much, Joey. And I love nothing more than taking my sweet time making love to you." He pulled back a touch so he could look at her before pushing his hands further, far enough to rub the pad of both his thumbs along her centre — before moving in slowly to press his lips to hers, speaking against them in a lust-filled growl. "But tonight, I'm going to fuck you so damn hard, you won't be able to walk for a week."

Joey swallowed down hard, Will's words pulsing and throbbing between her legs. How was it possible for him to be even more sexy than he was on a daily basis? She was sure she'd seen him at his most desirable, but he just kept on bringing more. Her eyes roamed over his face, her hands ran up and down the planes of his chest and her heart beat fast for him.

Seeing the desperate craving rippling through her, Will could hold back no longer. He crushed his lips to hers and left his hands to their own devices as they pushed up her stomach on a journey to find her breasts. The bodice of her dress stopped them from climbing much higher and he hurriedly pulled away, reaching around the back of her neck to find the top of the zip. He yanked it, hard, impatience grabbing a hold of him as Joey wrapped her legs around him and locked her hands around his neck, her need for him spiking.

The zip caught on the material half way down her back and Will clenched his teeth in frustration. "Fuck." He mourned the loss of her mouth, and as he pushed his lips to hers once more, parting them to match her open ones, he tried again.

It was still stuck.

The tips of their tongues sizzled together in a frantic samba and an electric pulse of sexual frustration clenched inside of him.

Without a second thought, he grabbed either side of the dress and pulled, ripping it clean open to the sound of another of Joey's gasps.

With his mouth still on hers, he whispered against her lips as he pulled the material from her shoulders until it pooled at her waist. "I'll buy you a new one."

He wasted no more time, using his hands to push her bra upwards so that the soft flesh of her breasts fell into his palms. His thumbs stroked across her already hardened nipples causing her to tip her head back with an ecstatic groan of pleasure. Will took the opportunity to run his open mouth down her throat and across her collarbone before dipping his head to circle her nipples in turn with his tongue.

Joey could no longer keep still under his touch, her body writhing uncontrollably, causing the piano keys to sing out of tune to them, a soundtrack to the desperate need that coursed through their bodies. Will's hands found their way between her legs again and she wriggled herself back slightly so that she could open them wider for him. He groaned into the crook of her neck as he shoved the material of her lace underwear to the side, pushing two fingers into her wet, hot heat.

"Shit." Joey's fingers gripped his shoulders tightly as her whole body tensed in pleasure at the feel of him. She dragged her hands down his chest and fumbled at his waist band, unbuttoning his jeans before pushing them and his boxers down his legs with her feet. He stood there, erect and magnificent, and she had never wanted anyone as much.

She moved her mouth to his ear. "Fuck me, Will."

Another guttural growl escaped his throat, and he snaked his arm around her waist, pulling her close to him, creating new music under her arse, and to the edge of the piano. "Hold on. Tight." A flash of mischief in Will's eyes had Joey biting down on her bottom lip and grinning at him before she locked her ankles around his waist and clutched at the back of his neck. A split second passed before Joey pulled in a sharp breath at the feel of Will pushing inside of her with a forceful thrust that took even his breath away. He stilled a moment, pinching his eyes closed as he relished her heat. His palms were splayed across her naked back, and he kissed along her jawline before holding her eyes with his. "I fucking love you." And

172

with that, a series of controlled but hungry back and forths had Joey panting and crying out in delicious euphoria. The keys were relentless in their music making, and with each buck of his hips, they cried out to the silence of the manor a love song that had never before been played.

His lids fluttering open and disorientation sweeping over his half awake mind, Graham pushed up onto his elbow and squinted at the clock beside his bed.

Two am.

He rubbed at his eyes and sat up, swinging his legs over the edge of the bed, confused for a moment as to why he had woken at such an ungodly hour.

And then he heard it.

At first he wasn't sure if he was imagining it as it was a sound he hadn't heard for many years, but when it happened again, he stood to his feet, sliding them into his slippers, and shuffled to his bedroom door. Opening it a crack, he stepped into the hallways as the mismatched chords and notes of the piano drifted up the stairs and to his ears.

"What is it?"

He turned his head at the hissed whisper and saw Bea hurrying down the corridor, fastening the cord on her dressing gown, her hair in rollers and a baffled look on her face.

"It's the piano, Beatrice."

"Well I know that, you big buffoon, but what is it that's making that horrible sound on it? Do we have rats? Good Lord, tell me we don't have rats."

Graham rolled his eyes. "Have you seen rats' feet? You really think they are big enough to press down on piano keys?"

"I wouldn't be too sure. You can get pretty big rats."

"Beatrice, my dear, I am pretty confident that you would need a whole *orchestra* of rats to be making such a noise."

The two of them stood together, side by side, peering over the balcony.

"Well is it an intruder?"

Graham shrugged. "A musical intruder."

"There's nothing musical about that sound. Rather tone deaf I would have said."

They glanced at each other and peered over again.

"So what do we do?"

Graham sighed. "Well, I suppose I should go down to investigate."

"Maybe we should wake Will?"

He shook his head. "No. I'll go."

Beatrice placed a hand on his forearm. "Wait here." She scuttled off back to her room returning a moment later with her umbrella and a brass fire poker.

Graham stared at them and then lifted his eyes to Bea's, his brows raised.

"Just humour me, man."

Graham reached out and gingerly took the items from her before turning towards the staircase.

"Wait."

A sigh huffed out of his chest. "What now?"

"I'll come with you."

"Don't be absurd. Get back to your room. This could be dangerous."

"Well quite. You may need backup."

"Beatr—" Graham's words were cut short as she bustled past him and started to walk down the stairs. He gave a defeated shake of his head and caught her up. "Fine. But let me go first."

On reaching the bottom, after trying to avoid the creaky floorboards, the pair stood still together, staring down the darkened corridor. The sound of the piano was louder now, and the noise it was making seemed rhythmic, if still far from melodic.

"Shall I turn the light on?" Bea whispered.

"What?"

"Shall I turn the light on?"

"Yes. Why don't you turn the light on and alert whoever is in there that we are armed and dangerous." His sarcasm earned him a slap to the forearm and he rolled his eyes. "Just get behind me if you are still insisting on coming with me, and keep bloody quiet."

The convoy of two crept as stealthily as they could until they reached the door to the dining room that sat ajar.

A split second decision had Graham barging in with his weapons raised like swords, a grimace on his face and Bea clutching the back of his pyjama top, a squeal erupting from her as she squeezed her eyes tight.

"Raaarrrrr!" He let out a growl as he swung his body around towards the piano at the back of the room.

Will's head swung round at the sudden noise, his hips still pounding of their own accord into Joey, whose head was thrown back in ecstasy, the noise from the piano almost drowned out now by her moans. "Graham?"

The old man was frozen on the spot, arms still raised as he wielded the umbrella and fire poker and a frown creased his brow as it dawned on him what he had walked in on.

"Will?"

Joey's head flew forwards and her eyes open as she flicked her gaze around the room, the feeling of pleasure still controlling the sounds that were coming out of her mouth. "Fuck, yes... shit. What the —"

Bea's face peered from around the back of Graham, her face lighting up. "Josephine?"

"Bea?" Will's expression grew more confused with every passing second and, his body finally caught up with what was happening. He stilled his movements and wrapped his arms around Joey in an attempt to preserve her modesty. "What the *hell* are you doing?"

Joey buried her head into Will's shoulder as shame and embarrassment filled her from her toes to the tip of her head. "Holy crap."

✿ ✿ ✿

The smell of breakfast had Joey's stomach growling as she stretched her body out under the covers and then curled herself back into Will's side. He was awake, as usual, but the look on his face screamed peace and contentment.

He turned his head and looked into her eyes. "Good morning, you sexy little thing." He curled the corner of his mouth up before kissing her hard. They had spent the rest of the night making up for the interruption in the sitting room, and just the memory of her perfect little body reacting to his touch all night was enough to have him ready to go again. His hunger for her was never satisfied, and he knew that he would spend his whole life enjoying that fact.

Lying naked together, their bodies sticky with sweat and smelling of each other, they spent another half an hour devouring each other with their mouths and their hands.

Sated and tired, they finally dragged themselves out from under the covers, throwing clothes on before heading down to the kitchen. As they neared the door, Joey grabbed a hold of Will's hand, pulling him to a stop. "I'm so embarrassed. I don't want to go in. I don't want to face them."

Will chuckled, dragging her along with him. "Got to face the music sometime, sweetheart."

"Will!"

"What? It's just Bea and Graham. They won't be bothered."

She huffed. "Well you go in first. I just can't."

"Come on, scaredy cat." He pushed the door open and Joey hung onto his arm, hiding behind him with her forehead pressed into his back.

"Oh God."

Graham was already sitting in his usual chair in the corner, a mug of tea steaming next to his plate of toast, and Beatrice was already half way through preparing lunch and dinner for later.

"Well good morning, William!" Her voice was more cheerful than Joey had ever heard it, and couldn't believe it was even possible. "How are we this morning?" She wiped her hands on her apron and walked around the counter to stand in front of them, peering behind him to catch sight of Joey.

"Leave them alone, woman. Stop fussing. Good lord. Last night was embarrassing enough for all of us without you making it worse." Graham slurped on his tea and gave Will an apologetic glance. He was quite frankly mortified and had contemplated staying in his room until the coast was clear, but there was also a feeling of relief that had swamped his chest as he realised what the previous night's fiasco had really meant.

Joey let go of Will and stepped out from behind him, a grimace on her face and a dry mouth. "I'm so sorry, Graham, Bea. I'm so sorr—"

"Come here, you silly girl." Bea reached out and grabbed her by the hands, pulling her into her huge chest. "You have nothing to apologise for. I can't think of a single situation that I would rather have walked in on than that last night."

"Bea!" Will and Graham simultaneously shouted out her name, their heads shaking with even more embarrassment before all four of them exchanged looks and finally burst out laughing.

"Come, come. Sit down. Let's get you fed."

Joey and Will sat opposite Graham and tucked into a hearty full English as they chatted about the reunion.

Bea began to chuckle again. "Deary me. The looks on your faces, and Graham… you're making a bit of a habit of this, aren't you, dear! I think these two had better start locking doors from now on."

Graham hung his head and shook it. "Please, for the love of God, yes. Lock your doors from now on. This heart of mine can't take much more shock!"

Will put his arm around Joey's shoulders and kissed her temple as Beatrice and Graham looked on fondly.

"It's good to have you back, my darlings." Bea smiled, her eyes a little glassy. "It's good to have you back."

Chapter 21

"I've got to keep an open mind. I can't dismiss business opportunities because you don't necessarily agree with them." Will placed a flat hand on the glass door to Cini's Italian restaurant and clutched onto Joey's hand as he pushed it open and moved them inside. "Does that make sense?" He turned to face her helping her out of her coat and handing it to the waiter who took it off to the coat rack.

Joey ignored his question, her eyes rolling over the interior of the place as she searched for the restroom, and spotting it in the far left corner, she looked at Will, excusing herself. "You go ahead. I'm nipping to the bathroom. I'll join you at the table as soon as I'm finished."

Will's eyes flicked over her pinched expression. "What's wrong?"

"Nothing. Nothing. I'm fine." She forced a smile onto her face for his sake and pressed her lips to his gently. "I'll meet you at the table."

"You're not *fine*, Joey. What's the matter?"

"I said, I'm fine."

Will huffed and pinched the bridge of his nose. "You know, you didn't have to come. I'm not forcing you to be here."

Shaking her head and rolling her eyes, Joey ignored him for a second time, leaving him standing there at the front entrance as she headed back in the direction of the bathrooms. She wasn't doing this right now. She was here for Will and that was the end of it.

He watched her walk away from him for a couple of seconds before he switched to his game head. He couldn't deal with the whims of female emotion right then, but a stab of guilt had him loosening his tie slightly so that he could undo his top button.

Using his hand to dismiss the waiter, who was waiting patiently to show him to the table, Will strode into the hustle and bustle of the restaurant and located the party of four who were seated at a round table set for six.

Spotting him from across the room, Simon stood to his feet and addressed the whole place in his usual bolshy manner as he announced his arrival. "Here he is. The man of the hour!" He picked up his wine glass and held it high above his head. "William. Join us!"

Gifting Simon a tight smile, he approached the table as David Bromley and Mitchell French from Green Frog Entertainment Group half stood to greet him. His smile turned genuine and he leaned in to shake their hands, his eyes flicking quickly to and then away from Nadine who sat with hooded eyes beside Simon. "Good to see you guys. Nadine." He pulled out the chair beside David and sat down, smoothing his hand along the length of his tie.

"And you, William. Thank you for agreeing to meet with us again." David smiled warmly and sat back down in his chair.

Simon nodded to the empty seat that sat between him and Will. "Table for six, Will. Who's the mystery gue —" His eyes widened involuntarily as Josephine reached the

180

table looking radiant as hell in a navy blue cocktail dress. "—est. Well hello, Cinders. Wasn't expecting to see you here."

Joey's lips reluctantly lifted into a smile—one secretly laced with disdain at the man she was forced to sit beside—as she pulled out her chair, slowly lowering herself on it. "Nice to see you again, Simon."

Will frowned over at his estate agent and shook his head discreetly. "What the fuck, man." His voice was a hissed whisper, and Simon held up his palms in defense mouthing a 'sorry' before turning to glare at Nadine who was sipping quietly on a glass of champagne and eyeing Joey carefully.

Joey's gaze flicked over to the blonde beauty sitting across the table, and her insides twisted as the last memory she had of her resurfaced. She nodded her head in friendly greeting, her expression faltering a little as she wondered what the woman was doing there. She hadn't realised she was involved with the Green Frog deal. "Nadine."

"David; Mitchell, this is Josephine Bell, my girlfriend." Will smiled over at Joey as the two men stood and reached over to take her hand. In the same breath, Simon's back teeth clenched at the term used to describe Joey and he turned his head sharply as Nadine gripped his hand tightly under the table at the same time.

David picked up his menu, the rest of them following suit, and addressed Will with a grin. "So. Let's get to it shall we? I'm assuming Simon here has been chipping away at you to the point of distraction, but I'm pleased he's made some progress at least. So what's the situation at the moment? Have you considered anyone else's offer? Or are we the lucky ones? I think I'll have the pappardelle." He slapped the menu close and looked around the table, still smiling and looking rather smug.

Will kept his eyes on the list of main courses as he spoke in a measured tone. "Nothing is set in stone, yet, David—"

"I like that word 'yet' don't you, Mitch?" He gave a chuckle and turned to look back at Will. "Sorry, you were saying?"

Will sat up straight and eyed him carefully. "Selling my family home and surrounding land is not a laughing matter, Mr Bromley, as I'm sure you can appreciate. I need to be absolutely sure I'm getting the best deal and that the property is going to be treated in the best possible way. I think I'll have the risotto." He slammed his menu shut in the same way, picking up his glass of wine and smiling over at Joey again. "Can you assure me that Green Frog can guarantee that, David?"

"You've seen the mock-ups, Will, more than once." Nadine's lip curled into a smirk and she flicked her eyes to Joey before continuing. "The amount of land that you have for offer is just the perfect setting for the theme park. Think of the enjoyment factor. You're a charitable man, Will. You understand the importance of family. Well our theme parks are the epitome of family and I think you'd be hard pressed to have your place put to better use."

"What's stopping you, man?" Simon leaned forwards and placed his elbows on the table in front of him, his fingertips making a steeple near his mouth. "We've talked this over so many times and you're here now. You've made that leap. Everyone is here. What's making you hesitant?"

"You know what."

Simon shook his head and sat back with a slump, picking up his napkin and throwing it back onto the table. "Damn horses. Just move them!"

Taking that moment to step into the conversation, Joey glanced over at Will before landing her gaze on the two men across from her. She cleared her throat, speaking almost timidly. "Mr Bromley; Mr French. As you may know, Wildridge is home to the country's top riding school—a school originally founded by Will's late mother. His top priority is that the school's superior and long-standing reputation will remain in tact no matter where its structure is located. The land on which it currently sits is a prime location, providing ample space for training as well as a high level of privacy due to the surrounding woods. But it's also so much more than that." She looked over at Will, gauging his reaction and hoping to God she wasn't stepping over a line she had no business crossing, and held his eyes with hers, imploring him to hear what she was trying to say. "It's his home. It's always been his home. And regardless of what's standing in its place, it will always *be* his home. So I think it's not unreasonable to accept that he is going to take his time in making sure that no matter what becomes of it, it's something he can look at and be proud of, not only for himself, but for the entire Marshall-Croft family."

"Build another fucking home!" Simon let out a raucous huff of laughter, glaring at Joey from the corner of his eye. "You have acres and acres just sitting there, Will. In fact, you should throw a few more into the deal. Make more money from this sale."

"More land! Now I like the sound of that." David turned to Will. "I'm a family man, Will. I understand the importance of keeping sentiment in tact, and I understand how important the riding school is to you, but like Simon says, you have so much land that you could move it wherever you choose — build a new home for you and..." He smiled at Joey. "Your little lady here." He slapped Will on the shoulder and leaned in closer to him. "Imagine the money, Will. Imagine what you could do with it."

The chime of a mobile phone halted the conversation, and Simon frowned, reaching into his jacket pocket. His eyes flicked to Nadine as he swiped across the screen and held the phone to his ear, plastering a huge grin on his face. "Hello Carter! How the devil are you!" He mouthed a sorry across the table at David and Mitchell and leaned back in his seat. "Sorry what?" His smile slid from his face and he began to stand, explaining non-verbally that he needed to take his call outside.

Will sat back in his chair, twirling his fork between his fingers and staring into nothingness. He was constantly back and forth with his decision, sometimes thinking that to be rid of the whole lot would be ridding himself of his past and that he would be able to move on so much more easily. On the other hand, life had turned a corner: Joey was back, things were out in the open, and new memories were being made in that big old house. Yes, the money would be a huge amount that he could invest in whatever he chose, but Goddamnit, did he need more money? Was he not rich enough?

"You'll have to excuse me a moment, gentlemen, Josephine. I must nip to the ladies' room." Nadine stood gracefully and tucked her clutch under her arm before sliding out from behind the table, walking hurriedly to the back of the restaurant with Joey's eyes on her every move.

On reaching the toilets, she glanced back over her shoulder and sneaked around the edge of the room until she reached the restaurant doors. Pushing out into the cool night air, she scanned the car park and almost jumped out of her skin when she was grabbed by the wrist and pulled around the side of the building.

"Jesus, Simon," she hissed.

He clamped his hand over her mouth and glared at her. "What now?"

Nadine freed herself from his grasp and shoved him in the chest. "Do you have to be such a brute? If you treated me like a lady once in awhile, we might get along better." She shook out her hair and stood up straight. "She needs to go."

Simon slammed his hand on his hip and rubbed his hand across the top of his head. "So what do you propose we do? The little bitch is going to sabotage this if we aren't careful."

184

Sighing, Nadine unclasped her bag and pulled out her lipstick and a mirror, carefully reapplying as she moved back towards the wall. "Well." She snapped the it closed and dropped both items back into her back, pouting her lips at him. "We need to get her away from the table, in a similar way to how I got you away from the table with that fake phone call." She grinned at him. "I'm such a clever girl."

Simon smirked at her and moved towards to her, snaking his arm around her waist and grabbing at her arse. "A very clever girl." He pushed his face closer and kissed her hard on the mouth. "So what clever scheme have you got up your sleeve for this next installment? We need to get back in there quickly before she does anymore damage."

Nadine wrapped her hands around his neck and pulled him to her, licking his earlobe and whispering into his hair. "You make it so that she has to get up and leave, and I will do the rest. Trust me." She pulled back and held his eyes with her own. "Can you manage that?"

Simon's hand dragged down to the hem of her dress and sneaked underneath, cupping her buttock so that his fingers caressed the heat between her thighs before he pushed the thin material of her thong out of the way and slid inside of her. A gasp left Nadine's chest as she pushed onto her toes and arched her back.

"Get inside before I fuck you against this wall until you can't walk." He shoved his tongue inside her mouth and pressed his thumb against her clit, before pulling away completely and running his wet finger under his nose and inhaling deeply. "My clever, clever girl." He gave her a snide smile and walked off back into the restaurant leaving Nadine to adjust herself and shudder at the feel of his hands on her.

"All in the name of business, Nadine. All in the name of business," she muttered to herself as she flicked her hair over her shoulder, plastered a smile on her face and headed back inside.

Once everyone was back at the table, Will looked over at Simon, his right hand man and the guy who, as yet, had not let him down. There was something bothering him, he could tell, and this possible sale seemed to have got him more excited than usual. He had been adamant that Green Frog was the company to go for.

Why was he so insistent?

Shaking the thought away, Will addressed David again. "Your offer is a pretty one, Bromley. It really is, and is highly tempting—"

"Will," Joey began to speak, cutting him off from what she feared was the biggest mistake of his life. "I think you should—" Her words died on her tongue as ice cold liquid rolled down her chest, causing her to jump up from her chair. "Shit!" She glanced to her left, a scowl pinching her features at the arrogant arse beside her who was holding a now empty glass limply.

"Jesus, Simon." Will stood up at the same time and put his arm around Joey's shoulders, kissing the side of her head. "You okay?" He glanced at Simon again and frowned. "What the hell has gotten into you?"

"Aww, I'm sorry, man. Joey, are you okay? Here. Let me..." He leaned over with a napkin and reached up to Joey's cleavage to mop up the spillage, his eyes drinking her in sleazily.

Joey slapped his hand away, speaking through gritted teeth. "I don't need your help, thank you."

"Joey." Nadine smiled quite genuinely from across the table. "Come on. Let's go and get you cleaned up in the ladies'." She stood and moved around to Joey's chair, holding her hand out and flicking her eyes to Will sexily. "I'll bring her back, don't worry."

With wary eyes, Joey stared down at the hand being offered to her. She glanced up at the plastic smile on

Nadine's face and shook her head. "It's okay. I can manage it myself." Turning back to Will, she pushed on to her toes and pressed a kiss to his cheek. "I'll be right back." And then she was off, making her way across the main floor of the restaurant and heading in the direction of the toilets.

Simon glared across the table at Nadine and she glared back, narrowing her eyes. She rested her hand on Will's forearm and smiled sweetly. "She looked a little upset. I'll just go and check on her."

Before anyone had a chance to protest anymore, Nadine strode confidently in the direction of Josephine Bell.

Huffing out through her nose, Joey pushed through the door of the ladies', smiling and apologising as she almost collided with an elderly woman who was making her way out. Her heels clacked along the tile floor, and she walked over to the sink, angrily turning on the water and reaching for a handful of paper towels. She ran them under the warm water and then brushed her hair—which had also been a victim to the sticky liquid—from her shoulders. Eyes cast downwards, she wiped at her chest, frustration heating her blood.

Who the hell did he think he was?

She knew his 'accident' hadn't been anything of the sort. She tossed the towels in the bin and reached for more, repeating the process as she swore under her breath at the arsehole and attempted to rid the potent smell of liquor and God knew what else from her dress.

"All okay?" Nadine peered around the door and gave Joey a smile that was laced with something sinister before walking over to her and leaning against the sinks, folding her arms across her skinny ribcage.

"Everything's fine." Joey bit the words out, the presence of this woman grating on her nerves. She didn't need her Goddamn help or her concern. In fact, she could take her Botox arse back to the table. "You can go. I'm fully capable of cleaning myself, I assure you."

Nadine looked Joey up and down. "Well, I told Will I would check on you." She paused a moment before turning around to lean over, her elbows resting on the countertop, catching Joey's eyes in the mirror. "You know, if you love him, you should let him just get on with selling. It's obviously what he wants. I don't really see why it has anything to do with you anyway. It's not like you're married. It's not like you've even been back together *that* long." She looked at herself in the mirror and pouted. "I mean, he could dump you again next week for all you know—trade you in for a—" She licked her lips seductively with the tip of her tongue. "*Different* model."

Joey continued to scrub at her dress, trying so damn hard to ignore the words leaving Nadine's mouth. The woman was trying to draw a reaction from her, she knew it, and she didn't want to stoop to that level, nor did she want to allow them to sway any of her thoughts when it came to her relationship with Will. "With all due respect, you don't know what the hell he wants."

Letting out a long moan, Nadine ran her finger around the top of the tap and then repeated the action around her own lips. "Tell me, *Josephine*, does his dick still taste like a lollipop?"

Anger moved through Joey's veins and she crumpled the paper towel in her hands, her eyes narrowing and darting to Nadine's. She wanted to grab the bitch by the throat, but for the sake of appearances, she smiled maliciously. "I'm surprised you still remember after all the ones you've sucked. I mean, it's part of your job description, right?"

Nadine stood up straight and whirled around to face Joey, her finger pointing in her face and venom darting from her eyes. "Listen here, you little bitch. You will stand by your man and encourage him to sell to Green Frog until he fucking agrees, do you understand me? If this deal falls through, I will blame you personally and you do *not* want that. I would hate to think what kind of malice this clever little mind of mine can conjure up. Trust me, Miss Bell, your life—and Will's—won't be worth living."

Nostrils flaring and every inch of her skin crawling with heat, Joey shoved past her, her shoulder knocking forcefully against Nadine's bony one as she spoke with a clenched jaw. "Don't *fucking* threaten me. Got it?" She gave Nadine one more look, pure hatred and disgust for the woman pouring from her brown eyes, before exiting the toilets and returning to Will's side at the table.

Chapter 22

Hunger by Ross Copperman
House Of Card by Tyler Shaw

Will lay propped up against the headboard with his hands under his head, watching as Joey pottered around the bedroom getting ready.

"You need a mirror in here." She lifted her hands to her ear and fiddled with the earring that dangled near her neck, turning over her shoulder to grin at him.

Will didn't respond. He continued to watch as she removed her jewellery, dropping it gently onto the top of his drawers. She walked the few steps to where her overnight bag sat on the chair near the wall, reaching around to unzip her dress and stepping out of it as it fell to the floor. "I'm going to use the bathroom. Do you need it first?" She reached inside the bag and pulled out her toothbrush and face cream and then turned to face him, stopping and frowning at him as she took in the serious look on his face. "What's up?"

Will hesitated, his eyes pouring over her face, down her body that was now only clothed in her underwear. The woman standing before him was his everything. She was it for him. There was no one else that would ever come close. He knew that. In the meeting that night, she had been his rock. She had seen into his heart and spoken its words out loud, telling everyone that she was by his side in every aspect of his life.

He wanted her by his side all the time, so as she crouched down to pull out her nightshirt, the words that fell out of his mouth did so without a second thought. "Move in with me."

Joey froze. Every muscle in her body turned rigid as she glanced over her shoulder to look at Will, unsure if the words he had just spoken were a figment of her imagination. She studied the lines on his face, searching for any sign of deception, miscommunication. "What?"

Will got off the bed and padded over to where Joey was still crouched. He sat down beside her on the floor, pulling her hands from inside her bag where they had stilled, and, holding them in his own, ensured she was looking at him. "Move in with me."

Move in with me.

She had heard him right. "Will, I..." She shook her head, the words she wanted to say stuck behind a mountain of hesitation.

She loved him. Of course she did. And she had never been as happy as she'd been over the course of the last few weeks, but moving in together was a huge step. It was a big deal, and there was so much to think about, to contemplate. "I... I don't know what to say."

"Say yes." He reached up and brushed his knuckles down the side of her face. "I don't want to watch you packing bags every few days. I want your toothbrush next to mine." He hesitated and looked down at their hands. "I want to wake up next to you every morning."

God, how was she supposed to say no? But how was she supposed to say yes? She had her father to think about, who, despite being able to manage on a daily basis with Emma's assistance, wasn't getting any better. As much as she loved Will, his proposal wasn't something she could just agree to on a whim. Reaching up and cupping his face, she looked him in the eye, hoping he would find it in his heart to understand. "You know I love you, right? Because I do love you, Will. I love you so much and I would love nothing more than to be able to fall asleep beside you every night, but it's not only myself and what I want that I need to think about."

Wil huffed out of his nose and cast his eyes down. He knew she had other commitments—John was her priority and he understood. "I know. I'm sorry. I just—" He pressed his forehead to hers. "I've never been able to see a future for myself, but now you're here. You're my future. I want a future for us."

"Oh, Will." Dragging his mouth to hers, Joey kissed him, hard. She couldn't say yes just then, but she wanted him to know that he was her future, too, and his offer wouldn't be one that was ignored. She just needed time to work out the logistics.

Pulling back but keeping his face in her hands, she looked at him with sincerity in her eyes. "We'll have our future. I promise."

Joey stood by the small chest of drawers in the living room of the only house she'd ever called home. Her eyes were glued to the framed photo that had sat in the same place for the last twenty-nine years, and she gingerly reached out, picking it up and smoothing her fingers across the thin layer of dust that had formed on its glass. It was one she look at often, and she couldn't help the smile that would always spread across her face as she'd stare at the young couple frozen in a loving embrace—the couple that was the exemplary definition of what love should be.

This time, however, a frown tugged at her lips.

"If there is something bothering you, sweetheart, I want to hear it."

Placing the photo back in its spot, Joey turned to look at her father who was watching her with concerned eyes from the couch. She licked her lips, not even sure where to begin or how he would react. Either way, she needed to get it off her chest, and more importantly, she needed his thoughts on the matter. "Will asked me to move in with him last night." With her arms crossed over her chest, she waited for Little John's reaction—a raise of his eyebrows, a lift of his chin, the jarring of his head as it reared back.

Nothing.

He gave her nothing. He sat there stone-faced as if the words that Joey had just uttered didn't have the power to change all of their lives, and he continued to sip from his mug.

She shook her head, perturbed by his lack of response. "Are you not going to say anything?"

Little John inhaled deeply. He took one more sip of his tea and then set it down on the small table beside the couch before clasping his hands together and giving his daughter that signature look of his, the one he wore whenever a serious talk was about to ensue. "Why are you still here?"

Taken aback by his question, Joey stared at him incredulously. "Why am I still here?" A dry laugh slipped from the back of her throat. "I *live* here, Dad. What kind of question is that?"

"Do you love him?"

"Dad—"

"Do you love him?"

Joey's shoulders sagged with the heavy sigh that left her mouth. "You know I do. Very much so."

"Then I think it's a perfectly reasonable question, Josephine. Why are you still here?"

She stood unmoving, contemplating the answer to that question. He knew why she was there so why did he even feel the need to ask? Surely he wasn't going to make her spell it out for him. He may have been sick and his age was crawling up in numbers, but he wasn't naive. "Because it's a huge step and—"

"Bullshit."

Her mouth snapped shut and her head reared back at his unusual brash tone. "Excuse me?"

An exasperated huff of air floated from John's chest and he patted the empty space beside him. She gave into his command, padding across the living room and sitting down on the couch, pulling her legs up so they were pressed against her chest, before wrapping her arms around them and resting her chin on her knees.

"Sweetheart, when are you going to stop?" John looked at his daughter.

She would always be his pride and joy, but she was no longer the little girl who followed excitedly at his heels. She had grown into a beautiful, young and independent woman; it was time she realised that. "I know exactly why you are still here, and I'm telling you now, it's not a good enough reason. You are almost thirty years old, Josephine, and Lord knows I'm not getting any younger. It is time for you to start living your life and worrying about me all the time is only going to hold you back." Tugging her hands from around her legs, he waited until she was looking at him and he was sure he had her attention. "You are in love with him, and I'm fully aware of how much in love he is with you. Don't wait, Joey. Don't wait to start your forever because I'm telling you right now, forever isn't nearly long enough."

Tears spilled from Joey's eyes before she even had a chance to realise they'd formed, and she shook her head, a thickness in her throat making it difficult to swallow. "*Dad.*"

He pulled her into his arms, his hand coming up to stroke the back of her head gently. "I'll only be a call away, and you know this will *always* be your home, sweetie, but I can't allow you to put your life on hold for me anymore. I *won't* allow it. So take this as your verbal eviction notice. You have approximately two hours to collect all of your things and remove yourself from the premises before I call that other half of yours and have him physically remove you."

Joey chuckled, her hold on her father tightening as she held him to her. "I love you, Dad. You'll always be the first man to own my heart."

"I know, sweetheart. I know."

Punching at the buttons on the calculator by his side, Will huffed as the number he was expecting to appear after pressing the equals sign didn't show what he wanted it to. He cleared the display and tried again, irritation spiking as the total was the same. He shoved the calculator away and tapped his keyboard, waking up his laptop before opening a new e-mail. Numbers and figures were his passion. He loved the thrill of the chase for property and land where he needed to use his brain to get the best deals—where he needed to be the best at his job, better than the next man. He loved haggling, and his gift of the gab would, in almost every circumstance, get him what he wanted. Sometimes, however, it took more brain power than usual, and today was one of those days. His phone vibrated across his desk and he answered it, shoving it between his cheek and his shoulder as he continued to type. "Yep... nope. No, I know. Well you'll have to just keep pushing. I'm not backing dow—"

Crash.

"Hang on." Will stood to his feet and moved to the window, parting the blinds and peering through them to the front of the house. He frowned at the sight of the back end of a white van and craned his neck to see who it belonged to. He wasn't expecting a delivery and so shrugged and moved away, deciding it was none of his concern and probably some maintenance worker that Graham had organised. "Sorry. So yeah, I'm not budging on this one. It's worth too much so just dig your heels in. I don't wan — "

Bang.

"What the... sorry. I'll call you back." He hung up and flung his phone onto his desk as he strode out of his office. On reaching the front door of the manor, he yanked it open and stood on the top step, his hands on his hips and a scowl on his face. Paul was at the back end of the van now, pulling at a cardboard box.

"What the hell is going on?"

Backing out of the van, Paul waved towards Will at the same time as Joey came around from the other side, her arms full of shampoo bottles and God only knew what else. Will's brow creased again. "What in God's name are you doing, woman?"

She smiled cheekily at him, and, moving closer to where he stood, she thrust the bottles from her arms and into his, almost laughing at the perplexed look on his handsome face. "Well are you going to just stand there or are you going to help me bring in my stuff?"

"Your stuff? What stu — " His eyes widened as he watched Paul dump the cardboard box by his feet. It's flaps were open, revealing its contents, and he snapped his gaze back to Joey's. "Your stuff. Like *all* your stuff? As in, you've brought all your stuff to my house? Like, your toothbrush and stuff?" He fought to keep his mouth from twitching into a grin in case he was reading the patently obvious situation wrongly, and he pleaded with her silently to put him out of his misery.

Joey gave Will a small nod. "Give us a kiss, roomie."

Will's face broke into a grin as he let the items fall to the floor, scooping Joey into his arms, spinning her around and crushing his lips to hers, whispering against them. "God I fucking love you."

Chapter 23

Pushing through the glass doors of the cafe, Danny close on her heels, Joey glanced around for an open booth for them to sit in. Spotting one over by the front window, she gestured for him to follow and navigated around the tables filled with patrons enjoying their early morning breakfast.

So…" She grinned at him as she sat down and grabbed the menu, her eyes roaming over the glossy pages and the array of food options as her stomach grumbled in hungry anticipation. "How did it go?"

Danny remained silent, and Joey peered over her menu, lifting a brow at his lack of forthcomingness. He chuckled at her incessant need to pry into his personal life, and more so, his date with Hannah's mum, Amy.

Lifting his shoulder, he shrugged nonchalantly. "It was good."

Joey slammed her menu down on the table dramatically. "It was good? Oh come on." She reached over and slapped his hand in a playful and teasing manner, rolling her eyes. "It was good. Now you sound like every other average bloke."

"Every other average bloke, huh?" A huff of laughter floated from his chest, and he smiled knowingly at the woman who he could tell just about anything to. "I'm glad you hold me in such high regard, Just Joey." He paused for a moment, flipping through his own menu, his eyes scanning over the endless selection and feeling the weight of her gaze still on him. He smirked, the corner of his mouth curling to one side. She was relentless. "It was great, okay? We had a wonderful time, and, unlike the date you and I had, I didn't get spit on this time by an angry llama."

Her nose scrunching and the corners of her eyes crinkling at the memory, Joey shook her head as she stared, amused, at her best friend. "Yeah. That was pretty gross."

They both shared another laugh, stopping only to give their drinks order to the waitress who was making her rounds, and then returned to their conversation.

It had been a struggle lately, attempting to juggle her time between Will, work, and her father, and she couldn't even recall the last time she had been able to sit down and talk with Danny, much less share a joke or two. Now that she was living at the manor and saw him every day almost, she was finally able to set aside a morning just for them and enjoy his company.

"So I take it everything is going well on the Will front."

The blood running through Joey's veins seemed to concentrate beneath her cheeks, warming them, and she gave him a small nod. "Yeah. It is. It's great. He um… well, we still have our moments, but what couple doesn't, right?"

"Right." Smiling, Danny tossed his menu down on the table, before clasping his hands on top of it. "I'm going to have a full English, I reckon. I'm starving this morning." He glanced around, curious as to where the waitress had wandered off to and why she hadn't returned with their drinks. The place was busy, but it wasn't *that* busy.

Closing her menu and sliding it aside, Joey rested her elbows on the table and dropped her chin in her hands. "I'll have poached eggs on toast."

The waitress returned a few minutes later, apologising for their wait and promptly took their food order before once again scurrying away from the table. Tuning out everyone around them, Joey and Danny continued to immerse themselves in the happenings of each other's lives. They talked about work and the horses, which ultimately led to the sale of the manor.

"Is he still considering selling?"

Joey sighed, wishing she could tell him no, but the truth was, Will was still undecided. After the meeting with Green Frog, he'd made it a point to give it some more consideration, but she didn't know how else to get through to him, to make him see that the manor was worth more than they were offering, and that it had nothing to do with money and figures. "Yeah. He is."

A simple nod was Danny's only reply. He couldn't change his boss' mind anymore than the woman who owned his heart, so all they could do was sit and hope, hope that Will would make the right decision.

"I don't trust them, Danny. I don't trust Simon."

Danny narrowed his gaze, his brow furrowing at Joey's unexpected confession, and he pressed back in his seat, bringing his hands up and clasping them behind his head. "I know he's a dickhead, Joey — believe me, *I know* — but he's also been Will's estate agent for years, long before I even started working there, and he's never let Will down. He's always steered him in the right direction."

"Yeah, but for Will's benefit or for his own?" As soon as the words left Joey's mouth, she wanted to take them back. She had her reasons for not trusting Simon and Nadine, but none of them were ones she could give voice to, even to Danny. Thankfully, she didn't have to. The waitress appeared at the table, placing their plates down in front of them, and Joey used it to her advantage, deciding to steer the conversation into another direction. "Oh good. I'm starving."

Sharing the same sentiment, Danny wasted no time in stabbing a sausage and stuffing half of it into his mouth, his hunger at an all time high. He had the entire thing devoured by the time Joey even took her first bite of toast and watched curiously as she stared down at her eggs, moving them around with her fork. "Everything okay?"

"Yeah." She nodded, plastering a tight smile on her face. "Yeah. I, um… I'm going to nip to the loo really quickly. I'll be right back. Just eat, don't wait for me."

Sliding out of the booth, Joey nearly broke into a full sprint as she darted around tables, heading for the ladies', her stomach suddenly in disagreement with the idea of eating breakfast. She pushed through the swinging door, rushing over to the first available cubicle, barely managing to close and lock the door behind her before she was hunched over, emptying the contents of her nearly empty stomach.

What the hell?

Her mind ran circles as she continued to dry heave, her head feeling dizzy as she wondered what had caused her sudden bout of sickness. She'd been fine all morning, starving even, but the moment the half gooey eggs were sitting in front of her, she'd felt the swirl of bile rise.

Wiping her mouth and breathing deeply, she pressed back against the cubicle wall and stared up at the ceiling. She couldn't afford to be sick, not that she relied heavily on the income now that she was living with Will, but she still couldn't miss work. They were short-staffed as it was.

She didn't understand.

She'd been fine.

Or *had* she?

Joey's pulse began to quicken as she reached up and ran her hands over her chest, her breasts feeling heavier and a soreness that she hadn't really paid any attention to before that moment causing her to squeeze her eyes shut and mentally count the days back to her last period.

No.

No, there was no way.

She was on the pill and she took it religiously, the same time every day.

Except...

Oh my God.

She'd missed a few—when she and Will were apart. She'd been so lost in her grief, some days not even getting out of bed unless it was to use the loo... and then there was work, and her father, and...

"Shit."

All the colour drained from Joey's face as a very real and probable realisation dawned on her, and before she had a chance to talk herself down from her incoming panic attack, she was once again leaning over the toilet, heaving for the second time in less than ten minutes.

Joey paced the floor in Will's bathroom, her eyes focused on anything and everything but the small white stick resting on the granite countertop that was taking its good ole time in revealing what was likely to be a life-changing result. Waiting to find out if it was one line or two was like waiting for a kettle to boil. Actually, that wasn't a very good comparison. A kettle was simply a kettle. Two lines meant that in nine months there would be screaming at all hours of the night and arguments over whose turn it was to change the nappy and clean the baby sick... lots and lots of baby sick.

As she closed her eyes and breathed deeply, air floated from her lungs on a huff of impatience. This was ridiculous, and the truth was, it was way past the three minutes the instructions had said to wait, so why was she still pacing?

She knew why.

She was terrified.

She was terrified to walk over and see what she already knew.

She was terrified of what it would mean for her and her schooling and her career, but more so, for her and Will.

They'd only been back together a little more than six weeks and while their relationship was in the best place it ever had been, she wasn't convinced that news of a baby would be greeted with joy and open arms. Sure, he'd told her he wanted a future, but her moving in was the beginning of that future, not a baby. There was too much going on in both of their lives and the last thing either of them needed was the added stress of an unexpected pregnancy.

Rubbing her hands up her face and dragging them back through her hair, she swallowed down the anxiety rising up her throat and walked over to the counter. With shaking fingers, she picked up the small white stick and turned it around looking at the little oval window that was suddenly the master of her fate.

Her heart stopped.

Her mouth dried.

Tears sprang to her eyes.

"Shit."

Bea reached down and picked up the basket of potatoes, moving along the vegetable patch. "Carrots next. How strong are you feeling?" She smiled over at Joey who was wiping the soil from her hands on the back of her trousers.

"I'm too old now to get down there and pull them out so it's all on you."

"I think I can handle it." Joey smirked as she followed behind Bea, careful to avoid any exposed roots or vines that lay across the dirt paths as they made their way over to the rows where the carrots were ready to be pulled.

Bea watched as Joey bent at the waist to pull the first one out and stopped her with a hand on her forearm. "Squat dear."

Joey turned her head to frown at the old woman but did as she was told, bending at her knees instead and grabbing the bunch of leaves that stuck out above the ground. She leaned backwards a little and pulled.

"We don't want you bending at the waist in your delicate condition."

Falling flat on her arse, Joey looked up at Bea, feeling the walls of her throat thicken at her words. "I'm sorry?"

Gasping as Joey, Bea reached out to grab her arms. "Goodness me, child. Please be careful. Perhaps this wasn't the best idea. Let's get you inside. Have you hurt yourself?"

Allowing Bea to pull her to her feet, Joey rubbed at her left arse cheek, feeling the sting from her fall as it soared up her lower spine. "I'm fine, Bea, but what did you just say? My delicate condition?"

Bea raised her brows a little and cocked her head as a motherly smile graced her lips. "Come now, Josephine. Don't take me for a fool. I may be old but I'm not stupid."

The colour drained from Joey's face as she stood there, at a loss for words. A few beats passed before she finally collected her thoughts and released them on a shocked whisper. "How do you... how do you even know?"

Bea gave a little shrug and another smile.

"How long have you known?"

Bea linked her arm with Joey's and walked them both down the path to the garden and towards the summer house. "I think, my darling, the question is how long have *you* known? Hmm?"

As they wandered side-by-side, the colour slowly returned to Joey's cheeks, bringing with it an uncomfortable heat. She looked away from the old woman and inhaled deeply, knowing there was no escaping the conversation. It was time someone knew. "A little longer than two weeks."

"And when were you planning to tell him?"

"Will?" Oh, God. The thought alone made her feel sick. Was it possible she could go the next nine months or even the next eighteen years without telling him? "I don't know, Bea." She sighed a sigh that was full of every last one of her fears. "I'm scared to tell him. Terrified. I don't know how he's going to react or how he's even going to cope with the idea that he's going to be a father. We've just got back together after being separated for nearly four months. I've just moved in. Not to mention he still has his past and his issues that he's trying to work through on a daily basis — that in itself is proving stressful for both of us — and I have my work and uni. I'm not ready to be a mum. This is all happening way too fast and I don't know how to slow it down or stop it. I feel like I'm on the train that's destined to crash with no way of getting off it, and I'm terrified because I don't know what to do." She finally returned her gaze to Bea's, desperate for the old woman to have some kind of words of encouragement to offer her. "What do I do?"

Bea waited until they reached the door of the summer house, stopping to open it and guiding Joey inside. She sat down on the bench and patted the space beside her, waiting for a nervous Joey to sit down. She turned towards her and took her hands in her own. "Men are strange creatures." She smiled and looked down at their joined hands. "I was pregnant once. I was young and afraid and back then getting pregnant outside of marriage was despicable. It wasn't something that you shouted out to the

world. My then boyfriend, Stanley, was the love of my life
and I went on to marry him a few years later, but even
though he was my one and only, telling him that I'd brought
shame on our families was the most terrifying thing I've
ever had to do. He wasn't ready to be a father. We were
babies. It wasn't an ideal situation to be in at all but I had to
tell him. He deserved to know. Did he accept the news with
smiles and open arms? No. He certainly did not. He
screamed at me and paced the room and spent the night in
the local pub with his buddies. But he came around, Joey.
It just takes time for these things to sink in and we have to
give them time. You've had your time and you need to
afford him his. In just the same way. But what you mustn't
do is make up his mind for him, don't write him off before
he even knows. Don't assume that he is not going to be over
the moon about being a father eventually. Give him some
credit. Give yourself some credit. Give your relationship
some credit. You are both wonderful young people with a
love so strong, and no matter what adversity you face, I for
one know that you will both hold onto each other and make
it through the other side. I've seen you blossom together
before my very eyes and I believe that you are stronger now
than you ever were. Sometimes life is sent to put us on trial,
to test us—and boy have you two been tested—but you
have love on your side, my darling. A big hunk of William
Marshall-Croft love, and I believe that's the best kind of
love to have. So. Stop listening to this old woman wittering
on about nonsense and go find him. Go tell him your news
but tell him with the enthusiasm you feel in your heart
about becoming a mother. Don't tell him when you're in a
panic. Tell him when you've accepted and embraced the
idea so that your love for your baby shines out of your eyes
to him. And I guarantee, he will love your baby too."

Joey sat still, allowing Bea's words to sink in. Maybe
the old woman was right. Maybe if she approached this
entire situation differently it would have a more favorable

outcome. She just needed to be positive and hope in return that Will would be too.

Chapter 24

Flushing the toilet, Will moved to the sink and washed his hands. He stared at his reflection in the mirror and splashed cold water on his face, rubbing his hands down his cheeks as he sighed. Things had seemed a little strange between him and Joey over the last couple of weeks, but after she'd come up to bed before him that night, he decided it was time to find out what was going on.

He grabbed a towel and dried his face before moving to stand in the doorway of the bedroom, his arms limp by his side. Joey lay curled up under the duvet, her back to him, still and silent. Letting out a huff of air from his nose, he stepped into the room and sat down on the edge of the mattress, pulling his t-shirt over his head and dropping it on the floor before swinging his legs onto the bed. He lay for a minute or two, staring at the ceiling, a rolling of unusual butterflies invading his stomach. Dealing with relationship blips was not something he was trained in, and he didn't know how to approach talking to her. He'd only just got her back and was scared that this was her way of telling him she'd changed her mind. He was scared that he'd fucked it up somehow—his drinking and his nightmares

208

still a real problem—and that she was so angry with him that she couldn't bare to spend time with him. Whichever it was, he knew he couldn't sit back and let it fester.

Rolling onto his side to face her, he smoothed his hand over the curve of her hip, down across her stomach, pulling her body into him so that he was wrapped around her back in a perfect fit.

They lay together without words, their chests rising and falling together, Will breathing in the scent of her hair. He felt like he missed her even though she was right there and he needed to let her know. He moved her hair from her neck and touched his lips to the skin on the curve of her shoulder. He returned his hand to her warm stomach and slid it upwards on a search for her breasts as he trailed wet and gentle kisses up the side of her neck. His hand found what it was looking for and he brushed his palm over her nipple as he pulled her closer still.

"Will. Please." Wincing, Joey reached for Will's hand, which was still planted firmly on her sore and tender breast, and pulled it away. "Not tonight."

He dragged his arm away and rolled onto his back with an irritated huff. Pinching the bridge of his nose, he squeezed his eyes shut. This was definitely not normal. Their sex life had never been something that needed work. "What's wrong?"

"Nothing." She inhaled deeply, readying herself for the lies that were about to jump off her tongue without any consideration for how they'd be received. Well, not all of them were lies. She was exhausted, the pregnancy draining every last ounce of her energy. "I'm just tired, that's all. And I have work tomorrow. I just want to sleep tonight."

"Bullshit." The word flew out without forethought and Joey's body tensed beside him causing him to close his eyes again, their past flashing before him. He wasn't going to hurt her. He wasn't going to go down that road again and so he pulled in a deep breath and turned his head to look at her, even though she still lay with her back to him. "It's more than that, Jo. You've not been yourself all week. Longer. What's going on with you?"

Just tell him, Joey. Just tell him.

Joey bit down on the corner of her lip so hard she nearly drew blood. Her entire body was hot and she felt as if she were suffocating under the weight of this truth she couldn't bring herself to reveal. "It's nothing, okay? There is nothing going on with me. I told you, I'm just exhausted." She reluctantly scooted herself closer to the edge of the bed and away from him, not really wanting to, but yet needing the space.

"Is it Nadine? Are you still upset about what went on at the restaurant? You know, you haven't even told me what happened and I know something did." He propped himself up on his elbow, damned if he was going to let her fob him off when he knew she was not okay. "What did she say to you?"

Joey huffed out, slightly annoyed this was being brought up now, weeks later. Nadine was the last person she wanted to think or talk about. "It doesn't matter."

Will sat up. "You're fucking lying to me." His voice got louder and even though he was aware of it, he couldn't stop himself. "What the hell did she say to you, Josephine?"

Joey flounced onto her back, glaring up at him, her stare lethal. "What the hell do you want me to say, Will? Do you want to hear how she told me she'd sucked and licked your dick like a Goddamn lollipop, huh? Because that's exactly what she said!"

"Fuck." Will got off the bed and paced the floor with his hand on his hips, his head low. "Fuck."

Joey swung her legs to the floor, grabbing her dressing down from the arm of the chair and shrugging into it.

"Joey. Nadine, she was… fuck. I don't even know what she was. A mistake. A stupid mistake that was borne out of weakness. It was before you. Before I wanted you, Jo."

She stood and walked to the end of the bed and headed towards the bathroom, a silent storm brewing in her mind.

"Joey. Please." Will reached out and grabbed her arm to stop her from passing, gripping the tops of both forearms so she would look at him.

She held his gaze for a moment and inhaled deeply before reaching out and slapping him across the face. "That's for being so stupid. That's for allowing yourself to be hooked by her filthy talons and causing me to have to listen to her telling me she'd had you. I didn't need to hear that, Will. That was rough."

Will flinched and rubbed his cheek. "Jesus. I'm sorry. I'm sorry you had to hear that from her. I'm sorry you had to find out at all. But she means nothing to me. You know this, right?"

Joey looked into his eyes and shook her head gently. "Of course I know. I'm not an idiot. I know how the world works. I know that people have sex with other people before they get into relationships. But Jesus, Will. Nadine?"

"So that's it. That's why you've been avoiding me, skipping off to bed early? Just cos you're pissed off that you heard I fucked Nadine before we were even in a relationship?"

Joey stared at him for a moment, her mind immediately replaying Bea's words and advice. She couldn't tell him now. She needed to be calm and happy, she needed that love to shine through her eyes so he could openly embrace it and there was no way that was happening tonight. Not with the arguing and misunderstandings. She gave him another small shake of her head, realising he was still waiting for an answer, some sort of confirmation. "No. This has nothing to do with Nadine, and I'd really just love it if you'd let it go for the evening, please." Flashing him one more look that said this discussion was over, she started to walk past him in the direction of the bathroom.

Will swung round to follow her, catching her wrist and spinning her to him again. "Like fuck I will. You're not fobbing me off if there's something wrong. I'm not doing this with you. I'm not—"

"I'm pregnant, Will!" The tears came out of nowhere, hot and heavy, filling Joey's eyes to the brim. All of the air punched from her lungs on one powerful scream as she repeated herself, knowing he wasn't going to let this go and she was tired of the back and forth. "I'm pregnant!"

Will dropped her arm and stepped back, his face contorting, his voice an incredulous whisper. "What?"

Joey gave him a small nod as she wiped the tears from her cheeks.

"Wh... h...how?"

She raised her eyebrows. "Really?"

Will shook his head and grabbed the back of his neck. "You know what I damn well mean. How have you allowed this to happen? How? When?"

Will's words shot through the air, grabbing her by the throat in a way she'd never anticipated. She'd known he wouldn't welcome the news with open arms, but she'd hoped... well, she wasn't even quite sure what she'd hoped for. "Are you serious right now? How have I *allowed* this to happen? The last time I checked it takes two people to make a baby, Will."

He dropped to the edge of the bed, holding his head in his hands and shoving his fingers through his hair. "That's not what I meant. You know that's not what I meant. It came out wrong. Just... how has this happened? How?"

"We weren't together. We weren't together and I wasn't taking my pill the way I should have been because I was an emotional wreck and it didn't matter. I wasn't expecting us to reconcile. The day you showed up at my house and we came back here and took Roya and Ginger out, I wasn't expecting us to make up, much less make love." The bile in her stomach swished and swirled and she didn't know if it was a result of morning sickness, which she had quickly learned didn't just occur in the morning, or the fact that she had finally come out with the truth. She swallowed down, desperate to rid herself of the unwelcoming sensation. "It's not like I planned this."

"I'm not suggesting you planned it, Josephine. I'm —" Will stood to his feet. "You know what? It's late. You need to sleep. And I haven't got the head space for it right this minute. So… get to bed. I'll see you tomorrow." He didn't look at her. He strode to the door, grabbing the handle and yanking it open, and left the room.

Joey watched with a crushing pain in her heart as Will walked away, leaving her to stand there alone with nothing but an eerie silence and the disastrous aftermath of her revelation.

She reached up to swipe at the fresh round of tears that were cascading down her cheeks before whispering sadly, "You weren't supposed to find out this way…"

A bottle in one hand, a now empty glass in the other, Will stood looking out of the sitting room window across his estate. The whiskey burned in his stomach and as he poured another one, Josephine's words rolling around in his head.

Pregnant.

She was pregnant.

Carrying a child.

Having a baby.

A baby.

His baby.

He threw the liquid back and swallowed it down as the enormity of the revelation hit him like a ten ton truck.

It was his baby.

He was going to be a father.

He wasn't ready to be a fucking father. Lord knew he was barely able to look after himself some days, never mind a helpless child who would depend on him for everything. He probably wouldn't even make a good one. Any child deserved a better father than he could ever be.

"Goddamnit, Will." He hung his head and inhaled deeply.

What a fucking mess.

They were barely back together and had so much to work through before... well before anything. He was one hundred percent positive that Joey was it for him. She was his rock—his future. There was no doubt in his mind. It wasn't a question of him never wanting a family with her, but they were not in the right place. The sale of the manor was in the air, he still needed to get a grip on his drinking and his nightmares that woke him. God. It would be like Josephine having two children to look after. On top of that, he was still guilt-ridden and angry, and that surely was not good if there was going to be a child in the house.

"Fuck. Fuck. Fuck."

He didn't know anything about being a father.

Not a single thing.

Chapter 25

Heal by Tom Odell

"If this is about the sale of the m —"

"It's not... Dad. It's not."

Nicholas pulled the peak of his flat cap further down over his forehead and stuffed his hands into the pockets of his wax jacket. "Well then. What is it?"

Will sighed, stopping beside a bench and gesturing for his father to take a seat with him.

The park was teeming with families enjoying the half term break, children weaving their bikes and scooters between legs and pushchairs. Will watched as a little boy climbed back onto his bike with the help of someone he assumed to be his father. The guy crouched down and brushed the boy's fringe back from his forehead and placed a kiss there before pulling a tissue out of his pocket and wiping the tears that were chasing each other down his little cheeks. He rubbed the boy's grazed knee, and spoke something softly to him before standing up and planting his hands on his hips. The boy looked back over his shoulder and grinned and then, with a big push, pedalled down the path. Will's eyes moved back to the man who stood there with a grin on his face that was so full of happiness, and

215

Will couldn't help but lift the corners of his own mouth into one that almost matched.

He turned to look at his own father, studying his face.

He couldn't remember the lines around his eyes being so deep.

When had he gotten so old?

He clenched his jaw together in preparation for the conversation that would follow and took a deep breath.

"What's it like, being a father?"

Nicholas frowned and leaned back against the wooden bench. He stared out at the parkland for a while, saying nothing, not sure where the question had come from. Affairs of the heart hadn't been present between them for so long now, and he wasn't sure where to begin. Taking his cap off, he rubbed the top of his head and huffed out of his nose. "When you were born, I was petrified. There you were, this bundle of pink flesh, wild black hair and making the most awful sound I'd ever heard. I just couldn't imagine what anyone found so appealing about babies. But then, I took you in my arms and looked into your eyes and I was utterly overwhelmed with love. It came out of nowhere, like a meteor or something."

Will glanced at him, a strange stirring in his chest keeping him glued to his seat and hopeful for more from his father.

"Now don't get me wrong. That's not where it ended. We got you home and then the tiredness started, the frustrations and the stress. You were never a great sleeper as a baby. You were too interested in what was going on around you and surely thought that sleeping was a waste of time." He stopped and lay his arm along the back of the bench. "Being a father is equal parts joyful and terrifying. And then of course there's all of the other words in between. It's like a sliding scale of emotions, and you can be guaranteed to revisit each one numerous times each day. But I can tell you one thing: it always, no matter how bad things have gotten on any given day—" Nicholas inhaled deeply and patted Will's knee. "It always comes back to love." He glanced at him. "It's unconditional, see."

Will swallowed down a lump of emotion and leaned forwards with his elbows on his knees. He twisted his head to the side to look at his dad. "I'm going to be one."

Nicholas stroked his finger and thumb down over his moustache a few times. "A father, huh."

Will nodded. "And I'm petrified."

Nicholas sat up straight. "Come on. Let's keep walking."

The two men stood to their feet, Will towering over his him as they walked side by side in silence for a little while.

"Who is she? The mother, I mean."

Will tipped his head back to look at the blue sky and let out a soft chuckle, his head shaking gently. "You couldn't write this shit." He glanced down at Nicholas, a pregnant pause hanging in the air. "Josephine Bell."

Nicholas stopped. "Joey? Little John's Joey?"

"Yup."

His eyes widened. "I think I need to sit down again." He walked on in silence, though. "And do… do you love her? Tell me this isn't the result of some sick game of debauchery, William."

Will rolled his eyes. "Dad, please. Yes. I love her. Like you wouldn't even understand. God, do I love her. There's no question. This is not what I'm scared of."

"So tell me what it is then. What has you spooked?" Nicholas slowed his steps to a halt and turned to face his son. "Does John know you love his daughter?"

"Yeah. Yeah, he and I have talked. A lot." Once the words left his mouth, a rolling of guilt hit him in the gut at how it must sound and feel to his dad with whom he'd made no effort to reconcile anything. "I mean, you know. We're good. The past has been wiped clean." He shook his head and squeezed his eyes closed. He was digging himself deeper with every passing second. "Dad, I'm sorry. I'm sorry I've not—"

Nicholas planted a firm hand on Will's shoulder. "I'm glad, son. I'm glad you have reconciled with John, and I'm even more pleased that you've found love. I have to say, I'm surprised that it's her, but if she makes you happy then that's all that matters."

"She does. She's it for me. God, she's so strong and so fucking beautiful, Dad. She's got this light inside of her that shines and draws you in. She's amazing. She gets me, y'know? She gets me, and yet she still sticks around, despite everything."

Nicholas smiled. "She always was a wonderful little girl. I look forward to meeting her again." He stepped back beside Will and began to walk. "So what are you so scared of, William? You have a woman who obviously wants to have a life with you, you've got her father's approval... what's worrying you?"

Will shoved his hand back through his hair. "I'm scared of me. I'm not ready. I'm not in the right place for this responsibility. God, I can sometimes barely look after myself, Dad. I drink too much, I get angry... what if... fuck, I don't even want to think about it." He looked sideways at his father, his eyes pleading with him to give him something that would help his situation. "I'm still a mess, Dad. After all this time, I'm still a fucking mess."

"It sounds to me like you've come a long way, son. I think you probably need to give yourself a little credit. You have to remember that you were not born with the devil inside of you. I mean, Christ. You could scream like him when you were hungry, but up until..." Nicholas trailed off and breathed deeply. "Up until that day, you were the brightest, biggest-hearted young man there ever was. I don't doubt for one second that that boy is still in there." Nicholas paused and walked to the next bench where the two sat down again. "Your mother's death was horrific. It cut everyone deeply and ties were also cut. These past years have been the loneliest time for me, and I expect for you too. I couldn't stay in that house, William. I'm sorry for that. Your mother was my rock, and without her, my life didn't make sense. Not the life I knew anyway. I've come to make a new life for myself now. I've learned that I can still be me without her, I just had to find my own path."

"And I couldn't leave." William smiled sadly. "The house was the only thing that made sense to me for so long and I just couldn't forgive myself enough to walk away from it. I felt like it was my penance to stay there and be reminded of what I had done every single day."

Nicholas' eyes remained straight ahead of him as he gently lifted Will's hand onto his own thigh and squeezed it tightly. "You didn't do anything wrong, son. You weren't to know that horse would buck. You weren't to know your mother in her... her bloody stupidity would come running at it." He shook his head sadly and bowed it before reaching up and pinching the bridge of his nose, the memory of his wife grabbing hold of his heart and squeezing it tightly. "Goddamnit, Diana."

"Shit, Dad. Don't cry. Please. I..." He sat up a little and removed his hand from under his father's, wrapping his arm around his shoulder instead. "I'm sorry."

Those two little words held so much in that moment. He was sorry for so many things: for taking away his mother, for being so angry at his father, for leaving him to manage on his own for so long when he was hurting... "I'm so sorry."

Nicholas lifted his head and wrapped his own arm around Will and rested his head against his. "Me too, son. Me too."

The pair sat quietly draped in each other's apologies for a while longer before Nicholas' stubborn male pride got the better of him. He cleared his throat and sat up. "Don't let your past define you, William. And don't define yourself by your past. You have to wipe the slate clean. Revisiting things that are long gone just twists everything and everyone. You just need to move forwards. You are your mother's son: strong and kind. Just remember that. Go home to your woman and tell her everything she wants to hear about how you're ready to rise to this challenge, because remember, all it boils down to is love, and you are riddled with it."

Will nodded and the pair sat together for a while in a companionable comfort, watching nature in all her glory, occasionally saying nothing very much at all as they enjoyed just being together.

After twenty minutes or so, Will sat forwards and pushed to his feet. "I have to go, Dad. Business calls, but I'll come see you again soon. Okay? You need a lift anywhere?"

"Nope. This old man is going to go blow some cobwebs away." He stood and faced his son, looking at him for a moment before patting his cheek. "Good to see you, kid." He gave a curt nod and turned to walk in the other direction.

He got a few steps down the path before turning back around. "William."

"Yep?"

"Bring that little lady to see me sometime." He smiled. "Oh, and thanks for making me a happy grandpa."

Will chuckled and raised his hand goodbye before dragging in a lungful of air.

He still didn't know anything about being a father, but with his dad's words to reflect on, at least he knew that he would be okay.

Dragging her finger along the surface of the table located in the greenhouse, Joey stared down at the dirt that collected on her skin and sighed. What was she even doing there? The manor had been quiet the last couple of days, both she and Will playing a game of avoidance, or so it seemed, and she needed some time to collect her thoughts. She hadn't allowed herself to think much about their argument or Will's reaction because doing so felt like a fist to the gut. The previous forty-eight hours had consisted of them burying themselves in their work and Will coming to bed long after Joey had turned in for the night, and if she was being honest with herself, she missed him.

Even now, she regretted blurting out the revelation in the heat of the moment.

This is all your fault, Joey.

Wiping her hands clean on the sides of her leggings, she glanced down at her stomach and frowned.

What if he never came around or warmed to the idea of a having the baby? Then what?

Where would she go?

What would she do?

Did she have it in her to raise the child on her own? Her father raised her all by himself. Perhaps, she could do the same.

All the questions racing through her mind made the corners of her eyes prickle with tears, and she sniffed them back, no longer wanting to entertain that line of thinking.

He'd come around.

He just needed time.

She continued to tell herself that as she pottered around the abandoned and dilapidated greenhouse, wondering how Will would feel if she took it upon herself to restore the structure to its former glory. She had no doubt she'd be able to make it a place that Will could once again look at with a smile on his face and a newfound warmth in his heart. She didn't want to erase the good memories he had of his mother, but she wanted them to be able to outshine the tragic ones that continued to haunt him, and something in her own heart was telling her that maybe, just maybe, repairing the greenhouse was a step in the right direction.

As she stood in its centre, allowing her gaze to roll over every corner, and her mind to envisage the changes she'd make, the unexpected sound of the door creaking open grabbed her attention.

She turned to see Will walking through it, and her heart beat faster at the mere sight of him.

Closing the door and turning to face her, he stopped and drew in a breath. "Hey."

"Hey." Joey stood still, every muscle in her body urging her to step forwards and throw herself into his arms. She refrained, crossing her own arms over her chest instead as if to protect herself from whatever he was about to say. "What are you—"

"I'm sorry." Will shoved his hands in his pockets and dipped his chin. A lungful of air escaped his chest and he glanced up at her through his lashes, assessing her mood and how receptive she was going to be to his apology. He knew the words he had blurted out weren't enough on their own and that he would need to give her more, but he needed to know she was going to believe every word first. He waited, the two of them at opposite ends of the small building, repeating his peace offering and hoping she would truly hear it. "I'm sorry, Joey."

Joey shook her head, those incessant tears now back and lining her eyes. "I'm sorry, too." She quickly swiped them away and glanced down at her feet, finding it difficult to look at him. "I'm sorry you found out the way that you did. I'm sorry I didn't tell you sooner, but I was afraid, Will. I'm still afraid, and I know this wasn't planned, and I know this isn't what you want, and—"

"Joey. Shut up."

"I don't want you to feel as though—"

"Shut. Up. Stop talking." Will strode towards her and on reaching her, he pulled her to him, wrapping his arms around her shoulders and pressing his lips to the top of her head. "You have absolutely nothing to apologise for. You have done nothing wrong." He closed his eyes and squeezed her tighter, his emotions beginning to get the better of him as he contemplated the fact that the love of his life, the woman he would die for, was in his arms and carrying their child. "I love you, Josephine. So damn much. I love you harder than I ever imagined I'd ever love anyone, but I fucked up the other day. I was selfish and I was impulsive. And I'm sorry."

Joey cried harder at his words, relief flowing through her as she allowed what he was saying to register.

Pulling back and holding her away from him so that he could look into her eyes, he continued to speak. "I'm scared. I'm scared stiff because I have so much growing of my own to do still, and I'm worried that I won't be good enough for you. I've always worried about that, but I'm even more scared now. I'm terrified of fucking up and messing everything up for you— for us—and my reaction the other night was born of this fear that I seem to carry around with me all the damn time. But despite all that, I am over the fucking moon, Joey." His eyes stung with tears and he blinked hard to keep them at bay. "I can't even begin to tell you how full you have made my heart with this news. You are my everything. You're my future and my life, and now… well now my future is going to be even more perfect."

"Oh, Will." Joey took Will's face in her hands and guided her lips to his in a kiss that spoke of all the love she had in her heart. She had hoped for the best, but with Will she never knew what to expect, and right now he was telling her everything she wanted to hear and more. "I love you so much, and I'm just as scared as you are, but that fear pales in comparison to how much I want this — how much I want you and this baby. Our baby."

Will moved his hand down and placed it flat on Joey's abdomen, his fingers splaying out to cover the whole area. His heart was pounding in his chest with a mixture of utter terror and the most heightened excitement he'd ever remembered feeling. His eyes were glued to her belly, and he pulled in a shaky breath before he moved them back up to meet her huge, expectant brown ones.

"Marry me, Joey." He swallowed down and continued to speak before his words had a chance to register with her. "Marry me. Not now, not yet. Not because of this — but because I love you so damn much and I don't want my life without you in it by my side, as my wife." He licked his lips, his heart still thumping away in his chest. "You're it for me. You're all I've ever wanted, and right here, right now, knowing our baby is growing inside of you, I've never felt it more." He took a deep breath. "Marry me."

Wide-eyed and completely hung up on his every word, Joey stared at him, her heart ready to explode right out of her chest. She willed her brain to make the necessary connections it needed to give voice to her one and only thought.

"Yes." Happy tears streamed down her cheeks, and this time she didn't bother to wipe them away. "A thousand times, yes."

An elated laugh floated out of Will as he grabbed her face and kissed her like his life depended on it, like she was the air he needed to keep him alive, before pulling back again, his hope-filled eyes roaming over every inch of her face "Yes?"

Joey nodded, her eyes alight with love and tears, a similar laugh hiccupping from her.

Will crashed his mouth to hers again, his palms sliding over her buttocks, pulling her hips flush to his own, and he spoke against her lips as their bodies ignited with need for one another. "God, I love you." He moved his hands to to clasp hers, running his fingers over her knuckles, until he suddenly pulled away again, a look of panic in his eyes.

Joey flicked her gaze across his face, a frown creasing her brow. "What? What is it?"

"A ring. I haven't got you a ring."

Joey giggled and rolled her eyes. "Just take me to bed you fool."

Chapter 26

Bea's hand remained on the door knob as she pushed her way into the kitchen. Her eyes were wide and her mouth hung open. "Sweet Lord above, Mr Kent. Why in Christ's name are you standing there in your smalls?"

Spinning around with eyes as wide as hers, Graham instinctively dropped his hands to cover his crotch. "Mrs Sykes." He scooted sideways and stood behind the counter. "I erm… I thought there was an emergency. I didn't think changing was a priority." He stared at her before he lifted his shoulders in a small shrug.

"You'll give an old woman a heart attack, for crying out loud." She moved further into the room and pointed towards the kettle at the other side. "I need to get over there, so I'm going to cover my eyes until you have removed yourself. Go and get some bloody trousers on." She wrapped her dressing gown a little tighter and placed her hand over her eyes as Graham started to move from his hiding place.

"They're here, come on." Will's voice filtered through the open doorway and as he and Joey practically skipped into the kitchen, Joey let out a squeal as her eyes landed on a scantily clad Graham, who was hurrying towards her. She dropped Will's hand and spun around to avoid looking at his crotch.

"Jesus, Graham! Get some fucking clothes on, man! What the actual fuck?" Will averted his eyes and shook his head as the old man shuffled past him apologetically.

"I nearly dropped dead, William. He thought there was some sort of emergency and didn't think to cover up. Imagine if there had been? Imagine if there had been something terrible happening and there he was, standing in his y-fronts? I tell you." Bea filled the kettle and shook her head. "That man."

Will turned to face Joey and bit down on his lip to stop himself from laughing. "Who are these people I live with?"

Chuckling, Joey moved over to the large worktable in the centre of the room and, as she pulled out one of the stools tucked beneath it and sat down, the smile on her face widened. "Bea, the kettle won't be necessary tonight. Come here. We have something we'd like to share with you."

Graham reappeared, fully clothed, as Bea cocked her head and walked cautiously towards the table.

"Don't look so worried." Will smiled at her and beckoned Graham to join them as he moved to the cupboard to grab four champagne flutes. "It's good news, not bad."

Once all four of them were seated, Will grabbed Joey's hand under the table and gave it a squeeze. "So. As you both know, Joey and I are going to be parents." The word almost got stuck in his throat as a lump of emotion threatened to consume him. He caught Graham's expression and smiled. The two hadn't really talked since the news had reached him via Bea, and he vowed to spend some time with him in the days that followed. "Tonight, about"—he glanced at the clock on the wall—"two hours ago, I made a promise to myself, and on the back of that promise, I erm…" He dipped his head a little as a huge grin

227

started to form on his face—one he was having trouble controlling. "I asked Joey to be my wife." His eyes caught Bea's and he nodded ever so slightly, confirming the news and answering all of the questions in her expression. "She said yes."

Bea's hands flew to her mouth as she stifled an elated sob of happiness and got to her feet. She hurried around to the other side of the table and wrapped her arms around the shoulders of the youngsters. "I could not be more thrilled. What absolutely wonderful news, my darlings. You have made this old lady so very happy." She planted a kiss on Will's cheek and wrapped herself around Joey as Will stood to his feet and popped the cork on the bottle of champagne.

Graham's smile was genuine, if a little reserved, and he held his hand out to shake Will's. "Congratulations, son. Not an emergency after all." He smiled again and held out two glasses for Will to pour the bubbly liquid into. Will filled his own and then the fourth with lemonade, winking at Joey as he handed it to her.

The four of them stood in a huddle of friendship and love as they clinked glasses and sipped their drinks.

"Have you…" Bea paused a moment, catching Will's eyes. "Have you spoken to your fathers? Both of you? Do they know yet about the baby?"

"No."

"Yes."

Joey's head whipped to the side, her brows narrowing at Will's response. This was news to her. "You've talked to your father?"

Wrapping his arm around her shoulder and eyeing her and Bea, he nodded. Both women watched his expression carefully as he told them how the afternoon with his father had played out. He finished with a small contented smile and took another sip of his drink. "There is still a massive gap to bridge, but the ice is broken at least. We are talking, and that's the main thing." He turned to face Joey, who was smiling fondly at him. "He wants to meet you." He absently ran his thumb along her bottom lip in the way that drove her wild and smiled, his eyes roaming over every inch of her face as he spoke. "Well. Not meet you, but, y'know… re-meet you."

"Oh gosh." A small bout of panic formed in Joey's stomach at the idea of going to see Will's father. "Really?"

He grabbed her chin between his thumb and forefinger and pulled her lips to his, pressing them softly together. "Don't sweat it. He's going to adore you."

The four of them returned to their drinks and chatted heartily and excitedly about the idea of a wedding and the sound of tiny feet running up and down the hallways of the manor, and Will's mind drifted for a few moments to the ever looming issue of the sale of the place. He was now in a totally different mind set and he had some serious decisions to make.

Sitting back in his chair he watched the three of them grinning at each other with happiness and he could have sworn he felt one of the cracks in his heart heal.

He smiled and slung his arm over Joey's shoulder before interrupting the comfortable lull in conversation. "Paisley? Really, Graham?"

The women burst out laughing and Will's chest rumbled with humour.

Graham rolled his eyes. "Oh, piss off."

"Right. Out with it. What's the matter?" Will glanced at Joey before returning his eyes to the road, flicking the indicator on and pulling into the driveway of John's house, turning his body towards her.

Joey shifted in her seat uncomfortably and sighed. "Nothing. It's nothing." She brushed her hair behind her ears and chewed on her bottom lip, knowing Will wasn't buying the lie she was trying to sell him. He knew her. He knew her well and could see right through her most days. "I'm nervous, that's all." She looked up at him as he began to speak.

"I am about to walk into the house belonging to my girlfr—my fiancé's father to tell him I have got her pregnant and that I want to marry her. This is all on top of me being his arch enemy for twenty odd years." He raised his eyebrows at her and cocked his head to the side. "Still nervous?" He didn't wait for her to answer. "I love you, Josephine Bell, and we are about to set out on a journey together that is going to be rocky, stressful, not to mention scary as fuck, and I will be right beside you every single step of the way, even on the days where my body might not seem to be—on the days where my past is in control—my heart is yours and will never falter. I promise you this. We are in this together, and I am just as nervous as you."

Taking Will's hand in hers, she threaded their fingers together and placed a gentle kiss to his knuckles. He was right. If anyone should be nervous, it was him. "I love you, too." She swept her thumb along his and allowed the next few minutes to play out in her mind. A small laugh erupted from the back of her throat, and she shook her head. "This is crazy, y'know? Who would have ever thought we'd even be having this discussion."

Will laughed, a sound that filled Joey's heart to the brim. "Don't I know it. Just a few months ago, I was a monster holed up in his castle, and now... well, now I'm just the luckiest man alive aren't I."

Joey moved closer and pressed her forehead to his before closing her eyes and kissing him gently. "I never thought of you as a monster, Will. Never."

Will shook away his darker thoughts and smiled brightly at her. "Come on. Let's do this."

They opened their car doors and walked hand in hand towards the front of the house where Little John stood waiting for them in the doorway.

After greeting each other, the three of them entered the house and sat in the living room as Joey made tea for them all.

"Here we go." She passed a cup to each of them and then perched herself on the edge of the sofa next to Will.

"So. To what do I owe this pleasure?"

Will flicked his eyes to Joey before turning his attention to her father. "John. I know this is a little... unconventional, but erm..." Will swallowed nervously and rubbed the back of his neck. "You know I love your daughter, right? You know she's the other half of me and that I would do anything to make her happy." He watched John's unwavering expression and took a deep breath. "Oh fuck it. John, I want her to be my wife. I want to marry her, but I want your blessing. I want you to be okay with it."

John slowly lowered his mug to the table and stared at the man before him. "Marriage isn't easy, Will."

Eyeing the old man, Will was steely in his determination and his decisions. He nodded and pulled his lips into a tight smile. "I don't want easy, John. I want love."

Seconds passed, or minutes, so it seemed, before John did or said anything. He looked over at his daughter, taking in the smile on her face and the hopeful gleam in her big brown eyes, and he saw it. He saw the love that used to filter back through Claire's eyes whenever she'd look at him, and he knew without a doubt that if there was anyone who was worthy of loving and providing for his daughter, it was William Marshall-Croft. "You both have my blessing, but are you ready? I don't doubt that you love each other very much. I see it. But are you ready for the ups and downs and everything that goes with being that person for each other forever? I am overjoyed for you both that you have got to this point where you want to commit to one another, but you have to understand that this can't be entered into lightly. You have to be ready physically and mentally." He looked at Will as he spoke the last words. "You have to be willing to compromise and put the other person first when they need it. You have to be willing to drop everything to give them your support. That means work as well as play. You have to be—"

"I'm pregnant."

The heads of both men whipped to the side to look at Joey with wide eyes, both sets with a 'what the fuck' look in them for completely different reasons.

"Joey, no! Again? Not like *that!*"

"You're what?"

"Oh God." All the colour drained from Joey's face as she sat there, her heart racing in her chest. She dropped her face in her hands and shook her head, mumbling under her breath. "I'm so sorry. That was so stupid of me. I…" She lifted her head, wanting to take it back and do it the right way. "I didn't mean to announce it like that." She flashed Will a remorseful smile and then looked over at her father. "Dad. You're going to be a grandfather."

"Oh God. Now he knows we've been having sex." Will pinched the bridge of his nose as the realisation dawned on him before slumping back in his chair, deflated.

"Well, no shit, Will. How else would the baby have gotten in there?" She looked at Will, not believing what he'd just said. "Thank you. Thank you very much. Now I'll never be able to look him in the eyes again." She pressed her lips together and inhaled deeply through her nose, not daring to meet her father's gaze.

"You two really are crazy, aren't you?" Little John brought his mug to his lips, taking another sip as Joey and Will sat there staring at each other. "I don't think either one of you are prepared for this, but I'm going to enjoy sitting back to watch." He placed his tea back down on the table and smiled. "Come on over here and give me a hug, sweetheart."

Joey rose from her chair, quickly rounding the table and falling into her father's warm embrace.

He stroked a hand through her hair and spoke softly in her ear. "I'm over the moon. I can't wait to be a grandpa."

The three of them spent the afternoon chatting and laughing at the awkwardness of the revelation, and after a couple of hours, Will and Joey sat buckled into their seats in the car.

Will revved the car into the road and smiled over at his wife-to-be. "Well. Just one more announcement to make and then we can start our happily ever after."

Chapter 27

Watching Josephine Bell walk up his garden path had Nicholas's heart squeezing tight with emotions he thought he'd locked away. She was a woman now, not the little girl of six who had been right at the very heart of the story twenty-three years ago. He inhaled deeply before opening the door ready to welcome her into his home.

"Goodness me, you took my breath away." He plastered a smile on his face and beamed at the beautiful young woman who was clutching his son's hand tightly. "Look at you."

Ushering them both inside, he instructed Will to hang their coats on the coat stand and showed Joey into the living room where drinks and biscuits were already waiting. "Please. Sit. Make yourself at home."

They sat together with awkwardness over their heads whilst Will told Nicholas about his proposal to Josephine, and after hugs and congratulations were over and done with, Will made the decision to give Joey and his father a little time on their own to get to know one another.

"How about I nip out and grab us all some lunch?" He looked pointedly at Nicholas, conveying his thoughts silently, and Nicholas nodded. It was time to move on from the past now and getting to know Joey as the bright young woman before him was imperative. Besides anything else, he was sure that she would be the bridge back to Will — he was sure that she would help them to rebuild their relationship and that he would learn so much about his estranged son from her.

With Will gone, Nicholas turned to Joey and smiled. "So. How are you feeling? Sleeping okay? Has the sickness kicked in yet?"

"Yes. It's manageable at the moment, but I'm feeling really tired all the time. All normal things, I suppose. We have the first scan in just over a week." She returned his smile, hers shy but genuine, and fiddled nervously with one of the silver bands on her finger. Now that Will had left, the awkwardness seemed to double, and she didn't know what to say or do to break it. She glanced around, searching for a topic of conversation. "You have a really nice home."

"Ah it's nothing much. Not compared to the manor." His expression saddened as memories of his old life came whirling back. "But let's not go there, hey. How would you like to see my garden? Although I do say so myself, that *is* something worth talking about." He stood to his feet and held out his hand for Joey to take.

"I'd love to." Joey allowed Nicholas to guide her out of the living room and through the small house to the outside.

The two of them wandered around the large garden talking about this and that until they found themselves falling unexpectedly into companionship. Their conversation was easy, and they laughed hard at each others jokes and anecdotes.

"So he hasn't decided yet then?" Nicholas bent at the knees and plucked a weed from the flower bed, chucking it over his hedge into the field behind.

"No. I understand his indecision, even if I'd prefer he reconsider selling at all. I fear his reasons stem from years of his own self punishment and he might be making a move he'd potentially regret." Joey paused, the spring breeze blowing warmly against her face. "Is it possible you could talk to him? Maybe offer some direction?"

Nicholas continued guiding her through the garden, towards the back where there was a wrought iron bench. "Yep. William stayed in that house to punish himself. I gather he has talked to you about this. I couldn't stay; it was too painful. But William decided he deserved the pain. If he has decided to sell, I might be hopeful in thinking he has forgiven himself. However, if he has found happiness at last, then I don't believe there is any need to sell. That place has been in our family for centuries and it would be a crying shame to see it transformed into some commercialised opportunity for money making. Does his estate agent not help in any way? What's his name? Simon is it? What are his thoughts?"

"Simon. Yes." Joey inhaled deeply, her chest tight at the mere thought of the man. "He wants Will to sell, but if we're being honest, I don't feel as though his intentions are honorable or in the best interest of Will. I don't trust him." She glanced over at Nicholas, waiting for his reaction.

They reached the bench and Nicholas invited her to sit down. "Funnily enough, I trust you, Miss Bell. So what is it that doesn't feel right where Simon is concerned? Is it something he has said? What gives you the impression he is not to be trusted?"

Squinting off into the distance, Joey sat down beside him. "Not exactly." How could she make him understand without exposing Simon for the snake he was? Will had every right to know what had happened—what Simon had done to her the night of the ball and how Nadine had confronted her during the Greenfrog meeting—but she wasn't sure how to tell him. Will knew her qualms as far as Simon and Nadine were concerned and she wasn't sure he'd believe her. "I don't know how to explain it, but I can't help but think Simon and Nadine—the marketing manager—are pushing Will towards this decision for their own gain. There is something going on between them. My gut is telling me there is, but I don't know how to begin to get to the bottom of it."

"And are your instincts usually sharp, Josephine? Do you think you're a good judge of character?" He glanced at her, knowing full well what the answer was.

"I'd like to think so, yes."

Nicholas nodded. "Yes. I don't doubt for one second that they are. You fell in love with my boy; you saw past his pain and found him."

A wistful look in his eyes made Joey's heart twinge. "You miss him?"

"I miss it all, Josephine. But life has a funny way of twisting and turning events to make you feel and think things that end up breaking hearts and putting distance between people. We have a long way to go, Will and I, but I think with you on board, it will be a much smoother ride." He turned to look at her and patted her hand. "Now." He pushed wearily to his feet. "What are we going to do about this Simon fellow, huh?"

Will glanced at the clock on the bedside table.

4.30am.

He sighed and linked his hands behind his head on the pillow, his eyes trailing across the old ceiling. Joey lay breathing softly beside him, sound asleep, and the need to wrap himself around her was almost irrepressible.

The nightmares that still woke him were something he would never get used to, and lying there, the aftermath of one still lingering in the back of his head, his mind switched to thoughts of his mother.

It was scan day—the day he got to see his son or daughter for the first time.

It was the day when all of this would become real and there was nothing he wanted more than to share his news with her.

What a wonderful granny she would have made.

He swallowed his emotion, knowing full well that if he allowed himself to dwell on the fact she was gone his anger would rise. He had to be anger free today. He had to have his head in the game and his heart open for Joey.

His past was exactly that—in the past—but his future lay right in front of him. He would be a fool to let what had happened to him in years gone by ruin anything now. It was time to buckle up and push forwards with everything he had in order to make sure the days that lay out before him were as full of light and love as they could be.

He closed his eyes and vowed that when the sun rose, it would be the start of a new Will. He needed to fight harder for her, for them, and it was now or never.

Rolling onto his side, he trailed his fingertip up the length of her arm, over the curve of her shoulder and then swept a curl away from her neck so he could place a kiss there.

When the alarm went off, four hours later, Joey turned to see Will asleep—still asleep despite the shrill sound of the alarm. He looked content, and she smiled. Something about him felt different and her heart filled with optimism. After watching him for a few more minutes, Joey quietly slipped out of bed and headed for the bathroom. As she went through her normal routine—brushing her teeth, showering, and fighting with her headful of curls—she struggled to contain her excitement. The idea that she was going to be a mother hadn't fully sunk in, not really, but she knew within two short hours, the reality would come in the form of a little baby flipping on the monitor screen.

Walking back into the bedroom, she glanced at Will, who was still—much to her surprise—sound asleep, and went about getting dressed. This was so unlike him, and she hated the idea of waking him, but she was anxious. And well, damnit, he needed to get up.

With a bounce in her step, she sprung on to the bed and landed directly on top of him. He woke with a grunt as she clasped his face in her hands and showered him with kisses. "Wake up! It's scan day!"

Will glared into her eyes before reaching up and squeezing her cheeks. He rubbed his stubbly chin down her nose and then swiftly flipped them both over so he was caging her in. With his mouth to her ear, he pushed her sundress out of his way, running his hand up the back of her naked calf and then round and up her leg until he reached the heat between her thighs where his thumb trailed gently. "You smell edible. Do I have time to fuck you first?"

"You're so damn irresistible when you talk like that." She kissed him hard, tangling her tongue with his before pulling back. "But no. You need to get up and get ready. We have a baby to go see."

Manoeuvring herself from his arms, she quickly rolled off the bed, blew him a kiss over her shoulder, and sauntered towards the door. "I'll meet you downstairs."

"Damn you woman!" Will flopped back down onto his pillow and dragged his hands down his face.

A cold shower was in order.

Once he was ready, the two climbed into the Bentley and Will drove them to the hospital, parked the car and then gripped Joey's hand tightly as they made their way to the prenatal department.

"You okay?" He looked down at her as they approached the receptionist's desk.

Joey grinned, smoothing her free hand up his arm. "Perfect. You?"

"Nervous as fuck, Miss Bell-soon-to-be-Mrs-Marshall-Croft" He grinned back and kissed the side of her head. "Nervous as fuck."

They stood patiently as the receptionist checked in the younger woman in front of them—who looked as though she was about to give birth at any second—and then were greeted with a beaming smile as they took their turn. After a brief exchange of names, tapping a few keys on her keyboard, and informing Joey she needed to drink until her bladder was full, she passed over a clipboard full of papers and gestured the pair of them towards the waiting room full of women. "Fill these out and we will be with you shortly."

They walked hand-in-hand to the small, white room.

There was a row of blue plastic chairs around the perimeter and all but a few were occupied by women in varying stages of their pregnancies. Will's eyes scanned them all, his nerves picking up even more as they watched the same woman from the reception clutch her stomach in pain.

Was this what Joey would go through?

Would she be in pain like this?

He looked down at her stomach that to him didn't look any different when she was clothed and protectively lay his hand across it. "You okay?" He shook his head. "Sorry. I keep asking. But you're okay, right?"

"I'm okay." Joey flashed him a warm but timid smile. "Are you okay?"

Will laughed. "I feel like this is all we are going to say to each other until this is over and done with. I'm good, baby. I'm just anxious, nervous, worried... I just..." He scanned the room again. "I just want everything to be okay, y'know?"

"I know. Me too. We just have to believe it will be."

It wasn't long before Joey's bladder was bursting and in the nick of time, her name was called.

"This is it." Will kissed the side of her head and squeezed her hand tightly.

Lying on the ultrasound table in the dimly lit room, with blue paper towel tucked into the top of her leggings, Joey smiled up at Will who sat, his leg bouncing, on the chair beside her. The sonographer introduced himself as Philip, and all formalities were out of the way quickly and efficiently.

As he smeared the jelly on Josephine's abdomen, she winced at the cold feel of it on her skin.

"Sorry about that." Philip smiled. "Okay. Are we ready? I'll just have to take some measurements etc., and then once I'm sorted and we have heard the heartbeat, I can turn the screen for you to see. There might be a little bit of pressure on your tummy, depending on what position the baby is lying in, but it won't hurt. Does that sound okay?"

Her heart beating fast and anxiousness swirling violently in her stomach, Joey looked at Will briefly before returning her attention back to the man who was talking to her. "Yes."

Smiling, Philip took hold of the probe and began moving the gel around with the end of it to ensure good movement. His eyes were fixed intently on the screen that was angled so that he had a good view of it. His left hand moved the computer mouse around and he periodically clicked it, pressing the odd key on the keyboard.

He gave nothing away.

Will and Joey didn't take their eyes off him.

After what felt like a lifetime, he removed the probe, swiveled his stool around to face them, clasping his hands in his lap. "Okay. So, everything looks fine. The measurements state that you're around eleven weeks pregnant. Does that sound about right with your dates, Josephine?"

"Yes. That's right."

"Good. So I'm going to get the fetal doppler out now and we will listen to the heartbeat, but before that, I'm going to turn the screen so you can see what I have been looking at for the last few minutes.

Will tensed in his seat and squeezed Joey's hand harder. This was the moment he was going to see his son or daughter for the very first time and he wasn't sure he was emotionally prepared.

"I do need to inform you beforehand, that the ultrasound shows you are expecting twins."

"Twins?"

"Twins?"

Joey's head whipped around, her wide eyes falling on Will whose colour had completely drained from his face. She looked back at Phillip, attempting to speak around the rock lodged in her throat. "Twins? Are you sure?"

Philip smiled, placed the probe back on Joey's stomach and turned the screen to face the pair of them.

Will gasped at the sight of two tiny little blobs on the screen, and as Philip placed the doppler next to the probe and the sound of two tiny little heartbeats filled the quiet space, an uninvited tear rolled over his lashes and down his cheek. "Jesus Christ."

There were no words after the two that had floated from Will's mouth, only shallow breaths, staring eyes, and beating hearts. Joey couldn't tear her gaze away from the monitor screen, not even to look at Will who she was sure was battling his own array of emotions. A million thoughts had raced through her mind leading up to this moment, but not one of them had been the possibility that she was expecting two babies. They had both been adjusting to the idea of one, and now there were two.

"I'll give you two a minute." Philip placed the equipment on the trolley, patted Joey's hand and left the room.

Licking the dryness from her lips, Joey chanced a glance in his direction.

Will's trance broke with the flicker of the screen, the image disappearing, and he pulled in a long breath, slowly moving his eyes to the face of the woman he loved with all his heart. "They're okay. The babies. They're healthy." He cupped her cheek and smoothed his thumb along her bottom lip. "Our babies are going to be okay."

Tears slid from the corners of Joey's eyes, and she nodded, any words she wanted to say stuck behind the emotion clogged in her throat. Reaching up, she took hold of Will's hand and pressed a gentle kiss to his palm.

They were all going to be okay.

Sitting wrapped around each other on the sofa in front of the fire, Joey and Will watched the television screen play out the film they had rented, but Will's attention was far from the plot. His life had taken a massive turn and he was in a position now where he had to get his priorities straight and his ducks in a row. He was going to be a father, the head of a family, and it was his responsibility to make sure that those he loved were cared for.

He patted Joey's legs. "Let me up. I need to go make a phone call."

Joey shifted her weight and looked at him curiously. "At this time?"

"Yeah. I need to discuss something with Simon."

She winced at his name and watched as Will moved towards the door.

"I need to tell him I'm not selling."

Joey sat up quickly. "What? Really?"

Turning his head to look at her over his shoulder, Will grinned. "You're happy about that, huh?"

"Will, I… yes. I'm absolutely delighted."

"It's our home, Joey. It's our babies' home. And aside from that, we don't need the stress right now. Back in a tick." He walked out of the sitting room and down to his office where he pulled his phone from his pocket and perched on the edge of his desk as he found Simon's number.

He answered on the third ring.

"William. How lovely to hear from you at this hour. It's the weekend. Why am I getting calls from you now?"

"I'm not selling."

The line went quiet and Will waited for Simon to respond.

Sitting up and swinging his legs over the side of his bed, Simon clenched his jaw. "I see." He pushed to his feet and began to pace the floor of his bedroom. "Are you going to elaborate?"

Will rolled his eyes. "Yes I can elaborate. Or I can let you go back to sleep and ring you with the details on Monday morning. I just thought you should know sooner rather than later so you can start—"

"Elaborate, Will."

Will stood to his feet and sauntered around his office as he spoke. "Joey and I need a home, and this is our home. And… well… we need it more than ever now. For the time being at least. Joey is pregnant." He paused to wait for the beam of congratulations he was sure would filter down the line from his right hand man.

"What?"

"Joey's preg—"

"I heard you, Will. I just meant, what. As in what the hell and why. Why the hell is she pregnant? Have you lost your mind?"

Will's eyebrows rose at Simon's words. "Wow. Thanks for the positivity, man. I'll be sure to make you Godfather."

"Fuck. Sorry. Congratulations. But I don't see how this means you can't sell. You are letting your heart rule again and you have to stop doing that. It's her. Cinder—I mean Josephine. She has got inside your head and she's stopping you from being business smart, Croft."

"It's not about business anymore. She's pregnant, Simon. I can't have her being stressed about anything. She needs to know she has a home and to not be worried about *me* being stressed about anything. You know damn well the horses are the biggest obstacle; moving them at this point would be ludicrous. I can't have Joey worrying about all of that in her condition. She needs to feel secure and she needs to know my head is with her and not full of the complications of such a massive upheaval. I'm not moving the horses for the foreseeable future, and therefore, I will not be selling for the foreseeable future. Elaborate enough?"

Simon slumped back down on the bed. "I'll call you Monday morning."

Chapter 28

"I need to see you. Now." Simon seethed down the phone, his voice low and his hand rubbing across his forehead. "I don't know. Wherever is close to where you are." He paced up and down the corridor outside his office, his eyes shifty and his body language nervous. "Fine. I'll see you in ten." He walked back into his office, grabbed his jacket and left the building in a cloud of annoyance and frustration.

Pulling into the carpark of the nearest supermarket, he glanced around to find Nadine's car and when he spotted it, he pulled up next to it, switching the engine off quickly and getting out. He was sure to do a scan of the area before he walked around to the passenger side of her silver-blue Porsche, opening the door and sliding in beside her.

"What's got your y-fronts in a twist?" Nadine had the visor pulled down and was touching up her lipstick, her eyes not once looking in his direction.

"What do you fucking think? He's not selling."

Nadine snapped the visor back up and turned in her seat to face him, her eyes blinking furiously. "What do you mean he's not selling? I thought this was in the bag. I

246

thought you'd convinced him that it was the best thing to do?" She pursed her lips and waited impatiently for him to respond.

"Well life has taken a turn hasn't it. So he has changed his mind. Fucking Josephine is pregnant so he won't move the horses. He says it's all too stressful and for the time being at least, he is staying put."

She huffed out of her nose and folded her arms across her chest. "The time being. What's that supposed to mean? I can't hold Dave off much longer you know."

"Fuck knows." Simon dropped his head in his hand and pinched the bridge of his nose. "For the foreseeable future is what he said. That sounds like a very fucking long time to me."

"Jesus, Simon." Nadine let her head fall back against the window and she closed her eyes. "This is my Goddamned promotion. This is our ticket. How can you have fucked this up so badly? You had *one* job."

Simon pushed his face into hers. "I'm not fucking God, Nadine. I can't control the contents of Will's ball sack for crying out loud." He slumped back in his own seat. "Jesus Christ."

The pair of them sat in silence for a few minutes, anger radiating from both of them before Nadine spoke again. "Joey, Josephine, whatever her fucking name is, she's your answer."

"What?"

"She obviously has a hold over him."

"We've tried that. She already doesn't trust us, I'm sure. So I can't see how trying to persuade her to persuade him is going to work another time."

A small, sly smile spread across Nadine's face. "Persuade is the wrong word, ma grosse petite saucisse."

Simon narrowed his eyes. "What are you thinking?"

"A threat."

"You already threatened her."

247

"No. That was a warning. I mean a threat. A proper threat."

Simon eyed her with an element of admiration. "I knew there was a reason I enjoyed fucking you." He leaned forwards, grabbing her face and pushing his tongue into her mouth before letting her go with a little shove. "So what do you propose?"

Nadine wiped the back of her hand across her mouth, smearing lipstick across her cheek. "That's your job."

Monday morning rolled around too slowly for his liking, and as Simon jogged up the steps to the manor, he straightened his tie and plastered on his best 'I'm happy for you' face. He passed Graham on his way to Will's office, slapping a hand on his shoulder and wishing him a good morning, and as he reached the large oak door, he halted, gave his tie another wiggle and pushed into the room without knocking.

Will's head kicked up from his work and he frowned at the grin on Simon's face. "Morning. What's got you all up in the clouds?" He looked back down at his laptop and continued to type.

"Well congrats are in order aren't they. Come here."

Will looked up again to see Simon standing with his arms wide open and his head cocked to the side. "Erm… I'm good. Thanks though."

"God, you're a miserable son of a bitch, Will. Y'know that?" He slumped into the leather chair in front of the desk, leaning his elbows on the arms and pressing the tips of his fingers together. "So you're not selling."

"Nope." Will didn't look up.

"And there's nothing I can do or say to convince you to change your mind?"

"Nope."

His sigh was audible but Will continued to ignore him. "I don't pay you to sit watching me work, Simon. Have you closed the Wilkinson deal?"

Simon pushed himself to his feet. "It will be closed by the end of tomorrow, I promise. Now where is that lovely woman of yours? I want to go congratulate her, too, on this wonderful baby news —"

"It's twins."

Simon's eyes widened. "Twins? Jesus, Will. Do you know what you're getting yourself into here?"

"Nope. And that's what I love about it. Now go and let me get on. She's in the greenhouse."

Simon left the office and headed back outside.

The greenhouse. Perfect.

He set off down the path and then over the incline of the garden to the greenhouse that, to his convenience, could not be seen from the house. The silhouette of Joey moved about and he picked up his pace a little, stepping over a couple of mole hills before reaching the glass structure. His shoes crunched on the gravel that surrounded the old building and he finally arrived at the door that already sat ajar.

"You've really got your claws into him now, haven't you, Cinders. You have your prince charming trapped good and proper."

Joey's head snapped to the side, her pulse jumping beneath her skin and the hose in her hand falling to the ground at Simon's voice. She swallowed hard, her eyes never leaving his as she stared at him. "What are you doing here?"

Simon stepped over the threshold, dusting his jacket sleeve off as he rubbed up against the decaying wooden structure. "To congratulate you of course. To say well fucking done for fucking everything up." He shoved his hands in his pockets and sauntered to where she stood, picking up a plastic plant pot and turning it around in his hands. "So he has you gardening, too. You're still just the hired help huh?" He put it down and turned to lean the small of his back against the high wooden table. "Giving him babies just makes you look like a whore if he's still paying you to clean his house."

At his words, Joey's hands balled into fists. He had real nerve showing up there and speaking to her that way, but with Simon, she didn't expect anything less. "Say what you will, Simon, but your words mean nothing. You may have the wool pulled over my future husband's eyes, but I'm on to you. I know you and Nadine are working together, and as soon as I figure out what you both have to gain from—"

Simon grabbed her shoulders and pushed her against the wall behind her. "You're nothing but a meddling little bitch, Miss Bell. You know *nothing*, and if you know what's good for you, you'll keep this"—he momentarily covered her mouth with his hand—"shut."

"Screw you."

His facial expression darkened and his eyes became hooded. He pressed the length of his body against the length of hers and ran his hand up the inside of her leg until he reached the hem of her sundress. "You will convince William to sell the house, Goddamnit, or I will do everything in my power to make sure your poor, frail father is homeless. I will fake paperwork, convince buyers, steal the deeds and sell the house from under his fucking feet." His hand continued to climb until he reached the apex of her thighs where he cupped her, and then dragged his fingers over her briefs. "Do I make myself understood?"

Every inch of Joey's skin heated with anger. She attempted to wiggle out of his grasp and when his hold on her tightened, her gaze flicked to the ground where the garden hose still lay running at her feet. She returned her eyes to his and slid her foot across the damp soil, her hand coming down at the same time she kicked the hose up, catching it in her grasp and blasting the icy water right in the bastard's face. "You can go to hell."

Watching as Simon jolted back, Joey flipped the switch on the hose, tossed it to her feet and stormed out of the greenhouse. She wasted no time slipping inside the manor and grabbing a set of car keys, before heading towards the garages.

She needed to speak to Nicholas, and she needed to speak to him now.

She couldn't risk calling him and having Will overhearing their exchange. Not until they figured this out—figured Simon out.

As Joey pulled out of the garage, she saw Simon trudging angrily down the driveway. She ignored her racing heart and pulled onto the main road, doing a double take as she saw Nadine parked alongside of the road in the Porsche.

What the hell are they up to?

Simon dropped into the passenger seat, next to Nadine, his eyes staring straight ahead.

"Wow." Her eyes roamed over him at the water trickling from his hair down his face and soaking into his shirt. "What the hell happened to you?"

"Just drive, Nadine."

A snicker and an eyebrow raise had Nadine reversing up the entrance to Wildridge and then driving the two of them back to Simon's office. "I'm assuming you saw Josephine then. Or was Will just in a bad mood?" Her eyes flicked to look at Simon's steely facial expression and she huffed out of her nose. "The fuck, Simon? What happened?"

Simon pushed his wet hair back and flicked the droplets of water off his fingertips. "She's a little witch."

"Well we know this, but did you convince her? Will she do it?"

Simon smirked. "Of course she will do it. I threatened her with homelessness for her father. How could she not? Give it a couple of weeks and William will be ringing me with his mind changed, trust me."

She stared ahead, an uneasiness in her stomach. "It looks to me like she doesn't give a flying fuck what you say to be honest. But whatever you say, Drippy."

"Josephine." Nicholas opened the door wider to invite her into his home. "This is a surpr—"

"They are up to something." Joey stormed past him and walked straight to his living room where she spun around with fury in her eyes. Her heart raced and her skin crawled uncomfortably with her and Simon's last encounter. "He threatened me, and he's working with Nadine, and they are up to something. I know it."

Nicholas closed the door quietly and turned to face her. "Come and sit down. I've just made a pot of tea. Wait a moment whilst I get another cup."

The two of them sat opposite each other a few minutes later, cradling hot cups of tea and Nicholas smiled at Joey. "Right. What's all this about? Simon I presume? And he threatened you? Please tell me more."

Joey fought to regulate her breathing. "He came to the manor. I was working in Diana's greenhouse when he approached me. He wants Will to sell the manor and started spewing all of these things about me messing up their plans. He demanded that I convince Will to agree to sell otherwise he'd take the house from my father. Can he? Can he do that if Will signed it over?"

Nicholas stood from his chair and moved to sit next to Joey on the sofa, patting her knee. "No. I don't know what rubbish he was talking or what he thinks that he can do, but no. It's not something that he can just forge. He's obviously putting the frighteners on you for some reason. I mean Simon will want the deal to go through; he would make a pretty penny in commission, I'm sure."

"This is true, but if it were just commission then why Nadine? Why is Simon so adamant about Green Frog?" Joey stood and walked over to the window, biting down on her lip. She needed to tell him, no matter his reaction. Turning around, she faced Nicholas and let out a heavy breath, one that she felt as though she'd been holding in since that night at the ball. "He assaulted me." She paused, waiting for Nicholas's reaction and then continued when she realised she had his full and undivided attention. "It was several months ago when Will and I had first got together. It was a business function — the ball. He had cornered me in a room and…" She couldn't force the words past the lump in her throat, but she didn't need to elaborate. The look in Nicholas's eyes told her he understood. "I never told Will. I wanted to, but I was afraid. He trusts Simon and our relationship has always been… well, let's just say it's never been easy, but I need you to trust me. They are playing Will as a fool, but he's too blind to see it." Pulling in a shaky breath, Joey crossed her arms over her chest and closed her eyes, her bottom lip trembling. "And he touched me again. Today."

Nicholas drew in a quiet breath. "You need to tell him."

"No." She shook her head adamantly. "I can't. We can't. Not until we get to the bottom of this. Will is hot-headed and impulsive; you know as well as I do that the moment he finds out it will be the end of Simon. We need to figure out what they are up to. Something tells me there is more to this, and, if there is, I'd rather see Simon put away for doing something illegal than Will being charged for assault." She paused. "Or worse. Murder."

Chapter 29

You Are The Sunshine Of My Life by Macy Gray

Every muscle weak from exhaustion, Joey trekked up the gravel path that led to the front door of the manor. The late afternoon sun bathed the grounds in its warmth, and she stood outside for a moment, basking in the spring air. As she stood there, she reached into her handbag and double checked her phone, curious as to whether Nicholas had made any attempt at calling her. Seeing as her work day had now ended, she knew the chance of him touching base with her anymore that evening was unlikely, the decision to not communicate while in the presence of Will was one they had both agreed upon.

It was better to keep things between them until they had some solid foundation to walk upon.

Stuffing her phone back in her handbag, she walked up the steps that lead to the main entrance to the manor.

As she grabbed hold of the door knob, turning it and and then pushing, her entire body flew forward as the door unexpectedly swung open at a force she wasn't anticipating.

"Damn doo—"

Strong arms broke her fall, and she lifted her head to see a chuckling Will.

"Jesus. A warning you were standing there would have been nice."

Will smoothed her hair back from her face and gave her a panty-dropping grin. "Just excited to see you." He pressed his lips to hers softly and ran his hand down her back and round to her belly where he rested the flat of his palm. "Are we all okay?"

Joey smiled and lifted up on her toes, kissing him for a second time. She'd never get enough of kissing this man. "Yes. We're all okay." She reluctantly removed herself from his hold and began to shrug off her cardigan, only to be stopped by Will.

He took hold of her shoulders, spinning her around before reaching and placing his recently removed tie over her eyes, tying it at the back of her head. He grabbed hold of her hand and walked towards the grand staircase. "Come on. I've got something to show you."

She reached up to adjust the blindfold and held on to him tightly, afraid she'd trip over her own feet at the urgency in his steps. "What are you up to?"

Will remained focused in his task of getting her up the stairs without falling on her face. "Foot up. Yep… and the next one. Keep going. Slowly does it."

Joey nearly tripped on the fourth, and a curse burst from her mouth. "Jesus, Will. Watch where the hell I'm going, will you!"

A chuckle rumbled in his chest and he stopped on the middle stair, sweeping her up into his arms to the sound of her giggles. "Come on you."

On reaching the landing, he gently placed Joey back on her feet and led her down the main corridor towards the north wing.

With her vision still obscured, Joey continued to follow Will around the quiet halls of the manor, the old wooden floor boards creaking beneath their feet. "What has gotten into you? Where are you taking me?"

They walked for what seemed like forever before he came to an abrupt stop, her front almost colliding with his back before he guided her in place. His fingers released the knot on the makeshift blindfold, and as it fell away, she stared at him with curiosity bright in her big brown eyes.

"Will, what—"

"Open the door."

She held his gaze for a few more heart beats before drawing her bottom lip between her teeth and grabbing ahold of the handle, her movements cautious this time in fear of the door flying open on her again. She gave it a slow push, her breath dying in her lungs as her eyes roamed the vacant space.

A broken chandelier hung from the ceiling, surrounded by a delicately complicated ceiling rose. The floorboards were bare, splattered with age old paint, dust and fluff sticking to the splintered wood. An old slate fireplace sat on the side wall, it's black, intricately decorative tiles cracked and chipped, and in the corner was what looked like old furniture covered in a dust cloth.

Will pushed himself into the room, jogging across to the huge bay window. "I can have the windows replaced— double glazed. The woodwork needs a good paint. I can do that. I can paint the whole room, replace the floorboards..." He moved back to the fireplace, Joey's eyes on him at all times, her lips slightly apart as he animatedly flapped his arms and hands around. "I know a man who can restore these old tiles back to their former glory, get that slate all polished. I am sure this fireplace till works." He walked over to her and cupped her face. "Come here." He led her to the corner of the room and the dust sheet, whipping it off quickly to reveal two huge boxes with *Mamas & Papas* emblazoned on the front.

Joey's jaw dropped as a gasp slipped from her mouth, her hand coming up in attempt to catch it before it completely floated free. Her gaze connected with his, and her heart felt as though it was about to burst from her chest. "Will." She shook her head, taking it all in. "What—"

He walked quickly over to the far wall. "I wanted them built before I showed you, but I just... well, I just couldn't wait." He gave her a shy smile. "I figured we could have one here." He moved his arms in parallel straight lines and then scooted to the left to do the same. "One here." Then moved again. "And we can get one of those changing things. The tables. We can hang things from the ceiling for them to look at. I mean, whatever you want. We can have it however you want it. Listen, I know it doesn't look much at the moment, but I figured—"

"Will, stop. Stop before you make my ovaries explode!"

Will did stop, a frown creasing his forehead. "What?"

Joey moved so fast she was almost a blur. She erased the distance between them and threw her arms around his neck, his coming up to wrap tightly around her waist as she crushed her lips to his. The kiss was hot and desperate, and each stroke of his tongue added more fuel to the fire burning through her veins.

Her hands moved of their own volition, pressing against his chest and pushing him until his shoulders and back collided with the far wall. She made quick work of the buttons on his shirt and then undid his belt, sliding it free from its loops.

As she tore through the button on his trousers and yanked at the zip, she broke away from his mouth and whispered against his lips. "I need you. I need you so bad."

Will's eyes darkened, and Joey's lower belly flipped at the hunger in his heated gaze. In one swift motion he spun them around, pinning her tiny frame to the wall he'd just been pressed against. He tugged at the straps of her sundress and bra, pushing them down her body and exposing her full breasts. Stubble from his beard scratched against her skin as he trailed his lips down her throat, his thumbs sweeping over her sensitive nipples. Joey's back arched at his touch, and Will's head descended, his lips and tongue nipping and sucking, caressing a path of fire over every naked inch.

Joey's senses were overwhelmed. She was surrounded by him. His scent, his hardness, his strength. He was her everything, and she felt as if she might physically combust if he didn't move this along faster.

She needed him, and she needed him now.

Reaching between them, she slipped her hand beneath the waistband of his boxers and wrapped her fingers around his erection, stroking him from base to tip. She spoke against his mouth, her voice coming in between pants. "Fuck me, Will. Please fuck me."

In answer, Will growled and shoved her hand away. He pressed his body deeper into hers and as he ground against her, he lifted his head to kiss her again. The kiss was harder and wetter, much more out of control. She instantly curled herself around him, fisting the hair at the back of his neck as she danced her tongue with his.

Without warning, Will dragged his palms slowly up her thighs and under her dress, pushing it up around her waist and then cupping her heat and trailing his thumb down her wet centre. He moved the lace aside and grazed the throbbing bundle of nerves. "Are you ready for me, baby?"

Her chance to respond was stolen by the drive of his hand, a whimper parting her lips as her head fell against his shoulder. "Oh, God..." Joey clutched his arms for support, and as Will continued to fuck her with his fingers—tension coiling at an unrelenting pace—her breathy pants and moans spurred him on. The need to be buried inside her had him impatiently gripping the fabric of her knickers and he tugged, hard, wanting to remove them from her hips but unintentionally ripping the material.

"Shit. I'm sorry."

At the sound, Joey laughed. "Jesus, you have to stop doing that. I'm not going to have any clothes left to wear."

He grinned wickedly against her lips, letting them fall to the floor before releasing himself from the restricting confines of his trousers, and then lifted her leg. In one deep and breath-stealing thrust, he slammed into her. They both gasped in unison, Joey at the feel of his thickness and Will at the feel of her tight heat surrounding him.

He held still, his chest heaving as if he was attempting to regain some control, and after another moment, he found a pleasurable rhythm for the both of them.

Joey's nails bit into the skin on his shoulders, a thin layer of perspiration collecting on their flesh as they gave in to each other, their hearts erratic and their bodies connected as one. Will pounded her into the wall, his hips gliding with increasing frenzy, and it wasn't long before Joey was moaning out her climax. Her muscles clenched tightly around him, gripping with the right amount of pressure, and Will grunted as his own release whipped through him, spreading from his dick, down his legs and to the tips of is toes.

Languid and weak, Joey's body collapsed against him. She buried her face deep in his neck, the scent of their love making coating his sweat-slicked skin. "God, I love you."

The world slowly came back to them as the euphoria from their orgasms faded, and Will pressed his forehead to Joey's, kissing her gently before pulling away. He grinned down at her. "So what do you say we build some cots?"

"Good God, man. Can I have a minute? Pregnant lady here!"

"My pregnant lady." Will's eyes glowed with post-coital bliss and a heartful of love, and Joey's heart flipped as she lost herself in them. They had come so far in such a short space of time, and there were days when she wondered if it were all too good to be true, but being here with Will, with him looking at her like that, she knew without a doubt that it was one hundred percent real. There was no faking how he felt for her, and vice versa.

The fairytale was playing out and she was slap bang in the middle of it.

She ran the tips of her fingers across his brow, down the side of his face and across his lips, drinking him in and committing the moment to memory. She was going to hold on with both hands as tightly as she could and never let go.

" Let me go get changed and grab something to eat. I'm starving."

He kissed her softly and backed away, heading towards the boxed cots in the corner of the room. "Order Chinese food and have Graham bring it up when it arrives. We might be here a while." He grinned at her over his shoulder and bent at the waist to pick the first one up, moving it to a space on the floor before crouching beside it to pull it open.

By the time Joey got back, the box was empty, there were wooden posts and slats all over the floor and Will was sitting cross-legged with a screwdriver in one hand and a metal rod in the other.

"All okay?" She plonked herself next to him, reaching over to grab the sheet of instructions that lay untouched in their plastic cover. "You might want to have a look at these."

"Nah." Will's eyes scanned the parts. "Pass me that bit there, please."

"This bit?"

"No, that one."

"Which one?"

"There. The long one."

"This one?"

"Woman. The long wooden one."

"This *is* the long wooden one."

"Jesus." Will leaned forwards over her lap and grabbed an almost identical piece of wood.

"Oh that one." She glanced at him and watched his pursed lips twitch as the cogs in his clever brain whirred and clanked. He began screwing the pole to the wood and

Joey glanced down at the paper in her lap, carefully but discreetly pulling it out of the plastic covering. She flicked it open to the first page, frowning as she looked at the diagram and then over to what Will was putting together. "Um, Will? I'm not sure—"

"Shhh. I need to concentrate."

She shrugged and flipped a page or two ahead, taking mental stock of all the pieces and matching them to the other diagrams.

Will lifted up the two pieces he had screwed together, held the box so he could see the photograph on the front and then reached for more bits. "Are you just going to sit there judging or are you going to help? I can feel you watching me, Miss Bell, and I can feel the criticisms on your tongue."

Joey chuckled. "I just think you should use the instructions."

"I don't need bloody instructions. It's just a cot. It's not rocket science."

He screwed more pieces together and held up the frame. "There. See."

"It's wrong."

Will rolled his eyes. "It's not wrong. It's exactly as it is on the box."

"Sweetheart. I love you. I admire you. I think you are the most cleverest businessman I have ever met, and I am not for one second insulting your intelligence, but you are wrong. It is wrong."

Will looked at her for a long time, his eyes narrowing, before whipping the instructions out of her hands. He flipped back to the start, compared it to his own work and then inhaled deeply through his nose. "Smart arse."

Joey laughed and took the frame from him, unscrewing what he had done whilst he collected the correct bits from the floor. "So how do you feel about Esmeralda as a name? For a girl of course."

"Good Lord, no. Esmeralda Marshall-Croft? Sounds like some sort of prostitute."

"Will!" She slapped his arm and huffed. "I just thought Esme for short was cute."

"Well why have Esmeralda, why not just Esme? Anyway, what's wrong with just bog standard names like, Jane. Or Elizabeth?"

Joey silently held out the piece she knew he would be looking for next as he finished tightening a screw. "Nothing. I'm just throwing ideas out there. I kinda feel like we should have some idea soon so we can test them out and get a feel for them, y'know? A name is so important. These babies will be stuck with whatever we give them for the rest of their lives. We need to choose carefully."

"Exactly. So no Esmeralda." Will kissed her cheek and grinned. "Anyway. I think we will be having twin boys. Peter and Paul."

Joey jumped as her phone began to ring and vibrate in her cardigan pocket. She fumbled around, pulling it out and answering the call. "Hey, Emma."

Will worked silently beside her for a minute or two but when he heard her sharp intake of breath and saw her hand fly to cover her mouth and stifle a sob, he stopped everything, pushed onto his knees and sat in front of her, his eyes holding hers as they filled with tears.

"I'll be right there."

Will frowned in question.

Joey blinked as she dragged the phone from her ear to let it fall in her lap, a tear following its descent. Her voice wobbled and her hands shook. "It's Dad. We need to go. Now."

Chapter 30

Not Alone by Red

"He's a little bumped and bruised from the fall and he's shaken up." The doctor took long strides up the corridor towards the cubicle where John was resting and Will and Joey followed quickly behind him.

"But he's okay? Right? Everything is okay?" The panic in Joey's voice was palpable, and Will squeezed her hand supportively.

"He has some internal bleeding and we are in the process of checking him over now, but he is comfortable. He's in the best place."

The three of them arrived at the last cubicle on the right and the doctor stopped abruptly. "Here we are." He reached up and pulled the curtain back swiftly to reveal an agitated Little John, clutching at his chest, his skin clammy and grey.

Everything happened at once.

A loud buzzer sounded and the doctor rushed inside.

Everyone's voices echoed in Joey's ears like she was underwater. The words 'cardiac arrest' rang around her head, piercing her thoughts, and the sudden rushing of new bodies that knocked into her seemed to be a never-ending stream.

Her mouth opened and her eyes flicked to those of the nurse, trying to read her expression and time seemed to slow to a halt in the seconds that followed.

"Get them out of here!"

The curtain was swished around the cubicle again, shutting them out—closing them off to the horrors that were unfolding—and it was then that her knees gave way.

"Shit." Will's hands caught underneath her arm pits, stopping her from hitting the floor before she finally found her voice. A high-pitched scream shot from the back of her throat as she begged for them to let her go to her father.

She was mildly aware of Emma's presence as she wrapped her arm around her shoulder and helped Will to haul her out of the way.

"Let me go! Please let me go!"

She continued to kick and scream, her small frame bucking frantically as she fought Will's strong hold. "Jesus Christ, Will. Let me go!" Hot tears streamed down her face. "Let me go!"

Will's heart beat wildly as he tried to keep it together.

What the fuck was going on?

Joey wriggled in his hands, her new-found strength almost too much for him to control, and so in one swift movement, he scooped her legs from under her and carried her down the corridor, wincing as she beat at his chest with her fists.

"Emma. Go and get drinks." His voice was gruff, angry, demanding, and Emma scuttled off obediently.

Once out into the waiting area, Will marched to the reception desk with a sobbing Joey still in his arms. "I need a room. Now. Tell me where I can take her."

"I'm sorry, Mr—"

"I said now. I am not here to bargain. Look at her. Find me somewhere private to go, immediately."

The young nurse nodded and stood to her feet. "One minute."

As she darted off, Emma returned to Will's side with paper cups. Her hands shook with emotion and Will closed his eyes before drawing in a deep breath and taking one from her. "Thank you. Go and sit down. I'll come and get you once I have Joey sorted."

Emma nodded and moved gratefully towards the seating area and watched as Will took charge of the situation, walking quickly behind the nurse who had returned to take him somewhere quiet.

On entering the small room, Will set Joey down on a plastic chair, handing her the cup of tea and crouching in front of her. A sense of deja vu washed over him as he remembered the last time they were in this very hospital. So much had happened since and he was struggling to come to grips with the situation they now found themselves in. Reaching up, he cupped Joey's cheek and dragged his thumb under her eye to catch the tears that continued to chase each other down her face. "I'm going to find out what's going on. Okay? I'll send Emma in to sit with you. You must stay here, Joey. Okay? You have to stay in this room."

Joey nodded, her legs ready to haul arse back to her father's cubicle, but she knew she needed to let Will handle this, and so she slumped back in her chair, numbly staring at the wall and sipping on the tea.

Standing to his feet, Will leaned over and pressed a firm, hope-filled kiss to the top of Joey's head before he walked with trepidation and purpose out of the room and into the waiting area again. He instructed Emma to take his place with Joey, and then he set off to find some answers.

The call that Joey had received not even two hours before had let her know that John had fallen as he was coming down the stairs. His slipper had slid off his foot, causing him to lose his balance and he had tumbled down the final four stairs. Will was no expert, but he certainly hadn't expected a critical situation because of a mere fall.

He waited impatiently behind an elderly woman and, who he presumed to be, her daughter as they spoke to the receptionist about their reason for visiting. He pulled his phone out of his back pocket and quickly shot a text message off to Bea and Graham, letting them know where they were, and then, upon reaching the reception desk, he snapped into gear and began asking questions.

"I'm here to find out about Mr John Bell. He was brought in here a couple of hours ago after a bit of a fall, and then twenty minutes ago I believe he went into cardiac arrest."

The nurse smiled up at him. "I'm sorry, but if he has already been seen by the triage doctor, we won't know anything until the information is passed to us."

Will inhaled silently and clenched down on his back teeth. "Miss," he squinted at the badge on the young woman's uniform, "Turner. You seem not to have heard me correctly. I'm here to find out. I need to know what is happening to him, where he is and what the bloody hell is going on. If you don't have the information here, then I require that you get up and go find it out. My fiance is beside herself with worry because she has no idea if her father is going to be okay. She is four months pregnant and I do *not* need her stressed. Do you understand? I need something to tell her—something to reassure her that everything *is* going to be okay. Okay?"

The nurse blinked and nodded before getting to her feet and complying with Will's demands for a second time in half an hour. She moved into the back and began talking to an older woman who promptly came out, her face pinched and stern. "Hi there. If you could take a seat, someone will be along shortly to give you the information that you require."

Will placed the heels of his hands on top of the counter, pushing himself back and dropping his head between his shoulders. He let out an exaggerated sigh before standing to his full height, leaning over and pinning the nurse with his stare. "I shall go and find out for myself." He pushed back again and began to stride through the waiting area in the direction of the cubicle that they had left John in, the sound of the nurse calling him back a mere irritation in his head.

He reached the double doors and held his breath as he pushed through them and began a nerve wracking journey to the last cubicle on the right.

He didn't even get halfway up the corridor before he was stopped in his tracks. His eyes had remained carefully trained on the tiles, but movement from the top corner had him slowing, and then stopping.

The doctor who had walked the two of them up this same corridor was slipping out from behind the curtain, a clipboard in hand, his sleeves rolled up and sweat dotting his brow.

Will swallowed as the doctor lifted his eyes to meet his own and he didn't miss the nervous bob of the guy's Adam's apple.

Fuck.

He was rooted to the spot, unable to take another step, and so he waited until the doctor reached him. He waited with his arms limp by his sides and his chest heaving with emotion.

"I was just on my way to see you and John's daughter. I'm so sorry—I didn't catch your names before."

Will licked his lips. "It's William. William and Josephine."

"Is she…" He pointed towards the waiting room.

Will shook his head. "No, she erm… she's in a room back there somewhere. I um…"

"Okay. Can you take me to her?"

"Just tell me." Will's voice was barely a whisper. He slipped his hands into his pockets and hung his head. "Please just tell me so I can go to her."

"William, I —"

"I want to tell her." He looked up at the doctor, imploring him. "Please. She's pregnant. I need to be the one to tell her."

The doctor held Will's eyes for a moment before nodding and glancing down at the clipboard in his hand. "Do you want to sit down somewhere?"

"No." Will moved towards the wall and leaned against it.

"Okay. So, John suffered a nasty fall. He tumbled down a good four stairs and in the process incurred internal bleeding in his chest. It's what we call Hemothorax: a collection of blood in the space between the chest wall and the lung — the pleural cavity." He looked up at Will whose head had fallen back against the wall and who was now staring at the ceiling. "There was a lot of bleeding, William, and the pressure of such meant that John's lung collapsed. We inserted a chest tube through the chest wall to drain the blood. In normal circumstances, we would leave that in place for several days to re-expand the lung. Like I said, though, there was a lot of bleeding, so John's heart was also essentially squeezed due to the build up and couldn't re-fill with blood very well. As a result, there wasn't enough blood to pump to the rest of the body. John went into cardiac arrest: that's what you witnessed when we arrived." The doctor placed his hand on Will's shoulder. "We couldn't revive him, William. We did all that we could, but he just didn't respond to CPR or the defib."

He wasn't sure if he had any control over his limbs, but Will began to slide down the wall until he was crouched with his head in his hands. His mind was blank, and his heart hurt.

"I'm so sorry, William. I'll give you some time, and then I'll come back to chat to you both."

Will listened to the doctor's footsteps as they retreated down the corridor and then pushed to his feet. He pinched the bridge of his nose and headed slowly back to where he had come from—he headed back to the love of his life so that he could tell her that her beloved father was dead.

The clock on the wall ticked as Joey sat in a state of unknown, her heart anything but steady and her veins laden with panic and fear. What was taking so long? Where had Will gone and why wasn't he back yet? She glanced up at the dreaded clock, watching as the hand moved round and round. Her knee bounced, a result of the nerves swishing anxiously in her stomach, and she stood, rubbing her hands together before pushing them through her tear-soaked hair. The brown strands clung to her wet cheeks, and her throat had shrunk in size over the last fifteen minutes, making it impossible to breathe.

Her gaze bounced to Emma, who seemed just as distraught as she, and she bit down on her bottom lip, her teeth sinking into the soft flesh so hard it nearly drew blood. Every part of her was desperate to walk out of the door and demand answers, but she'd made a silent promise to Will that she'd remain. She had to remain because emotionally, she was a wreck. She was in no state to deal with the doctors and nurses who had pushed past them to tend to her father, yelling words that became nothing more than muffled sounds behind the blood whooshing loudly in her ears.

So she paced.

And paced.

And paced.

Her heart squeezed painfully in her chest, her lungs burning with her inability to fill them properly, and she waited.

She waited for what felt like an eternity, her mind occupied with tumultuous thoughts, before the door creaked open.

Joey halted in her steps, scared to turn around—scared to look at his face. She didn't want to know what he had to say because not knowing meant there was still a possibility that everything would be okay.

Will's footsteps were quiet and they halted just after they entered the room. She could tell he was standing there, waiting—waiting for her to look at him.

She caught Emma's eyes that flicked over to Will and back again, giving away nothing, and in a moment of desperation, Joey turned.

One look in Will's eyes had her whole body crumpling, her face contorting. He didn't need to say a word. Everything she had been dreading was written across his forlorn expression, in the way he hung his head and the way his mouth twitched with emotion. For the second time in the space of a couple of hours, she dropped to the floor, her knees giving way beneath her as her whole world fell apart.

Within a split second, Will was on the floor with her, pulling her into his chest, wrapping his arms around her shaking body and smoothing his hands down her back. He rested his chin on top of her head, training his eyes on a crack in the ceiling as he concentrated on keeping his breathing calm. And as the love of his life fell apart in his arms, he listened to her silent cry of despair and allowed a single tear to trickle down his cheek for her—for her broken heart.

Chapter 31

A Place Near By by Lene Marlin

Dressed in a black suit, an untied tie hanging around his neck and his top button open, Will stormed the top north wing corridor, stopping to hang over the balcony, his eyes scanning the floor below. "Where the hell is he?"

Graham looked up to where Will's voice had come from. "Who, sir?"

"Paul." Will pulled back and jogged quickly down the stairs. "He was meant to be here half an hour ago. Where the fuck is he?"

Graham quickly fell into step alongside him, their hasty steps matching stride for stride. He checked his watch and pulled his mobile phone out of his pocket. "I'll give him a call." As he scrolled through his contacts and found Paul's number, he slowed to a stop allowing Will to march on ahead in search of his next victim.

The whole house was on edge.

There was a buzz of nervous energy that bounced off the walls as everyone scurried around at Will's command.

There was still plenty of time before the cars were scheduled to leave for the church, but Will wanted everything perfect. He didn't want to be rushing at the last minute, and he didn't want Joey worrying about a single detail.

As Will stepped into the entrance hall, the huge oak front door swung open and a bumbling, apologetic Paul burst through.

"I'm sorry. I'm so sorry. Sue's car wouldn't start, the kids needed to be taken to nursery... it was just really bad timing."

"I'm not interested in fucking excuses, Paul. The cars need washing and waxing. You have precisely an hour before we leave. I want the Merc and the Bentley. I want —
" Will stopped and turned his head to see Danny walking up the driveway in much the same attire as himself. "Watson. Nice of you to join us. Is she ready?" He jogged down the steps to meet him on the path between the house and the stables. "The answer I'm waiting for is 'yes'."

"Not yet. She will be though. I want to go and check on Joey first. I haven't seen her and I want to — "

"Sorry, what? Go and get Roya ready. It's not a request, Danny." Will turned to reenter the house but was stopped by a retort that had him swinging back around. His temper was frayed and he was not in the mood for insolent members of staff.

"I am going to see Joey." Danny shook off his boss's demands and attempted to make his way towards the house, his legs moving in long and measured strides as he brushed past a now fuming Will.

Will's whole body lit up with anger, his muscles tightening and his heart thrumming furiously. "Don't even fucking think about it. Do not take even one more step towards my house. You don't get to decide how today goes. Get the fuck back here right now."

Danny halted in his tracks, turning to face the man he had gained some respect for over the last few months. "You need to calm the fuck down, Will. Okay? Calm the fuck down. Walking around here, screaming and yelling like some Goddamn tyrant isn't going to make this any easier for her." The muscle in his jaw ticked and his hands clenched into fists to prevent him from doing something stupid—like knocking some sense into this guy. He knew the amount of stress resting on Will's shoulders was anything but an easy weight to bear, but he needed him to snap out of the downward spiral he was quickly losing himself in. "She needs you, man. Pull your shit together, would you? For her."

Will clenched his back teeth together, ready to fly off the handle at Danny again, but was stopped mid-thought by the sound of tyres on gravel. He turned his head to see the long, black hearse crawling up the driveaway towards him. It came to a stop and Will sucked in a breath, holding it high in his chest as his eyes found the windows that ran the length of the car. Inside was a mahogany casket, hand-picked by himself, and he felt his throat constrict. However, it was the flowers and wreaths that had him doing an about turn, striding into the house. This whole ordeal had had him on autopilot for the past week, but seeing the car had his mind careening into a dark tunnel that took him back to being a fourteen year old boy.

Will pushed his way through the front door, moving quickly towards the north wing and straight to the drinks cabinet in his sitting room. He couldn't do this. He couldn't walk out there again and be strong. It was too painful and he would only let her down. Doubt reared its ugly head, sneering and jeering at him for all his mistakes—past and present—telling him he was still not good enough and still not worthy of happiness. He reached for the whiskey, not even bothering with a glass, and after uncapping it, he tipped his head back to let the liquid trickle down his throat. His breathing laboured and his heart still racing, Will slumped into the nearest chair before taking another swig.

Would he ever be free of the shackles of his past? Would he ever be able to manage his emotions instead of living in fear of the day when he would snap and lose all control again in front of her? This was why he should have stayed away, no matter how much his heart had yearned for her. He was dangerously on the edge with no idea what might give him that final push.

And then it happened.

It came from nowhere but it came fast and furious.

Pull yourself together, Will. This is not about you anymore.

He shook his head, the realisation that the only person who was stopping him from being the man Joey deserved was himself. He stood up, hurling the bottle at the wall and letting out a war cry like no other as a promise to Joey, but more importantly to himself, that he was going to fight even harder. He would no longer allow his past to define him. He would battle and fight for his happy ever after because, damnit, he loved her and he deserved her for that fact alone. A strength like he'd never felt before burst through his chest, grabbing a hold of him and shaking him back to the present as he stormed back into the entrance hall.

"Bea." His voice boomed again, loud and authoritative, and his body followed the noise of it towards the kitchen. "Beatrice." He burst through the door and scanned the room quickly to locate the cook. "Is everything ready? The sandwiches? Cakes? Drinks?"

Beatrice turned slowly towards him, wiping her hands on her apron that today was hiding a long black dress instead of her usual attire. "Not quite dear, but don't worry: it will all be ready by the time it needs to be."

Will pushed his fingers through his hair and sighed. "I wanted it all done before we leave. I want everything to be stress free. She doesn't need to be worrying about anything." He pulled at the tie that still hung loosely around his neck, crossing and looping it with not much concentration. "She's pregnant, she's a mess and I want her to just be able to go and come back without—" He yanked at his tie angrily, pulling it off and starting again. "Just please have everything sorted. Please don't leave anything until we get home." He moved to the window, attempting again to get his tie into a smart Windsor knot. As he did so, he stared at his reflection, clenching his back teeth together as he tried to see the new, stronger man who stared back at him.

Why? Why would this happen to them? Joey deserved more than the shit that life had thrown at her so far; why had it been necessary to deal this final blow? Did she not deserve a fucking break?

Bea walked around the island and came to a stop behind him. "You need to stop, William. You have this in hand just the way I knew you would. Everything will be ready, everything will be where it needs to be, and you can concentrate on being the rock that Joey is going to need today." She urged him to turn around with a gentle hand on his shoulder and took his tie from him, swiftly and neatly doing it up as she continued to talk. "Have a little faith in all of us, please? Trust that we can do our jobs and do them well, and then you concentrate on looking after our girl. Do you think you can do that?"

Will's eyes were trained on Bea's nimble fingers and she pulled the end of his tie in the last step before she tightened it gently at his throat. She patted his chest and smoothed her palms down the lapels of his black suit. "I've always been so incredibly proud of you, my darling, but today, my heart is bursting it is so full. Look at you, rising to the occasion and showing your true colours—showing everyone what a fantastically wonderful man you are. You have had to contend with so much heartache, yet you still stand so tall and strong. Joey is lucky to have you, William. Now go. Go and see that she is okay."

Will caught hold of Bea's hands on their way back to her sides and squeezed them in his own. "Thank you." He kissed the top of her head and headed out of the kitchen to the North Wing where he and Joey spent most of their time together when they were home—headed up the stairs to support his fiance on the most difficult day of her life so far: the day she would bury her father.

There was no sound coming from their bedroom, and Will stood outside the door for a moment, anxious and worried about the Joey he would find inside. John's death had broken her. She was a mere shadow of her usual full-of-life self, and Will was struggling to find the Joey he loved so much in the shell that had been left behind.

Pushing the door gently, he stepped inside the still-dark room and watched her for a second or two. She was sitting on the edge of the bed, her fingers tangled together in her lap, her empty eyes staring at the wall opposite her. She wasn't showered, wasn't dressed and certainly wasn't ready to leave the house in twenty minutes.

He walked into the room and sat down next to her, picking up one of her hands and smoothing his knuckles over the back of it. His eyes remained trained on it, and he worked hard to keep his breathing even and steady.

"Hey." His eyes moved to the side to look at her. "We need to get you ready, beautiful. You think you can manage to get yourself dressed?"

Josephine didn't even blink. She continued to stare ahead, the only thing to move being her fingertips against Will's palm.

"We can fix your hair so that you don't need to wash it if you'd like. I can help you."

Still nothing.

Will's head dipped a little. He was desperate to get through to her. He was desperate for her to start grieving. Anything would be better than this silence that was hiding her away from him.

"I'll get you some clean underwear." He stood up and moved solemnly towards her drawers, pulling out a black bra and matching pants. He inhaled deeply and then turned back towards her.

Gently helping her to her feet, he lifted the hem of her pyjama top, pulling the garment up and over her head. She was compliant, utterly, like a lifeless doll, and it was breaking his heart to not have her fight him off or crack some wise remark about her being capable of dressing herself.

Slipping the straps of her bra onto her arms, he moved behind her, ensured the cups sat comfortably over her breasts and then fastened the clasp at her back. After encouraging her to sit back down, he worked just as deftly and just as gently until her pyjama bottoms were off and her pants were on. He sprayed a little perfume at her neck and lifted her arms to roll on some deodorant before manipulating her into her dress.

"Which shoes?" He didn't wait for a reply, the rhetorical question hanging there as he searched the shoe-rack for a pair of black flats.

A few minutes later and she was ready to go, aside from her hair which hung in limp, greasy strands over her shoulders. Will scrubbed his hands down his face, located a bobble, some kirby grips and her brush and set about trying to make her look a little more presentable. He crouched in front of her and was all fingers and thumbs at first, but it didn't take long before Joey's hair was scraped back into a sleek ponytail. Will placed his hand on her swelling stomach and held it there for a moment before standing to his feet and slipping his hands into his pockets. "Time to go."

"Time to go." Will squeezed hold of Joey's hand, the pair of them soaked to the skin from the relentless rain that had so thoughtfully decided to fall that morning. The ground underfoot was muddy and wet, and umbrellas had proved pointless due to the unusually high winds. The pair of them stood at the freshly dug grave, John's body now lowered inside. Everyone else had gone: Danny had stepped up as chauffeur taking Graham and Bea back to the manor to ensure everything was in order for the funeral tea that was to follow, taking Emma and Nicholas with them. Other members of family and friends had also dispersed after paying their respects.

Joey had remained silent and numb throughout, and as they stood side by side, Will was convinced that she would remain this way forever. He was scared that he had lost her to her despair and that bringing her back to him was an insurmountable challenge.

He turned his body as if to walk away, expecting her to follow him like the obedient puppet she had become. She had spent the last five days on autopilot, following the gentle directions of the people who loved her in order to get through each day without so much as nod of the head. So when he began to guide her away from the graveside, he was not in the least bit ready for her resistance as she dropped to the ground, her knees falling into the mud and her hands reaching in to grasp at the wooden coffin.

Another fissure cracked through Joey's already shattered heart, and as the pain poured out, numbing every muscle and limb, she forced her lungs to breathe through her heartbreak. Tears rolled in jagged lines down her cheeks, mixing with the still-falling rain, and she remained on her knees, watching as her entire world faded before her eyes.

Her father had been her everything.

Everything that she had done had been to help him, to protect him, and now he was gone.

He was gone.

"It was just a fall." She choked on a sob, her throat feeling as if it were caught in a vice grip. "It was just a goddamn fall! How can he be gone? How can he..." She fought to pull air into her lungs, but it got caught on the journey there, causing her to splutter on her next words. "I didn't even get to say goodbye."

Will wasted no time in scooping her up from the cold ground and lifting her into his arms. Together they stood there in the pouring rain, Joey cradled against his chest, as he kissed her forehead, soothing her with his silence while he thanked God that she was still in there somewhere.

Chapter 32

Lighthouse by Callum Graham

Will opened the car door and helped a bedraggled, muddy and tear and rain soaked Joey out. She clung to Will's arm, as he supported her fragile form, weak and tired from the emotion she was burdened with.

On arriving into the house, Will dropped her hand and turned around to close the door.

Joey stood still, her eyes roaming around the place.

Despite the dark clouds and the rain pouring down outside, everything was so bright. The light poured in through the windows, and without giving it much thought, she walked over to the first one, her fingers curling around the thick velvet fabric and hesitating for only a moment before she yanked them shut. The sudden shade of darkness was like a mask, a reprieve of everything she didn't want to feel, and so she moved to the next one, grabbing hold of the material and blocking out the light.

Hearing the sound of the curtain rings dragging across the brass poles, Will turned to see Joey moving into the corridor to grab another set of curtains.

"Joey?" He walked towards her, noticing the closed curtains in the entrance hall and dragging them open as he passed them. "Josephine, what are you doing? It's the middle of the day."

She frowned, casting him a look that revealed every corner of her broken heart. "It's too bright in here." She turned back to the curtains she'd just closed, her fingers clenching tightly around the fabric until her knuckles turned blanch white, and then moved. With an urgency in each step, she continued to work her way down the hall, shutting out what remained of the sun, shutting out what remained of the pain. "It's too goddamn bright."

Will followed her, undoing her work, opening each set of curtains with a yank. "Please stop." He moved towards her. "Just come here and stop. Come and talk to me, Joey."

"I don't want to talk, Will. I don't want to talk." Joey lengthened her strides, her pace faster still, not caring that Will was quick on her heels, letting the light back in. She was blinded by her own emotions, the heart-wrenching pain that she didn't know how to begin to handle, let alone soothe, and she carried on with her mission, doing her best to shut out the world and all the turmoil it brought with it. She was so wrapped up in her need to close it all off that when Will caught up with her—wrapping his hand around her wrist to stop her from running—she didn't realise she had pushed him away, shoved him hard in his chest with a cry of *leave me alone*, until she saw the look of hurt and rejection in his eyes as he stumbled back from her.

God no. She didn't want to hurt him.

She knew he was only trying to help, but she was broken, tattered, torn. She didn't know how to deal with any of this.

The corners of her eyes burned with fresh tears, and as they spilled down her cheeks, she crumbled to the floor in defeat. "I don't want to feel. It hurts too much to feel."

Will walked forwards, a painful knot in his stomach, crouching and lifting Joey into his arms. "I know. I know."

As she clutched at his shirt, he carried her up the grand staircase and down to the north wing where he kicked open the door to the bathroom. On reaching the huge roll-top bath, and with Joey still in his arms, he reached over and turned on the hot tap, bending at the knee to drop the plug into the plughole. He reached behind the toilet to the windowsill where he plucked a bottle of bubble bath, pouring a generous amount of the lilac-smelling liquid under the running water. Sitting down on the toilet seat, he manoeuvered her onto his lap, stripping her out of the clothes that he had dressed her in only a few hours before.

Once the bath was filled, he helped her to step in and watched as she sank into the hot, bubbly water. He flicked the lever and turned the tap on again, bringing the showerhead to soak her hair before shampooing it and then gently washing her skin clean of the grime from the day. After rinsing her hair clean of the suds and combing throgh it gently, he sood to his feet.

"I'm going to go get you a towel and to show my face downstairs with the guests. I'll tell Bea you're not going down to join them. You need to sleep: you're exhausted. I'll be back in a few minutes okay? Relax for a bit." Will ran his hand down the back of her head, his thumb coming around to stroke the apple of her cheek before leaving the bathroom.

Not ten minutes later, he returned with a fluffy white towel and held out his hand for her to take while she stepped out of the bath. He wrapped her up in it and once again picked her up, carrying her to the bedroom for her to get ready.

Joey moved methodically over to the dresser, pulling out a pair of pyjamas before slipping into them and wrapping a towel around her wet hair. She felt marginally better, at least in the sense that she was now clean and free of the cold wet and muddy clothes that had clung to her body, but Will was right: she was exhausted, emotionally and physically, and even she wondered if she'd ever be free from the agonising hell she found herself in.

Not daring to look in the mirror and see her sad reflection staring back at her, Joey turned and walked the few steps to the bed she shared with Will and crawled to her usual spot. She slipped beneath the duvet, pulling it up to her chin, and released a sigh that offered little relief.

Will was beside her in seconds, his warm lips pressing against her forehead in a tender kiss. He ran a gentle hand down the side of her cheek, his eyes holding hers in a cradle of understanding and support. "Sleep. I'll come and check on you a little later." His hand lingered for a few more moments, and as he went to pull away, to make his departure, Joey stopped him.

She grabbed hold of his hand, keeping him in place. "Stay. Please. I don't want to be alone."

Will wasted no time in climbing over her, lying down beside her and pulling her into him. He had been longing for the moment when she would wake from her nightmare and need him again, and his heart beat a little steadier when she nestled under his chin and wrapped her arm around him before falling soundly asleep.

A gentle knocking on the bedroom door had Joey and Will stirring in their sleep. Will pushed up onto his elbow and rubbed his eye with the heel of his hand before glancing at the clock to see that it was four in the afternoon. "Shit."

Another knock, this time louder, had him sitting up. "Come in."

The door opened slowly revealing Bea and a tray of food and drinks. "I thought you might both be hungry."

The sound of Bea's voice caused Joey's eyelids to flutter open and Will turned to smile at her. "Hey." He stroked the back of his fingers down her cheek. "Hungry?"

Joey gave a small shake of her head. "No. But thank you, Bea."

Bea's mouth pulled into a thin line. "I'll just leave it here then in case you change your mind." She placed the tray on the bedside table before leaning over to kiss Joey's forehead. "I love you, sweet girl." She stood up and left the room, closing the door behind her.

Will sat up against the headboard. "You really should eat something." He picked up her hand and planted a kiss in the middle of her palm. Y'know… I know this is heartbreaking for you, and I am not for one second trying to trivialise your pain—I of all people know what grief can do to you—but there's not just you to think about. I'm worried about you not being strong enough. I'm worried about the babies. Will you try to eat something? For them?"

Joey shifted to face him, a weary sigh floating from her chest. "You're right, and I know I need to eat for them, but I just feel sick to my stomach. This isn't easy, and I don't know how to get by without him. I didn't even get to say goodbye, Will." Her chin trembled and she pulled in a breath, blowing it out quickly to try to control her emotions. Tears fell, and she swiped them away. "How can he be gone? How could he be fine and then just gone?"

Reaching over to the tray, Will picked up a sandwich and put it on a plate, moving back to his position next to her and placing it on her lap. "I know. I know how hard this is. I promise I do."

Joey stared down at the food in front of her, not wanting to eat it but not wanting to disappoint him. She picked at the sandwich, tearing a tiny piece off and popping it into her mouth, rolling it around on her tongue while she continued to talk. "Growing up it was just the two of us, and now he's not here. He's not here to see our wedding or walk me down the aisle. He's not here to see and meet his grandchildren." The tears fell harder and she pushed the plate away, feeling like she was going to be sick. "I can't do this, Will. I don't know how to do this. He was all I had."

Her words made him wince a little internally before he shook them off, knowing that Joey wouldn't have said them to hurt him. "He was not all you had. You have me. I am yours to keep. Forever. For longer if you will have me. You have the babies. They are going to be your pride and joy and I have no doubt that your dad will live on in both of them." He slipped his arm around her shoulders and inhaled deeply. "You know, when… when my mum died" — he squeezed his eyes closed tightly, fighting through the painful memories of that day for Joey — "I spent so long not allowing myself to think of her — not allowing myself to remember who she was and the good times we'd had. I lived my life pushing everything about her away and only allowing myself to remember that dreadful day, punishing myself for my recklessness. And I regret that now. Because of you, because of your love, I have started to push my past away and I only wish I had memories of my mother to replace it, but they've faded too much now. I can barely remember what her voice sounded like anymore. I don't want you going through life like that. Eventually, this pain you're feeling, will subside and you will be left with wonderful memories that you will laugh about and talk about freely with me and our children, and your dad will always — *always* — be with you. He is in your heart, Joey. He is in you and he will be in our little ones." Will picked up the remaining bits of sandwich and handed them to her. "So please. Eat so you are strong enough to carry these babies and strong enough to tell them all about their wonderful grandpa."

Joey cupped Will's cheek, running her thumb down his jaw and across his lips, her gaze following the same path. "I love you."

"And I love you, future Mrs Marshall-Croft." He kissed her lips softly and sat back as she finished her food.

Chapter 33

"Pick up the fucking phone, Nadi—where the fuck have you been?"

"Well hello to you too."

Simon ran his fingertips across his forehead. "We have a fucking problem."

"Why doesn't that surprise me? This whole thing has been problem after problem. What the hell has happened now?"

"You're going to have to sweet-talk David; get him to hold—get him to wait some more."

An irritated sigh floated down the telephone line. "He's already got itchy feet, Simon. He's ready to pull out and look elsewhere. I don't know how you think I'm going to change his mind at this point in time. He's been waiting for months for Will to make up his mind. What do you want me to do?"

"I'm sure your hot arse can think of something."

"You're not my pimp, you slime. He's hardly going to make me partner if I lower my standards, is he."

"Well how do I know how you ended up in the running, huh? For all I know, that's how you got him to notice you in the first place."

Nadine huffed out a sarcastic laugh. "You might want to watch your mouth, otherwise your share in this imminent bonus and promotion might just find itself rammed up your—"

"He's dead."

"What? How? Jesus… Who does the manor go to?"

"Not Will, you stupid cow. The dad. Cinderella's dad."

"Oh…" Nadine sat down in her office chair, allowing it to spin her around gently. "Well that's inconvenient. Your threat means nothing now. What you going to do, genius?"

Simon paced back and forth, his hand gripping the back of his neck tightly. "Well I guess we have to go back to plan A."

"What was plan A?"

Simon perched on the edge of the desk and pursed his lips. Well…" He picked up a letter from the desk, scanning it before throwing it back down. "Will won't sell because Joey is pregnant—because he doesn't want her stressing about any upheaval with the horses. So…"

"Today would be good, Simon. I have things to do."

"So we get rid of the babies."

Nadine jumped to her feet suddenly. "What? What the fuck, Simon?"

He chuckled down the phone. "Or the horses." Flopping into his chair he grinned. "We get rid of the horses."

Chapter 34

Bea stood at the kitchen sink scrubbing at an oven tray and her eyes lifted to the window to see a blooming and heavily pregnant Joey walking the gardens hand in hand with Will. The past three months had taken their toll on the couple but just as Bea knew he would, Will remained stoic and brave for his fiance every step of the way. Bea was satisfied that they were coming out the other side much stronger and it made her heart burst to see them so happy. She was aware that Joey was presenting Will with a little surprise that day: she had been painstakingly restoring Diana's greenhouse and today was the unveiling.

She smiled to herself, ducking her head again to concentrate on the job in hand before taking another peek. Joey was glowing. With only two more months until the arrival of the babies—a little girl and a little boy, they now knew—she was looking more and more healthy by the day. The nursery was now completed, a job that Will had insisted he do by himself, and the room was filling quickly with baby grows and nappies ready for the big day.

They had worked so hard to get where they were, and each step they'd travelled had gained them a new piece of armour—armour that was going to protect them for the rest of their lives from the terrible luck that they had been gifted so far.

She was so proud of William and the way he had opened himself up to a future that no longer involved berating himself for acts he had not been in control of. She watched him hold himself taller and prouder each day with Joey by his side and she only wished Diana could see the amazing man he had grown into.

The couple disappeared around the corner of the building and Bea shook her wet hands into the sink before drying them and moving to the fridge to begin dinner.

Life was beautiful.

There was once again peace and happiness in the big old house, and she wasn't sure there was anything that could tear them down again.

"Josephine." Nicholas placed his hand on Joey's shoulder and kissed her cheek, taking hold of the shopping bags that weighed her down. "How lovely you look. And how are my grandchildren?"

"They're moving." She chuckled as one of them flipped over in her stomach, and she pressed her palm flat against it. "They haven't stopped." A beaming smile spread across her face as they stood outside of Betty's Tea Rooms in Harrogate. "How are you?"

Nicholas placed a gentle hand in the small of her back and held the door open with the elbow of his other hand—careful not to have the bags get squashed—and guided her inside. "I'm doing good thank you. Can't complain."

The two of them were shown to their seats.

"Thank you for meeting me." Nicholas pulled his half-moon glasses from the top pocket of his tweed jacket, popping them on and peering at the plethora of treats that were on offer on the menu.

Joey did the same, her appetite now once again in full force as she neared the end of her pregnancy. Everything looked so delicious and if she didn't control herself, she'd be tempted to order a little bit of everything. "No, thank you. Have you found anything out?"

Nicholas cleared his throat and sat back in his chair. "Well. After your last visit a few months ago, I got in touch with one of my close business friends. He knows people... if you know what I mean... and they have been working hard to uncover something based on your comment about your father's house. I thought that maybe if he was throwing ideas around about forging paperwork he might have left some sort of trail to other deals he was tampering with. But alas, nothing has surfaced."

Joey sighed, defeatedly.

"However. It got me thinking. And when I get thinking..." He chuckled. "I have been in touch with other friends of mine — businessmen, and people that I trust — and between us we have set up a fake deal."

Worry churned in her gut, and she gnawed on the corner of her lip. "How is this going to work? I mean, Will can't find out. If he finds out it's going ruin everything that we've worked hard to discover. You know his loyalty lies with Simon."

Nicholas gave her a reassuring smile. "William might be a smart businessman, but remember, I taught him everything he knows." He chuckled. "Don't worry, dear Josephine. He will not find out. We just sit back now and wait to see if Simon takes the bait. If he does, we can track him and monitor him — we can work out if he is up to anything more sinister than just a few idle threats."

Joey reached across the table, taking Nicholas's hand in hers. "Thank you. Thank you so much for doing this. I know I haven't been much myself with the passing of my father, but it hasn't changed anything as far as Simon is concerned. I still don't trust him."

"Well trust that I have it in hand. Now. What shall we eat? Those babies must be starving!"

Pulling on the handbrake, Joey killed the engine and stepped out, rounding the back of the car so she could gather the shopping bags from the boot. She was excited to show Will all the things she'd bought for the babies and anxiously hurried out of the garage and up the path towards the front of the house.

As her feet moved along the stone tiles, the sound of chatter near the front of the house grabbed her attention. She stopped, watching as Danny, Frank and Will stood at the top of the driveway, their body language a clear indication that something was wrong. Will had his hands on his hips, a look of concern on his face, and Danny's head was bowed, his chest rising sharply on what appeared to be a worried breath.

And Frank. What was Frank doing at the manor?

Her curiosity got the better of her and she followed the path to where the men stood, wrestling with her bags in the process.

Nearly out of breath, her energy all but completely depleted these days, she walked right up to their little circle and looked at them questioningly. "What's going on? Is everything okay?"

Will turned his head as Joey approached, wrapping his arm around her shoulders and pulling her to him before kissing the top of her head. "Hey." He turned his attention back to Frank who was shaking Danny's hand. "Thanks Frank, for coming out. We'll keep in touch if you don't mind."

Frank turned and gave Will a tight smile. "Of course. Call anytime." The three men exchanged nods and Danny and Will watched as he headed towards his car, Danny slipping his hands into his pockets and sighing loudly.

"What the hell is going on?" Joey pulled back from Will and looked between him and Danny. "Tell me."

Will took her hand and began to walk with her towards the stables, Danny by their side. "There's an infection in the stables. A very contagious infection."

Joey continued to look at both men, her mouth slightly agape as she listened to Danny take over the explanation.

"I noticed Berry and Tilly appeared quite lethargic the other day; their tails were limp and they appeared to have some weakness in their hind legs. I didn't think much of it until today when I saw that both of them have nasal discharge, which in my experience signifies a nasty infection. I called Frank, and he has confirmed that there seems to be an outbreak of equine herpesvirus." He stopped as they reached the stables and glanced at Will. "It can be quite serious and spreads really quickly."

"And Roya? What about Roya? She isn't sick is she?"

Will squeezed Joey's hand. "So far, no. But we now have a hell of a lot of work to do to ensure those horses that are healthy remain healthy." Will turned to Danny. "Whatever you need to do, do it. I can get you more staff, I can pay you more, whatever it is that needs to be done just let me know."

Danny dropped his head and shoved his hand back through his hair. "My main concern, aside from the manpower needed to completely blitz the place every day, is that I will need to be taking the temperature of every horse, several times a day every day until this thing is wiped out. The second we get whiff of an elevated temperature, we need to be getting that horse out and in quarantine. I am going to be back and forth continuously trying to get all that done, through the night etc. I just —"

"Stay here."

Danny kicked his head up. "What?"

Joey smoothed her hand up and down Will's suited arm as she turned to look Danny in the eye. "We live in a freakin' mansion, Danny. There are tens of rooms in there that are never used. I will get one sorted for you that you can stay in for as long as you need to. I'm not having you driving back and forth when you're tired, risking your own health and that of the horses. You'll stay here, in the manor."

"But you're pregnant, and there's—" He glanced at Will.

"Stay, Watson. Just stay; it's fine. She's right. It's ludicrous the idea of you being at home for this. We need you here."

Danny nodded and pulled in a deep breath. "Okay. Thanks. I'll finish up here and go home to get some stuff. I'll need to get the stable hands up to speed and have them start the cleaning process whilst I rehouse Berry and Tilly."

"So how serious are we talking?" Joey interjected as Danny was about to turn away.

He sighed again. "Well. Breathing problems is the most likely thing we would see; an infection of the respiratory system. But, it can be as bad as paralysis—problems with the spinal cord can cause that—and then abortion in the pregnant ones or death, particularly in the younger animals."

Joey's hand flew to her mouth as she gasped. "Jesus. And is there a cure? Will they get better?"

"There is a vaccine, but there are no guarantees that it will work. Our main priority is preventing an outbreak, hence my presence around here being vitally important. We need to be so vigilant. The staff need to be on it with hygiene. We can't take any risks. I can't stress how contagious this is."

Will pulled Joey into her chest. "Do we know how they might have caught the infection in the first place?"

Danny shrugged. "Who knows. Human contaminated hands or clothing, contaminated equipment and tack, trailers, cloths or other grooming equipment. Contaminated feed and water buckets. It could even be Silver—the new stallion. He's fairly old. He could be a carrier and we just didn't know when we bought him last week. In fact, I would probably bet on it. It's airborne but also spread through horse to horse contact through nasal secretions, and it's because it can live out of the body for seven days that we have to be so careful now with cleanliness. Speaking of which, I should get going. I need to hold a staff meeting."

Will nodded.

"Thanks Danny." Joey caught hold of his hand and squeezed it. "Let us know when you come back later on and I'll make sure Bea has some dinner for you and a room ready."

The three of them smiled tightly at one another and Will steered Joey and her shopping bags back towards the manor.

She pursed her lips and kept her eyes to the ground. "Will we ever get a break?"

Will kissed the top of her head, keeping his lips there as he spoke. "I don't know, Jo. I don't know."

Chapter 35

Burn It All by Hans Zimmer

Bea leaned over Joey's shoulder and placed a huge pot of bubbling stew in the middle of the table before taking her seat next to Graham. "Well isn't this lovely. I can't even remember the last time this table was full. Tuck in my darlings. Tuck in."

Danny, Will, Joey and Graham all hungrily reached for the serving spoon at the same time and laughter erupted around the circle of friends. They chatted lightheartedly together, filling their bellies full of Bea's mouth-watering food and enjoying companionable silences.

Almost a week had passed since Danny had discovered two of the horses had fallen ill, and he and his staff had worked tirelessly, every minute of every day, to keep the stables and the surrounding area infection free. Berry and Tilly had remained in isolated stalls, and the only contamination they had come across so far was of Ginger's foal who was showing signs of a respiratory infection.

"How's Fidget today?" Will shoveled a forkful of food into his mouth, raising his eyebrows over at Danny who was pretty much doing the same.

Danny sat back and wiped the corner of his mouth with a napkin as he swallowed. "She's weak. He temperature is struggling to regulate and her lethargy and loss of tone means she is struggling to balance and stay upright." He gave Will a sad smile. "I'll do what I can. She's obviously on her own and I think she's missing Mum."

Bea took a sip of water. "Fidget? That's Ginger's foal, right? Poor little mite. What a horrible thing. Did we find out where this all came from?"

Danny nodded. "Yeah. Uncle Frank did some tests on Silver and it seems he brought the infection to Wildridge without anyone knowing. He's a carrier. We are incredibly lucky that we caught it before we got an epidemic."

Joey sat back suddenly, wincing and moving her hand to rub her bulging stomach.

"You okay?" Will frowned.

She smiled up at him and nodded. "Braxton hicks. Nothing to worry about. It's just my body practising for labour apparently."

"Don't you be giving birth at the table, Miss Bell. I am not sure Graham's heart could take it!" Bea winked at her colleague and patted his arm as everyone laughed.

"I think I'm going to excuse myself and get an early night. Thank you for a delicious dinner, Bea." She stood from her seat and Will did the same.

"I'll come with you. We need to make the most of this sleep lark before it's too late! Night everyone."

Danny got to his feet followed suit almost immediately in order to get a few hours in before he needed to make his midnight trip over the courtyard to take temperatures and administer medicine.

Graham helped Bea to clear the table and wash the dishes and the pair of them smiled at the warmth in the air and the settled feeling that seemed to fill the old house.

"Well, Mrs Sykes, I have to say that I never thought I would see the day. All is calm and quiet at Wildridge

Manor, and I am honestly delighted. Our boy has done good, hasn't he."

Reaching into the sink to pull the plug out, Bea nodded, a proud smile gracing her lips. "I knew he had it in him. He just needed help finding it, and I knew she would be the one to do it. I'm so proud of them both. Let's just hope this imminent birth goes to plan, because I am not sure any of us can take anymore disappointment or heartache."

"Are you worried?"

Bea turned to face him. "No. Not really. I am putting my trust in our good Lord, but I can't help thinking of Claire."

"It wasn't a hereditary condition was it?"

She took the plate Graham had dried from his hands and placed it back in the cupboard. "I don't know. I really don't know. But let's not think about that, shall we?"

Twitching awake with his eyelids fluttering open, Will winced at the onset of a headache and rolled onto his side, reaching out and glancing at the screen on his phone.

It was almost midnight.

Danny would be heading out to see the horses. It would have been the sound of the front door that woke him.

He turned back to face a sleeping Joey and realised, quite suddenly, that it hadn't been a noise that woke him at all. Sitting bolt upright, he flung the covers from his legs as he sniffed the air again, the unmistakable smell of smoke filling his senses.

He reached the door to his bedroom just as it was flung open by a wild-eyed Danny, who almost threw himself into the room.

"The horses."

Nothing more needed to be said as the two of them darted out of the room and hauled themselves along the top corridor of the North Wing.

Seconds later, the bedroom door flew open again and Joey burst into the hallway, her heart beating wildly beneath her ribs as her head twisted from one side to the other, frantically searching for a cause of all the sudden commotion.

"Will!"

She took off in the direction of the staircase, the smell of smoke growing stronger and the fear in her chest climbing rapidly to her throat.

"Will!"

"Joey!" Bea scuttled down the corridor towards her with Graham at her side, the pair of them tying dressing gown ropes around their waists, looks of absolute terror on both of their faces. The two of them came to a halt in front of Joey, and Graham pulled the younger woman into a supportive embrace as their questioning eyes sought answers in each other's expressions.

Bea gripped Joey's hand. "Where is he?"

Joey didn't hesitate a moment longer.

She pushed out of Graham's hold and bolted down the stairs, her legs eating up the distance faster than her brain could process, and, as she ran across the tiles in the entrance hall, her chest heaving from exertion and her blood pumping fiercely with adrenaline, she came to an abrupt stop at the front door, which still sat wide open.

No. No. Oh God, no.

She stumbled back a step, a sharp gasp leaving her mouth as her wide eyes settled on the bright red and orange flames that licked up the side walls of the stable buildings, spreading across the roof, the pasture, creating destruction in its wake as it danced out against the night sky. Clouds of smoke billowed in the air, the smog so thick, Joey could barely catch her breath, much less fill her lungs. Her hand flew to her mouth to stifle a cry, and as Bea and Graham arrived at her side, her gaze searched the rest of the area, finally landing on Will.

Her heart, her life, her everything, was running straight into the chaos.

A primal, blood-curdling scream erupted from her throat. "Will!"

Turning to look over his shoulder at the sound of her cries, Will began to slow down, glancing back to see Danny ahead of him still running towards the horses. He opened his mouth to speak but stopped as Joey continued to scream and began running down the steps towards him, her hair flailing wildly, heartbreak plastered across her face. "Will, no!"

Without hesitation, he screamed back at her to stay where she was, running towards her until they ran into one another with blind force. The roaring of the flames and the howling wind caused him to shout loudly at her. He grabbed her by the shoulders, pushing his face into hers. "Get back in the house, Josephine! Go. Call the fire brigade and get back in the Goddamned house." His tone was angry and fearful all at once. It was authoritative yet worried and full of hurt. "Graham!" He looked over at the old man who had begun to make his way quickly towards them. "Take her back I do not want her out here."

"Will! No!" She clutched onto his arms with all her strength, not wanting to let him go. She refused to let him go. "I can't lose you too. *We* can't lose you. You're all we have."

Will held her eyes with his before pressing a fierce kiss to her forehead, and then, nodding towards Graham, he turned and ran back towards the stables, towards his mother's legacy, towards the raging fire.

Covering his mouth with his forearm, he ran closer, shouting Danny's name until he caught up with him just as he had started unbolting the stable doors. He shoved

Danny in the back to push him forwards, shouting above the noise of the fire and the wind that seemed to be blowing everything that was dangerous directly into their paths. "Roya. Go get Roya loose. I don't know which stall she is in. You do her side, I'll do the other."

Will got to work quickly once they were both inside, releasing Ginger from her stall, slapping her on her backside and shoving her towards the doorway and out to the fields at the back of the property with a forceful cry. "Go, Ginger!"

He worked his way down the line, moving out of the way and watching as each horse he released galloped past him in a frenzied disorientation to where he hoped to God they would be safe, at the same time edging closer to more stall doors that might open to bad news.

The panicked neighs and whinneys cut at his heart, and he forced the sounds to the back of his mind as he watched his prize black stallion rear and pelt his door with his hooves in attempt to get out. The smoke was thicker now, and Will bent his head lower, squeezing his stinging eyes together as he approached Equinox. In a moment of weakness, his mind flashed back to that fateful day when he had been sitting on the back of a crazed animal — much like the one in front of him — before forcing himself to move on.

Reaching up, he caught Equinox's mane and pulled his head down, stroking down his nose as calmly as was achievable and whispering in his ear. "Hey boy. It's okay. I'm going to get you out of here. Steady on."

Equinox's eyes rolled back and he let out a piercing neigh as he yanked his strong neck upwards, forcing Will to let go, and backed up ready to scale the stall door. In a moment of panic where his adrenaline took over, Will reached out for the bolt and yanked it open the exact second the stallion took a run at it.

Coughing and spluttering but moving out of the way in the nick of time, Will dropped to the floor, resting his back on the wooden structure as he watched his horse run for his life, down between the stalls and out of the stable door, across the paddock and then over the hedge into the field.

Will's chest heaved with emotion and exertion; it heaved from the lack of oxygen and he struggled to keep it together. Tears from the smoke rolled down his face and he wiped them away before standing back to his feet, urgency and his autopilot kicking in.

"Watson!" He coughed into the crook of his arm as he made his way down to the other end of the row of stables. He had no idea if Roya was safe. God, he had no idea if Danny was even safe. "Danny. For fucks sake!" Reaching over his shoulder, Will grabbed the back of his t-shirt and pulled it off over his head, balling it up and covering his mouth and nose to take a deeper breath so he could shout louder. "Danny are you there?"

"Will!" Danny followed the sound of Will's voice, his vision blurred by tears and smoke. He coughed loudly, the air now impossibly thick, and narrowly dodged a falling beam as he stepped over more debris.

"Will!" As soon as the call left his mouth, he collided into him.

"Shit man." Will reached out and grabbed Danny's arm as Danny did the same to him. "You okay?"

Danny nodded quickly. "Yeah. Yeah, I'm good. Did you get the horses free?"

Will wiped sweat from his brow with the back of his wrist as he nodded and tried to gulp in some air, the pair continuing to have to shout across to each other due to the horrific howling and roaring of the flames. "All of them from down this side are out. Fuck knows if they're safe; fuck knows if they've run out there into more danger, but they're out. What about Roya? Did you get her out? I didn't see her go past me, but I had a job on getting Equinox out. He was going mental. You managed to free them all down this side?"

"Roya's out, but there are still a couple of stalls I need to get to."

Will slapped him on his shoulder and cocked his head in the direction of the end two. "Come on. We'll do it now."

With their bodies slouched low and their mouths covered, the men picked their way across the floor of the stables, finally reaching the last two stalls.

"Shit. Fidget is in here right?"

Danny nodded.

"Fuck."

Sliding the bolt free, Danny swallowed down his fear and pulled the stall door open, the absence of the foal's cries on the other side causing him to hesitate only momentarily. He closed his eyes, breathed another lungful of toxic air, and then swung the door all the way open, the sight before him causing him to stumble back a few feet.

His expression crumpled. He reached up and fisted his hair, a cry in his throat that couldn't break free. "Fuck!" He shook his head, anger and sadness gripping his chest. "No." He couldn't breathe. He couldn't fucking breathe.

Collecting himself, he turned toward Will, who squeezed his shoulder and stood looking equally defeated.

"We've got to go. We need to get the others and and get the hell out of here."

Without any more exchange, the two of them moved along the line, sliding the bolts of the remaining doors open and releasing the last two horses to the distant sound of a siren.

"Thank fuck." Will coughed and grabbed Danny's arm. "Come on. Let's leave it to the professionals now."

They ran and hopped over fallen beams and had almost reached the doorway when Will halted and shouted over to Danny. "Wait."

Danny stopped, frowning and wiping his eyes. "What?"

"I need to get into the offices."

"What the fuck for?"

Will turned around and set off back the way he had come, shouting over his shoulder. "Because all of my mum's awards and trophies are in there. Along with some photographs that I need to save."

"Will, it's not worth it!" Danny's pleas followed Will, but when he realised his words were shouting to the wind and Will wasn't stopping, he shook his head and took off after him. "Jesus Christ." He couldn't let him go after the stuff alone. They had run into this mess together, and Danny was going to make sure that they walked out the same way.

The fire was licking up the walls now, fanning out across the ceiling of the stables—licking at the stalls that the men had been emptying only moments before—and as they burst through the door at the other end and into the office building, it became clear that there was worse to come.

With sentiment ruling his head, Will barged at the door of Danny's office with his shoulder in an attempt to force it open, the handle too hot to touch. "Fuck's sake!" There was no budging it to start with, and the exertion it took to give it another shove had Will coughing again. "Open the fuck up!"

Danny arrived by his side, his lungs on the verge of collapsing and beads of sweat rolling off his face. "Don't open the door, Wi—"

Will slammed his shoulder once more against the door like an enraged bull, and just as he crashed through the solid wood, Danny jumped on his back, pulling him out of the way and wrestling him down to the ground as an angry burst of flames was sucked from the office through the doorway into the corridor almost engulfing Will's entire body.

"For the love of God, Will," Danny shouted through the horrific noise. "When will you stop being so Goddamned mother fucking stubborn? For once in your life will you just LISTEN."

The men sat side by side, their knees bent and their arms resting on top of them. Both of them heaved the thinning air into their lungs in a desperate bid to catch some of the remaining oxygen, Will's naked chest glistening with sweat and smeared with soot.

A red mist had fallen in front of his eyes and it was blinding his ability to be rational. The buildings, the horses, everything that was tumbling around him was the only thing he had left that meant anything to him where his mother was concerned. Getting into the office and saving even just one piece of memorabilia was an absolute necessity, and in a moment of pure panic, he rolled to the side, pushed to his feet and ran through the flames into the room.

Danny allowed his head to fall back in exasperation before he too, pushed to his feet and took off toward a determined Will. "For fuck's sake."

It was chaos inside: beams were falling and the furniture was up in flames. The trophy cabinet that stood across the room had clearly been engulfed for a long time, the wood completely wrapped in the hungry red and orange tongues that licked and swished around it. Will's heart cracked as he realised that getting anywhere near it, nevermind inside it, was going to be an impossible feat, and even though his head had gone, he knew there was no chance. He dropped to his haunches and hung his head, coughing more and wiping at his stinging eyes.

At the sound of crashing and the splintering of glass, he kicked his head back up to see the huge framed photograph of his mother on the opening day of Wildridge Riding School falling to the floor and he jumped to his feet, battling through more fire and debris to rescue it from it's imminent death.

"Will, no!"

Chapter 36

You Go We Go by Hans Zimmer

Joey clutched her stomach as Graham pulled her into his arms, preventing her from running off in the direction Will had taken. Her screams and cries were as violent as the fire overtaking the stables, and he struggled to guide her back towards the house, back towards safety.

"Joey, please. We need to get you inside. It's not safe out here for you or for the babies."

"No." She shook her head, adamant in her response. The love of her life—the man her heart beat for—and her best friend had run straight into danger and there was no way she was moving until they were once again safe and Will in her arms. "I'm not going anywhere until I know they're safe." Her eyes were glassed by tears, but even so, the determination that lay just beyond their surface had Graham faltering.

Bea hurried up the stone steps and into the manor, thinking quickly about where the nearest telephone would be. She could go back to her room and fumble around in her handbag or cross the hallway and find the landline phone and dial from there. Deciding the latter, her heart in her mouth, she steadied her breathing and called the emergency services. She answered all the questions clearly and when she was asked if an ambulance was required, she closed her eyes tightly and nodded. "Yes. Yes I think that would be a good idea."

She placed the receiver gently and pulled in a shaky breath. She realised that there wasn't a chance in hell that Josephine would come back inside, so she set about collecting blankets from the airing cupboard and filling flasks with hot tea. And all the while, she sent up silent prayer after silent prayer, begging and pleading that Will and Danny would be okay.

Joey sat on the top step with her stomach churning with nerves as she watched the flames colour the sky with their orange hue. Her eyes darted from one corner of the ground to another, hoping and praying for a sign of life. The noise of distraught neighs had her sitting up straight and watching more intently when she saw the horses, one by one, galloping wildly out of the end door of the stables and over the paddock out of sight. A wash of relief had her breathing a little deeper, the sight of them meaning that Roya was safe, but more importantly, that Will was in there somewhere, alive.

Huddled in blankets and sipping on tea, Graham, Bea and Joey dived to their feet as only ten minutes later, the sound of sirens came wailing up the road in front of the manor and then turned into the long driveway.

"Thank fuck." Graham dropped his blanket and strode purposefully towards where a team of firemen were jumping out of the truck, unravelling hoses and doing their thing with speed and precision.

Words were exchanged between them and Joey watched as three heavily protected men began to run towards the stables. Her heart remained still in her chest, waiting, waiting, waiting—waiting until it could properly beat again, until two of the most important people in her life walked out of the mess they'd both blindly run towards.

She sat with her nerves in her stomach and her fingers clutching the blanket wrapped around her, the skin of her knuckles ghostly white in spite of the blood rushing furiously through her veins and thrashing loudly in her ears.

Time passed, time that seemed endless, and when the fear coursing through her was almost too much to bear, when the tears made it difficult to see and her thoughts were too heavy to push away, a sight she almost didn't dare to believe was true greeted her.

She rose to her feet and dropped the blanket to the ground, fighting the urge to run toward the two men walking in her direction. Her heart started to pick up pace, slowly at first then faster and faster, as they slowly made their way up the driveway. Will was supported by Danny and he clutched what looked like a framed photo in his hand.

Joey couldn't hold back any longer.

She ran as fast as her legs could carry her, hot tears streaming down her wet cheeks, and threw her arms around Will, crying into his chest.

Will's body tensed and he winced, hunching his shoulders as the pain in his lungs and torso flared. He hissed air in through his teeth and screwed his eyes closed, reaching his hands up to clasp Joey's shoulders and move her away from his body.

"Oh my God. Are you hurt?"

"Joey, please. Let me get him to the ambulance." Danny smiled gently.

Joey's gaze darted between the two of them, fear overtaking her, but she did as her best friend asked, and after he'd dropped a quick kiss to her forehead, watched as he guided the love of her life over to the waiting paramedics.

She watched while both men climbed into the back of the ambulance, were checked over and had masks attached to their faces to clear out their lungs and pump them full of much needed oxygen.

She watched as the professionals checked Will's pain, the conversation between them too far away for her to hear, and finally, after what seemed like forever, watched as Will climbed back out of the ambulance and headed towards her. "Are you okay? What happened? What did they say?"

Will reached the front steps and gently lowered himself so that he was sitting on the top one, clutching the blanket that had been handed to him by one of the paramedics. "I'm fine. Just bruised I think. They want me to go get checked out, but there's too much to do round here."

"Will." Joey sank her teeth into her bottom lip, attempting to stifle the sob pushing its way up her throat, but it didn't help. She shook her head, the tears still falling freely, and Will pulled her into his arms.

Graham put his arm around Bea and walked her towards the front of the house, stopping to squeeze Will's shoulder. He reached up and held onto his hand for a moment, the two men exchanging saddened smiles. Bea sat down on the step next to Joey, taking her hand in her own as Danny crouched down in front of the big oak door, his head in his hands.

The firemen were at work now, and the group of friends sat in silence as they watched fierce jets of water battling with the growing flames that caused huge clouds of smoke to rise into the orange sky, the distant sound of horses whinnying a soundtrack to the devastation that lay before them.

Will stared at the remains of his mother's memory and pulled in a shaky breath.

Perhaps he didn't deserve a break.

Out in the fields, Will and Danny worked for hours together to coax the horses to come back into the paddock, comforting them, soothing them...

The frightened beasts were wild and their jittery movements meant the whole ordeal tore at both men's hearts.

As the sun was beginning to peek over the horizon, Will looked up from where he was stroking the nose of a chestnut mare and saw a sight he thought he might never see. Snorting, his head pulling up and down, Equinox appeared over the cusp of the hill, trotting towards them.

"Danny. Look."

Danny stood from where he had been brushing Ginger's legs to clean the soot and debris from them and shielded his eyes from the morning sunrise. "Shit. Look at him."

Will dropped the rag he was holding and began to move calmly towards his horse. The stallion had a nervous look in his eye as he approached Will before circling and rearing onto his hind legs.

"Easy now."

Danny gingerly moved up behind his boss, making comforting noises as the horse began to calm down, and after dancing around each other for a few minutes, Equinox bowed his head and padded over to Will who took hold of his face, stroking down his nose and whispering softly.

"Good boy. It's okay. You're safe"

Leading the horses two by two back to the paddock, Will and Danny set about collecting bales of hay and water buckets to ensure they were fed and content. They worked silently side by side, sweat dripping from their soot-smeared brows, communicating with eye contact and nods of the head to get the job done.

"I've got Graham on the phone to find some temporary lodgings, portable stalls or something, until we get this mess sorted."

Danny nodded and bent to pick up an empty bucket. "I'll just go round the back and fill this last one."

On returning to the front with his full bucket, Danny halted to see a broken shell of the man he had been fighting with for so long crouched down in front of the remains of the stables, ash, soot and disintegrating timber standing bare and desolate against the early morning sky.

He had known Will for a long time, and the two of them had come to blows on more than one occasion, but watching him mourn for his loss brought everything into perspective. He walked up behind him and placed his hand on Will's shoulder. He looked on, taking in what Will was trying to come to terms with, and he pulled in his own devastated lungful of air. "I'm so sorry, man."

Will slowly lifted his head up and turned it to face his head groomsman. "Me too. Me too." He stood up and grasped Danny's hand, pulling him into his chest. "Thank you." He slapped him on the back before looking away. "For everything."

"William."

The two men turned quickly to see Nicholas picking his way across the grounds towards them and the mess they were surrounded by.

"Dad."

"Graham called. What the hell happened?" Nicholas let his eyes roam over the debris and the paddock full of homeless horses, emotion filling him up from his toes at what they had lost. "What the bloody hell happened?"

The three men walked together past the stables and Will explained how they had discovered the fire.

"Well was it a careless cigarette? A staff member forgetting himself and dropping it into a bale of hay? What?"

"I don't think so. It would have started earlier if that were the case. I mean, if it weren't for the fact Danny had needed to go check on the horses at midnight, God knows what might have happened. We might have been looking at a whole different situation."

Nicholas planted his hands on his hips and whistled through his teeth as he surveyed the grounds another time. "Jesus. What a mess."

Will dragged a hand through his hair. "I lost all Mum's trophies and awards." The muscle in his jaw ticked as he squinted towards the sky in attempt to rid the sadness that was just about destroying him from the inside out. "I was too late."

Glancing over at Danny, Nicholas frowned. "Too late? What do you mean, too late?"

"He went back into the fire to try to retrieve them, sir."

"Goddamnit, William." Nicholas shook his head. "When will you ever stop with this impulsive behaviour? You could have been killed!" He slumped down on the wall next to the stables and hung his head. "I just don't understand how this can have happened."

"You and me both, Dad."

Pulling air in deeply through his nose, Nicholas lifted his chin. "You don't think it was Simon do you?"

William looked at his father with his face scrunched up. "Simon? Have you just plucked his name out of the air because it's the first one you could think of? Why on earth would Simon burn down my stables?" He laughed and shook his head. "I think you're losing your mind, old man."

Nicholas stood and faced his son. "Josephine came to me a little while ago concerned about Simon's integrity and his intentions towards you and Wildridge, and—"

"What?" Will frowned and laughed again. "She what?"

"Hey, Nicholas." Joey came strolling up beside them, glasses of water in her hands that she passed to both Will and Danny. She pulled Nicholas into her arms and spoke softly. "I'm so sorry this visit couldn't be a happier—"

"Dad here was just telling me that you went to speak to him about Simon." Will planted his hands on his hips and glared at Josephine, his jaw ticking impatiently. "Behind my back."

"Will. It wasn't like that, okay? I went to your father because I don't trust Simon. I don't—"

"What is your problem? Huh? What is it exactly that you don't like about him? I know he can be a dick at times. I know he is obnoxious, but Joey, he helps me run my business. I trust him. He is the best out there. Why would you try to jeopardize that?"

Danny took a sip of his water, silently stepping back out of the conversation that clearly had nothing to do with him, and turned his focus to the horses.

Joey's heart slammed against her ribs, her expression faltering as a frown creased her forehead. "I wasn't trying to jeopardize anything. He just seemed adamant about you selling this place and I wanted to know why. I don't trust him. I'm sorry, but I don't."

Nicholas glanced at Joey from the corner of his eye. "There are things you need to know, William—things I have discovered in the last few weeks that I've been waiting for the right time to tell you. Please don't blame Josephine for her concerns. She came to me because she ca—"

"Morning all! What a fucking mess, eh." Simon grinned at the four of them who stood disheveled and tense. "Graham rang me this morning to tell me." He moved his mouth close to Nadine's ear and whispered. "Behold my genius." He stepped over burnt timber and halted in front of Will. "Sorry, Croft. Not ideal, huh." He clamped his hand down on his shoulder. "But… at least you don't have to worry about moving them now and the sale can go ahead. Silver lining and all that. Speaking of—"

"Simon has been skimming money off the top of all of the deals he has closed for you. For a very long time." Nicholas stepped forwards and pulled a wad of papers from inside his jacket pocket. "Josephine was right to not trust him, and I've been investigating since she came to me. I set up a fake deal and Simon took the bait. It's all here for you to look at."

Will took a step back, holding his hands up, trying to stop the barrage of words from reaching him. "Just stop. All of you. Stop. What the fuck is going on?" He turned on Simon. "You've been doing what?"

Simon let out a nervous laugh. "Bullshit." He shrugged and slipped his hands into his pockets. "Bull. Shit." Dropping his head and shaking it with a smirk on his face, he moved back to Nadine's side, slinging his arm around her shoulder. "Tell them, babe."

Closing her eyes and inhaling through her nose, Nadine stepped away from Simon, lifting his arm from around her and letting it drop before shaking her head in disbelief.

Simon did a double take and whispered at her with gritted teeth. "What the fuck are you doing?"

She teetered in her high heels to stand further away from him and pushed her blonde hair from her shoulders. "It's true. I've been helping him. And I would probably still be helping him, had he not brought me here today to show me how low he will stoop to get what he wants." She turned to face him. "What the fuck did you do? Are you sick?"

A wash of realisation coloured Will's face white as he took in the ridiculousness around him, joining the dots and understanding for the first time what was going on. "Simon?" His voice came out as a croaked whisper, his eyes scrunching up with disgust as he questioned the man who had helped to make him rich over the last ten years. "You did this?"

Another laugh erupted from Simon's chest. "What do you think, huh? You think I am that desperate for your money that I would go to such lengths? Think about it, Croft. Really think about it." He pointed to Nadine. "*She's* the one to blame around here. She's been trying to get a promotion at Green Frog and has gone to ridiculous lengths to get where she wants to be. It wouldn't surprise me if she's the one who burned your damn stables."

Nadine scoffed. "Really? So you didn't threaten Miss Bell as a way to get her to convince Will to sell to Green Frog?" She folded her arms across her chest and glared at Simon.

"Oh, Little Miss Innocent, are we. I fear you are forgetting your part in all of this threatening business."

Will dropped to a crouch on the floor, ragging his hands through his hair. It was all too much for him to process and after no sleep, he was struggling to keep it together.

Nicholas moved towards him. "He did more than threaten her, William. He—"

"No. Nicholas, no. Leave it. Please, leave it."

Nicholas spun around to face a distraught-looking Josephine. "He needs to know."

Will pushed to his feet again. "I need to know what? What the hell else do I need to know? Please, fucking enlighten me, because I am done with this now. Whatever you have to say can't possibly surprise me anymore. Spit it the fuck out, Dad."

Nicholas held his son's eyes with his own. "He sexually assaulted her, William."

Tick… the whoosh of blood in his ears…

Tock… the pounding of his heart as it just about beat through his ribcage…

Tick… the adrenaline that surged through his veins, and propelled his body forwards…

Tock… the raging roar of anger that screeched from his throat as he lunged…

Grabbing Simon by the throat, he pushed him to the floor, his knee landing on his chest to hold him in place. Drawing his arm back, he curled his fingers into a fist and smashed it into Simon's face. "I'm going to fucking *kill* you." His breathing was laboured and the sound of Joey's muffled screams from behind him were dismissed as that black, murderous fury took a hold of him.

He smashed again.

Smash.

The crunch of his knuckles against Simon's cheek echoed in his ears.

Smash.

The splatter of blood as he broke his skin splashed onto his t-shirt.

Smash.

The grunt from Simon as he struggled to escape from beneath the weight of a raging Will was completely ignored as he lifted his hand for a fourth time.

Danny caught his fist mid-air, and with all his strength, dragged an enraged Will off of the man who lay on the ground now covered in blood and dirt. He wrestled against Will's broad shoulders, fighting to pull him back and create enough distance between him and Simon to prevent him from murdering the arsehole. "Stop, Will. You need to fucking stop." Danny spun them both around, attempting to gain Will's attention, which was still pinned on Simon, his eyes wild and blinded by rage, and he shook his shoulders. He rounded the front of him and pushed him backwards, walking Will away from the rest of the group before stopping, ducking his head slightly and attempting to get his boss to look at him.

Will's chest heaved, and he brought his hand up to wipe under his nose and the sweat from his brow. "I'm going to kill him, Watson." He glared at Simon —who staggered to his feet while wiping blood from the corner of his mouth — and pointed at him over Danny's shoulder, shouting with forever-building anger. "I'm going to fucking kill you!"

Simon continued to stumble around, getting dangerously close to Will again. He sneered, and a sarcastic laugh huffed from his chest. "I told you she'd got inside your game head, Croft. You're fucked."

Seeing the fury build in his eyes all over again, Danny clutched the top of Will's shoulders, using his own body as a shield between the two of them as Will pushed against him in an attempt to reach Simon again. "Let it go, man. He's taunting you on purpose. Just let it fucking go. He's not worth it, do you hear me?"

Simon continued to move forwards towards the two men, reaching down to swipe his phone from the floor where it had fallen in the scuffle and then moving closer still. Simon shook his head and laughed again, deliberately knocking into Danny's shoulder as he walked past, muttering under his breath. "Fucking lunatic."

Clenching down on his jaw, the blood in his own veins now pumping at an alarming rate, Danny kept his gaze locked on Will's. "Are you good?"

Will nodded and swiped under his nose again, his eyes never leaving Simon.

"Are you sure? You're positive?"

His chest still heaving, Will finally glanced at Danny. "I'm good."

"Okay. Good." Danny clapped Will on the shoulders one final time and whirled around, his fingers forming a tight fist and slamming into Simon's jaw. The crack of bone on bone rang out in the air, and Simon hit the ground in one heavy, lifeless heap. Danny straightened himself, shaking his hand out as pain flared across his knuckles. He glanced back at Will, who stood with his eyebrows raised. "Fuck. Haven't had to do that in a while."

Chapter 37

This Is Not Goodbye by Kristin Kalliope

"What are you doing, Will? Stop. Look at me. Please."

Will ignored Joey's pleas and continued to shove clothes into his bag. She stood in front of him, and he refused to look at her, moving her body out of the way so he could get to the bathroom.

Panic clawed at her throat as she rounded the corner of the bed and hurried after Will's steps. "Why aren't you talking to me!" Her chest rose sharply with building emotion and tears coated the surface of her eyes. "Goddamnit, Will! What are you doing? Stop this. Please stop this. Talk to me, damnit!"

Exiting the bathroom, he threw his toothbrush and shower gel into his holdall and slung it over his shoulder, moving towards the door. He grabbed the handle and halted, dropping his chin to his chest before sighing. "We said no more secrets, Josephine. After everything, you must be able to understand how this feels to me. I need to go."

Joey's chin quivered uncontrollably. "Are you coming back?"

He swallowed down, knowing that if he even looked in her eyes, she would keep him there, and he needed to get out.

He opened the door, stepped into the corridor and left.

Joey watched as Will walked away from her, a crippling pain in her heart. She had done this—she had ruined everything he'd held dear—for a second time. Maybe she'd been wrong. Maybe she *was* the poison.

When he'd completely disappeared from view, she walked back into the bedroom and closed the door, leaning against it for support. Her entire world was crashing down around her and she felt powerless to stop it. She had no idea how to prevent the emotional trauma from the day from crushing her beneath its weight.

She could get angry—yell, curse and scream—but it wouldn't matter. It wouldn't bring him back. It wouldn't reverse the last twenty-four hours or the destruction that seemed to have occurred within a blink of an eye.

Tears raced down her cheeks, hot and heavy, one after the other, and she swiped them away, her lungs burning from her inability to breathe. Forcing herself away from the door, she padded over to the bed and lay down on Will's side, cradling his pillow in her arms and falling asleep to the sound of her own cries.

Climbing the stairs sometime later, Bea pulled in a determined breath, a mug of tea in her hand and words of comfort on her lips. A telephone call from Will had had her promising to look after Joey, and so that was what she was doing. Knocking gently on the door, she pushed into the bedroom and walked over to the bed, perching on the edge and brushing Joey's hair from her forehead to wake her up.

Joey blinked awake, her eyes still puffy and sore, and as the old woman came into focus, she pushed herself up, looking around. "Bea? What's wrong? Is everything okay."

"How are you feeling? I brought you some tea. Dinner will be ready in an hour or so, and I wanted to make sure you were awake for it. How are you holding up?"

The corner of her eyes stung, and the lump in her throat made it impossible to speak. Joey ignored Bea's questions, instead directing the conversation back to the only thing that mattered. "Has he really gone? Does he ever plan on coming back?"

Bea sat back a little and clasped her hands in front of her. "I do not know the ins and outs of Williams heart, my darling. What I do know is that he loves you; I believe you know this too. I didn't press him for answers when he called me because the tone of his voice told me he didn't want questions. That boy is like my own son, and I have to be there to support him when he needs it. What I do believe is that he needs a bit of time. So much has happened recently. So much has taken its toll on his heart and I think that him leaving is a massive step in the right direction. There was a time when he would have turned to drink, thrown things, screamed and shouted, but you being here, you taking him in your hands and caring for him, has helped him to see that that's not the best way to deal with things. He has grown so much since loving you, Joey. And for that you should feel good. Your priority now is these babies, who I imagine will be making an appearance in the next week or so. Let Will have this time to think, to reflect on his devastation, to reflect on the things that have come to light today and he will come around. I am positive. He's done it once and he is in an even better place than before. He loves you, Joey, and I can not for one second imagine that he would give that up for anything."

"I did this, Bea. This is all my fault. He's lost everything and it's all my fault. If I had have just told him about Simon, if I had have been honest with him—"

"Did you listen to a word I just said?" Bea raised her eyebrows and shook her head a little. "We humans are a funny old species. We make decisions in the heat of the moment to protect the ones we love, and yes, sometimes those decisions backfire on us. But hindsight is a wonderful thing. No one could have predicted this, Josephine. No one would ever think that you did this on purpose to hurt him. Least of all him. He won't be hurting because he thinks you caused the fire to happen." She took Joey's hand in hers. "He will come back. I'm sure of it, because this is not how the story ends."

"Does she know you're here?"

Will hung his head and cradled his mug of tea between his legs. "No."

"And is that wise? In her condition?"

Sitting up and leaning against the back of the sofa, Will sighed. "I don't know, Dad. I just walked out so that I didn't hit something or down a bottle of whiskey. I just acted on—"

"Impulse." Nicholas looked over at him and smiled. Chuckling to himself. "You always have done. Impulse has ruled your life since a very young age, and if I'm honest, it amazes me how good your business head is when you find it so hard to sit back and think things through."

"Business is different, isn't it."

Nicholas nodded. "That it is. Affairs of the heart are much more likely to have you making rash decisions."

"You think I'm being rash? Not as rash as sinking a bottle of Bruichladdich, though. Eh?"

"Who am I to say? It's your life, William, and you have to deal with it. I can offer you my advice, but that doesn't mean it's the right advice to take. I'm just one man with one opinion."

Standing to his feet, William walked over to the window. "I'm just so mad. This whole journey, this whole thing, we have promised that honesty comes first. After all that happened before, I thought that would be one thing I could rely on. I didn't think for one second that she would hide anything from me." He took a sip of tea and pushed his other hand into his pocket as he watched a group of sparrows bathe in the bird bath in his father's garden.

"I'm sure she never thought she would be anything but honest either, son. But life has a great way of scuppering our plans. I don't doubt that she had your best interests at heart from day one. In fact I can assure you she did. When she came to me, she was worried about so many things, not least how you would react."

William turned around and looked at his father. "I just hoped that she trusted me. And now I don't know if she does. And if she doesn't, then what? How do we carry on?"

Nicholas stood and joined his son at the window, grasping the back of his neck and smiling. "If it's not there, then you rebuild it."

"I seem to be rebuilding a lot these days."

Nicholas chuckled again. "Welcome to the real world."

"Can I get off?" Will smiled at his dad.

"You have babies coming. I don't think getting off is an option."

"Can I at least stay here for a couple of days? Just til I get my head straight?"

Nicholas nodded. "You have come a hell of a long way, son, and I am proud of you. But you have responsibilities that you need to uphold and Joey and the babies are your priority now. You have to put yourself last. So yes. You can stay. But you have to call her first. Tell her where you are and tell her you'll be home soon."

William nodded. "So, Columbo. How did you find out about the embezzlement?" Will flicked his eyes to his father and gave him a quick smile. "I seriously had no idea. I knew he was a twat, but he's always been reliable."

Nicholas tapped the side of his nose. "Your old man knows people. I may be retired, but my mind is still sharp as a whistle. As I told Joey, you mustn't ever forget that I taught you everything you know."

The pair of them chuckled.

"I can't believe he would stoop so low as arson. Jesus." Will shook his head.

"People do strange things for money. Greed is an ugly thing, and from what we can gather, greed was Simon's middle name. Not only was he skimming off the top of your deals, he was set to gain a whole extra income through Nadine. She was fighting to be made partner at Green Frog, and securing the sale of Wildridge was pretty much securing her promotion. She was in cahoots with Simon, relying on him to push the sale through, and was bribing him with a huge lump sum and... well... her body by the looks of things."

Will shuddered at the thought of Nadine's body, the way she had practically thrown herself at him now making complete sense. What an idiot he had been. "Jesus. What a fucking mess." He stood to his feet, taking his father's empty cup from his hand and walking towards the living room door. "I guess the alternative to all of this would have been the sale of the manor. And now... I am certain I don't want to get rid of it. It's my home; it's Joey's home. I can't even imagine life elsewhere." He smiled wistfully and walked into the kitchen.

Placing the cups in the sink, he cast his mind over the events of the last year.

Enough was enough now. He was determined to not let life lead him a merry dance anymore. He *did* deserve a break, and he was going to make damn sure that he got it.

Chapter 38

Moon And Back by Alice Kristiansen

Pushing through the large metal gate that led into the rose garden, Joey walked along the stone tiled path and breathed deeply. Her gaze drifted over the bushes, now trimmed and cut back for winter, and her mind immediately took her back to the first time Will had shown her this place.

Her mother's rose garden.

Oh how so much had changed since then.

She had been a naive and confused woman, falling for a man who on the surface appeared to be nothing more than a monster, but what a beautiful monster he had turned out to be. They had come a long way and endured so much in the year that had passed, and although it had only been a few days since the fire and Will walking out of the door, she missed him beyond words. Her heart ached in his absence, but she understood. She knew he needed this time to process all that had happened and everything that he'd lost — *they'd* lost.

It was so much, but in a few weeks they'd be gaining so much more — a family. No matter what happened or what challenges life would throw at them, it didn't matter, because they had each other. Right?

Rubbing her hand over her stomach, Joey continued along the path, stopping and squatting in front of her mother's favourite rose bush. "Just Joey."

She smiled to herself but the smile quickly slid from her face as a painful ache pulsed in her heart. Tears pricked the corners of her eyes, the loss of her father pushing itself to the front of her mind from the place she had it buried. It was something she struggled to keep at bay every second of every day, but she couldn't pretend anymore. She couldn't be strong because all of her strength had left her and so she collapsed to her knees and let the tide of emotions wash over and consume her.

God, she missed them.

She missed them all—Will, her father, the mother she'd never known. How had she screwed this up so bad? How had she let fear rule her thoughts when she should have put her trust in the person she had given her heart to? She should have told him. She should have been honest. But God, Will was impulsive and his fierce need to love and protect her was at times dangerous, and him knowing or finding out any other way than he had would have meant a different ending for everyone.

She couldn't have allowed that to happen. There had been too much at stake.

So there she was, waiting anxiously and for what seemed like an eternity until the love of her life came home.

Rising from her position, Joey moved along the path.

A few short steps later, she crouched down in front of another bush, one hand on her swollen stomach, and reached for the small tag planted in its soil. She closed her eyes, trying to guess what bush it might be, and as she did, the memory of her and Will making a game out of it surfaced, bringing a sad smile to her lips.

She inhaled the cool autumn air and flipped the tag around, reading the name printed on its side.

"Simply the best."

Joey's breath caught in her throat at the sound of the deep, gravelly voice echoing in her ears, and she rose from her position and whirled around. "Will?"

"Hey."

"You're home."

Will pushed his hands into his pockets and nodded. "I'm home." He squinted over Joey's shoulder at the skyline. "I was always going to come home. I'm sorry if I upset you that day—I just needed some time, y'know?" He reached out and ran his thumb along her bottom lip. "I'm trying to be a better man for you, Joey, and I guess that was part of it. If I'd stayed, I was scared that my anger and frustrations would have manifested themselves differently. I don't want to be that guy anymore."

A lone tear slid down her cheek. "I'm sorry. I'm sorry for not telling you about Simon, I just didn't know how, and I felt like I needed proof. Like you wouldn't have believed me otherwise, so that's why I went to your father. That's why I asked him to help—"

"You hurt me, Jo. I don't give a damn about the deals. I don't give a damn about you needing proof. You hurt me. I walked out of our bedroom that day believing that you didn't trust me—that everything we had built our new start on meant nothing to you. No more secrets. We promised we would be open and you weren't. You hid it all away from me and made me look like a fool." He looked at the ground and bit down on his back teeth. "At least that's how it felt."

Glancing back up at her, he took her hand and pulled her closer, reaching up to hold her face and look in her eyes. "But you know what was worse? You know what killed me the most?"

Joey could barely see him through tears filling her eyes, but she gave him a small shake of her head anyway.

Will squeezed his eyes shut and pursed his lips. "The pain in my heart at the idea of losing you again is not something I can bear, and the thought of you putting yourself out there in the line of fire, putting yourself in danger. Jesus. He could have hurt you, Joey! The idea that he had his hands on you... fuck. But you didn't stop to think, did you? You didn't stop to think that if things had have gone wrong, you could have been seriously hurt. All three of you could have been seriously hurt. I can not lose you again, Josephine. I can not. Do you understand me? I love you with everything that I am, and my life would cease to carry on if you slipped through my fingers one more time. Are you listening?" He gave her face a shake out of pure frustration before pulling her to his chest and wrapping his arms around her. "I fucking love you, you silly, silly girl. Do not *ever* do anything like this again. Please. I can *not* lose you."

Joey cried into his chest. "I'm sorry. I'm so sorry, Will."

Moving his hands from around her, Will pulled her chin up so that she was looking at him and clasped her face with his palms again. "Do you trust me?"

"With my whole heart."

And it was all he needed. He bent his head and pushed his lips to hers, inhaling her and allowing himself to be engulfed by the taste of her. Opening her mouth with his own parted lips, he dipped his tongue inside, catching the tip of hers with it as they swirled and danced, figure-eighting in soft strokes. He nipped at her lip and pulled her close before lifting his head and placing one last kiss on the top of her head.

Standing back from her and holding her at arm's length by her hands, he watched her for a moment or two, taking in her beauty and her grace. He rolled his gaze down her breasts to her swollen stomach and an overwhelming sense of pride and contentment washed over him.

He let go of her hands and fished inside his pocket before slowly dropping to one knee before glancing up at her with squinted eyes, a cocked head and a sexy lopsided grin. "Miss Bell. I think the only thing left to ask you now, is whether or not you will officially accept my previous haphazard proposal of marriage, by accepting this ring." He pulled out a blue velvet box, flipping the lid open and holding it out to a wide-eyed and blooming, Joey. "Marry me, Josephine."

"Will…" Her eyes lingered on the diamond solitaire as it sat perched in its box and the gold band that showed wear. Her gaze darted around the facets and the way they sparkled under the afternoon sunshine and she couldn't help but feel as though the ring looked familiar. "Is this…"

Will stood to his feet and nodded. "Your mum's ring. Yeah." He smiled. "I hope you don't mind. I just —"

Joey brought shaking fingertips to her lips to stifle a cry of emotion-filled delight. "Of course I don't mind. I absolutely love it." She smiled through the tears still glassing her eyes. "How did you get it? I mean, when did you get it?"

Will stepped closer, pulled the ring from it's velvet nest and took hold of Joey's left hand by her fingers. He looked her in the eye as he slid the ring to its forever home and kissed her lips. "A couple of days after we told…" He pressed his lips to hers once more. "After we told your dad about the babies, and the proposal and… the sex." He smiled and then chuckled.

Joey rolled her eyes at him and the memory before she looped her arms around his neck and brought his mouth closer for another kiss. "I love you, William Marshall-Croft. I love you something fierce."

Epilogue

You Got Me by Gavin Degraw
Collide by Taylor-Ann

"Oh, God." Joey groaned and rubbed her eyes. "Not again." She pushed herself up onto her elbows glaring at the Godawful time of three fifty-eight am.

"I'll go. I'm already awake." Will leaned over and kissed Joey's nose before flinging the covers from his legs and padding out of the bedroom to the room next door, shaking off the nightmare he had woken from just half an hour before.

A soft glimmer of moonlight streamed through the the voile curtains into the spacious room, and the soft snuffling and wimpering of babies had a love-filled smile spreading across Will's face. "Hungry again are we?" He leaned over and scooped Diana from her cot, bringing her tiny face to his where he pressed a smattering of delicate kisses on her warm cheek. "You eat more than I do."

Hitching her up onto his shoulder, he picked up a wriggling Jonathan, his mop of jet black hair sticking up in tufts as his tiny fingers curled into fists to mark the beginning of a full on hunger meltdown. "Oh hush. I'm here. Anyone would think we don't feed you." He snuggled his little boy under his chin and kissed the top of his head, inhaling that unique baby smell before he jiggled the two of them up and down for a few moments.

He was in love, smitten and completely besotted.

Each second of his days since the twins had been born just three weeks earlier had been more full than he could ever remember or ever imagine.

He rocked the babies a little longer, whispering promises to them and relishing the private time he had with them before picking up cloths, wipes and clean nappies. "Come on then let's go wake the bear."

He walked out of the nursery and back into the bedroom, sitting carefully on Joey's side of the bed in order to wake her back up again. "Mummy. We are *very* hungry and would like to suck your boobies. And then, when we have finished, Daddy would like to suck them too."

Looking at Will through tired eyes, Joey smacked him playfully. "Don't be such a weirdo."

He grinned and handed a squirming Jonathan to her, waiting until she was comfortable before passing Diana over and climbing onto the bed next to her.

As the screaming settled and the twins fell into their nightly feeding routine, Joey glanced over at the man beside her who sat awake, watching with love in his eyes. "So tomorrow. We haven't really talked about it. What time is everyone supposed to be arriving?"

Lying on his side, Will smoothed his palm gently over Diana's head and he looked up at Joey. "Well, Bea said she would come over mid-morning to get the food ready. I told her we would get catering in with it being a Saturday, but she insisted, and you know there's no telling her when she has made her mind up." He placed his lips gently where his hand had been and sat up a little. "I guess Graham will arrive around lunchtime with my dad, and Danny will be here from early in the morning. I got the plans through for the new stable building and I wanted to get his thoughts on them."

"Tomorrow?" Joey frowned in disappointment. "It's Christmas eve, Will, must you worry about work over Christmas? Can't it wait until next week?"

Will shrugged. "It won't take long. I just want to get them approved and then we can start the work as soon as New Year is out of the way. Half an hour in the morning. An hour tops, and then I will relax for Christmas. I promise."

Resting her head back on the pillow Will had propped behind her, Joey sighed. "Okay." She licked her lips and glanced at him. "Are you looking forward to it? Christmas, I mean."

Will held her eyes for a few moments—the huge brown pools that he had fallen in love with so quickly. They were expectant and hesitant all at once, and he smiled, reaching up and running the pad of his thumb across her bottom lip before nodding gently. "I am actually."

"Are we ready then?" Beatrice picked up the two small boxes from the coffee table, handing one to Will and the other to Joey.

"No. We need to wait for Danny. He's in the loo."

Pushing the door of the sitting room open with his foot, Danny appeared, his hands still doing up the buttons on his jeans. "I'm here. I'm here."

Joey shook her head and chuckled before turning to look at Will. She picked the bauble up from its protective box, holding it by the hook and letting it dangle in the air whilst losing herself in the moment with the man who owned her heart. "Ready?"

Will dropped his eyes to the old box that he held in his hands and let out a weary sigh. He gently pulled the lid until it came off and then squeezed his eyes closed as he

331

shook his head. "No not really." Lifting his head again, he turned to look at his beautiful fiance and smiled. "But I'm okay." He moved the delicate tissue paper aside and took a hold of the ribbon and watched the glittering sphere spin as the light caught it, a lump forming in his throat as what it stood for washed over him like a tsunami. Pushing aside the past, though, he thought instead about everything the words would mean from now on. New baby... two new babies... his babies...

He lifted his arm and hung his mother's babule on the nearest available branch and then took a step back to allow Joey some room. He kissed her cheek and whispered in her ear. "I love you."

With tears in her eyes, Joey reached up on her tiptoes and hung the bauble they'd had specially made in memory of her father.

She missed him.

She missed him so much, and while they had so much to celebrate this year, there was a pain in her heart that would always linger as a result of the sudden loss of him. Nevertheless, she knew that wherever he was, he would be reunited with the love of his life and they would both be smiling down and watching not only her and Will, but their grandbabies as well.

Pulling in a deep breath, she stood back, looking at the tree that was now complete. It was beautiful, just like her home, her family.

Stepping up behind the two of them, Nicholas placed his hand on the back of Will's neck, giving it a gentle squeeze. He reached out and spun the bauble that he remembered so clearly from twenty-five years ago. "I'm proud of you, son." His lips pulled into a tight smile as he nodded his head at Will, the two men silently exchanging the words in their hearts.

Turning to Joey, he put his arm around her and read the lettering on the bauble she had hung. "Grandpa." He smiled and then kissed the top of her head. "Let's hope I can be Grandpa enough for the two of us."

The lights from the Christmas tree continued to twinkle into the evening, and Will pointed up at them as he held Diana in his arms. "What can you see? Can you see the pretty lights?"

Diana's big brown eyes blinked and Will kissed her tiny button nose.

"Come and play, Daddy." Joey looked up at him from her position on the floor where Jonathan lay kicking his legs on his play mat, gurgling. Will dropped to the floor lying his precious daughter next to her brother before stretching out on his side next to Joey.

"He's just like you were, William. It's quite alarming really." Bea smiled over at him from her seat on the sofa before draining the last of her sherry. "A feisty little thing from day one."

"I can't imagine what you are talking about, Mrs Sykes." Will winked at her.

"She's right, you know. I had my fair share of kicks to the groin when you were a toddler."

"Don't encourage her, Graham! Please."

The four of them laughed and Will pushed his hand through Joey's hair, cupping her cheek and smoothing the pad of his thumb across it. Kissing her lips, he moved to his knees and then whispered into her hair. "I'll just be a minute."

Will collected people's empty glasses to refill them and moved to the back of the room to the drinks cabinet. He poured himself a shot of whiskey and followed it with a tumbler of soda water.

There were days when the horrors of his past would come barreling towards him still, but he was most definitely on a different path now. He looked up in front of him at the photograph he had rescued from the fire, now in a brand new frame, and smiled. He looked forward to the day where he could hang it back in its rightful place in his mother's stables and be proud of all he had accomplished in order to uphold her name and reputation.

Danny appeared at his side. "So any news on Simon and the blonde?"

Will shook his head. "Not anything new. They're out on bail, pending investigation, so I guess when the police find out more they'll get in touch."

Danny nodded. "Fuckers." He reached his hand out. "Need any help with those?"

"Sure." Will passed him two glasses of sherry. "For Bea and Graham." He plucked a bottle of red out and pulled out the cork. "Thanks, Watson."

"It's no trouble."

"No. I mean, thank you. Again. For everything."

Danny smiled. "Again, it's no trouble."

Nodding, Will returned to the other side of the room and handed out the rest of the drinks before dropping back to the floor and immediately turning his attention on his little family.

So much had gone wrong in his life, but this feeling of utter contentment washed every moment of hurt away.

It had all been worth it, all of it, because it had led him to now.

It had led him to his break — the one he finally believed that he deserved.

This was it.

Everything he had wished for was in the form of two tiny bundles that were his whole world, and a sexy brown-eyed, brunette who had given him a reason to try. His life was complete and all his reasons to be the best version of himself were here within the walls of his family home.

Beatrice looked on adoringly at the scene at her feet and turned her head to her long-standing colleague. She reached out and picked up his hand, squeezing it in her own and leaning over to press her lips to his.

"*This*, Mr Kent, is how the story ends."

Graham smiled and smoothed his thumb across the apple of her cheek, capturing her sparkling blue eyes with his. "I do believe this is just the beginning, Mrs Sykes."

Acknowledgements

To our Alpha, our Betas, to our die-hard supporters, to our friends and fellow authors, to anyone and everyone who stands by us on this journey, we thank you.

And to you, the reader, you keep our dreams alive.

All our love, ELJ & Fox

Printed in Poland
by Amazon Fulfillment
Poland Sp. z o.o., Wrocław